John Fothergill

An Account of the Life and Travels in the Work of the Ministry of

John Fothergill

Second Edition

An Account of the Life and Travels in the Work of the Ministry of

John Fothergill

John Fothergill

An Account of the Life and Travels in the Work of the Ministry of John Fothergill
Second Edition

ISBN/EAN: 9783337345341

Printed in Europe, USA, Canada, Australia, Japan

Cover: Foto ©Raphael Reischuk / pixelio.de

More available books at **www.hansebooks.com**

AN ACCOUNT

OF THE

LIFE and TRAVELS

IN THE

Work of the Miniſtry,

OF

JOHN FOTHERGILL.

To which are added,

Divers EPISTLES to Friends in *Great Britain* and *America*, on various Occaſions.

The SECOND EDITION.

L O N D O N:

Printed and Sold by MARY HINDE, at Nº 2, in *George-Yard, Lombard-Street*, 1773.

THE

PREFACE.

IT was not till within a few Years before the AUTHOR's *Decease, that he entertain'd a Design to leave behind him a Memorial of this Nature : But being requested, about the Year* 1742, *to turn his Thoughts this Way, by one of his Sons who had been much less under his immediate Tuition than the rest of his Children, and consequently less acquainted with many Particulars of his Life, replied, that* tho' he had been mostly easy, in relation to writing any thing by way of Journal of his Labours, as some other Friends had done ; yet it had not wholly passed unattended to, nor without Thoughts often darting into his Mind concerning it, and so frequently of late, as to have somewhat turned his Inclinations that Way. *From this Time it fixed more closely upon him, and he employed great part of his leisure Time, when Health permitted, in drawing up the first Part of the ensuing* Memoirs, *which extends only to the Time of his Return from his first Visit to* America, *and was finish'd but a few Weeks before his Decease under great Weakness of Body. But the plain, sensible, and*

lively

lively manner, in which this Account is drawn up, occasions the deeper Regret, that he had not earlier engaged herein, and that the many interesting and instructive Observations, that must have occurr'd during the remaining part of his Life, are new lost irretrievably.

The succeeding Part of this Collection has been compiled from the short Notes he kept of his several Visits, and some other Papers and Letters, as it were providentially preserved: And as this Part required some Care in digesting, as well as Labour in transcribing, the Work has been retarded longer than was agreeable to the Editors, or the Publick, for whose Satisfaction, as well as Benefit, they were not unconcerned.

It was not without Hesitation, that some Parts of the following Collection were committed to the Press; such as the summary Journals of several of his Visits. Nevertheless, as even these short Hints may possibly occasion, in the Minds of divers who remember those Visits, and his Labours therein, some useful Considerations, it was thought most proper to retain them.

A painful, deep, searching, laborious Ministry was oftentimes the AUTHOR's Portion; accompanied with a zealous Concern, that all might come to the certain Knowledge, and inward Experience of an holy, living Principle operating in the Hearts of Mankind; in order to lead them

from

from Error and Unrighteousness, into all Truth, and into the Practice of every Christian Virtue: And to those who read with a View to profit, not barely Amusement; and in order that they may both be informed of, and animated by Example, to come up in their respective Duties, the Perusal, we hope, will be beneficial.

This was the general Tendency of his Labours in the Ministry, as many now living can testify; and in the following Sheets the same important Doctrine is strongly and frequently inculcated, and is now earnestly recommended to the Reader, with Desires, that the many Truths herein delivered may have a due Effect upon every Mind; and that those especially, who have been Witnesses of his Zeal and Fervency, may, in calling his Services amongst them to their Remembrance, be incited to follow him, as he followed Christ, and thus secure to themselves the Benefits he diligently laboured for, and at the same time pay the most expressive Regard to his Memory.

A N

A N
ACCOUNT
OF THE
LIFE and TRAVELS
OF
JOHN FOTHERGILL.

I Was born in *Wensleydale* in *Yorkshire*, 1676, of Parents not only convinced of the blessed Gospel Dispensation of God to Mankind, in sending the Spirit of Christ to enlighten and reprove for Sin, and to lead the Believers in it into Truth and Righteousness, as testified unto by the People called *Quakers*; but also, who endeavoured carefully to feel after, and live up to the powerful Principle of Truth, whereby they were both instructed and enabled to be exemplary in Life, and in a religious Concern to attend Meetings for the Worship of God; and in an humble, steady, diligent waiting upon him for the Appearance of his enlivening Presence and Power, to enable them to worship acceptably. This also led them into

 a godly

a godly Care to train up their Children in the Fear of the Lord, and to take them to religious Meetings frequently, both on Firſt-days and other Days of the Week, which they ſeldom failed in attending ; eſpecially my Mother, whoſe Care herein, and her ſpiritual, reverent Travail of Soul in Meetings, often in Silence, for the Sacrifice of a broken Heart to be prepared in her by the Lord, had, very early, a deeply affecting Impreſſion in my Conſideration : So that I was convinced fully, when very young, both of the Exiſtence of an all-mighty, holy, all-knowing Being ; and that there is a Part in Man that is immortal ; and from hence aroſe a Fear to offend him in Word or Deed.

I have made this mention of my Parents, and the Benefit accruing to me through their religious Life, as well as of ſome other Friends, manifeſtly exerciſed in Spirit towards the Lord, and feeling after his humbling Love and Life to renew their Strength from Time to Time, for this End chiefly ; to inſtruct our Youth, who have religious Parents or Tutors, to prize ſuch Privileges, and to conſider, that if ſuch Advantages be diſregarded and made light of, thoſe who ſo do have much more to anſwer for, and will have heavier Condemnation to bear, than thoſe who have not had ſuch convincing Opportunities. And *Secondly*, To ſtir up Parents and others profeſſing the holy and bleſſed Truth, to labour carefully to

feel

feel after and obey it for their own Advantage ; and also to be good Examples and certain Way-marks before their Offspring and the Youth, who may see them both in Meetings and out of Meetings.

For as I have had to remember divers of the Elders, and the Instruction which their Conduct afforded me in my very young Years ; so it hath often brought a fresh Care, and inward Concern of Soul upon me, that I might be such a Light, and such an Instance of Diligence, as might carry some true Demonstration with it to my Children and others : And in this Concern of Mind we are often renewed in a Capacity to pray, or desire for others, with some Access.

And I am not easy without leaving this Testimony behind me, that I fully believe one great Hinderance to the Growth of our Youth in true Godliness, is the Want of that true Spiritual-mindedness which ought to be regarded by all, but in an especial manner by the elder and more knowing.

From this Fear to offend the Lord, which I mentioned above, to be early raised in my Heart, I loved religious Meetings and true Ministers ; and as many such Ministers, who travelled in the Service of Truth, often lodged at my Father's House, I greatly loved to be near them, and to remark their Conduct and Conversation, which hath often been beneficial to me, both then and in the after Part of my

 Life :

Life : It hath likewife made me glad to fee the like Inclination in Youth, and taught me to be careful to converfe with, and behave before them with godly Prudence.

But although inward Fear and Care, with fome heavenly Touches of the Life of Truth, enabled me to live more felf-denyingly and gravely than fome others of like Years, which my Mother particularly noted to herfelf with fome comfortable Hope, and mentioned it to fome in private ; yet fhe was removed by Death when I was about eleven or twelve Years old, which was a great Lofs to me : For though my Father's Care continued, yet being more from under his Eye, and he being obliged to have other Houfe-keepers, who were not duly feafoned with the Truth ; fome of them, with other Servants, proved Inciters to Airinefs and a loofer Conduct, inftead of being Examples of a religious and godly Sobriety : And fo the evil Power took Advantage of my natural Activenefs and Propenfity to Sports and Play, and often ftifled the heavenly Defire and Care towards God, which I ought to have retained. And fo I became more thoughtlefs about my Soul's Intereft, and fubject to be led into Folly ; which yet was often made a Burthen to me, and an occafion of Sorrow fecretly, which caufed me to beg Mercy for my Negligence, and to make Covenants to be more watchful againft Temptations ; but alas ! I often failed in performing them.

Yet

Yet divine Mercy, by renewed Convictions and awakening Visitations, gave me to see and consider my Unfaithfulness and Weakness in such a manner, that I often with secret Lamentation bemoan'd myself under his Judgment, much fearing that I should not be regarded in Mercy any more; nor durst I make any more Promises, as I had done, left I should by failing increase my Soul's Bondage.

Yet as I was kept for a Time thus low and watchful to this heavenly Principle of Truth, which let me see my Sin, and the Danger of it, I was favoured with Springings of Hope for Mercy and Salvation; and then my Cry was frequent and strong to be purged throughly, whatever I had to bear, if the Almighty would but enable me. Thus I wrestled several Years, and durst not believe that I gained any effectual Victory; and as the Baptism of Christ by his Spirit had begun to operate in me, to bring a Death to Sin, and the Lusts of the Flesh, that thro' Faith, and a diligent Attendance to his Power, I might live to him in Newness of Life, I had some Hope that the Fan in his Hand would throughly purge me, which was the very earnest Cry and Longing of my Soul. But the winnowing, refining Work of the Spirit of Judgment, and of Burning, now kindled to take away my Dross, was so heavy upon me, that I was often tempted to conclude I was forsaken of Mercy, and that Judgment and Darkness were to be

my

my Portion. Under such Apprehensions the Enemy of Souls would have turned my Heart against the righteous Almighty, or prevailed upon me to give myself a Loose into present fleshly Pleasure ; but oh ! blessed Regard from on high was near, to manifest the wicked Design of the evil Spirit, and the Tendency of his Suggestions. A Resolution, in a Degree of living Faith was firmly fixed in my Heart, to endeavour to lie and to wait as at the Almighty's Footstool, if haply he might regard me in Mercy to Salvation, and if not, but that I must perish, I would perish as near it as I could get.

And as this Desire after divine Favour and Mercy, and Devotedness of Heart to lean towards, and wait for his Arising for my Salvation, was of his own begetting ; so he was graciously pleased to stay my Mind in humble Resignation, until he brought forth Judgment into Victory by degrees, and caused the Sun of Righteousness at Times to arise upon me, with Healing in his Wings : Yet he often saw meet to hide his Face from me again, and to strip me, not only of any Sense of his Favour, but even of Hope of obtaining a Place among the Redeemed. At this Time the Scripture which saith, *It is good to hope, and quietly wait, to see the Salvation of God in the Land of the Living* ; and some other like Sentences was brought to my Remembrance, accompanied with Glimpses of heavenly Goodness, which

graciously

gracioufly helped to ftay me in fome patient Hope under the heavenly refining Hand, which fometimes, as it were, fet me upon my Feet a little, and withdrew again : And fo I was left in a Senfe of Weaknefs, Fear and Sorrow. But the bleffed Prefence of the Saviour of the World, which at Times filled and over-fhadowed my Soul, in my thus following him, though mourning, is never to be forgot by my Soul. This was about the feventeenth Year of my Age.

But I am not eafy to proceed much farther in this Account, without making mention of fome few Cafes refpecting my younger Time ; and though they may feem little in fome Readers Thoughts, yet I cannot but think they may be of Service to others, and at leaft ftand as a Teftimony to the Purity, and Spirituality of the bleffed and glorious Gofpel Difpenfation of God, in pouring of his Spirit upon all Flefh, and writing his Law in Men's Hearts.

When I was between fix and feven Years old, as near as I can collect, being at fome little Play with another Boy, through the Force of a fuddain Temptation, I fwore an Oath, which notwithftanding it was to a Truth, yet fuch fecret Conviction of the Evil of fo doing in the Sight of the almighty God, fo affected my Mind with Sorrow and Remorfe, as made a lafting Impreffion on my Judgment ; and alfo imprinted that Warning and Fear in my

Heart

Heart in this Refpect, that I never did the like fince on any Occafion.

Wherefore as I cannot but believe that the pure Law of God, which is Light, makes its Appearance againft Evil in all, and often in tender Years ; fo if a careful Regard were yielded in Youth to this Infhining of the Day of God in fecret, many evil Practices and defiling Liberties would be prevented, and would never get that room in the Mind, and in Ufe, which with Sorrow we too often obferve they do.

Another Thing I am inclined to mention is, when I was about twelve or thirteen Years old, which was after my Mother's Deceafe, a ftrong Inclination took Place in me to have a Coat made with fome more Refemblance of the Mode or Fafhion of the Time, than in the plain manner which I had, with other Friends, ufed, and prevailed upon my Father to grant it ; but I was made fo uneafy in it, almoft at the firft wearing it, and the more fo in ufing it, feeling the certain Reproofs of the Spirit of Truth, for my fo leaning to, and joining with the vain and reftlefs, flefh-pleafing Spirit of the World, and turning from the fteady Plainnefs of the unchangeable Truth ; that I was indifputably fatisfied, both that the Enemy of all Good work'd in the earthly Affections of thofe wherein he could get place, to draw out the Mind at times, of the Youth efpecially, after the unfteady Corruptious

of

of the depraved World, in its changeable and vain Fashions in Drefs and Cloathing, in order to lead into the broad Way, and by degrees into the wide World, one Step making way for another. And on the other hand, I was in meafure then, and have been fince more immoveably affured, that the Light of the Gofpel-day, the Spirit of Truth doth appear againft, and reprove the very Conception of fuch vain Defires and Inclinations; and would lead and prefeve out of them, if People did but attend thereto, and labour honeftly to bear the Crofs of Chrift in this refpect : Which as it hath done before our Age, hath alfo in our Time, bleffed be the Name of the Lord therefore, faith my Soul, crucified many to the World's Spirit and Ways, in thefe enticing and adulterating Fafhions, as well as to others of its Evils. And oh ! well would it be (and for this End hath it been with me to mention it) if Youth would duly confider thefe Things, and learn to bear the Yoke of Chrift in their tender Age, while they are teachable and innocent ; before many wrong Liberties harden the Mind, and darken the Underftanding, and embolden in a Difregard to that one ever bleffed Spirit in the Heart, which only doth and muft lead Man to God and true Godlinefs.

Another Thing is frefh in my Remembrance, which I am not eafy without mentioning : There was in our Meeting an ancient and truly valuable Minifter ; and when I was about fix-

teen

teen or seventeen I was often affected with discouraging Reasonings in myself, *How we should do? And what would become of us when he died?* Under this anxious Thoughtfulness I was induced to consider, how and by what Means he was made so valuable and serviceable: That it was through his Faithfulness, his waiting to feel after, and adhering to that Manifestation of divine Power and Life from almighty God, whereof he declared; that this Principle, to which he laboured to turn and gather Peoples Minds, appeared in all: And as hereby he was made truly serviceable, so that heavenly, living Principle was well able to help, feed, fit, and preserve all who truly sought to know and be subject to it, and make them truly serviceable also. Which Consideration both instructed and encouraged me to look to the Lord, and beyond outward Instruments: And I have reason to believe, the like Thoughts affected some others of our Youth in that Meeting also to Advantage.

For as the said Minister was taken away by Death in about a Year after, the heavenly and merciful Springings of divine Life, so owned and relieved many of us, in our humble Hungerings after it, though much silent in our Meetings, that there soon appeared a lively and truly religious Growth among us; and in little more than two Years after the aforesaid Friend's Decease, there were Five of us engaged by the Truth to open our Mouths in the Ministry of

the

the Gospel, to the Satisfaction and Comfort of the Meeting. So that instead of a Decay and a Declension, about which I had been distressed with Fear, our Meeting increased in Number and in true Godliness.

Now as discouraging Thoughts, from several Sorts of Prospects, may at times attend even some well disposed Minds, and which the evil Spirit may be busy in making Use of to their Hurt, and weakening their Faith; so it is necessary to endeavour to watch against him, and call to mind with sincere Devotedness, wherein the alone Sufficiency of God's People is: And by duly seeking to witness divine Help and Succour from Christ the good Shepherd, even one Person, tho' poor and often dejected, may become instrumental to excite and encourage others in a rightly religious Application, drawing down more of divine and truly strengthning Help; by which Means many People and Meetings have been revived and helped, and have become more fruitful, to the Praise of God.

For as I have sometimes heard Complaints, or a Bemoaning of the State of some Places, for the Fewness of Ministers and truly religious Helpers in the Churches, and I believe not without Cause; yet it hath long been my Judgment, that this is principally owing to too many of our Brethren (in Profession) indulging themselves, in neglecting a proper Labour to improve the Gift or Manifestation of the Spirit

of

of Truth, given to every Man to profit with ; and ſo hold their Profeſſion of the Doctrines of Truth, in a barely rational Apprehenſion and carnal Underſtanding ; which as our Saviour Jeſus Chriſt taught in the Parable of the *unprofitable Servant*, was attended with taking away that which he had, and ſo came on a dark, reſtleſs Condition : While thoſe who diligently regarded the Giver's Direction, to attend upon the Gift, improved it, and more was given : And it is promiſed to the faithful in the little, that more ſhall be entruſted to them ; which often hath been, and yet will, I believe, be fulfilled to the honeſt, diligent and ſpiritual-minded. Thus as many Perſons and Meetings, by labouring to be found in their Duty, ſeeking their Souls Intereſt, have been regarded ; and by degrees, thro' the humbling Operation of the Power of Chriſt, the bleſſed and everlaſting high Prieſt, fitted for, and engaged in the Service of the Lord in his Wiſdom ; ſome in one Station and ſome in others, to the Edification of the Body, and the building up and beautifying his City *Zion* in the Sight of Nations. And oh! that this right Thoughtfulneſs and Application of Heart, which is both the Duty and certain Intereſt of Mankind, may more and more prevail when I am no longer here ; and be a Means of ſuch Fruitfulneſs in Righteouſneſs and heavenly Qualifications, to ſhew forth the Praiſe of God in the Earth, that Multitudes may ſee and flock to *Zion* with

everlaſting

everlasting Joy upon their Heads. *Amen, Amen.*

When I was about the eighteenth Year of my Age, a nearly affecting Exercise befel me; my Father being prosecuted on Account of his *Christian* Testimony against Tithes, and carried to Prison at *York*, forty Miles from our Dwelling; and I being the eldest he then had living, both the Care of three other younger Children, and our Business and Servants fell upon me; this with my Father's Imprisonment at such a distance, and he in a poor State of Health, brought a deep and heavy Concern upon me, that Things might be well outwardly; and I well remember a Kinsman (not of our Society) came to see me, labouring to improve the Thought of our present Difficulties, and urged me strongly to give him Liberty to agree with my Father's Prosecutor, and that I would reimburse him the Money; which when I considered a little, my Understanding was of a sudden fully satisfied, that it was the Mind and Cause of God that this Testimony against Tithes in this Dispensation should be born, and that what Suffering soever might attend our Faithfulness to him, he could readily make up, and I then believed he would; as on the other hand, that he could soon blast and consume any seeming Advantages that might be hoped for, by giving way to selfish Reasoning, or shrinking from the faithful and reverent bearing of that Testimony. Thus Truth itself, as

it

it were in a Moment, both cleared my Judgment, and brought a holy Boldnefs, with heavenly Comfort over my Soul ; in which I anfwered the Man fo, that he went no farther in the Cafe.

I am the more ftrongly induced to mention this, in order to leave an additional and experimental Teftimony to the Nearnefs and Clearnefs of the Inshining of the Light of the Gofpel, *the true Light that enlightens every Man*, to convince the Underftanding of what is evil, and to lead into the Practice of Truth ; and I fully believe, that as a truly innocent and honeft Defire hath due Place in the Mind and Soul to know, and be enabled to do the Will of the Lord our God, the Profeffors of the bleffed Truth efpecially, would have their Judgments rightly open'd and clear'd, refpecting this *Chriftian* Teftimony againft paying Tithes in any fhape ; and would find it to be their Duty, and be encouraged in themfelves, in feeling the Arifing of divine Life and heavenly Power, to ftand firmly and act chearfully with their faithful Friends, in confeffing Chrift before Men in this refpect, in Actions as well as Words. That as it is an everlafting Truth that God is One, and his Way is One; fo the People profeffing the One Truth, may walk and act confiftently with that One Way in all Things.

During my Father's Imprifonment, for want of his ftaying, guarding Eye, and prefent Help

to

to watch against and resist Temptations to hurtful and deadning Liberties, I suffered some Loss inwardly; and as it was chiefly by regarding Company too loose and airily disposed, particularly some of our Servants, I again earnestly desire, that all possible Care may be exercised by Parents who have at Heart their Childrens Growth in Godliness, to keep them from corrupting Company, and the Dangers they are exposed to from irreligious Servants. The want of which hearty, zealous Care, having certainly been an Inlet to many ruinous Temptations, often destructive both to Religion and Morality; the Sense of my own Loss, and the Danger I was in of suffering more, induceth me to leave this Remark, both as a Caution to others, and with deep and awful Reverence to acknowledge the merciful Goodness of God, in secretly disquieting and bringing a Dread over my Heart, to deter me from Liberties, which though not generally condemned, yet the Lord would not allow me in, mercifully following me at times with heavy and severe Reproofs; and as I endeavoured to sit down under his chastising Hand and Power, revealing itself against the Remains of the Lusts of the Flesh, he was pleased to deal gently with me, mixing Mercy with Judgment, and filling my Soul again and again with reverent Hope, as well as humble Supplication, that he would throughly purge me, and spare nothing alive in me that was offensive to him. Thus was
my

my Heart often excercifed both by Night and by Day, in the Fields alone and in Company, often likewife when about my Bufinefs; and fometimes the Brightnefs of the Salvation of God, and Enlargings of his Love were fo abundant in my Soul, that I could fcarce (nor did I always) keep from falling down upon the Ground to adore and worfhip his glorious Prefence. And at fome Times I apprehended it might be required of me, to open my Mouth for the Lord in the Congregation, which was an exceedingly humbling matter to me to think of.

My Father being releafed from Prifon after about fix Months Confinement, I had fome outward Eafe, though I had a deep mournful Travail inwardly, often feeling little living Comfort, but a heavy humbling Weight, which at times I ftill feared was in Difpleafure: But as ncthing but divine Favour could give me any real Satisfaction, fo a fteady Submiffion to bear his purging Hand was my Defire and fecret Hope.

When I was about the Age of nineteen my Father was removed from us by Death, which again increafed my Exercife in divers refpects; but as I endeavoured to feek the Favour and Counfel of the moft high God, he was pleafed to remember me with merciful Help many Ways: And I believe he open'd my Way to have lefs temporal Bufinefs, which was not only fome Eafe to my Mind, but more fafe in feveral

refpects,

respects, it giving Opportunity for more un-
disturbed Retirement of mind to feel after the
Salvation of God.

And now in my twentieth Year I was often
more apprehensive, that something of the Ministry of the Gospel would be laid upon me;
and some Words and Matter would often come
before me, in waiting attentively upon the Lord
in our Meetings: But I was very much afraid
of being mistaken, as well as backward about
so weighty a Work, and put it off one time
after another; but I was often exceedingly
distressed after Meetings, under a Thought
that I had refused to answer the Requiring of
God, and had thereby incurred his Displeasure
so as not to be forgiven. Under these Tossings
and Fears I often concluded in my Heart, that
if I was but certain that it was the Requiring
of the Lord, I would endeavour to obey, whatever was the Event. Thus I often concluded
both out of Meetings and in Meetings; and
some Matter would often be before me, but
in a more transient manner, or less certainly
distinct and positive, than what I reverently
and sincerely begged for.

And after this poor, distressing, sifting manner, I waded near about a Year; but when
the Time came indeed, that I was to open my
Mouth in a few Words for the Lord among
his People, it was so indisputably clear, that I
had no Scruple of its being certainly the holy
Requiring: And yet in fear I reason'd it away

D   one

one Meeting, to my deep Sorrow. But the all-feeing One knew it was from an innocent Fear, and not a rebellious contemning his fmall Appearance, and therefore he gracioufly owned me again ; and in another Meeting fhortly after, a frefh, ftrong Motion, or Concern, came upon me, and I broke forth in a few Words, but fcarcely durft ftand up upon my Feet: And after the Meeting I got quietly away, with fome Eafe and an holy Peace of mind, but thought I fhould perhaps never be farther concerned that Way: Yet now and then a Neceffity came upon me to fpeak a little again, which I moftly endeavoured to anfwer, but with great Fear and Care not to enlarge beyond the Requiring ; which Fear often prevailed upon me, fo as haftily to deliver a fmall Part only of what was fet before me, by which many times I got but little Eafe and Satisfaction ; fo that I was ftill ready to fear, and fometimes to conclude, I was wrong fome way, but knew not wherein : And under thefe Apprehenfions I was often much dejected, and humbled in deep travail to be, and to do what Truth would have me, be the Event as to myfelf what it might; which hearty Care and Fear I was made fenfible, was favourably regarded by the all-wife Being, by the humbling Senfe of his awful Prefence being near, notwithftanding the threatning Danger of being overfet by fore Toffings fecretly, and various Temptations which the evil Spirit was per-

mitted

mitted to aſſault me with ; ſo that for ſome Months I could not either eat or ſleep much, but was often alone in the Fields both Day and Night, mourning under a Load of inward Sorrow and deep Fear, leſt I ſhould yet become a Caſtaway ; but by degrees I was brought to a Deſire after Stilneſs, and a patient waiting for the ſaving Help of God to appear ; that if happily the bleſſed Saviour might ariſe and rebuke thoſe diſtreſſing Waves which lay heavy upon my Soul, occaſioning a viſible Declenſion in my Health.

But in thus labouring after Stilneſs, and thro' Submiſſion to the Day burning as an Oven, one Difficulty after another, and the diſturbing, afflicting Uncertainties and Imaginations wherewith I was beſet during this dark Time, gradually vaniſhed, and more powerful and living Light, with an humbling yet joyful Hope ſpread in and over my Soul ; which, as on one hand the ſenſe of the Mercy, and a feeling in degree of the Salvation of God, was made the more unutterably glorious and precious to my Soul ; ſo I was, on the other, more preſſingly and clearly inſtructed and warned to be fearful and watchful both againſt unrighteous vain Self, and againſt Self creeping in, and acting in the ſhape or ſhew of Religion. Thus it was given me to ſee and conſider, that the holy One was not only ſetting up his Judgments in the Earth for condemning Sin and obvious Evils in the Fleſh, that the Righteouſneſs of the Law might

be

be fulfilled in me ; but that he would over-turn, overturn all Rests or Dependencies meerly human respecting Religion, that he the Lord in whom alone is Sufficiency, might rule and have the Pre-eminence in all things ; and in a special and particular manner, in the Ministers of the Gospel.

And I am concerned to observe this farther, in relation to the uncertain manner in which some Matter and Expressions were before me in Meetings, as is hinted above, at times for near a Year : When the clear and evident Time and Requiring came, I then saw distinctly (and I have often considered it since) it was a Trial suffered to attend me, whether I would venture to act in the Uncertainty, (though a measure of the Presence of Truth was about me for my own Help to worship) and by bringing forth untimely and unripe Fruit, soon fall to De-cay, and become rather hurtful than strength-ning to others. But tho' the Lord our high Priest suffered this exercising Trial to attend me, he did not leave me to fall and miscarry here, but he renewed Fear and Resolution to do my best, to wait for distinct Assurance of his Injunction, if I must be so concerned : Which as it was and is my Duty, so I believe it to be the Duty of others also, and acceptable to the Lord, who fails not, nor ever will fail to manifest his Mind, as he is duly sought unto, for Understanding to do what he requires.

But

But I am not without fear, that such a due Attention for diſtinct Certainty of the immediate Call or Requirings of the Word of Life, hath not always been ſuitably practiſed ; and for want hereof, ſome have appeared as Miniſters before ripe, and have brought forth Fruit of very little Service, if not detrimental ; becauſe none can give what they themſelves have not : Whereas if theſe had waited with proper Diligence for the living Word to open and engage, in the entire Subjection of Self, they might have been great and good Inſtruments, as Clouds filled by the Lord with heavenly Rain. And as the divine and certain Requiring of Truth, is the only right Entrance into the Miniſtry, becauſe the Lord ſaid, *Some run and I ſent them not, therefore they* ſhall *not profit the People :* So it is only his freſh and renewed Requiring, not only opening Matter to ſpeak, but engaging to ſpeak it at this Time, whereby the Church or Particulars are edify'd, as our Father would have his Children edify'd. Theſe Obſervations reſpecting the Entrance into, and proceeding in the Miniſtry of the Goſpel, I could not be eaſy without leaving behind me, believing they will afford Inſtruction and Encouragement to ſome low and careful Travellers ; and likewiſe afford ſome neceſſary Caution to ſuch as may be in more danger of being too active.

I may now proceed farther to mention, that tho' I was nearly try'd, and had many hidden
Sorrows

Sorrows under the weight of the heavenly re-fining Hand; yet a degree of living Hope was often revived that I might in time, through humble Attention and godly Care, be ſet more at liberty in the Freedom of a Son; and thro' a true Labour to wait carefully for the diſtinct Openings of the Light of Life, and being faith-ful thereto, I ſhould gather Strength to diſcharge myſelf to more Eaſe and Satisfaction, in the little Appearance in publick I was engaged in: But I had ſo many diſcouraging Views, and was often almoſt wholly caſt down after ſome little Spring of Eaſe and Comfort in the Love and Peace of God, that I often thought I had ſurely more Droſs and Refuſe in my Nature than other Men, and therefore I muſt go oftner into the Furnace, and be melted down again and again: But I often begged the Lord not to ſpare any thing in me that was offenſive to him, how low ſoever I was brought, ſo that he would but deal with me in Mercy and not for-ſake me: And gracious Goodneſs was pleaſed to vouchſafe regard, and ſtaying Help, as a tender and wiſe Father, knowing me better than I did myſelf, and acquainting me feelingly with my Nothingneſs, and with the abſolute Neceſſity of his own Power to enable me both to live, and eſpecially to act in Religion, on any Account truly to his Praiſe.

About this time I found my Mind drawn to viſit ſometimes one neighbouring Meeting, ſometimes another, tho' much afraid to go

becauſe

becaufe of the Expectation that would be to-wards me, thro' a fenfe of my own Weaknefs, and a fear left I fhould do more hurt than good: But as I thus endeavoured to anfwer fuch Drawing, I was, beyond my Expectation often owned, and ftrengthned by and in the Word of Life to fpeak a little with that Demonftrati-on, which was edifying to others and eafy to my Spirit; begetting humble and living Reverence in my Soul, with fecret worfhip and praifes to the almighty Helper: Yet it was exceedingly awful to me, and what I could not readily get to obey the Truth in, to open my Mouth in Supplication to the infinite holy One in pub-lick Affemblies, tho' I was often full of Praifes to his mighty and glorious Name: But as he faw the reafon of my putting off fome ftrong Motions to call verbally upon the Lord, fo he dealt tenderly with me, and renewed Strength to comply with the Motions of Life in this refpect, but with inexpreffible Fear and Awe-fulnefs: Which holy Dread and due caution I beg may ever be properly renewed upon all Hearts from time to time, in the Exercife of this folemn Duty.

A Concern at this Time (being then about the twenty-fecond Year of my Age) came upon me to vifit Friends in *Scotland*, and I acquainted fome of our Friends, the Elders efpecially, therewith, who chearfully encouraged me in it; and I hearing of fome other Friends like-wife fo concern'd, I gave up to go along with
them,

them, with their free Consent; and the monthly Meeting approving my Proposal, gave me a Certificate according to good Order: And setting forward in much fear and lowness of mind, I met the other Friends at *Carlisle*, and travelled with them into the West of *Scotland*, to *Glasgow* and some other Places, where we had satisfactory Meetings, and came to *Edinburgh*: From thence we went into the North, visiting the Meetings of Friends to *Aberdeen*, and where any Meetings were settled: Friends every where appearing glad of our Visit; and being easy thereaway, we return'd by *Edinburgh*, and so by *Kelso* into *Cumberland*. We travelled together in true Unity and Comfort, divine Regard, and fresh heavenly Help being graciously afforded us, from place to place, enabling us to perform the Service for which we were drawn thither: And tho' we met with abusive Treatment in several Places, especially at *Glasgow* and *Edinburgh*, by the mobbish part of the People disturbing Friends Meetings, by casting Stones or any other matter at hand amongst them; which was a very frequent practice and continued many Years, yet we were preserved from any material Hurt: And for my own part, as I had nothing to depend upon, but as it might please the Lord our God to open and supply with his own Hand; so attending patiently upon him, that his Will might be done, he failed not to afford both daily Bread to live upon, and often Help and Engagement

gagement to labour in the Miniftry, which feemed much to Friends Satisfaction, and very much more to my own than I dared to hope for, fo that I returned with Peace and Encouragement humbly to truft in God, and to follow the Drawings of his divine Love.

I had given up Houfe-keeping fome time before this Journey, yet kept a little Ground in my own hands for fome neceflary Employ, which I loved and believed was good for me, both for the Body, and a beneficial Stay to the Mind. Yet being much alone, I had often comfortable Retirements, through the merciful regard of divine Goodnefs, opening heavenly Inftruction, and increafing clear Difcernment betwixt the transform'd and betraying Suggeftions of the evil Spirit, and the fteady, pure, heavenly Openings and Motions of the Word and Spirit of Truth.

But fome farther Concern and Drawings to leave home coming upon me, I thought it beft to difpofe of that Land and Bufinefs alfo ; yet for Employment I work'd often for fome others, both for a living, and that my Mind might not be too much difengaged from fome temporal Concerns ; wherein there appeared to me then, and more fo fince, a danger of being tempted to be eafily drawn abroad (after having been fomewhat engaged to travel) even before or without that diftinct Requiring of Truth, both *to go* and *return*, in which only the Minifters of Chrift move in true Safety, and to

                          right

right Edification : And by indulging such an Inclination, may be in danger of missing or losing the clear Knowledge of the pure Requirings of the everlasting high Priest ; and so make way for Formality, a barren Ministry and unprofitable Labour, whereby some have hurt themselves, with respect to real Service in the Church, and true Esteem among the living and sensible Part of the People.

And yet on the other hand I was afraid (and so should all Ministers) of being involved in temporal Concerns so much, as to hinder me from true inward retiring often to feel the Life of Truth, for the daily Supply of my Soul, and where I might understand when he called to Service abroad ; and made willing and ready to leave any thing to follow the Lord's Drawings.

Some Months after the aforesaid little Journey, I found it my Concern to visit more of our own County, and the County of *Durham*, and afterwards several other Northern Counties: And it pleased the Lord, the blessed Fountain of Wisdom and all truly sufficient Help, not only to engage me in that Service, but to furnish with Supply for inward Life and publick Labour, to my humbling Admiration before him, I being altogether poor and empty, but as he renewed Help afresh in my careful waiting upon him for it. And indeed his goings forth in my Ministry in that Visit, were often wonderful to me, both because of the humbling and

and encouraging Effect that my Labour had upon the better minded, the younger especially, and which was not forgot by many while they lived ; and likewise the terrible and awakening Calls to some bold Libertines, and those who were sitting down in the deadness of Formality. Though this Labour was like a Fire to the house of *Esau*, and therefore unpleasant to some ; yet the inward and living among the People were relieved and made glad in the Lord, whose Favour and Peace often filled my Heart with awful Reverence toward him, with strong Desires purely to know, and be helped to do his Will faithfully.

About this Time several were convinced in the Northern parts where I was drawn to visit, and were gathered into the Knowledge of Truth ; of whom some became valuable Ministers of the Gospel.

But I still loved to be as much at home with our own Friends as I could with ease, and to labour with my hands in the Creation, though some Concern was growing upon me towards part of the South ; which as I kept still in my mind, desiring to see my Duty clearly, both Places and Time were set plainly before me, and a hastning to go forward. So with the Approbation of our Friends at home, I set out in a poor low frame of Spirit, full of fear, and reverent Desire after heavenly Help, and went through most of the Meetings in the Western

 side

fide of the Nation, and to *London* : And after fome Weeks ftay and Labour there as Truth gave Ability, I travelled Weftwards, through the feveral Counties to the *Land's-end* in *Cornwall*; then back by *Briftol* to their Yearly-meeting, and fhortly after that turned into *Wales*, vifiting (as I remember) all the Meetings of Friends there, alfo in *Chefhire* and part of *Lancafhire*; and fo home again with Gladnefs and Thankfulnefs of Heart for many Reafons, having been about nine Months on that Journey, though I travelled diligently : My Health being preferved almoft to me wonderfully, though as I came through *Somerfetfhire*, I was for fome Days very ill, but preffed forward in the Service to *Briftol*, and the Day I got thither after the Meeting, the *Meafles* appeared upon me, on which Occafion I kept houfe only two Days ; and being clear of the Place, in a few Days more I fet forward again. For an earneft Defire and Care was very early imprinted upon me, and hath continued to this Time, to occafion as little Trouble and Charge to Friends, in my Travel as could be, which I believe is but mine and every other Minifter's Duty.

This Journey afforded various Occafions of profitable Inftruction to me : Sometimes divine Goodnefs and heavenly Life was gracioufly and plentifully opened in my Soul, both for my own feeding and renewing of Strength to worfhip ; and furnifhing me with Matter and

Power

Power to minister prevalently to others, that the Name of the Lord our God might be felt and glorified : Yet at some other times Access to Food was much more restricted, and with Patience as well as Diligence to be wrestled for : Sometimes it was longer before any thing was given to minister to others, and the Openings were with less Clearness for a time, and not so strong, nor Engagements so lively or sensibly to myself as I much loved : But often as I attended upon the Lord in due Stilness and Resignation of Mind, at such Times hath he opened a Supply of Food, though less plentiful, and something, though small in appearance, to offer to the People ; which I found my Duty to seek for satisfactory Evidence, that it was a degree of the Word of Truth, before I durst open my Mouth, and then contentedly to labour according to the measure of present Ability : Yet some such Seasons, through the merciful, though gradual Arisings of heavenly Greatness and Wisdom, were made both comfortable and strengthning to me, reverently to trust in the Lord ; and signally beneficial and memorable to the Congregation. And thus I was made a Witness, what it was to abound, and how to suffer want ; and taught to be resignedly content with the various Dispensations, and Operations of the heavenly Power : Neither in more plentiful Seasons to forget God the blessed Author and Giver thereof ; nor in times of Poverty to put forth a hand to steal :

And

And oh ! good and gracious was that divine Arm of Power, which engaged my Spirit in that Travel, in many refpects fhewing me plainly many Dangers and By-ways, which Youth efpecially are liable to fall into ; and that our Safety only confifted in keeping in watchful Fear, and in carefully feeling after, from day to day, the Influences of divine Life in the eternal Word, wherein is the Light of Men for all Stations and religious Services through-out all Generations. And as it was made, through divine Mercy and Help, a teaching, ftrengthning, encouraging Time to myfelf ; fo the Lord of Mercies, by the Attendance of this Power renewedly, made the Labour I was engaged in, profitably awakening and relieving to many : Several were convinced and ga-thered to the Truth, in this Journey ; fome of whom, in time, were made zealous and ufeful Minifters in the Church.

I was now eafy, and comfortably glad of being at home among my Friends, as they were alfo therewith : And here I continued moftly vifiting adjacent Meetings, as I found Draw-ings thereto, and attending our Monthly and Quarterly-meetings, which for fome Years I had had an honourable Efteem for ; being often indifputably fatisfied, that the Lord God in his Wifdom and Power had directed to, and eftablifhed them in Love and Mercy to his Church ; inafmuch as I was livingly fenfible, in fitting reverently behind the Elders in

Meetings

Meetings for the good Order and Difcipline of the Church, that the divine Wifdom and Prefence of the Higheft was often with Friends for Counfel and Strength, enabling them to lift up a Standard againft the Enemy of all Godlinefs, when likely to prevail through the various evil Liberties of the Flefh.

In about a Year after, I found a frefh Concern growing weightily upon me, to vifit Friends in *Scotland* again, and likewife in *Ireland*; with the Approbation of my Friends, and (having a Certificate from our Monthly-meeting) I fet forward in the fixth Month 1701, with humble defires of Soul before the Lord for his Prefence and Wifdom to guide and enable me : I went thro' *Cumberland*, to *Edinburgh*, and fo to the North of *Scotland*, vifiting the Meetings of Friends every where in thofe parts, and return'd by *Edinburgh* to *Glafgow*, and the Meetings thereaway : Being in many Places truly comforted with Friends, and they encouraged and glad in a living Senfe of the continued fartherly Regard, and Extendings of the Love of God toward them in that Nation, amongft a hard, felf-conceited, and in fome Places an envious People : And ftill a wicked Spirit prevailed with the mobbifh People both in *Edinburgh* and *Glafgow*, to delight in difturbing Friends in almoft all their Meetings; fometimes throwing Stones, &c. whilft others with all the Noife and vain Sport they could invent, efpecially endeavoured to drown the

Voice

Voice of any who were concern'd to minifter publickly among them : Yet at times the Power and Authority of Truth arofe over thofe wicked Endeavours, and the evil Spirit was overborne and fo weighed down, that fome of the worft would go away, and others lend fome Attention to the Teftimony of Truth ; and Friends were the more edified, and their Faith and Hope in God ftrengthned. This difturbing, envious, perfecuting Spirit, was fuffered to exercife the Faith and Patience of Friends there, in that manner, during many Years : But a Cafe happen'd at *Glafgow*, when I was there, fomewhat remarkable ; on a Firft-day of the Week, the People had very much difturbed us, in the afternoon Meeting efpecially, in their ufual wicked and vain manner, and followed Friends after Meeting along a large open Street, where their Number increafed, fome fhouting and fcorning, others throwing Stones and Dirt ; one Stone of fome pounds weight paffed with great force very near one of my Legs, which if it had been hit, muft, I believe have been broke by it ; yet we were preferved from much harm : Whilft the People who were gather'd in great Numbers about their Doors, and faw what paffed, feemed rather to be pleafed with the abufive Behaviour of the Mob towards us, than to offer any Difcouragement to them : Whereupon a Soldier, an *Englifhman*, began to cry aloud three times, as if he had fome publick Proclamation to

make,

make; and when he had thereby drawn the Peoples Attention to him, he called aloud again, *Behold the godly Town of* Glasgow, *how they entertain Strangers!* and repeated it three several times. Which Reproof made the People so ashamed, that they mostly took to their Houses and got out of sight; and the more grown People drawing away, the rest soon left us and made off likewise, so that we had no farther Disquiet that Day; and I heard, when I was at this Place some Years after, that the People had never offer'd the like Disturbance again, either in their Meetings or in the Streets.

From hence I went down the River *Clyde* for *Ireland*, and landed near *Belfast*, and thence went to *Lisburn* where several Friends lived, who received me lovingly. I began to labour diligently amongst Friends, hoping to get clear of the North part of that Nation before the half-year's Meeting in *Dublin* in the ninth Month, which I was enabled to answer, in a good measure to my Satisfaction. At *Dublin* there was gather'd a large body of Friends, not only in a very consistent and grave Appearance; but a living and truly religious Concern and Zeal for the Truth was upon many of them, and great Harmony amongst them. Here I met with our ancient and honourable Friend *William Edmundson*, whom I had a great desire to see, having a deep and reverent Value for him from seeing him before in *England*, tho' he knew little or nothing of me. For I believed, if I

F was

was not what I fhould be, he would not only obferve wherein, but would deal plainly with me : I went with fome other Friends to fee him at his Lodgings, where he looked fternly and earneftly upon me, and faid little ; I fat down, and little was fpoke amongft us, but I obferved he often caft his Eye upon me : But when we parted from him, he feemed more free and chearful to me ; and in feveral of the publick Meetings I was concerned to teftify for the Truth among them, which both he and other Friends gave free way and time for, and fo openly manifefted his Regard to, and Satif-faction with me, as made my way eafy among Friends through the reft of the Nation ; and had a deeply humbling, and yet encouraging Effect upon my Heart, to feel carefully after divine Help and Wifdom, which alone can fufficiently qualify for real Service, and preferve in the Way and Work of the Lord.

I then vifited the Meetings of Friends thro' the other parts of the Nation with diligence ; but forgetting natural Ability too much, I fell into a dangerous Ilnefs from a violent Cold, which forced me to ftop about ten Days at *Mountmelick* ; I fet forward again in the Work I was engaged in, though before fome Friends thought it was fit for me, but got well along till I was clear of the Nation at that Time : My Labour in the Gofpel Power and Word of Life being chearfully received, and made profitably awakening to fome, reviving to the

Living ;

Living ; and a means of divers of the Youth amongſt Friends being inwardly affected with the Power of Truth, to their laſting advantage, and the Churches comfort. And ſo with the Love of my Friends, and an humble and thankful heart before the Lord of all true Help, I took leave of Friends at *Cork*, and went over to *Minehead* in *Somerſetſhire*, having ſomething remaining upon me to a few places there-away, and about *Briſtol*; and from hence came pretty directly home again, with reverent Awe towards the ever bleſſed Helper.

And now I ſtaid moſtly about and near home with my Friends, in true Comfort, (for we were made and preſerved truly dear one unto another in the Love and Life of Truth) employing myſelf in bodily Labour with diligence, which I ſtill loved, for the reaſons above-mentioned : But in leſs than a Year after, a Concern came upon me to viſit the Eaſt-part of the Nation ; I ſet forward through *Lincolnſhire, Norfolk, Suffolk, Eſſex,* and went over the *Thames,* and through *Kent* and *Suſſex,* returning through *Surry* to *London,* and through the middle part of the Nation home, as I remember, in about five Months, the ſupplying Preſence and Power of Chriſt being mercifully renewed for Aſſiſtance from time to time. Yet a deeply exerciſing Trial for about two Weeks was ſuffered to attend me, by a heavy weight of Trouble and diſtreſſing Doubts lying almoſt continually upon me day and night,

F 2

eſpecially

especially out of Meetings, which brought very narrow Searching of heart, and much fear of being forsaken of all-saving Help, and left I should thereby become a Reproach to the glorious Name I had made mention of : Yet I was not left void of some hope in his Mercy, who is all-knowing. This so far affected my Behaviour, that I could not conceal my Sorrow in mourning alone, and conversing little, though unexpected Relief and Supply mostly attended in Meetings. But as I was brought to endeavour and desire after a thorough Search, to know the cause wherein I had offended, or missed the right way in any case, and to double a watchful waiting and walking ; so I was strengthned in a Resolution, or Desire at least, to labour to be duly devoted to follow the Almighty's requiring, if he would but give a clear understanding thereof, with necessary Help, whatever it was to do : And by degrees Life sprang up in my Soul through death ; and a peaceful Devotedness, with a chearful, yet awful Trust in the almighty Searcher of hearts, overspreading my whole inward man, imprinting Instruction upon me not to be forgotten.

And not long after this, a Concern, which had been at times moving in my mind, but at some distance, to visit the Churches in *America*, now grew more constant and weighty upon me ; and my late exercising time had contributed to bring me into the more quiet and ready yielding to follow the Truth any

way,

way, if it was but caſt up to me clear ; ſo that when the matter was freſh before me, I endeavoured to be duly ſtill and devoted ; and when it ſeemed almoſt out of ſight, or gone away, I was pleaſantly eaſy therewith ; which Reſignation and Quietneſs I have found to be my Duty, and the ſafeſt way to attain a clear diſcerning of the Motions of Truth in thoſe caſes, and alſo of the Time ; for I am very ſenſible the Lord directs as to Time, as well as the Thing in this reſpect.

This was in the fore part of Summer, and the next ſecond Month ſeemed to fix with me to be the Time, though I yet kept the thing moſtly to myſelf ; but as it ſeemed to remain ſettled with me, I grew inclined to acquaint ſome particular Friends, ſome eſpecially who had been engag'd in that Travail, with the Concern I was under, who encouraged me to be given up properly in that reſpect ; and a young man of our County, *viz. William Ar-miſtead,* finding his Mind likewiſe drawn that way, gave up to go along with me. And I having ſome Acquaintance with a Friend, who was Maſter of a Ship, who uſed to go to *Maryland,* I had a thought of going with him, and wrote to know when he expected to ſail, and had Anſwer, he intended to go about the twelfth Month, (1705) which account put me out of expectation of that Opportunity, becauſe I durſt not move before the Time that appeared to me the right one. But as the matter
remained

remained with me I continued to make myself ready, and having the Approbation of, and a Certificate from our Monthly-meeting, and the Meeting of Ministers and Elders at the Quarterly-meeting, we set out in the second Month towards *London*; when we came thither we soon heard that the above-mention'd Ship and Master were not sailed, and tho' near ready, yet we had a seasonable Opportunity of more than two Weeks to visit Friends in the City before we departed.

This Circumstance I mention because it afforded me matter of secret Encouragement, both in confirming me that it was the Lord's requiring, also that it was his Time; and likewise that this was the Vessel order'd for us to go in: I had therefore the stronger Hope we might be preserved. All which Considerations humbled my Heart before, and revived my Hope in the Lord; and the more relievingly, as it was at that time War between *England* and *France*, and the *French* had abundance of Privateers out at Sea. This occasioned us to be longer in the Channel than usual, that the large Fleet might get together, being three Weeks e're we parted from the Land's-end, and we were ten Weeks more in getting to our Port in *Patuxen* River in *Maryland*; yet we had a safe and good Passage tho' long: And the exceeding Difficulty arising to me from so long a Confinement with little business (having been much accustomed to be stirring) was abundantly eased, and render'd

often

often joyful to me, by the gracious Regard and comforting nearnefs of the heavenly Prefence to my Soul, never I hope to be forgot.

After we had ftaid a few Meetings with Friends thereabouts, who receiv'd us with great Chearfulnefs, finding our Minds drawn towards *Philadelphia*, and fo northward to *New-England*, we croffed *Chefapeak* Bay and had fome Meetings with Friends on the Eaftern-fhore of *Maryland*, and fo into the lower Counties of *Penfilvania*; we got to *Philadelphia* before the Yearly-meeting there, which was large and comfortable to us and Friends, by the gracious and powerful Influences of the Love of God, whofe glorious Name was worfhipped and praifed for his Mercy and Salvation.

We fet out for *Long-Ifland* with fome Friends who came from thence to this Yearly-meeting, and tho' I had an *Intermitting Fever* upon me, which diftreffed and weaken'd me very much, yet being defirous to be forward in the Work we were there upon, I was not willing to be hinder'd by it, whilft I could any way avoid it. After ftaying a few Meetings on *Long-Ifland* we fet out for *New-England*, having near two hundred Miles to travel by land through the Colony of *Connecticut*; in which Space there were few or no "Friends, and the People generally very fhy of us, and partly by reafon of fome fevere Laws then in force there, they were afraid to converfe with Friends; though I was enabled to bear the Journey, yet it was

not

not without difficulty and being much weakened ; having almoſt no Appetite to any Food : But getting to *Rhode-Iſland*, we were gladly received by our Friends there to our Encouragement ; after a Week's reſt, and the trial of ſome Medicines, tho' to little effect, I reſolved to go forward in the Service, in the Ability that Truth would be pleaſed to afford ; we viſited the Meetings down to *Sandwich*, and thence through *Plimouth* Colony to *Boſton*, being favour'd with the Preſence and Help of Truth, often to our own and Friends Comfort and Encouragement in the Lord. We went forward by *Salem*, and to the fartheſt Meetings of Friends that way, and had ſeveral Meetings about *Dover*. It was then a very exerciſing and trying time with Friends here, by reaſon of the bloody Incurſions that the *Indians* then frequently made upon the *Engliſh*, being hired by the *French* about *Quebeck*, which lies behind *New-England* to the North-weſt ; ſo that many of the *Engliſh* Inhabitants were frequently murder'd in their Houſes, or ſhot, or knock'd down on the Road or in the Fields ; ſome were carried away Captives ; and thoſe whom they killed, they cut with their great Knives round the Head about the Skirt of the Hair, and then pulled the Skin off the Head ; and for every ſuch Skin, which they call a *Scalp*, they were to have a Sum of Money. Theſe Barbarities cauſed many People to leave their Habitations with their Families, and retire into

Garriſons,

Garrisons, which the People built in many places for their greater Security. Yet that which was sorrowful to me to observe, was that few of them seemed to be affected with due Consideration, so as to be awakened to think rightly of the Cause of this heavy Chastisement, and be induced to seek the Almighty's Favour, as they ought. But it was a profitable, humbling time to many of our Friends, who generally stood in the Faith, and kept at their usual places of Abode, tho' at the daily hazard of their Lives : And it was very remarkable, that scarce any who thus kept their Habitations in the Faith, were suffer'd to fall by the *Indians*, tho' few Days passed but we heard of some of their cruel Murders, and destroying Vengeance. We were in these parts backwards and forwards a considerable time, having many Meetings, before we could be clear to leave them ; which thro' the merciful Regard and succouring Nearness of the almighty Power and Presence, was satisfactory to us, and very strengthning and comfortable to Friends ; we and they being all graciously preserved though in the open Country, and we lodged several times at one Friend's House, at some distance from the Garrison ; and we had reason to believe a Party of *Indians* was for some time about it, the Marks of their Feet being plainly to be seen next Morning, but they went away without doing any Damage, tho' it was but a mean little timber House, and easy to break into.

G   We

We alſo got a few Meetings in ſome Towns where few Friends lived ; but not many People durſt come to them, becauſe of the Laws of the Country then unrepealed, which had been made to prevent the Spreading of Truth, and alſo becauſe of the dark and envious Induſtry of their Preachers to hinder them, by monſtrous Miſrepreſentations of Friends : Yet ſome did come, and behaved with Attention, and the Love and Power of Truth being meaſurably with us, they carried ſuch ſatisfactory Accounts to their Neighbours, as tended much to beget more favourable Sentiments with regard to Friends and the Doctrines of Truth: Yet I often thought that a thick Cloud ſeemed to be over the Country, and eſpecially about *Boſton* and Parts near it ; tho' Light ſeemed to me to be breaking through in ſeveral Places, and I fully believed would more prevail after the Remains of that wicked and perſecuting Generation was gone off the ſtage. We had nevertheleſs in *Boſton* ſome bleſſed Meetings with a few innocent Friends there, and ſome others, who would often come, in the Evenings eſpecially.

From *Boſton* we travelled back up the more Weſtern - parts, towards *Providence*, having Meetings with Friends ; and I was not eaſy without going up to ſome of the later ſettled Towns, to ſee if we could have ſome Meetings among them ; the People there-away being little acquainted with Friends, or their Principles.

Principles. We accordingly went to several Towns, being accompanied with two Friends, and sought for Liberty to have some Meetings among them, but the People were afraid either to grant Room, or to come to a Meeting ; yet we found several willing to converse with us, (asking Questions, and receiving Answers) and who seemed pleased to be better informed. Several gross Misrepresentations concerning Friends and Truth, which had been spread amongst them, were confuted and cleared away ; with which many seemed well pleased in several places ; so that we returned in Peace and Satisfaction, believing we were in our Duty, and that our Labour there-away was of some Service.

We came back to *Rhode-Island*, and after having a few Meetings on that Island and near it, (where there is a good and valuable body of Friends, with whom we were comforted in the heavenly Father's Love and Regard) we came back to *Long-Island* and *New-York*, and had some large and heavenly Meetings there-away ; where some were convinced of the Truth, and joined honestly with Friends. We also had Drawings to visit some Towns towards the East-end of that Island, being some Days Journey from the Places where almost any Friends dwelt : We accordingly went to several Towns, and procured Liberty to have some Meetings, though there was a rigid *Presbyterian* People there-away ; and at one Town

the

the Preacher and the Juſtice conſulted together while we were at a Meeting in the Evening, and contrived to give us ſome Trouble : And next Morning the Juſtice (whoſe Name was *Hubbert)* ſent forth a Warrant to bring us before him : We went, and many of the Town's People hearing of it, gathered about us, and went in. He began to examine us of our Names, Places of abode, and our Buſineſs there, to which we gave him Anſwers, ſo that he ſeemed to be at a loſs what farther to ſay to us ; but he bethought him to examine us about taking the Oaths ; we deſired to know what Oaths he meaned, but he was as much at a ſtand to tell us, nor could he find them in his Book, which he turned over carefully, but met with nothing to his purpoſe ; whilſt the People who were there, ſeemed pleaſed to ſee him ſo faſt, and in a manner confounded. Then another Juſtice of the peace came in : The firſt being behind a Table, ſtood up and ſaid, Come Mr. *Wheeler,* pleaſe to come here, this is a Part of your Buſineſs : To which he replied ſternly, *I know not that it is, or yours either* ; and ſo they fell to argue the caſe one with another with ſome heat, we ſtanding ſtill with an innocent Chearfulneſs ; for the Love and Preſence of Chriſt was meaſurably with us, and much beyond our Expectation comforted us ; the People were pleaſed to ſee the poor, dark, envious Man, who gave us this Trouble, confounded. Then the other Juſtice who

who came in, said ; I have been at our own
Meeting three Sabbath-days one after another,
and did not hear Chrift named from the Pul-
pit ; and I confefs I was at the Meeting with
thefe People yefternight, and heard Chrift
preached truly. A pretty deal more paffed betwixt the Juftices, and fome of the other People
alfo began to fhew their Diflike of him and his
Proceedings with us, fo that he feemed much
to want to have the Difcourfe over, and us gone,
though we were then in no hafte : But after a
little he difcharged us, and fet us at liberty,
though he had threatned us with a Prifon before. So after fome time fpent fatisfactorily,
among the more friendly difpofed People in
the Town, we being eafy in our minds, left
that part and returned up the Ifland, having
fome Service, and feveral Meetings in other
places, till we came again to where Friends
were fettled.

But we could not find ourfelves clear without
returning again to *Rhode-Ifland*, tho' a long Journey, in order to be at the Yearly-meeting held
there for that Government and *New-England*,
which we got to, through fome Hardfhips in
travelling ; there we faw Friends from moft
Parts of thofe Provinces, it being an exceeding
large Meeting, and very eminently comfortable
to many, through the ftrong and lively fpreading of the Love and Power of God therein
for feveral days ; and the edifying Accounts
brought from the feveral Parts belonging to
this

this Meeting : Friends generally keeping their Places and Habitations in the Faith, and were eminently preferved in that diftreffing, bloody Time, when the Sword, like a Scourge, afflicted the Country. We then were free to go from thofe Parts, and return toward *New-York*, we took our Leave of Friends in much Nearnefs of heart, under a Senfe of the Lord's blefled Prefence and Fatherly Care, and with holy and hearty Rerurns of Thankfulnefs, and Praife to the almighty Deliverer.

. As we pafled through the Colony of *Connecticut*, we found fome Concern upon us, to endeavour to have a Meeting in *New-haven*, the chief Town in the Government : We enquired at the Inn if we could have a Room, or where we could procure one to have a Meeting in ; but were told, that none in the Town durft allow fuch a thing, and that but very few would dare to come to one of our Meetings, except the Minifter (as they call their Teachers) firft gave leave : One Man in the houfe feem'd defirous that we fhould have a Meeting, and faid he hoped the Minifter would not deny it, if he were fought to for it ; and offer'd himfelf to go with us, if we defired to fpeak with him, which I found my Mind inclined to : We went accordingly to the Prieft's Houfe (his Name was ——— *Pierpoint*) he fpoke to us civilly, and invited us in ; I told him, that as we as a People, and our Doctrine had in many places been very much mifreprefented, and

and unjuftly reproached ; we were often defirous of Opportunities that People might hear
us, and fo be the better able to judge for themfelves ; and that we defired to have fuch an
Opportunity in that Town, but did not find
the People durft allow it, unlefs he would con-
fent thereto, and the Occafion of our coming
to him was to make that reafonable Requeft :
But he fmoothly excufed himfelf from giving
fuch a Liberty, with divers Allegations, but after a feeming civil manner ; for by this time
a pretty many of the Upper-fort of the Towns-
people were gather'd in : Then he was told,
that we had nothing in our Hearts towards
them, or any elfe, but the *univerfal Love* of
God : On which Expreffion he began to obferve, that he fuppofed they did not underftand
the Love of God to be univerfal in the *manner*
that we did ; To which I return'd, That feeing
the Scripture is pofitive that Chrift our Saviour
gave himfelf a Ranfom for all Men, and *by the
Grace of God tafted death for every Man* ; and
that *he became a Propitiation not only for their
Sins (viz.* the Believers at that time) *but for
the Sins of the whole World* ; and alfo, that he
fpiritually *enlighten'd every Man coming into the
World* ; *that a Manifeftation of the Spirit was
given to every Man to profit withal* ; and that
*the Grace of God which bringeth Salvation, hath
appeared to all Men :* From hence we had good
reafon to believe the Love of God in Chrift to
be *univerfal* ; and defired him if he thought
fit,

fit, and could, to shew from Scripture the contrary : He anſwered, they underſtood that Salvation was extended to Mankind, as the Goſpel
was *outwardly* preached : Proof of which Opi-
nion from Scripture was then deſired : He mention'd that of the *Law coming to* Iſrael, *and the
Statutes to* Jacob, and that God had not dealt
ſo with any other Nation : He alſo mention'd
Gallilee *of the* Gentiles, *the People that ſat
in Darkneſs ſaw a great Light*, &c. which
was, he ſaid, the Goſpel was preached *verbally*
amongſt them : We anſwer'd that we ſcrupled
not to allow, that the Almighty manifeſted a
particular Regard to the Houſe or Family of
Iſrael ; and alſo favour'd the People of *Gallilee*
of the *Gentiles*, in cauſing the Goſpel to be
inſtrumentally preached unto them early : Yet
that did not prove, to our Underſtandings, that
others had not Offers of *ſaving Help* from God ;
becauſe the Apoſtle *Paul* had aſſerted, that *the*
Gentiles *who had not the Law, yet did thoſe things
contained in the Law* ; thereby ſhewing forth
the Law of God written *in their Hearts*. Then
he began to ſay, he ſuppoſed we were come
prepared for diſputing matters, and that he was
not appriſed of any ſuch thing ; or to this
effect : We told him we were but newly alighted
from our Horſes, and came to him to aſk his
Conſent to have a Meeting for the Peoples Satisfaction ; that this Diſcourſe was altogether
unexpected by us, and that we conſidered we
were in his Houſe, and would not impoſe upon
him.   By

By this time the House was almoſt full of
ſoberly behaved People, which occaſion'd both
more fear and care upon the Prieſt ; and I believe the Truth both ſupply'd and ſeaſon'd our
Spirits for their good : I think we might have
about an hour's Conference at leaſt, moſtly in
a commendable Calmneſs and Civility ; we
parted, and with an holy Comfort and Thankfulneſs of heart before the Lórd for his merciful Aſſiſtance.

We were then eaſy to go forward, and came
to *Fluſhing* in *Long-Iſland,* and having ſome
few more Meetings there-away, we came thro'
part of the *Jerſeys* into *Penſilvania* ; in which
Provinces we travelled, viſiting Meetings moſt
of the Summer, having many large and heavenly Seaſons : Which very much ſpent my
bodily Strength, (and ſo far that I think, I never recover'd it.) But the Lord added a Bleſſing to our Labours in theſe parts ; ſome were
convinced and gathered to the Truth ; and one
young Woman, who after ſome time became
engaged in the Miniſtry of the Goſpel, wherein
ſhe was made a very eminent Inſtrument to
the help and comfort of many, in divers parts
of the World.

We were alſo at the Yearly-meeting in the
ſeventh Month at *Burlington,* for Friends of
Penſilvania and the *Jerſeys,* which was exceeding large, and to good Satisfaction in the dominion of Truth.

H   We

We then turn'd towards *Maryland*, and visited Friends and some others in several places down the Eastern - shore, into *Virginia*, to pretty good Satisfaction, though the Affairs of Truth among Friends there-away, were at that time but low, partly thro' a Neglect of Discipline.

We got over the great Bay of *Chesapeak*, so thro' the lower part of *Virginia*, and into *North-Carolina*, and had many strengthning and comfortable Meetings in those parts, thro' the gracious Extendings of the Love and Power of God towards a well-disposed People, both Professors of Truth, and some others; among whom we had some good Service.

We then came up into *Maryland* again, upon the Western-shore, but got over some large Rivers with great difficulty and hazard, in the severity of the Winter; we then visited some few places in *Pensilvania* and the *Jerseys*, which we were not clear of, greatly to our comfort: and so prepared to take leave of those parts in order to visit *Barbadoes*. But I hope never to forget the heavenly Nearness and Openness of heart, wherein we had to take leave of our Friends there-away, with the Offers of Thanksgiving and Praise to the almighty Helper and Protector.

And as particular Marks of the Interposition of divine Providence, should be had in remembrance, I think it fit to mention here something that I esteemed such. There were two

Vessels

Veſſels both near ready to ſail for *Barbadoes*, and many were inclinable to our going in one of them rather than the other, believing the Maſter would behave reſpectfully to us: The other was accounted a moroſe ſour-temper'd Man, yet we could not be eaſy but in concluding to go with him: The other Veſſel went out firſt, but quickly loſt her Maſt, and lay many weeks tumbling at Sea; we went well, and were near ſix weeks before the other, which was owing to the providential Care over us.

We were kindly received by Friends at *Barbadoes*, and enter'd upon our Service amongſt them, labouring therein near two Months to pretty good ſatisfaction: But thro' the Heat of the Climate, and my diligent Labour, I was ſeized with a violent *Fever*, which, moſt of thoſe who ſaw me, expected would have taken me off; but it pleaſed the Lord of all Mercies to reſtore my Health again, in about a Month's time; and ſhortly after, being clear of the Iſland, took leave of Friends in much nearneſs in the Love of the Goſpel.

We ſailed to *Antigua*, but in our Paſſage were attacked by a *French* Privateer, which after firing a few Guns, without doing the Ship or Men any damage, made ſail and left us: We were ſome of us very thankful for the merciful Protection; and that Evening we landed in *Antigua*, where we had ſome good Service in divers reſpects among Friends; ſeveral of whom had been out of good Order, but we

were

were helped to leave things better, and were clear to depart in about three Weeks, and sailed for *Jamaica*, where we arrived in the eighth Month.

There were at this time four Meetings of Friends in *Jamaica* mostly kept up; tho' they were several of them remote from each other; we visited them frequently, and had some Meetings at times amongst the People, so that our Labour became of good Service for the Truth. There was a Priest toward the farther part of the Island who grew very angry about us, calling us *Deceivers* and *Deluders*; and gave out that he would dispute with us: We thereupon let him know, that tho' we were not much in love with such Opportunities, they often proving more noisy than really edifying; yet as he had frequently taken the liberty to calumniate and asperse us as a People, and the Doctrine of Truth which we had to publish, in a publick manner behind our backs, we were willing to meet him in a publick Place, when and where he would appoint, that we might make our Defence: He then sent us word by Letter, that he would only have a private Conference before six of our People, and he would bring as many with him: But we chose that the Meeting might be so publick as that all might come and hear who desired it; which as it was his own Proposal at first, he could not fairly refuse.

Time

Time and Place being agreed upon, he and many People came ; he had fixed upon four Things to difcufs, in order to prove us errone- ous, *viz.* the *Difufe of the two Sacraments,* as they call them ; our holding *Perfection* ; and allowing *Women to preach* ; and to *keep to Scrip- ture* for proof. He firft enter'd upon *Water- baptifm,* in order to prove it a ftanding Ordi- nance in the Church of Chrift, which he en- deavour'd to do by a Chain of Arguments, artfully link'd together ; but when thefe came to be taken afunder, and their Inconfiftency difcovered in much Calmnefs of mind ; he fell into a furious Paffion, ufing angry Threats in- ftead of Arguments ; afterwards becoming fomewhat more cool, he wanted to proceed to another Article : I told him, I would allow him to proceed to the next as foon as he pleafed, if he firft yielded up that, or could advance fome more convincing Proofs of his Affertions, but not till then. He was fo uneafy and afhamed with his Management of the Debate, that he foon left the Houfe and Company : We and many of the People ftay'd, and had a good and edifying Meeting, and parted com- fortably. The Prieft in a little time after left the Ifland, and got a Place, as I heard, aboard a Man of War.

We labour'd near three Months, in this Ifland among the few Friends in it, and fometimes among the neighbouring People ; but Grandeur and vain Liberties very much obftructed the

Growth

Growth of true Religion at that time, and more so afterwards : But we were favour'd with heavenly Help, and much holy Comfort and Peace in our Labours amongst them.

When we became clear in our Spirits, and easy to leave the Place, we prepared for our Departure for *England* ; and a Ship bound for *London* being almost ready to sail, we had some Thoughts of coming in her : My Companion being indisposed, desired that I would go on board the said Ship to take our Passage ; I went accordingly to speak with the Master, but quite unexpectedly to me, I found myself so disquieted and uneasy in mind, that I durst not say much to the Master, tho' the Vessel had the Character of the best sailing Ship in the Trade. I learn'd that there was another Vessel almost ready to sail for *Bristol* ; I went on board her to see how things were, and here I found my Mind easy and quiet : I let my Companion and Friends know what I had met with, and the Occasion of altering my Intention : My Companion readily agreed with me, to come in the *Bristol* Ship, and we embarked for *England* the 18th of the eleventh Month 1707, but were eighteen Days in beating thro' the Windward - passage to *Crooked - Island*, from whence it is called thirteen hundred Leagues to *England*, which distance we run in twenty-six Days. The Master and Mariners agreed they had never had so expeditious a Voyage ; and through heavenly Protection it was safe.

I mention

I mention *heavenly Protection* at this time, I think from very evident reason: The Ship which we firſt thought of coming in, had we not been reſtrain'd by a ſupernatural heavenly Hand, founder'd ſomewhere at Sea, and was never heard of more, which was a very teaching thing to me: And *ſecondly,* when we were got within the *Iriſh* Channel, the Maſter intending to keep as near the *Iriſh* Shore as he could, one of the Seamen on a ſuddain called out *Land*; the Maſter aſk'd *where?* and was anſwer'd on the *Larboard*; the Maſter reply'd, *God forbid that Land ſhould appear there*; then almoſt all running to look at the Land, I walk'd upon the Forecaſtle, and looking into the Sea, ſaw a Rock a-head of us, not above ſix feet under Water; of which I gave notice to the Maſter, who immediately ſaw it, and called out to the Man at the Helm, with the moſt lamentable Cry I ever heard, *Helm a-lee, Helm a-lee, for God's Sake, or we every Man of us periſh*; which he quickly did, and ſo the Ship ſteer'd by it, but within half the length of the Veſſel: A dark Fog with drizzling Rain had occaſion'd the Maſter's Miſtake; it clear'd up a little before this Danger occurr'd, and enabled us to diſcover it, but it ſoon return'd again thicker than before. We got a good way up the Channel, but our Wind failing us, we drop'd Anchor, and early next Morning got into the Fort of *Minehead*, with deep and humble Thankfulneſs before the Lord of Heaven

and

and Earth, who had his guardian Angel manifeſtly regardful of us. It was now a time of hot War betwixt *England* and *France*, and great Numbers of Privateers were out, yet we were preſerved out of their Hands, as well as from the Perils of the Sea, which was owing to divine Mercy, and to no Merit of ours.

TO this Period of time our dear and honourable FATHER had brought down the Account of his Life and Labours in the Service of Truth ; and finiſh'd it only a few Weeks before his Deceaſe : The remaining Part chiefly conſiſts of Chriſtian Epiſtles to the Churches and ſome particular Friends in divers Places, together with ſuch an Account of his Travels, as could be collected from the ſhort Journals he kept, and in which he ſeldom put down more than the Times when, and the Places where he had Meetings, with ſome general Obſervations upon them ; as theſe might in ſome reſpects aſſiſt him to give a particular Account of his Travels, and the State of the Churches, to his Brethren at home ; to whom at his Return he was wont to communicate it, with a peculiar warmth of Gratitude and reverent Thankfulneſs to him, who had called him to labour in his Vineyard, and accompanied it with ſuch inſtructive Obſervations, as made theſe Opportunities often very precious and edifying. But

But as these Lessons were too deeply fixed in his Mind ever to be forgot, so as he had not, at least, during great part of his Life an Intention of writing any thing by way of Journal, he omitted inserting them ; we are therefore deprived of many valuable Observations, and Christian Experiences, and are obliged to present the Reader with such an Account of some of his Visits, as, tho' worthy of notice, yet will be the less satisfactory, as it appears from the preceding Sheets, that the remaining part of a Life, so usefully employ'd, must have afforded much important Instruction.

Yet lean, as some parts of the following Accounts may appear, it was thought proper not to suppress them. They may serve to revive in the Minds of many now living, a useful Recollection of the Seasons they have spent with him ; to renew a Remembrance of the Doctrines he has had occasion to deliver ; and to excite them to a Consideration, how far they have since profited by them and by his Example.

We have inserted here the Copies of such Epistles, wrote by him during this Visit to *America*, as we could find among his Papers, or in the Hands of his Friends, and were thought proper to be added to this Collection, reserving to the Conclusion some pathetical Exhortations, which though wrote very early, may be till then postpon'd, without prejudice to Order or Utility.

I

To

'To Friends *of the Monthly-meeting* 'of Richmond *in* Yorkshire.*

'DEAR FRIENDS,

'IN the bowings of living Virtue, 'my Spirit
'doth freely reach towards you, in earneſt
'Travail for the Proſperity of the Lord's work
'among and in you all : My heart being hum-
'bled-before the Lord Almighty to magnify
'him for his Mercy, in bringing me to have a
'Share of that ſolid Comfort which the living
'enjoy, in the ſweet Goſpel - fellowſhip of
'Jeſus Chriſt ; herein my Life is ſtrongly
'with you very often, tho' I am outwardly far
'ſeparated from you for the great Name's Sake,
'as he has hitherto given my Soul large and
'plentiful Confirmation, in being pleaſed fre-
'quently to viſit with his humbling Preſence
'and

* *In a private Letter to a Friend, to whom this
Epiſtle was ſent, he writes thus ;* 'I have been under
'a Concern of Spirit on behalf of the Monthly-
'meeting of *Richmond,* and all its Members, and
'thro' ſecretly ſeeking to the Lord, my way was
'opened to viſit you with a Letter, which I deſire
'thee to take to the Monthly-meeting, and if Friends
'think fit, I would have it ſolidly read both to the
'Men and Women ; and alſo Copies of it ſent and
'read in the particular Meetings, for the ſtirring up
'of all ; or however that I may be ſo far cleared.'

' and Life, which doth support thro' various
' Difficulties : To his almighty Power let my
' Soul bow for evermore.

   ' And *dear Friends*, both male and female,
' I cannot easily forbear signifying to you, that
' I have been under deep Exercise of Soul on
' your behalf many Days, and for some time
' wanted to see my way opened to speak to
' you : But in my inward and secret Attention
' upon the Lord, my Heart was opened, my
' Life set at liberty, and my Spirit engaged to
' remind you all, of the inexpressible Love and
' Mercy of the God of Heaven, in manifesting
' his saving Truth to our Understandings,
' whilst many as worthy as we were, do not yet
' know it. And now, a Consideration of the
' end of so great a Favour from on high should
' engage us all, and be always before us ; surely
' it is for no less a purpose, than that we by
' the Power of it, should be redeemed from
' all Iniquity, and be purified as unto himself,
' a peculiar People. Oh! this Word *Redemp-*
' *tion* is often in my mind, and lives closely
' with me at this time, and I intreat you all to
' take notice of it ; it is a Word soon spoken,
' but requires deep Travail to experience it to
' be fulfilled ; and without this Experience,
' all other Enjoyments can never make us truly
' happy : This is the Word of Life that is
' in my heart at this time to all ; that you
' may be *redeemed* from the Power of all such
' Humours and Inclinations as are carnal and

I 2

' fleshly,

‘ flefhly, and confequently oppofite to the pure
‘ Nature and Will of the Lord God ; that
‘ fo, anfwerable to primitive Doctrine, every
‘ Thought may be brought into Subjection,
‘ and Obedience to Chrift. This is the State
‘ into which the Lord is gathering his faithful,
‘ tho’ often mournful Followers. For though
‘ prejudicial and hindering Thoughts and In-
‘ clinations may fometimes appear and arife ;
‘ yet they being brought to the Light, the
‘ Spirit of Chrift, the Spirit of Truth we make
‘ profeffion of, to be tried and proved, he
‘ fhews the Nature and Danger of them, and
‘ alfo makes way for the Deliverance of fuch
‘ inward Chriftian Travellers ; and as they
‘ yield Obedience to his leading, they go on
‘ from Strength to Strength : Thefe are they
‘ who experience what *Redemption* is, and dare
‘ live no longer unto themfelves, but to him
‘ who has called them. Thus the blefied end
‘ of the Lord’s mercy in vifiting us will be
‘ anfwered, to the Glory of his great Name,
‘ and our Souls will have the Comfort and
‘ Enjoyment of his Love. But I do again fay,
‘ and it is an everlafting Truth, that tho’ we
‘ fubmit in our Judgments, and give up to
‘ profefs the blefied faving Truth, yet if we fit
‘ down fhort of witnefling *Redemption*, by the
‘ humbling Power and Virtue of it, we can
‘ never reap the Benefit of God’s Salvation,
‘ which is indeed therein ; nor be brought into
‘ Covenant with God, nor partake of the fweet

‘ ar d

' and holy Communion of Saints, and the true
' spiritual Union which is among the living
' Members of the true Church. Oh ! the
' want of right Devotedness of Heart and Di-
' ligence in this momentous Concern, is the
' reason why many fall short of the Enjoy-
' ment of that engaging Life which doth de-
' scend into many bowed Souls, and fills them
' with holy Zeal ; and on the other hand, not
' feeling this, is the cause of so much Coolness
' and Indifference in many, about the Lord's
' business, so that the necessary Care and Con-
' cerns of the Church, for it's Preservation and
' Growth in Righteousness and Holiness, in
' order that *Sion* may become the Beauty of
' Nations, according to God's determination,
' is almost become a wearisomness to them :
' I say this Concern, I am afraid, is become
' like a Burthen and Uneasiness to some among
' us, and I have often borne a part with the
' living, of the weight of such careless easy
' Spirits ; my Soul cries, that the almighty
' and powerful God may awaken such by his
' eternal Word of Truth, which, tho' People
' may change, and become less fervent and
' zealous for his Cause, is the same that ever
' it was, and remains so for ever.
' And *dear Friends, Brethren* and *Sisters*,
' my Soul intreats you, as tho' I was present
' with you, every one see to the discharging
' yourselves in the time allotted you, of your
' respective Duties and Services in the Church

' of

‘ of Chriſt ; for you are not called to be idle,
‘ neither to ſerve yourſelves ; but that with
‘ your Abilities and Qualifications, you ſhould
‘ above all, and in every Undertaking, labour
‘ to exalt and ſhew forth the Glory and Ex-
‘ cellency of the everlaſting, undefiled, glorious
‘ Truth ; which God in his Mercy has given
‘ you to believe in, which muſt be over all,
‘ and ſhine to the very Ends of the Earth ;
‘ and thoſe who are faithful livers to it, ſhall
‘ be dignified with Riches and Honour that
‘ ſhall never fade away.

‘ *My Friends*, my Heart is open in the Ex-
‘ tendings of eternal Life towards you, and for
‘ the diſcharge of my Duty I am plain with
‘ you : And further ; I cannot but deſire you
‘ to conſider, how induſtriouſly careful, and
‘ earneſtly concerned ſome, both Men and
‘ Women, are about *temporal Things*, ſome in
‘ one ſort, ſome in another, in their Trades
‘ and Dealing, and about the very Cattle, and
‘ by ſuch Induſtry attain to great Skill and
‘ Acuteneſs in their divers Profeſſions and Em-
‘ ployments ; though moſt of this is to gratify
‘ human Deſires and Inclinations, and to make
‘ them and their Poſterity appear great in this
‘ World.   If ſuch did but employ the Capaci-
‘ ties and Qualifications which God has given
‘ them, with the like Earneſtneſs, about hea-
‘ venly things (proportionably to the weighti-
‘ neſs of matters) and to be great in favour
‘ with the Almighty, rich in Faith and good
‘ Works,

‘ Works, and to endeavour to bring up their
‘ Children in the Nurture of the Lord ; and
‘ as much as in them lies, to prepare their
‘ Minds to receive the Power of Truth, with
‘ out which they can never be happy : Oh !
‘ then we should soon have many, both Men
‘ and Women, excellently qualified with clear
‘ Understandings, found in Judgment, not
‘ wanting Zeal for the Lord (which at present
‘ is too much wanting) because the engaging
‘ Love of God would be shed plentifully in
‘ their Hearts, drawing them to serve the Lord
‘ heartily : And may we not justly say, if
‘ some were as zealous for the Lord and his
‘ Truth, as they are for themselves and their
‘ own Concerns, they would soon be mighty
‘ Men and Women for the Lord, and great
‘ would be their Comfort and Reward both
‘ here and hereafter.

‘ *Dear Friends*, my Heart is reverently
‘ bowed, that the Lord has opened my way,
‘ to ease my Spirit a little to you, from the
‘ Concern I am under for all your good ; and
‘ I beg earnestly of you who are more elderly,
‘ to let what I have here writ, have a place in
‘ your solid Consideration ; knowing there is
‘ no reason for the truly living to be offended :
‘ And you who are young, lay things to heart,
‘ for now is your time, and as you wish to
‘ be happy, bow inwardly to Truth, that you
‘ may be saved by it, and become of the *Re-*
‘ *deemed of the Lord*, so will he be a tender
‘ Father

‘ Father to you, providing for you what he
‘ fees you have need of, which, without him,
‘ you cannot provide for yourfelves.

‘ And oh! you truly living Souls, you Tra-
‘ vellers in the deep, that nothing can fatisfy
‘ but God’s arifing, firft in yourfelves, and
‘ then in others; fo that he alone may be ex-
‘ alted, and may have Liberty to fway his
‘ Sceptre in Righteoufnefs, that whatever is
‘ contrary to him, wherever it is, may come
‘ under Judgment: As I know there are fuch
‘ among you, my Spirit is ftedfaftly with you.

‘ And *dear Friends*, this one thing is yet in
‘ my heart to you; (tho’ I have been already
‘ unexpectedly enlarged) keep in mind, *that*
‘ *it is the Life of Truth which quickens the Soul*
‘ *to God*; if ever we become of his People in-
‘ deed, ’tis by retaining a Thirft after the re-
‘ newed Springings up thereof in the Soul;
‘ and this alone can keep us to be of his People;
‘ and whoever lofeth this true Thirft after
‘ Life, humbling, bowing Life, they lofe their
‘ Accefs to God, and that wherein alone is
‘ Acceptance with the Father. It is the Life
‘ that is the Light; ’tis the Life that is our
‘ only Strength, and alone the Sanctuary and
‘ place of Safety in all Befetments: And tho’ it
‘ may fometimes feem as if it were fealed up,
‘ and the Heavens may appear like brafs, yet the
‘ truly thirfty Soul, that retains its earneft
‘ travail, and cries after the Enjoyment of
‘ Life, will never be tried beyond what it will

‘ be

' be helped to endure, to the increasing of its
' Experience of the Lord's Goodness, and ad-
' ding Obligation upon it, to serve him faith-
' fully, who is Lord God Almighty, worthy to
' be served and obeyed by all People for ever ;
' into whose hand of Love, I commit you all
' with my own Soul : And in the Sense of his
' uniting heart-tendring Love, I bid you *fare-*
' *well*, and remain your near Friend according
' to my measure, who earnestly seek the Good
' of all People,

Cliffs in Maryland in   ' JOHN FOTHERGILL.'
America, the 17th
of the Sixth Month
1705.

' *To* Friends *in* Rhode-Island *and* ' New-England.

' DEARLY BELOVED FRIENDS,

' IN the Love of our heavenly Father,
' whereby through his Son the Lord Jesus
' Christ, our blessed Saviour, he hath graciously
' visited our Souls, and by the merciful Draw-
' ings thereof, hath gathered a People into Ac-
' quaintance, and measurably into Covenant
' with himself, and one with another, my
' Spirit doth at this Time tenderly salute you ;
' earnestly praying, as at many other times
' since our outward Separation, that the eternal

K   ' and

' and divine Spring of Love and Life may
' abound among you ; and I firmly believe it
' will be fo, as you wait for it with diligence
' and patience ; as it is the incumbent Duty
' of both old and young, becaufe daily Bread
' to our inward Man we all have need of :
' And that our bleffed Father may guide and
' keep us, and may ever be with us on all
' Occafions is my fervent cry.

' And, *my dear Friends*, as it is divine Love
' that hath overcome our Souls, and gathered us
' to be a People to fhew forth the Praife of the
' living God ; the fame divine Love draws his
' Servants from Country to Country, to vifit and
' ftrengthen one another in the Way to Peace.
' The Strength of this Love often engaged
' my Spirit when with you, in a deep Travail,
' both by Night and by Day, for the Exalta-
' tion of the Government, and Righteoufnefs
' of our gracious God ; that he may delight
' to dwell among us, and through our Faith-
' fulnefs to him, his glorious Name may be
' magnified among them who are afar off.

' And very often fince has my Heart been
' drawn towards you, and it remains engaged,
' with thofe who are truly concerned among
' you, and fuch I know there are, both elder
' and younger, male and female ; whom I
' befeech in the Bowels of engaging, uniting
' Love, fome as Fathers and Mothers, and
' fome as Brethren and Sifters, as to age ; to
' labour that nothing may hinder your Growth

' and

' and Progrefs in due care and diligence ; firft
' refpecting your own Souls, and then in faith-
' ful care and fuitable dealing with thofe of
' your Houfhold, your Off-fpring efpecially, if
' fuch you have ; endeavouring not to be be-
' hind in due Labour, not only in living Zeal
' to advife, but to reftrain from what you fee,
' or may have feen to be inconfiftent with the
' mind of Truth, and pernicious to them, in
' refpect to their Souls Happinefs : And in the
' next place, relating to the Churches in the
' refpective Places, where your Lots may be
' caft ; having efpecial care that thofe who
' come among you, and are reputed to be of
' you, may live to Truth, and come up in
' Obedience to the holy Leadings of it :
' Which true and diligent Care over one ano-
' ther hath often proved greatly helpful to
' fome weak and ftaggering People, and a
' Comfort to the Admonifhers : For, *Friends*,
' many have heard *line upon line, and precept
' upon precept*, in a publick or general way ;
' and they believe that Truth is Truth, and
' are willing to make Profeffion of it, and love
' to hear its Teftimony ; yet from time to time
' continue in what the truly living know is
' condemnable, and not of the Nature of
' God's bleffed Truth.

' I fay, *my Friends*, we muft come to this,
' to tell fuch *thou art the Man*, who art un-
' faithful in this or the other thing, which we
' know the Spirit of Truth, if regarded, doth

K 2

' fhew

' fhew to be evil, and would lead out of : It
' is a Hurt to thy own particular, a Reproach
' to the bleffed Truth, and a Caufe of Sorrow
' to the true Seekers of *Sion*'s Profperity ; be
' they rich, or ancient, or near Acquaintance,
' or under what Circumftances foever, who
' ftay behind : This I believe is the Way in
' which the Lord will have them dealt with,
' if concerned Perfons fhrink not from their
' Places.

   ' Bear with my plainnefs, *dear Friends*, I
' muft be fo, if I be right ; think on thefe
' things, and look to the full Difcharge of that
' Truft and Service, which the living and holy
' God has repofed in you, and fitted you for,
' many of you in divers Places, both male
' and female ; and he would fit many more,
' if they would but ftand loofer from the load-
' ing, clogging, reafoning World, and the
' Hindrances that attend thofe who earneftly
' purfue it. Arife, arife, you who know that
' the Almighty would make Ufe of you in his
' Houfe, his Church, if you would but caft-
' your Care upon him ; mind heavenly things
' more than earthly, and fhake off your rea-
' foning and entangling enjoyments, and the
' Lord will then make Ufe of you, and you
' fhall not want your Reward, but fhall have
' what he, who is wifer than Man, fees con-
' venient for you here, and an eternal Glory
' with him hereafter. But if all the Labour
' of Love thus every way beftowed, doth not

                           ' prevail

‘ prevail with the earthly minded, or thofe
‘ who mind themfelves too much, the Lord
‘ will pafs by them, and choofe others into
‘ their places, and will give them their Re-
‘ ward : Thus I am eafed on this Head, being
‘ truly plain in God’s Love.

‘ Yet I have farther to treat with fome among
‘ you, who may perhaps be of the elder rank,
‘ but have not gone on in the Way, that in the
‘ Vifitation of the Love of God, they were con-
‘ vinced was right, fo honeftly and uprightly as
‘ they fhould have done ; but have ftooped a
‘ little here, and a little there, and rather fhrunk
‘ from the Work of the mighty God, fome-
‘ times with one fhoulder, fometimes with the
‘ other, and ftood not upright like Men for
‘ him, in the day when he would have made
‘ principal Warriors of them ; by which means
‘ and doings they have marred and wounded
‘ themfelves, fo that they have not the clear-
‘ nefs of Sight, nor Underftanding, nor are
‘ they to be leaned upon, as according to their
‘ age they might have been. For if they had
‘ walked uprightly and faithfully before the
‘ Lord, regarding his Honour and Teftimony
‘ as they ought to have done ; he would un-
‘ doubtedly have made them capable of being
‘ thus ferviceable and honourable in his hand,
‘ as he hath made a Remnant among you,
‘ through their Faithfulnefs to him in a day
‘ of Trial, unto whom my Soul cleaves in
‘ immortal Love.

‘ But

' But this is not all the Damage which has
' enſued, by giving way in this manner ; the
' Spirit of the World, and its corrupt Fruits,
' which Truth has to make war againſt, here-
' by have been ſpared and got Strength, and
' were the harder to encounter by ſuch as God
' raiſed up, and who muſt ſtand for the Truth
' in good earneſt ; their Work was harder,
' their Burthen heavier, and the Warfare in
' ſome Reſpects made longer through ſuch
' Unfaithfulneſs ; but the Lord is on his way
' in good earneſt, and is and will be mindful
' of all who truly wait for his Counſel, both
' old and young, and who give up their All in
' true Dependency upon him : He has been
' the God and Helper of his People in all their
' Straits and Beſetments, and he will never for-
' ſake his little Ones, as they confide in him.
' My Heart is filled and overcome with the
' living Senſe of immediate Extending of his
' Love and Fatherly Care over all his Family ;
' eſpecially the faithful Warriors for his Righ-
' teouſneſs, and holy Teſtimony againſt the
' Corruption of the World : Whether they are
' ſuch as are immediately engaged in perſon,
' or are ſuch as have been valiant in their day,
' and have done their day's Work truly ; or
' are true in Faith, and Sufferers in Spirit, and
' right in Heart with thoſe who are ſo en-
' gaged, though not required to be much
' perſonally concerned ; ſuch are all the
' Lamb's Followers and Warriors ; and the
' Lord

‘ Lord of heaven and earth has a careful Eye
‘ over them for good ; and in keeping true to
‘ him, he will be with them, and they shall
‘ have the Victory.

‘ Thus my Heart is open to all my faithful
‘ Brethren and Sisters, in a pure stream of Love,
‘ which sprung up, and a little drew me from
‘ another matter; and from Persons under some
‘ other Circumstances, who for age might have
‘ been more serviceable, and more worthy of
‘ true Honour, than now they are. Some of
‘ these have had a Service in their Time, and
‘ I know, Kindness from a tender Father has
‘ often reached towards them for their good,
‘ and in order to stir them up closely to consider
‘ where they had stooped, and given way to the
‘ wrong thing, and altho’ I am led to treat
‘ after an unpleasant manner, I doubt, to some,
‘ and I am sure, as a Man, it is so to me, yet
‘ my Heart was engaged on this wise, some-
‘ time since, to treat with such; and my Spirit,
‘ tho’ at first attended with Sorrow on their
‘ account, yet was presently full of the Reach-
‘ ings of immortal Love to them, with an
‘ Invitation from the God of Mercy to such
‘ holders back, and rather hinderers of the
‘ Work of the Lord ; for such you may soon
‘ find yourselves to have been, not only by
‘ your giving way yourselves, but when any
‘ thing has been to be discoursed of as a
‘ Branch of our holy Testimony, have you
‘ not generally rather opposed it, and been
‘ Pleaders

' Pleaders for eafe and liberty, and with-
' holding of right Judgment from being placed
' upon things that were inconfiftent with
' Truth ? Oh ! that you may fee yourfelves,
' and lay hold of that fearching, purifying
' Power of the living God, which is extended
' towards you, which though it would lay
' hold in Judgment, yet Mercy follows very
' near: Let a Time of fearching and humbling
' have its way, I befeech you in that Love,
' which I know comes from the holy One:
' For he will bring Men to Account when he
' pleafeth, and in Judgment will not regard
' their ftations in this World : The faithful,
' upright Walkers, the Lovers of God's Tefti-
' mony, more than life or liberty, or eftate,
' or any other enjoyment, thefe will be ad-
' mitted into the Lord's Reft ; when fome
' more knowing, (in their own eyes) or older,
' or richer, and of more account amongft
' Men, will be difowned by him, if they do
' not come up in more Faithfulnefs.

   ' I am earneft with you upon this head, be-
' caufe a Concern faftned clofe upon me, well-
' knowing that the Lord would have fuch
' truly awaken'd ; that as fome are haftening
' to the Grave, they may go away living and
' bright, and leave an encouraging Example
' to the younger, whom the Lord is ftirring
' up. And that others, who to appearance
' are not fo near their latter-end, may be
' roufed up out of their unfafe Refts, and ftand

' up

‘ up like Men for God indeed: And he would
‘ make some of you, I fully believe, who have
‘ rather been Retarders of the Work, valiant
‘ for his Cause, and serviceable in many re-
‘ spects ; whereby you will at last receive the
‘ good Sentence of *Well-done*.   That the Lord
‘ God of Mercy and Salvation may thus prevail
‘ upon you all, is my earnest Prayer, with an
‘ Heart full of true Love ; believing there will
‘ be but few, if any, offended at my plainness,
‘ except such as have some need to lay fast
‘ hold of this renewed Visitation : For it will
‘ not touch the Lord’s deeply engaged Servants,
‘ and faithful Burthen-bearers for *Zion*’s sake.

‘ And as I have been drawn to intreat, and
‘ tenderly to caution both Older and Younger,
‘ Men and Women, whose Spirits are engaged
‘ to seek the Honour of God every way ac-
‘ cording to their Capacities, the Prosperity of
‘ his holy blessed Truth, and the Growth of
‘ those who make profession of it, in the Righ-
‘ teousness which it would lead, and doth lead
‘ the faithful Followers of it into ; that they
‘ who have this Care upon them, (as I know
‘ many have) may see to the full discharge of
‘ their Duty : So I have to speak to such as
‘ have been convinced in their Judgments that
‘ *Truth is Truth*, and make some profession
‘ thereof, yet live out of the Life of it, and shun
‘ the Cross of Christ, that would break them
‘ off from their former vain Conversation ;
‘ in Words and Actions which are of the Flesh

L   ‘ and

‘ and the World, and not of the Father ; and
‘ tend to nothing but to gratify the fleshly mind
‘ and desires in yourselves and others, whom
‘ you may strive to please either for worldly
‘ Profit or Pleasure, tho’ in so doing you slight
‘ and neglect what would make for your future
‘ Happiness and eternal Peace. Oh ! my
‘ Bowels are full of Love and Pity for you ;
‘ and I am engaged, tho’ absent in body, to
‘ call unto you once more, to consider of your
‘ *latter-end*, the Time whereof is uncertain ;
‘ and that you must give Account to a righte-
‘ ous God, who has long waited over and in-
‘ vited you in mercy, and who will be just in
‘ his Rewards according to the Deeds you have
‘ done. Look into yourselves in coolness, I
‘ beseech you, and see whose Will you are
‘ doing, and whether you live to the pure
‘ Word of Truth, the Spirit of holy Jesus ;
‘ or to the Flesh, and the vain corrupt Spirit of
‘ this perishing World. You have had many
‘ Reproofs, by the Grace of God; you have also
‘ had many Opportunities of hearing the ever-
‘ lasting Gospel and Word of Truth plainly
‘ declared, in the Love and Power of the
‘ Father ; all which has been for the gathering
‘ you to Truth and Righteousness, and out of
‘ the Corruptions of the World, to be a People
‘ to bear a faithful Testimony, in Words and
‘ Actions against apostate Practices, and to that
‘ Power which never fell, and is come to re-
‘ deem the fallen to itself. And you have
‘ many

' many of you been advifed and plainly dealt
' with, by the Servants of God, and of his
' Church; tho' fome to their own hurt, as it
' will be found at one time or other, have
' flighted their Advice, and rather defpifed
' them. But be it known to all fuch, as would
' have no Bounds fet to their corrupt Inclina-
' tions and Humours, that the Lord will yet
' concern others to treat plainly with them,
' yet for no other end, than the honour of his
' Truth and their good : And if all will not
' prevail with fuch to obey the righteous and
' holy Truth, the Harveft will pafs over their
' Heads and they will be ungathered ; and
' will then, tho' too late remember, who were
' their Friends, and acknowledge the great
' Mercy of a long-fuffering God towards them.
' That you may be brought forwards in true
' Faithfulnefs, while Time for it is continued,
' I am thus engaged to treat with you in the
' Father's Love, which I heartily defire you
' may embrace, and be fitted to enjoy it both
' here and hereafter.

' There yet remains upon my mind, a near
' Concern for fuch as have been moftly edu-
' cated and brought up in the Profeffion of
' Truth, and are Children of believing Parents,
' whofe Care it has been, both to advife their
' Off-fpring faithfully, and to fet before them
' good Examples. Tho' you might be inclu-
' ded in what is above written, yet I have to
' treat with you in particular, in hopes that

L 2

' the

' the Cautions may be more prevalent. There
' are feveral, I fear, if not many, who take
' more delight to be like the vain World in
' their Conduct and Converfation, than to
' grow up in Obedience to Truth which
' worketh in you, and in a Gravity and Com-
' linefs anfwerable to the Care, the Labour,
' and the Example of your honeft Parents: But
' remember, that both thefe inward Convicti-
' ons, the Care and Advice of Parents and
' others, are merciful Vifitations to you from
' your great Creator ; in order to gather you
' in your young Years, into Righteoufnefs,
' without which none can enter the Kingdom
' of God : And be affured, the Time will
' come, and it may be unawares, when you
' muft be accountable for them all to the Judge
' of Heaven and Earth. Therefore be intreated
' to feek after acquaintance with, and Sub-
' miffion to the pure Principle of Truth in
' yourfelves, which you make profeffion of ;
' that by the power and virtue of it, you may
' come to be Witneffes of its faving you from
' Vanity, and delivering from corrupt Incli-
' nations ; and fo you may be brought into
' Communion with the living God, and be-
' come faithful Teftimony-bearers for him in
' your Generations, in the room of your Pa-
' rents and others who are paffing away : The
' Bleffing of the Lord fhall then be upon you
' while here, and at laft an Inheritance among
' the fanctified will be your Portion.

' And

‘ And tho’ some young People among you
‘ may not have had those Advantages of due
‘ care over them, nor the Benefit of Examples
‘ in Sobriety and Faithfulness, from their Pa-
‘ rents, which some others have; yet I believe
‘ these can see that it has been their Parents
‘ Fault, and that if they had been true to
‘ their Principles, or rather to the Principle
‘ of Truth they professed, it would have
‘ taught them, both to have been better Ex-
‘ amples, and to have advised and restrained
‘ you more, from vain Ways and Company,
‘ and youthful Pleasures, which we know war
‘ against the Soul. Wherefore be persuaded,
‘ I beseech you, as you are I believe convinced
‘ concerning the Truth, to learn of it, and
‘ suffer it to lead you, tho’ it be from your Plea-
‘ sures; and instead of taking liberty either
‘ from your Parents indulgence and neglect,
‘ or their loosness and misconduct, rather let
‘ them serve as Caution and Instruction to you
‘ not to do the like; seeing you know or believe
‘ that they should have done otherwise. My
‘ Heart is engaged for your good and happi-
‘ ness every way, Oh you young People ! who
‘ have been brought up in some profession of
‘ the blessed Truth of God, in particular at
‘ this Time; and I am sensible as I treat in
‘ plainness with you to cleave to Truth, that
‘ you may be broken off from Vanity, and
‘ vain and idle Company, which its impossible
‘ to use frequently and unnecessarily without
‘ damage

' damage and hurt, if People look with a
' right Eye : Therefore be warned and ſhun
' it in time, before you be like it, as I fear
' ſome are already too much. Let the extend-
' ing of divine Love, both ſecretly in your
' Hearts and inſtrumentally, win upon you,
' and humble and ſoften your Spirits before the
' Lord of Mercy, who is gracious abundantly,
' and waits to ſhed his Love abroad in many
' Hearts, if they would but make room for it :
' In the iſſuing forth thereof towards many of
' the Youth, who have been lovers of their
' own ways, more than the ways of Goſpel
' Truth, I thus diſcharge myſelf to you ; with
' Prayers that this renewed Viſitation from our
' heavenly Father, who would make you his
' Children indeed, and Heirs of the Kingdom,
' may have its due weight with you all.

' And to you dear and tender ſpirited Ones
' among the Youth, Male and Female, upon
' whom the ſweet Influence of the Love of
' God hath made ſome Impreſſion, and hath
' begot Deſires in you after the Enjoyment
' of it, and that you may grow up, ſuch as
' God would have you to be , tho' you are
' often beſet with the ſtrength of your own
' Inclinations, and the ſecret allurements of
' Satan, render'd more enſnaring by the means
' of Aſſociates and former Acquaintance, draw-
' ing your Minds out after one little thing, or
' another little matter, according to your vari-
' ous circumſtances and tempers, and pleading
' the

' the Harmlefnefs of it too : Beware of fuch
' things I intreat you, and as your Faces are
' turned from them, when your Hearts are
' moft tender, and your Spirits the moft fweet-
' en'd with divine Love ; be careful not to
' tamper with them when that may be a little
' withdrawn ; for then is the time of the
' Enemy's working : And love, I befech you,
' and as much as poffible keep to folid Com-
' pany, there you will find Help ; and fhun
' the Company that love idle, jangling, and
' airy Difcourfe, for this draws back and
' hardens.

' Thus, *dear young Friends*, be careful that
' the Work which the Lord has begun in you,
' in order to fit you for himfelf, and to enjoy
' his holy living Prefence, may not be hin-
' dered : If you cleave clofe to him, and
' regard him diligently, he will be with you,
' and you know not what Ufe he may make
' of you in his Family, or to bear his glorious
' Name to other People.

' And you, my *Brethren*, and tender *Sifters*,
' who have fomething of this Work commit-
' ted to your Charge, to appear in publick in
' and for the great Name ; fome of whom are
' fitting for more and more Service, yet are
' attended, as I know fome of you are, with
' many Fears, and know Times of far with-
' drawing, as it feems to you, fo that you
' think you are emptier and leaner than other
' People ; and fometimes the great Difturber

' feems

' feems almoft to be let loofe upon you ; thefe
' are indeed diftreffing, humbling, proving
' times, yet they are times of learning great
' Experience, and of fitting for divers Services,
' as well as plunging thoroughly down, that
' we may fee what we are, when the Power
' of Truth hides itfelf from us, and to exer-
' cife our careful Dependance upon the Arm
' and Power of the Lord. I know there are
' among you, who are Witneffes that this hath
' been the Way, in which God hath led them,
' and fitted them for his Work ; and in lean-
' ing upon the divine Hand that fhuts and
' opens as it fees good, they have been preferv-
' ed living and fweet to this time. And I wifh
' that all who take the mighty Name in their
' Mouths in this refpect, were rightly prepared
' for it, and had come in at the right Door,
' and kept a due Dependancy upon renewed,
' divine Opening, and would open and fhut
' with it : But I fear with fome it is other-
' wife, tho' thofe who ftand moft in need of
' Caution, are often the moft backward to re-
' ceive it ; and thofe who want rather taking
' by the hand, are the moft fubject to fearch
' and get under undue Difcouragements.
   ' *Dear Friends*, I am led fomewhat farther
' than I was inclined to go in this refpect ;
' but I fee not how to eafe my Spirit otherwife,
' and fhall add this Intreaty to you my dear
' and truly efteemed *Brethren* and *Sifters*, whofe
' Hearts and Souls are engaged in Care for God's
' Honour,

' Honour, and the Churches growth in Righ-
' teoufnefs, and Soundnefs in every refpect: Let
' this laft mention'd Obfervation be under your
' Notice; and let all unfavoury and unfeafon'd
' Spirits, who do, or would bring forth their
' dry, dead and killing Offerings in publick,
' be difcouraged, let their Words be as fmoothly
' compofed as they may; for this, you know,
' may be done by the Wit of Man, but they
' can never beget rightly to God. And as this
' ought to be difcouraged, being a Diftemper,
' as I may call it, that hath attended your
' Country, and is a very great hindrance to
' Peoples Growth; fo the tender and fimple
' who are living in the Truth, tho' little, muft
' be encouraged: And I pray God, that he may
' ftir you up whom he has qualified for his
' Work, and help you with his powerful Pre-
' fence to labour in his Vineyard; that People
' may have the Opportunity of feeling and
' tafting the Difference, betwixt that which is
' but the *Words of Man*, and the *Miniftry of*
' JESUS CHRIST, which quickens the Soul.
  ' Thus, my truly near and efteemed *Friends*,
' *Brethren* and *Sifters*, in the Covenant of Life,
' and Fellowfhip of the everlafting Gofpel, I
' open myfelf unto you; as I know Truth has
' many times open'd my Heart, in fecret hope,
' that tho' there is fomething of Advice and
' ftirring up herein, from a younger Brother
' to many of you; yet you will not fet it wholly
' afide, but give it room in your Minds. In

M   ' immortal

' immortal Love from the Father and Foun-
' tain of all our Mercies, I tenderly embrace
' the truly living among you ; being brought
' under an Engagement of Spirit, for many
' Days and Weeks, to vifit you with this *Ge-*
' *neral Epiftle*, as it fettled upon my Mind in
' that which drew me from my native Country,
' to leave with you now before I take my
' Leave of *America*. I remain your Friend in
' the Truth, and a Traveller for *Zion*'s Prof-
' perity and *Jerufalem*'s Peace, and that her
' Glory may fhine forth to the Ends of the
' Earth.

' JOHN FOTHERGILL.'

Antigua, the 1ft of the
Ninth Month, 1707.

Not long after he returned from this his firft Vifit to *America*, he married *Margaret* the Daughter of *Thomas Hough*, of *Sutton* in *Chefhire*, a Family of good Efteem in the world, and walking anfwerable to our holy Profeffion : She was a Perfon of an exemplary Piety and Prudence from her tender Years, and eminently diftinguifhed by that moft valuable Ornament, *a meek and quiet Spirit.*

From this Time we meet not with any Account of his being engaged in much publick Service abroad, till the Year 1709, when he found himfelf engaged in Spirit to vifit Friends in the South-weft Parts of *England*, of which Journey the following fhort Account is pre-ferved. The

THE 12th of the seventh Month 1709, I set forward on my Journey, to visit the South-west parts of *England*, having been under some Concern of Spirit, engaging me thereto, some time before: I left my dear Wife and Friends at home, in a Sense of our heavenly Father's Love and Care; and met my Uncle *Gilbert Thompson*, who had been under the like Con-cern, at *Middlewich* in *Cheshire*; where we joined together in the Service, and had a good edi-fying Season with Friends there, in the at-tendance of the Virtue of Truth, to our Com-fort; and went to *Namptwich*, where we had a Meeting the 15th, to which came several of the People; with whom we had a pretty open Time. From hence we went to *Wolverhampton*, and to *Stourbridge*, where we had Meetings; and so to *Worcester*, where on the 18th, being the First-day of the Week, we were at two Meetings; that in the Afternoon especially, was a good Season, through the free extending of Truth, both towards Friends and others.

After this we had Meetings at *Tewksbury*, *Gloucester*, and *Painswick*, where we had a pretty satisfactory Meeting, through some deep Labour of Spirit; and so to *Nailsworth*, and had a large Meeting; in which the Love of God engaged us in a deep Labour, and sup-plied with Strength to discharge our Spirits, tho' in a rousing, shaking manner, and Truth prevailed much to our Comfort, and to the Help of the Faithful. From hence we went

 to

to *Thornbury*, where we had a seasonable Opportunity in the Meeting there; and so to *Bristol*, and were at both their Meetings on the 25th, being First-day; wherein Truth owned us freely, both in giving its Testimony forth, and in coming up in a good degree of Dominion. On the Third-day following, we had another good solid Meeting, through the Labour of both, tending to bend some too lofty, and to stir up some who embraced this World more than the Life of Truth, to more Care in their Duty to God, and for their own Good. From hence we went to *Glastonbury*, where we had a Meeting, attended with some heavy Labour in the Extendings of the Love of Truth, in order to stir up some dull-spirited Professors, as well as to strengthen the Faithful; and so to *Grinton*, where we had a pretty edifying Season with Friends in their Meeting; and also the next Day at *Long-Sutton*, which Truth owned with its Presence, much to ours and Friends Comfort.

The 2d of the eighth Month, being the first of the Week, we were at a Meeting at *Wellington*, which was pretty large, but very exercising, by reason of a dull, earthly Spirit having prevailed upon the minds of some of the Professors of Truth: But the divine Power in Mercy, worked strongly in a rousing manner; tho' attended with much Tenderness towards the Faithful, who were glad, and praised God in Reverence. And that Evening we had a

good

good open Meeting, both among Friends and many sober People, and the Power and Testimony of Truth was exalted.

We had also a Meeting at *Minehead*, (where there was a Marriage) and the Testimony of Truth went freely forth amongst the People, there being of divers Professions, and our Spirits were comforted with Friends. We then went to the Quarterly-meeting for *Devonshire* at *Collumpton*, which began that Day for Worship, and was solidly comfortable. The next Day was their Meeting for Business, and a seasonable edifying Time. From hence we went to a Meeting at *Spiceland*, where Truth accompanied us mercifully, to the stirring up of those who were at ease, and to the Encouragement and Help of the Upright; and so to *Exeter*, and were at Friends Meeting, which was pretty large, and Truth opened freely towards them, engaging us to declare, that in becoming subject to the Power of God's Spirit, we only can become his People indeed; and that to live under the Sense thereof, was our Preservation: At *Stickle-Path* we likewise had a Meeting with Friends and many other People; amongst whom we were favoured with a pretty open Time. From this Place we went to *Launceston*, *Pershore*, *Falmouth*, and the *Land's-end*, and had a Meeting at each Place; as also at *Marazion*, where several other People came in, and through the attending of Truth, we had a good edifying Season. We

We then went to *Falmouth*, and had a Meeting there that Evening, which Truth owned very eminently, to our, and Friends folid Comfort; as alfo at *Key* the next Day, to which Place many Friends from *Falmouth* accompanied us; from whom we parted in great fweetnefs, and fet out for *Trigany* and *Lefkard*, to a General-meeting, which was large, and a blefled Opportunity we had, through the gracious Attendance of Truth, and the Lord's holy Name was magnified. From hence we went to *Plymouth*, and had a Meeting there, and the next Day at *Kingfbridge*, where a confiderable number of other People came in, and the Power and Teftimony of Truth was exalted. From hence we went to *Topfham*, *Chard*, *Thorncomb*, *Bridport*, and to *Dorchefter*; in all which Places we had Meetings, and at the laft Place many of the Town's People came in, together with a confiderable number of Friends, and the Lord's Power and Teftimony prevailed to our Satisfaction in a good degree, and the Lord was praifed.

On the 4th of the ninth Month we went to *Pool*, from thence to *Ringwood*, *Fordingbridge*, *Southampton*, *Alesford*, and fo through *Alton* and *Guildford*, to *London* the 12th; in all which Places we had Meetings, and in moft to the help and comfort of Friends, and the Honour of the great Name.

The 13th, being the firft of the Week, we were at the *Bull* and *Mouth* Meeting in the Morning;

Morning; wherein the ancient Power of Chrift our heavenly Head, came over Friends Spirits, much to our Comfort and Strength : In the Afternoon we were at the *Peel* Meeting, which was very large, and many fober People came into it ; and the Lord's Power was over all in a great and folemn manner, and his holy Name was magnified. We vifited the Week-day-meetings, and on the 20th, being Firft-day, were at *Savoy* in the Morning, which was a very large Meeting of Friends and others, and an open good Time, through the bleffed Pre-valency of the Power of Truth ; and alfo in the Afternoon at *Weftminfter*, to our great com-fort and fatisfaction. We continued to vifit the Meetings in courfe through the Week, and on the 27th were at *Devonfhire-houfe* in the Morn-ing, which was a very great Meeting, and were very bowingly opened by the Power and Virtue of God's bleffed Truth ; in the After-noon at *Grace-church-ftreet*, which was very large of Friends and others, and was, through divine Goodnefs, a truly edifying and ftrength-ning Time to the Upright, of whom I took leave in great fweetnefs.

On the 28th we fet out on our way home-wards, and had a Meeting in the Evening at *Watford*, and the next Day another at *Jordans*, where feveral Friends met us from fome other Meetings; and it was an edifying, ftrengthning Time in the Prevalency of God's Power. We had a good open Meeting the Day following at
Ailefbury,

Ailesbury, where there were some newly convinced of Truth, and some other sober People, to whom the power of Truth reached freely, and came into good dominion, blessed be the Name of the Lord God. We had a Meeting at *Banbury*, which was pretty large, and a good comfortable Time, through much deep labour with divers sorts of Spirits, and circumstances of People. From hence we went homewards by *Warwick* and *Birmingham*, where we had Meetings; on the ninth we parted, and on the 10th I got home, and found my dear Wife well; and we were humbly and truly comforted together, in the consideration of the Lord's Providence to us, and in a sense of his great and unspeakable Goodness, in affording us his blessed Presence, both abroad and at home.

From the time of his returning from this Visit in 1709, to his second Voyage to *America* in 1721, it does not appear from any Memoirs in our possession, that our FATHER was engaged in much publick Service abroad: It seems most probable that he was now at liberty to discharge the necessary care over an encreasing Family: In this Interval however, he visited Friends in several of the neighbouring Counties frequently, attended the Quarterly-meetings at *York* pretty constantly, and the Yearly-meeting at *London*, as he found himself engaged for that Service; for though few were more diligent in Business, more carefully

affectionate

affectionate to every part of his Family, or loved more to be at home, yet whenever he perceived it was his Duty to leave them, he could chearfully caſt his Care upon One that was able to ſupply all wants, and on whom he ſecretly and ſteadily relied, not with preſumptuous boldneſs, but with humble, reverent truſt ; and often, yea very often, would he take occaſion to recite to his Family the ſignal Interpoſitions of divine Providence in many· Trials and Exerciſes of various kinds.

In the Year 1719, he met with a very cloſely affecting Diſpenſation, in being deprived of a *faithful* and *affectionate Companion* ; as were ſeven young Children, the Eldeſt not Ten Years old, of a *religious* and *moſt tender, careful Parent*, before they were capable of knowing their Loſs. This he bore with holy Reſignation, and Acquieſcence to the divine Diſpoſal, as appears from his Anſwer to a Friend, who was ſympathizing with him on this mournful Occaſion : *The Lord gives, and he takes away ; his Will be done, he is worthy.* But, *what if I muſt be called from my little-ones alſo ?* For at this time he was apprehenſive, that it would e're long be required of him, once more to viſit *America :* Which muſt render the Trial ſtill the harder, as few, or perhaps none, ever exceeded him in paternal Care and Affection for his Children. Yet when he became fully ſatiſfied that it was the Lord's requiring, he gave up freely, ſaying to his Children, as ſome of

N

them

them could rember, *that though he had all the anxious Concern of a Father for them, yet he muſt obey the holy Call of the Lord, who he believed would care for them in his Abſence.*

Tho' an Account of our MOTHER's religious and exemplary Life, hath already been publiſh-ed in the *Dying Sayings of Friends,** yet we think it may not be without its Uſe to inſert it in this place, *viz.*

' MARGARET FOTHERGILL, late
' Wife of *John Fothergill* in *Wenſleydale,*
' *Yorkſhire,* was carefully educated (when a
' Child) by her Parents, amongſt the People
' called *Quakers* ; and while ſhe was but very
' young, did not only delight to go to Friends
' Meetings, but came under a Concern of heart
' that ſhe might become acquainted with the
' Lord for herſelf, and be made a Partaker of
' his quickning Power and Virtue in her own
' Soul : Which Concern the Lord was pleaſed
' to regard, and graciouſly came in upon her
' Heart by his Power and Love, and thereby
' Helped her to draw near him, and worſhip
' him knowingly, while ſhe was but very
' young. And as ſhe grew up, ſhe continued
' to delight in waiting upon God, and feeling
' after his Goodneſs ſecretly, thro' the pure In-
' fluence wherof, ſhe came to be cloathed
' with a meek and quiet Spirit, and alſo helped
' to

---

* Piety Promoted, Part VI. Pag. 90.

' to ſhew it forth in a grave, modeſt and ex-
' emplary Behaviour ; becauſe whereof, ſhe
' was much beloved by moſt that knew her :
' And ſome time before ſhe was married (be-
' ing likely to leave her own Country) ſhe came
' under ſome Exerciſe to exhort Friends, in
' ſeveral of their Meetings, to a cloſe walking
' with, and a true depending upon God ; and
' to beware of an unconcern'd Mind when
' they appear'd before him in Meetings ; which
' Exerciſe ſhe made mention of (being freſh in
' her mind) on her Dying-bed.
' After ſhe was married, ſhe continued a
' true lover of Meetings, and an humble waiter
' for the Reſurrection of the Life of Truth,
' right-well knowing, therein is all Ability for
' the Performance of Worſhip acceptable to
' the Lord. And as ſhe was often attended
' with Fear and Care, leſt any thing ſhould
' divert her Mind from the fervent Search after
' the Truth itſelf, which is abſolutely neceſſary ;
' ſo would ſhe often expreſs her Sorrow of heart
' concerning a Dulneſs and Indifferency ſhe ap-
' prehended to be growing upon ſome Peoples
' Minds, who had profeſſed the Truth long.
' And notwithſtanding her being often unfit
' for attending Meetings, as ſhe had a good
' Will to do, eſpecially Monthly and Quarter-
' ly-meetings, by reaſon of having ſeveral young
' Children, and ſometimes being very tender
' and weakly as to her Conſtitution of body ;
' yet would ſhe often expreſs her Care, that

N 2   ' the

‘ the Affairs of Truth in thofe Meetings might
‘ be managed with fuitable Zeal and Care for
‘ the Glory of God ; fometimes faying, *She*
‘ *could be glad, and was not without Hopes of*
‘ *living, to be a little more at liberty to attend*
‘ *thofe Services, and to difcharge herfelf more*
‘ *fully amongft Friends for Righteoufnefs-fake.*
‘ Whereof fhe was a Pattern in her Converfa-
‘ tion, being humbly careful, that the Lord’s
‘ holy Name might be glorified.   And when
‘ fhe was delivered of her laft Child, and got
‘ to Bed, fhe exprefs’d much Thankfulnefs to
‘ the Lord, faying in a reverent Mind, *How*
‘ *fhall we be thankful enough for all his Help*
‘ *and wonderful Goodnefs !* And altho’ fhe was
‘ as hopefully got fo far as at any other time,
‘ (that being her eighth Child) yet did fhe
‘ grow fufpicious of herfelf, and the third Day
‘ after did difcover her Apprehenfions of being
‘ taken away in thefe Words : *I wonder that I*
‘ *cannot be troubled that I am like to leave my*
‘ *little-ones, and my dear Hufband* ; which Ex-
‘ preffions nearly affecting her Hufband, fhe
‘ added, *they* (meaning her Children) *will be*
‘ *cared for* ; *and thou* (meaning her Hufband)
‘ *will be helped* ; *and there is a Place prepared*
‘ *for me.* And after continued in a fteady Ex-
‘ pectation of being taken away, and fpoke of
‘ Things relating thereto, with fuch Chearful-
‘ nefs and Refignation as was much admired :
‘ And fpake to divers Perfons in particular, ad-
‘ vifing, *To prize their Time, and make right*

‘ Ufe

' *Use of the Visitation of God to them.*   And she
' also express'd herself in a living Concern,
' that young People [amongst *Friends*] might
' not content themselves with bare going to
' Meetings: And said in a weighty manner,
' *It will not do, it will not do*; and so spake of
' her own Concern, and Desire to meet with
' the Lord in her young Years, when she went
' to Meetings; and that she could not be con-
' tent without his Presence or his Love; and
' humbly acknowledged his Mercy and Good-
' ness to her, from her youth upward :   And
' also said, that *She had often thought herself*
' *poor and bare, but she followed on after him,*
' *and could not let him alone*; and humbly ac-
' knowledged, *He had often appeared to her as*
' *a Morning without Clouds*; and her Heart
' then being filled with the Love of God, with
' unspeakable Joy in the holy Spirit, she sung
' Praises and Hallelujahs to the Lord God,
' and the Lamb her Saviour, for his Loving-
' kindness and Goodness to her, in many Re-
' spects till that very Time.

' Another time one coming in to see her, of
' whom she quickly took notice, called her by
' Name, and charged her to *be careful about*
' *going to Meetings among the Lord's People;*
' *and that she did not go in a careless or uncon-*
' *cerned Mind, but sit down at his Footstool, and*
' *wait to hear his gracious Words*:   And char-
' ged her to tell her Daughter thereof; and so
' spake farther of the Sorrow which had seized

' upon

‘ upon her Spirit, becaufe of an unconcerned
‘ Mind, and Indifferency, with refpect to
‘ waiting for the Knowledge of the Truth itfelf,
‘ that fhe had feen coming in among Friends,
‘ which that Day (or then abouts) fhe faid.
‘ *She well remember'd fhe had to advife Friends*
‘ *againft, the laft Time fhe had any thing to fay*
‘ *in Meetings before fhe left her own Country.*
‘ And with great weight farther faid, *It is*
‘ *great, or abfolute Mockery, to go to fit down*
‘ *before the Lord in Meetings in a carelefs*
‘ *Mind :* And after fome little Stilnefs, in the
‘ Strength of the Word of Life, fhe faid, *There*
‘ *was a terrible Day of Judgment coming, or*
‘ *haftening upon the Backfliders in* Sion. And
‘ after that fhe feemed to be eafier in her Spirit.
‘ and lying fome time more ftill, her Hufband
‘ foftly afked her, How fhe was ? She reply'd,
‘ *Well,* or *pretty well, my Love ; I find nothing*
‘ *but Eafe and Peace.* And tho' her Weaknefs
‘ had then prevailed much upon her, and
‘ fhe lay pretty ftill for fome time, yet her
‘ Strength was renewed in the Power of Truth,
‘ wherein fhe brake forth in Supplication, in
‘ a very humble and fervent manner, for the
‘ Church in general ; and alfo mentioned her
‘ little-ones. And further faid, *Let me be*
‘ *bowed down before the Lord, that the Fruit of*
‘ *my Body may be enriched with the fame Favour,*
‘ *Love, and Goodnefs ;* and fo went on in
‘ praifing and glorifying God, in the Abound-
‘ ings of his Love, and merciful Goodnefs, to
‘ the

' the tendring the Hearts of moſt about her.
' And after ſome time, ſhe being intreated to
' endeavour after Reſt, or Sleep, ſhe anſwered,
' *I had a fine* or *eaſy Day, Yeſterday, but this*
' *will be a hard Day* ; *for I think I ſhall reſt*
' *little more, till I reſt for altogether* ; that be-
' ing about or before the Middle of the Day ;
' and ſo ſhe continued in humble Acknow-
' ledgments to the Lord for his Goodneſs and
' Mercy, and in Praiſes to him, who ſhe often
' ſaid, was *worthy, worthy of it for evermore,*
' ſo long as her Words were intelligible.

' And though ſhe had a hard Struggle with
' Death, yet the Sting of it being taken away,
' ſhe ſeemed not to regard it, or complain, her
' Spirit being borne over it, by the Senſe of
' Joy and laſting Pleaſure ſhe was near to
' launch into the full Fruition of ; and that
' Evening ſhe departed, being the fifth Day of
' her lying in Child-bed, and the 16th Day
' of the ſecond Month 1719, in the Forty-
' ſecond Year of her Age, and was buried the
' 18th Day in Friends Burying-place, accom-
' panied with a great Concourſe of People,
' amongſt whom the Teſtimony of Truth was
' borne, in the Power and Goodneſs of the
' Lord Almighty, to the Comfort and ſtrenth-
' ning of many.

Not long after this, it came before him to
pay another Viſit to *America* : For which
Journey he began to make the neceſſary
Preparations,

Preparations, committing his Children to the Care of Relations and proper Perfons. But a dangerous Accident which befel him about this time, feemed likely to have retarded his Journey: By a Fall in the dark, upon an Inftrument made ufe of for cutting Hay, he received a deep and large Wound in the flefhy part of his Thigh; as he lived in a part of the Country where no proper Affiftance could fpeedily be had, he directed his Servant to few up the Wound, whilft he held the lips of it together himfelf. Of this Accident he recover'd fo faft, as to get Abroad in lefs than two Weeks, to the Admiration and Surprize of many of his Neighbours, who being little acquainted with any other Calls than thofe of temporal Intereft; or any Duties where this is not the Object, ignorantly interpreted it as a Judgment inflicted upon him by divine Providence, for leaving his Family and outward Concerns.

Being hinder'd by this Accident from attending the Quarterly-meeting at *York*, as he had defigned, he acquainted his much efteemed Friend *Benjamin Hornor* with the Occafion of his Abfence, in the following Letter, addreffed partly to him, and partly to the Quarterly-meeting at *York*.

‘ *Dear Friend*, B. Hornor;

‘ IT has happened that I have been ftaid
‘   about home, fomewhat longer than I ex-
‘ pected when I was laft with thee, partly in
‘ that

' that my own Affairs have not seemed to rid
' out of my way, so much to my Satisfaction,
' as I have desired to leave things ; and also
' having been enlarged beyond what I then
' saw to visit divers Places in my own Coun-
' try, in the Movings of the blessed Truth,
' which has been graciously sanctified and
' made truly profitable ; all which gives me
' Satisfaction.   I have hitherto been order'd in
' the Will of the all-wise Disposer, which to
' me is enough, being all I desire on my part ;
' and it was pleasant to me, to see a like-
' lihood to have the Comfort of being with
' my near Friends in the Quarterly-meeting at
' *York* again, before I leave my native Land ;
' but now I am like to be prevented, by reason
' of an Accident, whereby I am like to be
' unfitted for travel, a Week or two at least :
' Yet my Friends may know, that tho' I have
' been beset with some Straits and fresh Diffi-
' culties in this pinching Time, altogether
' unlooked for ; having been plunged in Ex-
' pectation of having to wade through a nar-
' row passage to the Service before me ; yet I
' am not dejected, or unsettled in my Spirit,
' under the Siftings which are suffered to at-
' tend me ; because my Mind is preserved
' intirely quiet under renewed Sweetness, be-
' lieving the Lord Almighty is near, and
' will go before in his due Time.
    ' And, *dear Friends*, altho' I desire not to
' magnify myself among my Brethren, yet is

O

' my

‘ my Heart engaged in travail to be more and
‘ more known among the Lord’s Family of
‘ all ages, in the hidden Root of immortal
‘ Goodneſs ; which is the only true Engager
‘ of Hearts for the Lord’s Cauſe and Teſti-
‘ mony, and which rightly fits, and maintains
‘ ſtrong for the work of our Day : And as
‘ my Heart is made often to ſtoop in awful
‘ Reverence before him, for Help to live ſo as
‘ Acceſs to the pure Spring of Sufficiency may
‘ be renewed ; ſo my Bowels, in true Brother-
‘ hood, move within me for my Brethren’s
‘ Sake, that a ſuitable Watchfulneſs and Fer-
‘ vency of Spirit, in feeling after immortal
‘ Goodneſs, may grow and be maintained,
‘ through all degrees in the Lord’s Family ;
‘ and if we ſlack not in attending upon the
‘ pure Spring, I am well aſſured, the Lord
‘ our gracious and mighty Helper will be near
‘ to ſupply with Life and Favour, Wiſdom
‘ and Ability, to ſerve him acceptably ; and
‘ to ſhew forth his Mercy and Salvation, to
‘ the Enlargement of the Borders of his Sanc-
‘ tuary, ſo that his Name may be more and
‘ more known and renowned in the Earth ; *ſo
‘ be it*, ſaith my Soul.

‘ Tho’ I am like to be diſappointed of the
‘ Opportunity of being preſent with you at
‘ this Time, yet I am thankfully glad, and
‘ ſtrengthned in my Hope, both on your
‘ and my own Account, if I ſhould not meet
‘ with you here any more ; in that I find my
‘ Soul

' Soul enlarged, and flowing in a current to-
' wards you, in that pure Love wherein *New*
' *Jerusalem*'s Children have their true Confo-
' lation ; and wherein, my *dear Friends*, I
' tenderly falute you, hoping to be better'd
' for your tender Remembrance, when we
' may be far feparated ; and thus I fhall con-
' clude, remaining your loving and near
' Brother in pure Fellowfhip.

Carrend, the 11th of the   ' JOHN FOTHERGILL.'
firft Month 1720.

At the Time propofed he fet out for *London*,
in order to take Shipping for *America* ; of
which Voyage, and of his Labours in the
Work of the Miniftry in that Country, he
kept the following Journal, which tho' fhort,
was judged worthy to be preferved, *viz.*

IN the Year 1721, an Exercife of Spirit, in
the moving of the Word of Life, came
upon me to vifit Friends in *America* again ;
and tho' the Matter feemed fomewhat ftrait at
the firft, becaufe my Wife being taken from
me, I was left with a pretty many young
Children ; yet the moving of the Word in my
Heart was fo powerful, and fweet, that I was
foon made perfectly willing to give up all, and
to follow the Lord freely : I laid the Concern
before the Brethren at our Monthly-meeting,
and then at the Quarterly-meeting, where
Friends readily fignified their Unity with me

                                                    in

in the Exercife. I then fettled my Affairs, and placed my Children under proper Care, and in the latter-end of the firft Month 1721 took leave of Friends in our own County, in the Love of God, and fet out for *London*, having *Laurence King* as a Companion in the Service: We had fome Meetings among Friends in the way, in which the Lord owned us, and ftrengthned us by his holy and living Prefence; greatly confirming us, that we were on the way in his Counfel and Requiring. We came up to *London* in the fecond Month, and ftaid there about three Weeks, vifiting the Meetings, the Lord opening a door for our Service among Friends in the City, and mercifully attended with his bleffed Prefence, much to ours and Friends Comfort, and the Name of the Lord was glorified.

Then finding our Minds fet at liberty to go forward, and a Veffel bound to *Virginia* being ready to fail, we took leave of Friends in the Love of Chrift, and left *London* the 6th of the third Month. We were favour'd with a fafe Paffage, and arrived in *York-river* the 6th of the fifth Month 1721. The Lord's Countenance was often gracioufly manifefted, to my great Humiliation and Comfort, often filling my Soul with Praifes to him.

We got up to *Skimina*, and the 9th of the Month, being Firft-day of the Week, we had a Meeting there, where there are but a few Friends, tho' feveral fober People came in and

were

were very attentive to hear the Teſtimony of Truth ; and it was made a good Seaſon to us, thro' the Preſence of Truth. On the 11th we had a Meeting at *Warwick*, where a pretty many ſober People came in with Friends, and we were favoured with the free Extendings of the Love and Goodneſs of God to our Comfort, and the Satisfaction and Encouragement of the Meeting in general. On the 13th we went to a Monthly-meeting at *Chuckatuck*, where was a fine Appearance of Friends, and the Lord's good Preſence, and the opening of his Word and Counſel was with us ; and his holy Name was magnified. The 16th we were at Friends Meeting at *Perquimons* in *Carolina*. The 18th we had a Meeting at *Joſeph Barrow's*, to which many ſober People came, and the Lord's Power and Goodneſs was gracioully preſent with and amongſt us, to our great Comfort, the Peoples Satisfaction, and the mighty Name of the Lord was glorified. We came back from thence to a Meeting at *Little-river*, where we were favour'd with ſacred Help, and the Teſtimony of Truth prevailed amongſt the People.

On the 20th we were at the Monthly-meeting of Friends at *Paſpitank*, whither came many Friends ; and we had an edifying Seaſon together, thro' the abounding of goſpel Life and Wiſdom, bleſſed be the holy and great Name. We had a Meeting amongſt ſome tender Friends the 22d, at *Joſeph Henley's*, and

went

went from thence to the other side *Paspitank*, to a Meeting we had appointed, and where some Hundreds of other People were gathered; the Meeting was held under the Shade of a large Tree, it being extremely hot. My heart was much enlarged in the Power and Testimony of the Gospel of Salvation towards the People, to the Glory of the Lord of Mercies. We came over the River to *Mary Glaister's*, and on the 24th visited some Friends Families there-away. The 25th we came to *Little-river* Meeting again, which was very large of Friends and others; and the Testimony of Truth opened freely and plentifully towards the Meeting, and prevailed sweetly over many Hearts; and I so far forgot my bodily Strength, as to be very much spent, the Weather being very hot; but the Life and Goodness of the Lord God was magnified, and the Might of his holy Arm supported me beyond reasonable Expectation.

The 26th we came to the lower Meeting-house upon *Perquimons-river* again: The Meeting was very large, and very solid and edifying. The 27th we came over the River again to a Meeting not far from *Gabriel Newby's*; but so great a number of Friends and others were gathered, that the House could not contain them; the Meeting was therefore held under a large Mulberry-tree; and we were greatly favoured with the glorious Presence and Power of the Lord God, to our great Help and

Comfort;

Comfort; the Testimony of the Gospel prevailed in an establishing, strengthning manner over many Souls; and the Name of the Lord was magnified.

On the 28th, being accompanied by many Friends, we went among some new Plantations, where we had appointed a Meeting, which considering the Place, was very large, (it being towards *Virginia)* and the Lord was pleased to bless the Time unto us, by opening his Life and Testimony to the Edification of Friends and the Satisfaction of the People, who were very attentive. We took leave of most of the Friends of *Carolina* here, in a sense of the Love and tendring Power of Truth, and in much nearness one to another. From thence we came to *Nathan Newby*'s in *Virginia*, where we had a large Meeting the 30th, mostly of other People, who were, as in many other Places there-away, attentive to the Testimony of Truth, which in the Openings of the Power of Christ, went freely forth among them that Day, to the Glory of God. We went the 31st to *Robert Jordan*'s, and on the 1st of the sixth Month we had a large and solid Meeting near *Nancemund-river*, and on the 2d at the *Western-branch* Meeting-house, which was large, and mercifully favoured with divine Attendance, to the Help of some tender Friends there; tho' there were many other People, with whom Truth itself had but very little place.

The

The 4th we went to a Meeting at *Rafco-neck*, which is a fmall Meeting, but the Name of the Lord was with us to declare its Excellency, and Safety for Refuge. The 6th, being Firft-day, we were at Friends Meeting in *Le-vy-neck*, which was large, as many Friends and others came to it many Miles: It was a fearching, exercifing Time, but through the Lord's Goodnefs, it proved a good and ferviceable Meeting. On the 8th we went towards the head of *Elizabeth-river*, where there were a few Friends, and had a Meeting at *Sarah Whitehoufe*'s, to which came fome pretty innocent People, with whom I had a good open Time. From thence we went to a place called the *Great-bridge*, and had a Meeting at a friendly Man's houfe, to which likewife came many fober People, and fome of the more Confiderable there-abouts, and we had a fatisfactory Seafon amongft them: And there being one *Henry Woodward* at the Meeting, he invited us to go with him to lodge, which I was very eafy to accept of, and three other Friends who were with me, accompanied us. Both he, his Wife and Children, were exceeding friendly and loving; and both the former went with us to another Perfon's houfe, where we had a Meeting amongft feveral fober and tender People; and it was made a profitable Time to many of them, through the Lord's Goodnefs. We then went to vifit one *Robert Stewart* (a loving friendly Man) and his Family, and had

a good

a good Opportunity with them, and lodged there that Night, as he would not willingly part with us.

The 11th, bring clear of that part of the Country, we came back to *John Holliwell's*, near *Nancemund-river*, and had a Meeting that Evening with a few Friends who lived near him, much to my Satisfaction. The 13th we were at Friends Meeting near *Nancemund*, to which came many Friends from several other Meetings; and though I was but weak in Body, and much indisposed, yet the Lord's Goodness and Life strengthned me, and we had a solid, settling Meeting, to the Lord's Glory, and the Comfort of many. The 14th we visited a Widow Woman, whose Name was *Baker*, and her Children; where our gracious God was mindful of us, and by the springing up of his Love among us, made glad our Souls together.

The 15th we had a Meeting in a Barn at *James Copeland's*, whither came a considerable number, both of Friends and others, from among the Woods; and the Power and Dread of the Lord of Hosts, mercifully owned us, and prevailed over many; the Testimony of Truth being over all. The 16th we passed over a River called *Black-water*, to a Place newly settled, and had a pretty large Meeting among some Friends and People there-abouts. The 17th we rode thro' the Wilderness to another new Settlement, where on the 18th we had a Meeting with

P   some

some People who lived difperfed among the Woods, and tho' many of them feem'd to know very little about Religion, yet the Lord was good to us, in owning us with his Prefence, and enabled us to preach the Gofpel of Chrift in the Power of it, among them, wherewith divers of them feemed much affected. The 20th, being the firft of the Week, we were at Friends Meeting, in their Meetinghoufe in *Surry* County, which was pretty large ; but too many of the Profeffors of Truth there, as in fome other Places, for want of living to the Truth, ftood in the Way of the Gofpel-life, and hinder'd its Prevalency among the People ; yet the Lord helped to declare the Truth in the Power thereof, and filled my Heart with Praifes to him.

The 23d we had a Meeting at the Widow *Butler*'s Houfe, to which came feveral foberly-behaved People ; and through the Lord's Goodnefs and Help, we had a good Opportunity among them. We came back from thence to *Robert Hunnicut*'s, and had a Meeting near his Houfe, among the few Friends who live there-abouts, and a pretty many other People, wherein the Lord's Power, and the Teftimony of Truth, made fome Impreffion on them, to the Glory of the Lord of all our Mercies. From hence we went with a Friend called *James Benford*, in whofe Family we had a good little Meeting that Evening. The next Day we croffed *James-river* to *William Lead*'s,

Lead's, where a small Meeting is usually kept; and we had one that Day, in which the Lord mercifully owned us with his living Power, and furnished with Ability to preach the glorious Gospel of Christ in a good degree of Dominion, to the Praise of our gracious God. The 27th we had a pretty large Meeting at *Curles*, and lodged at *Thomas Pleasant*'s; and on the 28th, with some other Friends, we rode up the Woods to a place called *Dover*, where few Friends live; we lodged two Nights with one *Joseph Parson*, who with his Wife entertained us chearfully, tho' not professing with us. On the 29th they went with us about four Miles, where a pretty large Meeting gathered; in which the Power and Testimony of the blessed Truth reached freely to the People, to their general Satisfaction, and the Comfort of many. The 30th we had another Meeting, seven Miles higher up in the Woods. The 31st we crossed over *James-river*, and had a Meeting amongst some People who requested it; to which many came out of the Woods, and the Lord favoured us with his Presence and Help, so that Truth prevailed. That Evening we came down to a *French* Settlement called *Manikin* Town, and on the 1st of the seventh Month we had a Meeting there; to which divers of the *French* People, with others, came; and the Lord was graciously mindful of us, his Gospel Testimony freely reaching forth in his free Love towards the People, and Truth

P 2   was

was magnified amongſt them. We lodged with one *Daniel Groom*, a Man upon whom the Truth had made an Impreſſion in a Viſitation of Mercy, and we left him tender and loving. After the Meeting we took leave of that part of the Country, in much Eaſe of Spirit, and came to *Thomas Pleaſant*'s that Night.

On the 2d we went to the Monthly-meeting at *Edward Moſby*'s, where many religious People, beſides Friends, were gathered ; and the Power and Goodneſs of the Lord appeared among us, to the Satisfaction, Comfort, and Eſtabliſhment of many ; as alſo in faithful Warning to Backſliders and lukewarm Profeſſors of the Truth : Friends went through the Buſineſs of their Monthly-meeting in a peaceable tender manner. We lodged that Night with *John Johnſon* at the *Swamp*, and on the 3d, being Firſt-day, had a large Meeting of Friends and many others, where divine Mercy and Goodneſs owned us, and helped to declare the way of Life and Salvation, in the Demonſtration of the holy Spirit ; many were comforted, and the Name of the Lord magnified in the midſt of his People.

The 4th we went to *Black-creek*, where we had alſo a large Meeting, and many People not of our Society (tho' generally very ſober) were preſent. But thro' the Backſliding, or Indifferency of ſome, who had been convinced of Truth in that part, the Way of the Teſtimony of the Goſpel ſeemed very ſtrait ; yet the bleſſed

Power

Power of Christ did by degrees prevail, to the Praise and Honour of Truth, the Encouragement and Comfort of many. We lodged at *Garrart Ellyson*'s, and on the 5th, we had a Meeting over the *Monky-river*, where few or no Friends had ever been, or had a Meeting before; the People who came were generally sober, and attentive to hear the Truth declared, and we had a satisfactory Time among them: Several were very loving. We came back to *G. Ellyson*'s, and had another Meeting the 6th at *Black-creek*, more select to Friends or friendly People, where the Lord apppeared mercifully mindful of them, opening both Counsel and Warning to the Loose, Encouragement to the Honest, and in the Riches of his ancient Love, made the time very comfortable to us.

The 7th we went to the Meeting at *William Lead*'s again, where the Lord graciously owned us with his Presence, and opened Counsel for the Establishment of the Well-minded. We lodged at *John Crew*'s, and went again to a Meeting at *Curles*, where we had a mercifully open time in the Love of Truth, to exhort Friends to Faithfulness to the Lord; we took our leave of them in his Love, and lodged at *J. Pleasant*'s, where the next Morning we had a truly edifying Opportunity, in the Openings of the Power of Christ, with some Friends who came to take leave of us.

The 9th we went over *Jame*'s and *Apamattock* Rivers, lodged at the Widow *Butler*'s, and

and went to *Joseph Paterson*'s, a friendly Man, who lived on the Bank of this laſt River, up in the Woods, his Wife being a Friend ; we had a pretty large Meeting on the 10th among a tender People, being almoſt at the outſide of the Inhabitants that way ; and the Lord was pleaſed to open my Heart and Mouth to preach the Goſpel of Life, in much Openneſs of Spirit, to his Praiſe : The People appeared ſatisfied, and ſeem'd very deſirous of another Meeting, which I gladly ſubmitted to, and appointed it to be at *Timothy Harriſon*'s ; it was held on the 11th accordingly, among a larger number than before, of ſober People, and the Lord of Mercies was tenderly mindful of us, and gracious in extending of his Love and Goodneſs to the People. I left that part of the Country with much Peace and Comfort of Spirit, and came back again to the Widow *Butler*'s that Night. The 12th we had a little Opportunity with her, her Children and Family, wherein Truth opening my Heart in Counſel and Encouragement to them, to our Comfort, bleſſed be the Lord for his Help and Goodneſs. Taking leave of them, we came down to *James Benford*'s, where we had appointed a Meeting, which was held there accordingly the 13th ; a conſiderable number of Friends and others came thither, and Truth was pleaſed to own us, in its Power and Wiſdom, to the eſtabliſhing of many in the way of Life.

The

The 14th we took our Journey towards the Yearly-meeting, and came to *Matthew Jordan's* at *Pagan-creek*. The 15th to *Chuckatuck*, where the Yearly-meeting was held, which continued three Days : Part of the firſt being for the Buſineſs of the Church ; wherein divers Things were inquired into, and offer'd to Friends Conſideration, relating to the building up and preſerving Friends from the Corruption of the World ; and maintaining the Teſtimony of Truth amongſt them in that Country ; which was done and received in a Spirit of Love. The publick Meetings were very large, both of Friends and many ſoberly-behaved People ; And thro' the merciful Help of the Lord's Power, the glorious Goſpel, both in its Teſtimony and holy Life, was exalted over all ; and Friends had to part under the Senſe of the Love and Goodneſs of God, whoſe holy Name was magnified, as it is worthy to be for ever.

The 17th, being Firſt-day, and the Concluſion of the Yearly-meeting, we came back again to *Matthew Jordan's*. The 18th we took our Journey Northward, and came to *James Bate's* at *Skimina*. The 19th to *William Trotter's*, a Friend who lives remote from any Meeting, and had a Meeting in his Houſe next Day, to which divers of his Neighbours came, and we had a good open Time in the Love of Truth. We went that Evening to *Thomas Pricklow's*. The 21ſt to *Warwick*, where we had a Meeting with the Friends who live there-abouts, there-abouts, and lodged at *Miles Carey's*. The 22d we went to *Skimina* again, where we had appointed a Meeting to be that Day, and tho' it is a low, decay'd place refpecting Religion, yet the Lord was good to us, and helped us to declare the unchangeable Truth, and way of Life; and to exalt its holy Teftimony over all Unrighteoufnefs. We lodged with *James Bates*, and on the 23d took our leave of him and his Wife, and went to *Black-creek* to *Garrart Robert Ellyfon's*. The 24th, being the firft of the Week, we had a large Meeting, Friends coming thither to meet us from many places there-abouts; we had a good edifying Seafon in the Love of God; and took leave of one another in much Tendernefs of Spirit, as Children of one Father. We went to a place call'd the *Swamp* that Night, and the 25th, being accompanied with a pretty many Friends, we went up the Country to fee fome friendly People, newly fettled at a place called *Cedar-creek*.

The 26th we lodged at *Thomas Stanley's*, and had a Meeting there, wherein divine Goodnefs favoured us with a fatisfactory Opportunity. A few there were, who made fome Profeffion of Truth, and many foberly inclined People, towards whom the Love and Teftimony of Truth extended freely, which was greatly comfortable to us.

The 27th we took our Journey thro' the Country towards *Potomack-river*, and came at Night to *William Duff's* in Prince *George's* County.

County. The 29th we had a Meeting among a few Friends, and some other sober People, at *Peter Skinner's*, where we had a good and seasonable Opportunity.

The 30th we went to a Meeting held at *Mattocks*, at *Justice Washington's*, a friendly Man, where the Love of God opened my Heart towards the People much to my Comfort, and their Satisfaction ; and the holy Name of the Lord was glorified. We came back to *William Duff's* again that Night, and the 1st of the eighth Month, the first of the Week, we had a large Meeting there, to which came many other People : Many of them were very attentive to the Testimony of Truth, and the Lord's Love and Power were greatly magnified and exalted over all. The 2d we had a little Meeting with Friends living there-abouts by themselves, which our heavenly Father owned with his Presence, and made it a good Time to them and us ; and his great Name was praised.

The 4th we took our Journey over *Potomack* and *Patuxen* Rivers, and came to the Widow *Hutchins's* that Night, and the 5th we were at the Week-day Meeting at *Cliff* Meeting-house ; we had a sweet Season in the Love of God : And went to *Robert Robert's* that Night. The 6th we had a Meeting at *Patuxen* Meeting-house, several being with us from the *Cliffs* ; and a comfortable Time thro' some deep Travail, but Truth prevailed over all. The 7th we came back to *Kensey John's* House at the *Cliffs*,

Q   and

and the 8th we were at their Meeting again ; which was large and precious, to our Comfort, the Help of many, and God's Glory.

The 9th we had a large Meeting at *Herring-bay*, where the ancient Love of God, and its holy Way and Teftimony reached freely, and was exalted among Friends ; divers of whom were much hurt by the libertine fpirit of the World too much prevailing ; yet the Love and Power of God was over all, to their Comfort and Help.

The 10th we had a large and edifying Meeting with Friends at *Weft-river*, in the free extendings of living Power, tending to build up the Living, and gather the Wanderers who had gone from the Simplicity that is in Chrift, nearer to it again.

The 11th we came to *Samuel Chew*'s. From hence we crofs'd the Bay, and lodged the 12th at one *Edward Ellicot*'s, not a Friend, but were kindly entertained by him. The 13th we went to *Daniel Richardfon*'s, and the 14th to *Tred-haven* Meeting-houfe, to the Yearly-meeting there, which continued five Days fucceffively, where a great number of Friends and others were gathered ; and the Lord's Goodnefs and Majefty were eminently manifefted among us, to the Glory of God, and the Comfort and Confirmation of many Souls.

The 18th we went after Meeting to *Rebecca Pitts*'s, where we refted the next Day, and from thence through *Chefter* to *Cecil*, where cn

the

the Firſt-day, being the 22d, we were at a large Meeting, and came back to *William Thomas*'s the 23d, and had a Meeting at *Cheſter*, wherein the Power of Truth prevailed, to the Comfort and Strengthning of many. The 24th we came down to the Widow *Pitts*'s, and the 25th to *Tredhaven* Meeting-houſe again to the Quarterly-meeting, and the Monthly-meeting which was held the next Day; wherein the Life and Goodneſs of Truth attended us, to the Encouragement and Help of thoſe who loved it, and its Teſtimony.

The 27th we went to *Tuckaho*, and had a large and profitable Meeting, through the eminent Manifeſtation of the Lord's Power and Goodneſs, to the Comfort of the living, and to the Awakening of the careleſs; the looſe were faithfully warned, and Truth was exalted. The 28th we went to the Bay-ſide, and were at the Meeting there the 29th, being Firſt-day, and at a Marriage there the 30th, to which came many ſober People; and the Lord mercifully owned us, and magnified his own Name and Teſtimony, which prevailed over many Hearts, greatly to our Comfort. The 31ſt we went to *Choptanck* Meeting, which tho' ſmall, yet was made very comfortable and edifying to Friends.

The 1ſt of the ninth Month we went over *Choptanck-river*, to a Meeting at *Joſhua Kinnerley*'s, where many others beſide Friends were gathered, among whom the glorious Goſpel-life and Teſtimony ran freely forth, and

Q 2

prevailed

prevailed in a great degree over many Souls : I was much comforted, and the Lord's holy Name was glorified.

The 2d we went to *Tranſgeekin* Meeting, which was large, many others not of our profeſſion being preſent, and it was render'd to us a profitable Seaſon. The 3d we had a Meeting at the Widow *Fiſher*'s at *Nanticook-river*. The 4th we croſſed that River and *Nickocomico* to *Mannie*. The 5th we had a Meeting there, wherein the Lord's Power and Goodneſs helped us, and his Teſtimony went freely forth to the Information and Encouragement of the Religious-minded ; and powerfully againſt a backſliding worldly Spirit, which has almoſt overrun the few Friends there. The 6th we went to the Widow *Waters*'s at *Annimeſſet*, and on the 7th had a good little Meeting there, to which divers other People came.

On the 8th we took our Journey downwards into *Virginia*, and on the 12th had a Meeting at *Neſwadax* Meeting-houſe, to which came a conſiderable number of ſoberly inclined People, and the Lord's Power and Teſtimony were exalted, to our Comfort and the Glory of God.

The 13th we went to one *Arthur Upſher*'s, a friendly Man's Houſe, and had ſome Service in the Love of God in his Family, and lodged there that Night. The 14th ſeveral of the Family went with us to a Meeting at *William Nocks*'s, to which came many ſober People, and the Lord gave us a good and ſeaſonable Time

Time among them : Tho' we were much afflicted in a sense of the prevailing of an earthly
Spirit, leading some that had been convinced
of the Truth, into Indifferency and Slackness
respecting its Testimony ; by which the Progress of Truth and Righteousness has been
much obstructed in divers parts of that Country. The 15th we went to *Muddy-creek*, and
had a good open Meeting there that day, thro'
the gracious Nearness and Help of the powerful Presence of the Lord God, whose Name
was exalted over all. We went that Night to
Mary Johnson's, an honest Woman's house,
and on the 16th to *Thomas Preeson*'s Plantation
near the Sea-side, to a Meeting appointed before ; to which many sober and well-behaved
People came, and the Testimony and Life of
the Gospel, in the Love of God was opened
towards them, to their Satisfaction and our
great Comfort in the Lord.

The 17th we went up to *Maryland* again,
and the 19th, being the First-day of the Week,
we had a Meeting at the Widow *Truit*'s, which
tho' but small, was favour'd with the Extending of merciful Regard for the Peoples Help.
On the 20th we set out towards a part of *Pensilvania*, and the 21st went to *Robert Lodge*'s, a
Friend living at *Cold-spring*, thro' some dangerous Swamps. The 22d we had a good and
comfortable Meeting near his House, and were
at several others in the remaining part of this
Week.

The

The 26th we went to *Duck-creek* Meeting, being the First-day, and Truth favour'd us and Friends, with a good and strengthning Season, in the free opening of divine Power and Goodness. We had divers Meetings betwixt this and the 1st of the tenth Month, when we were at *Chester* Meeting, which was large and solidly comfortable, in the free Attendance of divine Goodness and Counsel: Many Friends met us here from several other Meetings. The 3d, being the First-day, we had a large Meeting at *Derby*, wherein seasoning Goodness, from the Lord of Mercies, was comfortably manifested, and the holy Name of our gracious God was magnified amongst us. The 4th we went to *Philadelphia* to *William Fishburn's*, where I met with many near Friends of my former Acquaintance, and we were much comforted together, in the Love of our gracious God: I staid there about a Week, and had several good and truly edifying Meetings in that Time, thro' the Lord's merciful Goodness.

The 12th I had a Meeting at *Springfield*, which was very large and solidly profitable, and on the 13th another large and good Meeting at *Providence*. On the 14th I had a Meeting at *Middle-town*, which was likewise very large; but was an exercising Time, because a worldly Spirit, and love to vain Liberty, seemed to have unfitted many hearts for the Love and Life of Truth: Yet the Lord's blessed Power prevailed, and was exalted over all.

all. The 15th I went to a Meeting at *Chichester*, wherein God's Love and Testimony likewise prevailed over hurtful Things, to the Comfort and Strengthning of many.

The 17th, being First-day, I went to *Concord*, where a great number of Friends and some others were gathered, and the Lord's Power and Goodness came over us, and were magnified to the Comfort of many, and to the Awakening of others. The 18th I had a Meeting at *Center*; a laborious Time, but Truth prevailed, and came over loose Spirits. The 19th I went to a Meeting at *Kennet*, where the Lord gave us a good and edifying Season, and on the 20th I had a Meeting near *Abraham Marshall's*, being a newly settled Place, and the Lord gave us a good Time among the People there. The 22d I went to another new Place called *Caln*, where a pretty many People were gathered, towards whom the Love and Mercy of God extended freely, to their Help and Comfort.

The 23d I had a Meeting at *Youghland*, to which came a considerable number of Friends, and in the Lord's Goodness we had an edifying Season. The 24th, being First-day, I was at Friends Meeting at *Goshen*, which was large, and a heavenly informing and truly edifying Time it was, in the Demonstration of the Lord's Power. The 25th I was at the Monthly-meeting for Business at *Providence*, which was large, and the ancient Goodness,

and

and living Power of the Lord God, was comfortably among Friends, and therein the Service of the Meeting was carried on in much Unity and Peace.

The 26th I went to *Newtown*, and tho' it was extreme fnowy, yet we had a large and bleffed Meeting. The 27th to *Hartford*, where we had a very large Meeting, and Truth was near to help thro' much Exercife, to my Comfort and Eafe. The 28th I went to *Radnor*, where was a large and folidly profitable Meeting, and the powerful Teftimony of Truth was exalted to the Help of many Souls. The 29th to *Merion*, where a large number was gathered, and the bleffed Gofpel-teftimony, and humbling Power, greatly prevailed that Day, to the great Joy and Help of many, and the Lord God was magnified. I went that Evening to lodge with *J. Roberts*, where I had a good and edifying Seafon with the old People, many Friends alfo coming there to fee us. On the 30th I came to *Philadelphia*, in order to take my Companion along with me in a Vifit further up the Province, he having remained here about three Weeks, being unwell. I ftaid here over the next Day, *viz.* the 31ft, and Firft-day, and had pretty good Meetings.

The 2d of the eleventh Month we had a Meeting at *Frankfort*, which the Lord bleffed to us, and made it a comfortable Seafon. We lodged at *Jonathan Dickenfon's*, where Truth open'd a way to extend a merciful Vifit to the Family.

Family. The 3d we went to *Byberry* Meeting, which was very large, but a strait suffering time. The 4th to *Nishaminny*, which being the Monthly-meeting for Business, many Friends came, and the Lord strengthned and encouraged us together, by the attendance of his blessed Power and Goodness. The 5th we went to *Bristol*, where many Friends gathered, and the Lord gave us an heavenly relieving Time, in the reachings of his Wisdom and Power. The 7th, being the First-day of the Week, we were at the *Falls* Meeting, which was very large, and thro' the blessed attendance of the Lord's Power and Goodness, we had an edifying Season. The 8th we went to *Macclesfield*, and had a good Meeting that Afternoon with some Friends, and many friendly People who came in. The 9th we went to *Wright*'s Town, where we had a large Meeting that Day, wherein the Testimony of Truth reached forth in an Awakening manner; and to the Comfort and Strengthning of many.

The 10th we had a Meeting at *Buckingham*, and went the 11th to *North-wales*, where we lodged at *Jonathan Evan*'s, and had a good Meeting that Evening, with a large number of Friends who came to see us. The 12th, being accompanied by several of those and some other Friends, we went to a new settled Place called *Great-swamp*, and though the Snow was deep, and the Frost very severe, yet thro' the Lord's Goodness we got well through, and had a good

R   little

little Meeting with some Friends and other People, who came in that Evening, at *Peter Leicester's*. The 14th we were at the Meeting of Friends at *North-wales*, which was very large, several other Professors coming in, and the Gospel was preached in its own Authority and Wisdom, and was exalted in many Souls, to the Comfort of the living, and the Glory of the Lord of all our Mercies. We had another Meeting that Evening, at the House of *Hugh Folke's*, which was much to our Satisfaction. The 15th we had a Meeting at *Plymouth*, a good, informing and profitable Season. And the 16th we were at *North-wales* Meeting again : A large solidly edifying Meeting it was, and the Lord's Power spread weightily over many Hearts.

The 17th we had a Meeting at *Horsham*, wherein the Wisdom and Power of Truth prevailed greatly to our, and many Friends Comfort. We lodged that Night at *William Stockdale's*, where we had some good Service in the Love of Truth that Evening, among a pretty many Friends. The 18th we were at *Abington*, where the Meeting was large, and an awakening rouzing Season. We lodged at *Morris Morris's*, where several Friends came in, and we had some Service among them.

The 19th we went to a Meeting at *Germantown*, which was a large and blessed Meeting, thro' the Prevalency of Truth. The 21st, being First-day, we were at the Meeting at
Burlington,

Burlington, where we were favour'd with a good and solid Meeting; and the 22d at *Springfield*, where the holy Arm of the Lord was revealed, to the Comfort and Help of many Souls, and his Name was magnified over all. The 24th we had a Meeting at *Mountholly*, which was pretty large; and the bleſſed Arm of Power was manifeſted therein, tending to ſtir up ſome ſlack and looſe People, and to encourage the Upright. The 25th we went to a Meeting at *Anchocas*, where there was a Marriage, to which many People came; and Truth made it a profitable and eſtabliſhing Seaſon. The 26th we had a large and bleſſed Meeting, thro' the ſtrong ariſings and goings forth of the Teſtimony and Life of Chriſt. The 28th, being Firſt-day, we were at *Newtown* Meeting, wherein Truth appeared in Mercy and Goodwill to revive and build up a weak and ſtaggering People. The 29th we had a good and prevailing Meeting, in the Help of the Life and Goodneſs of Truth, at *Woodberry-creek*. The 31ſt we had a Meeting at *Alloway-creek*, which was an eſtabliſhing, ſtrengthning Seaſon, thro' the merciful Attendance of the Power of Truth. The 1ſt of the twelfth Month we had a very large Meeting in *Salem* Town, which the Lord made an awakening Time, to the Comfort of many.

From hence he wrote the following Epiſtle to Friends in own Country, but more eſpecially his

To

‘ *To* FRIENDS *of* WENSLEYDALE
‘ *Meeting.*

‘ DEAR FRIENDS,

‘ WHom I very often remember, tho’
‘ now separated far from you out-
‘ wardly ; yet as I am a Part of you in many
‘ respects, especially in that we have, many
‘ of us, been begotten by one heavenly Father,
‘ into one Faith and near Kindred ; and by and
‘ in his Love and living Power, many of our
‘ Souls have been fed, and nursed up as Bone
‘ of Bone, both in true and near Love, and
‘ Readiness to serve one another with Plea-
‘ sure ; which as it is the Effect of divine
‘ Love, so we shall never lose the Comfort
‘ and Profit of its being renewed to us, and
‘ upon us, both to our own particular Help
‘ and Supply, whatever any of us may have
‘ to wade thro,’ or be tried with ; and also to
‘ nourish and maintain a holy, strengthning
‘ Fellowship, as Brethren and Sisters, if we in
‘ ourselves keep but the pure Faith, in the
‘ everliving Power, and walk in due Fear and
‘ Care before the Lord God of Mercies and
‘ All-sufficiency. For this my Heart often
‘ humbly breathes to the Lord for myself, and
‘ for you all ; and in a tender, near manner
‘ for the humble, inwardly needy, and bap-

‘ tized

' tized Souls among you, towards whom my
' Bowels, often as it were, turn within me ;
' you being almoſt daily before me, and dear
' to me in the Love of God, whoſe compaſ-
' ſionate Eye is ſurely over you in a Fatherly
' manner, and his mighty Arm extended to-
' wards you, both to feed and waſh, and fit
' for a further Service in your Day, if you
' wait but patiently and diligently upon him,
' in true Reſignation of Heart, to be made
' what he would have you to be ; for Love and
' Care from the Lord Almighty, I am often
' very ſenſible, reacheth graciouſly towards
' you to do you good.

' And, *dear Friends*, as you are in general
' often freſh in my Remembrance in Brotherly-
' love, ſo I have been influenced to write a
' little to you, and therein I now ſend my near
' Salutation in engaging Love from the holy
' Spring of pure Edification ; praying that you
' may all wait diligently, to feel a holy fervent
' Thirſt to be raiſed in your Hearts, after cer-
' tain Experience of divine Life, and enlarging
' Goodneſs in yourſelves, and more and more
' to be prepared for it ; ſo will you come to
' have Bread in your own Houſes, pure
' Water in your own Veſſels, and ſo to have
' Rejoicing in yourſelves, and not in another :
' Thus will all grow towards God, and become
' fruitful in Righteouſneſs, to the Comfort and
' Help one of another, and to ſhew forth the
Nature

' Nature of Truth, to the Praife and Glory of
' the one moft holy Head.

   ' And it is alfo frefh upon my Spirit, with
' fome weight, earneftly and tenderly, to ad-
' vife all of you, to fee carefully to the Im-
' provement of your own Gifts or Talents;
' which is not only your Duty, as they were
' given for this Purpofe, but is alfo the alone
' Way to a truly happy End. And altho' all
' have not received Gifts alike, neither with
' refpect to Meafure nor Operation, yet all are
' from one God, one Spirit, and are to be
' improved, whether five, two, or one: The
' faithful Improvers, the diligently exercifed
' Hearts, according to the Meafure given, only
' will have the Sentence of *Well done*, and
' *enter into the Joy of the Lord* at laft; as well
' as be often favoured with Accefs to Life here.
' It is the careful Waiters for the Spirit of
' Truth, and its quickning Power, fuch as fow
' and live to the Spirit, who will reap Life ever-
' lafting, and from time to time have the free
' Earneft of a never-fading Inheritance. And
' thus, Strength in Faith, and Vigour in Zeal
' for the Lord God, his holy Teftimony, and for
' the Peace and Profperity of his Family, is
' renewed and maintained; and thus we grow
' up truly fubject to one holy and living Head,
' and near to, and careful over one another.

   ' And, *Friends*, be fure to be careful that
' heavenly Things have fuitably more Room
' than earthly, with you all; and walk in the
' Spirit,

‘ Spirit, as well as talk of it, and then the
‘ Lusts or unprofitable Desires of the Flesh
‘ will not be fulfilled, but the great Mount of
‘ our elder Brother *Esau* will be gradually, and
‘ effectually judged in all ; and the Kingdom
‘ and Government of Hearts will be the Lord’s,
‘ whose Right it is : Then will your Hearts
‘ enlarge one towards another, and grow
‘ stronger in an heavenly Mind. Oh, thus
‘ will the Elder among you be built up and
‘ maintained bright in Spirit, and in Life :
‘ And the Younger will be gathered from the
‘ lofty Mountains, where the World’s deceiv-
‘ ing, dazzling Glory is viewed and coveted ;
‘ where the hurtful things mostly range; where
‘ Coldness and Barrenness often reign ; and
‘ then the Lord alone will be exalted in feel-
‘ ing Knowledge among them, and he will
‘ become a Fountain of Blessing to them, that
‘ they may be a Generation for God in their
‘ Time, to shew forth his Salvation and re-
‘ deeming Power in the Earth. My Hope is
‘ strong, that many of the Youth will thus
‘ grow up to their own, to yours, and the
‘ Comfort of many others. I am well satisfied
‘ that divine Care and Regard is, and will be
‘ extended towards you in general, to do you
‘ good, according to your several Wants ; t
‘ be assured, it must be in the Lord’s Wa   l
‘ Terms, and not in Man’s. And one
‘ farther take good Notice of, which
‘ both Caution and Encouragement in it,   t

' altho' *Saul* was sent against a great People,
' and with close Orders to destroy *Amaleck* ut-
' terly, yet was he attended with Ability suit-
' able to the Service : And so is the Lord care-
' fully near to help you in every respect, in
' the Performance of what he requires, both in
' resisting and eschewing whatever he shews to
' be hurtful or evil ; and also in pressing on,
' tho' through a crowd, and drawing near for
' right and effectual healing of every Distem-
' per : He will also be with you, and near to
' help forward in answering his Requirings, in
' any Thing or Service for his holy Name, the
' Good and Comfort of his Family.

' I say again, in a steady Sense of holy
' Goodness in my Heart, at this Season reach-
' ing towards you, that the Lord God, who
' manifests unto Man what is good, and what
' he requires, doth and will attend and assist
' you to go forward, in performing and an-
' swering the blessed End ; to our Peace and
' his Glory, how weak soever any may appear
' in their own sight, if they do but duly la-
' bour to follow him with full Purpose of
' Heart : And that this may be more and
' more all our humble Care, is my sincere
' Advice to you, and Prayer to him who can
' do all Things. *Amen.*

' Thus, *dear Friends*, I have freed my Spirit
' a little towards you in our Father's Love,
' wherein I am almost daily mindful of you,
' tho' at this great outward Distance, and in

' it

' it once more dearly greet you, and remain
' your sincerely loving Friend and Brother, in
' the unchangeable Covenant of Life,

Salem in Weft-Jerfey,   ' John Fothergill.
    the 1ft of the twelfth
Month, 1721—2.

' I may farther acquaint you, that thro' di-
' vine Goodnefs and Mercy, my Health and
' Strength is every way maintain'd and renew'd,
' to mine and many Friends Admiration, con-
' fidering my Diligence and the Depth of
' Labour : And altho' I am led to trace out,
' and wade through many exercifing Circum-
' ftances attending the Churches, yet the
' Lord's Arm often makes way to great Do-
' minion in the Refurrection of the Power
' of Truth, to my humbling Joy ; and the
' moft holy and worthy Name is magnified.
' We get forward pretty well, tho' not very
' fpeedily, but my Hopes are renewed that I
' may yet live to fee you again in the Lord's
' Time, unto whofe Hand I am freely refigned,
' having many Evidences, or Confirmations,
' thro' divine Help, that it is well I am here.'

The 2d of the twelfth Month *(continues the
Journal)* we had a Meeting at *Pilefgrove*,
where many foberly-inclined People were gathered, and the Love and Teftimony of Truth
reached freely towards them, and made it a
profitable Seafon.

The 3d we came up the Country again, and in the Evening croſſed over the River *Delaware* to *Philadelphia*, where on the 4th, being Firſt-day, we were at the Burial of an ancient Friend, *Nicholas Waller*, at *Fair-hill*; at which Place a great Concourſe of Friends and others were met: We had a large Meeting that Evening in *Philadelphia*, which the Lord was pleaſed eminently to own with his glorious Power, and the Goſpel Teſtimony and Life was over all in a great and bleſſed degree. The 5th we were at the Quarterly-meeting for Buſineſs for the County, where the Lord owned us, and opened divers weighty Things, to recommend to the Meeting, in the Power of Truth, which Friends received in Tenderneſs; and an holy Reverence, with deep Thankfulneſs, was brought over our Souls before the Lord.

The 6th we were at a General-meeting for Worſhip at *Haverford*, wherein the Lord's Power glorioufly appeared, and ſhook the Earth in many Hearts in divers reſpects; and it was made a Day of Gladneſs and Comfort to others, bleſſed be the Name of the Lord God for ever.

The 7th we were at a Monthly-meeting for Buſineſs at *Derby*, where we had a good and edifying Time, in the Love of God. The 8th we went to *Springfield*, viſiting ſeveral Friends by the way, to ſome Advantage, and had a large Meeting there, wherein the Lord's Power and

and Life was exalted and magnified, to the Encouragement of many. The 9th we had a Meeting at *Middletown*, wherein the powerful Word of Life arose and prevailed greatly, to our Comfort, and the Help of Friends. The 10th we visited several Friends Families, and went to *Chester :* The 11th, being First-day, we were at. Friends Meeting there ; to which Friends came from many Places, and a solid settling Time it was in the Power of Truth. The 12th we went to the Quarterly-meeting for Business at *Providence* ; where the Lord's Power and Love were eminently among Friends, to our Encouragement in the Service of Truth. And the 13th were at a General-meeting for Worship at *Middletown*, which was very large, and a blessed, humbling Season, in the sensible Prevalence of the Gospel of Christ, and the holy Name was magnified.

The 14th we went to *Lewis Walker's*, in the *Great-valley*, where we had a large Meeting out of Doors, with many other Professors ; all were very attentive, and the Gospel Power and Testimony went freely forth to general Satisfaction and Comfort. The 15th we went over to *Perquiomin*, where we had a good Meeting in a sense of the Prevalency of the Power of Truth. We lodged with *Joseph Richardson*, in whose House we had a serviceable, humbling Season with his Family, and some others who came in that Evening.

The

The 16th we went up the Country to a new-settled place above *Manhatonia*, where were gathered some Friends and others; we had a good Season amongst them in the love of Truth, much tending to their Establishment. The 17th we had a Meeting in the *Baptists* Meeting-house near *Skippolk*, at the Request of some of them, where the Lord owned us in his Wisdom and Power, and gave us a comfortable time to general satisfaction. We parted lovingly, and came that Night to *Evan Evan's* at *North-wales*, and were the 18th at Friends Meeting there, which was large, and it being First-day, we had another in the Evening; in both which, the great Lord and Fountain of Life and Wisdom graciously owned us, and prevailed upon the Hearts and Understandings of many, both of Friends and some who professed not with us.

The 19th we went to visit an ancient Friend who had lost her Sight, being accompanied with several Friends, with whom we had a profitable Season in the attendance of the Love of God. We went to *Philadelphia* that night, and the 20th into *Jersey* to a General-meeting, which was very large both of Friends and others; and tho' I met with some Affliction and Suffering of Spirit, because of the prevailing of a careless and libertine Disposition amongst many professing the Truth; yet the Lord shewed himself gracious, in extending Help to many Conditions; and many Souls were

were comforted in the Love of Truth, the Power whereof was exalted. We came back to *Philadelphia* that Night, and went the 21ſt to *Niſhaminny*, to the Meeting of miniſtring Friends and Elders, where we were comforted together in the Love and Power of Truth.

The 22d we. were at Friends Quarterly-meeting for the County, wherein the Lord's Power greatly prevailed, in humbling and ſtrengthning many Souls. We lodged at *J. Stackhouſes*'s pretty near, and on the 23d viſited ſeveral Friends families there-about, wherein we had ſome good Service, and returned that Night to *Adam Harker*'s, and went the 24th over the River to *Burlington*, to a Meeting for Miniſters and Elders, where the Lord God opened many things to them thro' my Heart, for their Help and Encouragement in the work of the Day. We went back to *Briſtol* by Boat, and rode to *Joſeph Kirkbride*'s.

The 25th, being Firſt-day, we got over the River in a Boat near the *Falls*, but were driven down a great way by the Strength of the Stream ; ſo that it was not without difficulty and danger that we paſſed. We got in pretty good time to *Stony-brook*, where we had a good Meeting among a few Friends, and many other Profeſſors, at *Joſeph Worth*'s Houſe.

The 26th we came down to *Burlington* again to Friends Quarterly-meeting, which was very large, and a ſtrengthning encouraging Seaſon in the Love of God, and a peaceable

Spirit

Spirit was sweetly over many Hearts, to the Glory of the Rock of all our Strength.

The 27th we were at a Youths-meeting at the same place, where many Friends were gathered, and the blessed Order and Testimony of the Truth, in the Power of it was exalted and extended to many Hearts. The 28th we went to *Mount-holly* to a General-meeting of several particular Meetings, which was large, and the Lord was pleased to make it a solidly strengthning time, in the free Spreadings of divine Love and edifying Life, much to our Joy in the Lord. We lodged at *Nathaniel Crip*'s, where the Lord's Goodness arose among us in the Family to profit.

The 1st of the first Month we were at *Chesterfield* Meeting, wherein the Power and Doctrine of Christ reached eminently forth to the great Comfort and Help of many Souls. That Evening we went to *J. Sykes*'s, intending to set forward from thence toward *Egg-harbour*.

The 3d we took our Journey through the Deserts to little *Egg-harbour*, and came to *Gervas Farrar*'s, and on the 4th were at a Meeting there, and had a pretty good time in the extending of the Love of Truth to the poor People there-away. The 5th we travelled part by Land, and thro' dismal Marshes, and part by Water in Canoe's to great *Egg-harbour*, and on the 6th had a Meeting among some poor dark People that came thither ; yet the Lord was pleased to draw near, and comforted divers

of

of us fweetly. The 7th we had a Meeting at one *John Skull*'s, where a confiderable number of different Profeffors came in, and we had a pretty good time among them. The 8th we endeavoured to go over a great River to *Cape-may*, but the Wind was fo violent that we could not get over till Evening, when with hard rowing and much toffing we got fafely to land.

The 9th we got to a Meeting which was appointed at the Widow *Townfhend*'s, and gave notice to have another Meeting there on the 10th, which was Firft-day; and a large one we had, wherein the Lord gracioufly owned us with his Counfel, and the going forth of his Goodnefs to our Comfort, and the Satisfaction of the People, moft of whom were of other Profeffions, and but few Friends. The 12th we took our Journey thro' the Wildernefs and a great boggy Marfh, and fwimming our Horfes over *Morrice-river*, we came to *Cohanfey*, and on the 13th had a Meeting at *Greenwich* with a few Friends and feveral other Profeffors; and had a good opening, confirming time in the Love of God, which was gracioufly extended to us.

The 14th we went to a Meeting at *Salem*, which through the Lord's Goodnefs was made an edifying Seafon; and on the 15th we had a Meeting at *Pilefgrove* again, where pretty many People were gathered; and the Doctrine and Power of the Gofpel of Chrift reached freely towards them, to the Satisfaction of many.

The

The 16th we came up to a Meeting at *Woodberry-creek*, where the Wisdom and Mercy of the Lord our God was evidently manifest in dividing the Word of Life to the several States and Benefit of many; and his holy Name was magnified.

In his Passage thro' West-Jersey, *he wrote the following Epistle, viz.*

' *To* Friends *of the Quarterly-* ' *meeting at* York.

' *My dear* Brethren *and* Sisters *in the* ' *Covenant of Life !*

' ALTHO' I am now outwardly far sepa-
' rated from you for the Gospel of our
' Lord Jesus Christ's Sake, yet as I have
' been favoured with Mercy to obtain a Share
' of near Brotherhood amongst you in the
' heavenly Relation; so you are very often truly
' fresh in my Remembrance, in the springing
' of heavenly Love from our Father, wherein
' I believe I am often bettered for your tender
' Breathings to the living Rock of all our Abi-
' lity and Comfort : And the Remembrance of
' that near Unity, and sweet Fellowship, which
' many of us have been nursed and built up
' in, and wherein we had to take Leave one
' of another, is often renewed in my View,

' and

‘ and made somewhat like a Staff to lean upon
‘ (in part) in my Travel : And in feeling the
‘ Renewal of quickning Virtue from the ever-
‘ lasting Root, my Heart is often filled with
‘ Supplication to the God and Father of all our
‘ Mercies, that his powerful Presence may
‘ often be with all your Spirits, to strengthen
‘ heavenly Zeal and Care in every Heart for
‘ your own good, and for that of the Family
‘ of God : And that pure Wisdom and Unity
‘ of Heart may be, and continue to increase
‘ among all.
　‘ I doubt not but that it will be a degree of
‘ Joy to you, to hear of me and my Com-
‘ panion’s being well, and on our way in the
‘ Lord’s Work ; and I may likewise add,
‘ that pure and living Love often moving in
‘ my Heart towards you, has encouraged me
‘ to send a few Lines as a Token of my Re-
‘ membrance of you, and therewith my dear
‘ Salutation in the Love and Fellowship of
‘ Christ our Lord ; and in humble Reverence
‘ to let you know, that the living and power-
‘ ful Word, that drew us away from amongst
‘ you for the present, hath been graciously
‘ near in our Services hitherto, to our great
‘ Comfort, (notwithanding it has been our
‘ Lot sometimes, to wade through Sorrow and
‘ suffering of Spirit for Truth’s sake) and has
‘ prospered the Work in several Places ; both
‘ in awakening some of the forgetful and
‘ lukewarm ; in reaching to many amongst

T　　　　　　　‘ the

‘ the poor, airy, and wanton Youth, by his
‘ baptizing Power ; alfo in gathering fome
‘ from *without* in divers Places : And the living
‘ and concerned Hearts for *Zion's* Profperity,
‘ are ftrengthned and encouraged.

‘ And tho’ a forgetfulnefs of the Lord's
‘ Goodnefs, and merciful Vifitation, in fome,
‘ and of the Duty of living near the Truth,
‘ and an Unwillingnefs to walk *within*, and a
‘ flight of the Bounds of Truth in others, have
‘ forrowfully prevailed in too many Places ;
‘ yet bleffed be the Lord God for ever, he is
‘ at work, and arifing to turn the Stream of
‘ divers hurtful Things which have crept in ;
‘ and I am ftrong in Faith, that the Power
‘ and Life of Righteoufnefs is prevailing, and
‘ will fpread in the Earth, and in the Ccun-
‘ tries, even in this Generation, to the Glory
‘ of God, and the Comfort of the Living.

‘ And, my *dear Friends*, I have it in my
‘ Heart to requeft of you, and tenderly to ad-
‘ vife all Fathers and Mothers, Minifters and
‘ Elders, in particular, carefully to wait to feel
‘ the Love and Life of the bleffed Truth to
‘ arife in your Hearts ; to ftrengthen and in-
‘ creafe a heavenly Zeal and Concern to do the
‘ Work of your Day, according to your Abi-
‘ lities, with due Diligence, while you have
‘ Time and Opportunity. And I believe the
‘ Lord will enlarge your Capacities for your
‘ feveral Services, and will blefs your Labour
‘ and Care in and for the Church ; and will alfo

f loofen

' loosen some from these lower Enjoyments,
' and striving too earnestly after them, both
' with respect to the Gain, and the Great-
' ness of this enticing World, either for your-
' selves or your Posterity ; the grasping after
' which, has hindered divers amongst us from
' being so serviceable in their day, as they
' might have been, and not only so, but a
' Way hath been opened thereby to greater
' Damage, in their becoming Snares and Hurts
' to their Off-spring.

' And you who are Mothers, keep in a dili-
' gent watchful Labour, that the Youth, who
' generally are more immediately under your
' Eye, and sometimes your ordering too, in
' several respects, may grow up, and be pre-
' served in such Society and Conversation, as is
' most likely to influence them to love the
' Truth, Purity, and the Adorning, and Be-
' haviour agreeable to it ; which is the most
' beautiful of all : And Fathers likewise should
' carefully unite together in this Concern.——
' Suffer, *dear Friends*, this Word of Ex-
' hortation to have due place with you ; for
' pure Love from the Bosom of the Father
' moves in my Heart often, and at this Time
' towards you.

' And you tender, and concerned Youth,
' who are very dear to me, be encouraged to
' follow on to feel the humbling Love and
' Goodness of God to arise and prevail in you,
' and to hope in the Strength of his powerful

T 2

' Arm ;

' Arm ; which tho' it may fometimes lead thro'
' exercifing Siftings, yet will it carry forward
' that bleffed Work, and Way to Bleffing,
' which is begun in many amongft you : For I
' am well affured, that the Love and Favour of
' the God of Bleffings, is mercifully extended
' towards the younger Generation, to make
' you ferviceable in his Houfe, both Males and
' Females, and truly honourable in your Day :
' And I have ftrong Hopes, that the Lord will
' raife up many among you, who often walk
' with heavy, and doubtful Hearts ; and
' make you as polifhed Shafts in his mighty
' Hand, and Inftruments of honourable Ser-
' vice in the Church ; to the Comfort of many
' Souls, and the fpreading the Fame of Wif-
' dom in the Earth, if you patiently wait and
' depend upon the Sufficiency of his holy
' Power.

' And that thus, my *dear Friends*, the Lord's
' Power and Love may be with you, his own
' Life rife higher and higher among you, and
' the Glory of the Reign and Government of
' *Zion*'s King fhine through you, in all your
' Services, to the Glory of the Lord God of
' our Salvation ; is the humble Travail of my
' Spirit, who remain your near Brother in the
' heavenly Covenant : *Farewel, Farewel.*

Weft-Jerfey, the 5th of the   ' JOHN FOTHERGILL.'
  firft Month 1721—2.

The

The 17th of the 1st Month we came over *Delaware* to *Philadelphia* to the Meeting of Ministers, it being their Halfyear's-meeting, principally for Worship, for the Provinces of *Pensilvania* and *Jersey*; to which came a great number of Friends, and our gracious God was pleased to favour the Meetings with his holy Presence, and opened many things thro' us, to their Comfort and Help; tending to stir up and engage many Hearts to Diligence in following and serving the Lord. Friends parted in thankfulness towards him, and true nearness one towards another.

After some other Service among Friends in the City, and preparing for our Journey towards *New-England*, we set forward, having many Friends with us, the 22d to a Meeting at *Bristol*; where a Man and his Wife, from among the Seventh-day *Baptists*, had been convinced when we were there before: The Woman was there now, and in a solid, tender frame: The Meeting was, in the main, comfortable and edifying, though under some Exercise with a dull unfaithful People.

The 23d we went over the River *Delaware*, and called to visit a Friend (*Thomas Lambert*'s Wife) who had been long indisposed, with whom we had a comfortable Opportunity; we then went forward to *John Watt*'s at *Stony-brook*, and had a Meeting there that Evening, which was helpful and seasoning. The 24th we went to *John Kinsey*'s at *Woodbridge*, and

on

on the 25th, being First-day, were at a Meeting there, to which came many other People, and the Lord gave us a good and prevailing Season among them. The 26th we set out towards *Long-Island*, and on the 27th had a Meeting at *Newtown*, where many Friends met us, and several other Professors came in : And it pleased the Lord to give us a good time to the profit of many. The 28th we were at a large Meeting at *Westbury*, where the Gospel Doctrine and Life was freely extended and declared in its own Authority, to the Help and Comfort of many.

The 29th we had a Meeting at *Matinicock*, where many People not of our profession came in, and a blessed Opportunity it was made to us ; many Hearts being reached with the Life of Truth, and were bowed before the Lord God Almighty. The 30th at *Cow-neck* we had a very large Meeting of divers Professors ; and the blessed Testimony and humbling Power of Truth, in the love of it, affected many Hearts.

The 31st we called to visit several Friends, and on the 1st of the second Month 1722, being First-day, were at Friends Meeting at *Flushing*, which was very large ; it was a time of faithful Warning to some, and of solid Edification to many, through the Lord's Goodness.

The 2d we set out on our Journey towards *Rhode-Island*, and had a Meeting with Friends at *West-chester* upon the Continent, and the 3d at *Rye*, to which several People came, and

Truth

Truth favoured us with its Help and living Prefence to our Comfort. The 4th we proceeded on our Journey towards *Connecticut*, having that place in view, and got on the Firft-day, which was the 8th, to a Friend's houfe *(John Richmond)* in *Rhode-Ifland* Government, where we had a good little Meeting with a few Friends and others who came in. The next Day we vifited feveral Friends in our way to *Kingfton*, where on the 10th we had a Meeting, to which pretty many People gathered, and the Lord gave us a good time among them. That Evening we went over to *Cannanicot-Ifland*, and had a Meeting with Friends there, and on the next Day in the Evening we came to *Newport* in *Rhode-Ifland*, and were the 12th at the Meeting there, which was pretty large and comfortable. The 13th we went to *Portfmouth* to Friends Quarterly-meeting for the Bufinefs of the Church ; wherein Truth was renewedly prefent in Counfel and Help under fome Exercife attending Friends, from fome brittle, unfettled Spirits ; but the Power of God was over all in a good degree, to the Comfort of the right-minded. The next Day we were at their Meeting for Minifters and Elders, and came from thence to *Newport*, and on the 15th, being Firft-day, we were at the Meeting there, which was very large ; and the Lord's Power and glorious Teftimony reached eminently forth, making profitable Impreffions on many

Hearts,

Hearts, to the Glory and Praise of the Lord our God, who alone is worthy for ever.

The 16th we went to a Meeting appointed at *Tiverton* at *J. Wanton*'s, to which came pretty many Friends and others; and the Lord gave us a good Opportunity, in the Ability of his Power, to declare the Truth, and its holy Testimony was exalted over all earthly and loose Spirits. The 17th we had a Meeting at *Little-Compton*, wherein the Testimony of the everlasting Truth went freely and powerfully over the loose and lukewarm, to the awakening of some; and much to the Encouragement of the living Travellers for Truth's Prosperity. The Day following we had a good and solidly edifying Meeting at *Coanset*, and the next Day another very large one at *Penniganset*; and a blessed time it was, in the fresh Extending and Prevalency of the Lord's Power.

The 20th we had a Meeting at *Rochester*, which through the gracious attendance of the Power of Truth was made a good Opportunity to many, and the Lord's holy Name was magnified. The 21ft we visited a Family of Friends in the way, where we had some good Service, and went to *Sandwich*. The 22d, being First-day, we were at the Meeting there, wherein the great Duty and Advantage of loving God and his Truth, in Sincerity of heart on one hand; and the Mischief and Hurt with respect to Religion, by loving the World, the Things and Spirit thereof, on the other, were largely

declared;

declared ; to the help and ſtirring up of many Minds, the Exaltation of the Power of Truth, and the Praiſe of the Lord God Almighty.

The 23d we had a Meeting near this Place, at the Houſe of a Perſon who was indiſpoſed, to which ſeveral who did not profeſs with us came, and the Lord was pleaſed to own us in his Power and Goodneſs, greatly to our Satisfaction, and the Comfort of many. The 24th we had a Meeting near *Yarmouth* among a few Friends, and ſeveral others who ſeem'd to attend to the Teſtimony of Truth with diligence ; but it went forth againſt a looſe negligent Spirit that was given way to, by divers called *Friends* here-away, much to the Diſhonour of Truth : Yet we were comforted in the Lord who helped us. The 25th we were at Friends Meeting at *Sandwich* again, wherein the Lord opened our Hearts and Mouths in Counſel and Admonition, alſo in Encouragement to the honeſt-hearted ; and gave us a bleſſed Opportunity together to his Glory and Praiſe, who is alone worthy for ever.

The 26th we went to *Succaneſſet*, where was gathered a pretty large Meeting of Friends and others ; and the Teſtimony of Truth and Righteouſneſs, in the Love and Power of Chriſt, extended freely among them, both to inform, reprove and confirm in the way of Righteouſneſs, to the Profit of ſeveral, and our Comfort. The next Day we rode to *Pembroke*, and on the 29th, being Firſt-day, were at

U

Frienc

Friends Meeting there, in which the Lord was near to help us in his Service ; tho' we found that a great deal of Dulness and Indifferency about Religion, had prevailed among Friends ; whereof they were warned, and ftirred up to confider its Tendency, and to be more careful in feeling after the Power and Life of Truth in themfelves : And we had our Reward of Peace and Sweetnefs in the Love of God.

The 30th we had a Meeting at *Scituate*, to which came many fober People, and the Gofpel-power and Teftimony rofe and went forth amongft them freely, to the great Satisfaction and Comfort of divers. We took our Leave of Friends there, and came up to *Pembroke* again, and from thence to *Jofeph Eddy's* near *Taunton*, where on the 2d of the third Month we had a bleffed and open Meeting with the few Friends there ; many People not profeffing with us came in, who feem'd much fatisfied with the Teftimonies delivered. The 3d we had a Meeting with Friends at *William Chafe's* at *Swanfey*, wherein the Lord's Goodnefs was manifefted, much to our Comfort ; and the next Day we had a Meeting over a great River, in a Place called *Fair-town*, where few Friends live, but a confiderable number of other People came, and heard the Truth declared attentively ; but in general they are a hard dark People. We came over the River again, and went towards *Providence* Woods, where on the 6th, being Firft-day, we were at a large Meeting
in

in Friends Meeting-houſe near this Place, and Truth helped us to declare the way of Life and Salvation, among a wild raw People who came in, and the religiouſly-minded were comforted and encouraged, the Life of Truth ſeeming low among them. The next Day we went towards *Mendam*, where on the 8th we had a Meeting, in which we had a good and profitable Seaſon in the Love of God; and on the 9th were at the Monthly-meeting of Friends in the upper Part of *Providence*, wherein the Lord opened Counſel in his living Power, and gave us a good and heavenly time with Friends and ſeveral others. Friends afterwards went thro' their Buſineſs in peace, and we had ſome Service with them therein, to their Help.

The 10th we came down to *Benj. Smith's*, viſiting ſeveral Friends in our way, and on the 11th we had a Meeting in the Town, to which came many ſober People, and the Lord's Power and Goſpel-teſtimony went freely forth, in a tendering manner; we had good Service, and the People were glad of the Opportunity. We went that Night to *Warwick*, where we were at a large Yearly-meeting on the 12th; to which came many of other Profeſſions, and the Lord's Power and bleſſed Teſtimony reached freely, and was eſtabliſhed over all, to Friends Satisfaction. The 13th we went to *Greenwich*, where a Yearly-meeting began that Day, and was held the following. The Meeting was very large, many hundreds of People being

U 2

gathered

gathered, fo that the Houfe could not contain them : Wherefore we kept the Meeting in a Friends's Orchard, and tho' there was a great Multitude of young wild People, yet the Lord's bleffed Prefence and glorious Power favour'd the Meeting, and the Teftimony and Doctrine of the Gofpel was declared in great dread, and went over moft there, ftilling the Spirits of the People wonderfully. And it was made an alarming Seafon to the carelefs and forgetful ; a tender Vifitation to many of the Youth, and a time of ftrengthning of the Hearts of the true Seekers of *Zion*'s Profperity, to the Glory and Praife of the Lord God, who is worthy for ever.

The 15th we went up into the Woods to *Ifhmael Spink*'s to a Meeting, where feveral friendly People were met, and we had a good Opportunity with them. The 16th we went farther back into the Wildernefs, to a new fettled Place called *Volintown*, having fent to have a Meeting appointed there for that Day ; but very few of the People came to it, being very rainy : The Lord was pleafed to open his Hand of Love amongft us in the little Meeting we had, to our Comfort and the Peoples Satisfaction ; we went that Night to another Town where were no Friends, and on the 17th we had a Meeting there, in which the Lord our God was gracioufly near, and opened us in the Life and Doctrine of the Gofpel to our great Comfort ; the People were very loving, and

feem'd

seem'd much satisfied. The 18th we had a Meeting at the House of one not a Friend, who was desirous thereof ; where the Lord's Power reached forth freely, and the Testimony of Truth prevailed to our mutual Comfort. The next Day we came to *William Robinson's* at *Kingston,* and on the 20th, being First-day, we were at Friends Meeting there, and notice having been given some time before, several Friends from other Places, and many of the Country-people came in ; so that it was a very large Meeting, and the Testimony of Truth went forth among them in great dread ; tending to awaken them out of a slothful ease, which many in that Country had long sat down in ; several of them having been convinced some Years, but shunned the Cross of Christ : And a Meeting of good Service it was made, in the Love and Mercy of God, and much to our Satisfaction.

Being clear of these Parts at present, we went along with Friends over a Water to *Cannanicot,* to *David Green's,* and on the 21st we crossed another Ferry to *Newport* ; and there a Passage offering, we set out directly for *Nantucket-Island,* whither we then inclined, and got there, thro' the Care of divine Providence, the next day in good time, but wearied with hard travelling, and poor lodging ; but all was well, Truth being with us, and sweeten'd all. We lodged at *Nathaniel Starbuck's,* and staid a Week upon the Island, having several large
publick

publick Meetings, and many others in several Families; and the Lord Almighty was pleased to own and attend us with his living, strengthning Power, and holy Counsel, for the several Services, to the Glory of his own Name; and blessed our Labour, to the great Comfort and Help of Friends, and the Satisfaction of many of the People, who came freely and pretty generally to our Meetings, especially on the First-day of the Week: And we took our Leave of Friends in much sweetness and nearness of Spirit in the Love of God, with true Thankfulness of Heart to him, for the Help and Comfort of his living and glorious Presence.

The 29th we set out for the main Land again, accompanied by several Friends in a Sloop, and got well ashore, and were the 30th at Friends Week-day Meeting at *Penniganset*. The 31st we went to *Thomas Hathaway*'s at *Cushanet*, and on the next Day, which was the 1st of the fourth Month, we had a pretty large Meeting there of Friends and others; with whom we had a profitable, informing Season in the Power of Truth, but very heavy and strait amongst such as might have been a Comfort. The 3d we were at the Meeting at *Penniganset* again, where most of those in that part of the Country, and some Friends from a great distance, met together; and it pleased the Lord of Mercies so to help us with Power and Wisdom, that the Doctrine of the Kingdom, in the Life of Truth went freely forth,

and

and prevailed in a good measure over many Hearts, and the Lord's Name was magnified, being worthy for ever.

The 4th we went to *Swanzey*, through the Woods and bad way, to *Joseph Chase*'s, and were the next Day at a large Meeting, where a Marriage of two young People was solemnized; a considerable number of People of different Professions came to it, and the Lord was pleased to magnify his own Name and Testimony to our Comfort.

The 6th we went towards *Rhode-Island*, and the next Day were at the Yearly-meeting at *Portsmouth*, wherein the Father of all Mercies greatly owned us with his Power, encouraging to hope for his Help for the Service of the other Part of the Meeting, which was held at *Newport*, to which Place we went that Night. On the 8th the Meeting gather'd at *Newport*, and continued four Days; it was supposed to be the largest that was ever held there, it being computed, that near two thousand People were present; and the Lord Almighty, the never-failing Helper of his depending Children, graciously opened his glorious Gospel Testimony to the People freely and plentifully, in the Demonstration of his eternal Power and Wisdom, greatly to the Comfort and Confirmation of many Souls: There appeared to be a general Satisfaction, and awful Reverence on the Minds of People; divers Matters came under the Consideration of Friends, relating to

the

the Propagation of Truth and Righteousnefs, and the comely Order of the Gofpel, in the Meetings for Bufinefs ; all which were carried on in Peace and Amity, and the great and moft worthy Name of the Lord was magnified over all. After this Meeting was over, we fet forward towards *Bofton*, and the Eaft, and came to *Swanzey* the 12th, vifiting feveral Friends in the way.

The 13th we went to *Taunton*, where we had appointed a Meeting at *Jofeph Eddy*'s, to which many Friends accompanied us, and a pretty many People likewife came in ; fo that we kept our Meeting in a Barn, and had a good open Seafon, and the Word of Life went freely forth to the People, who feemed to hearken with Gladnefs, and the Life of Truth affected many Hearts with folid Comfort. After Meeting we went about feven Miles, and got the 14th to *Bofton*, where we had a Meeting that Day, to which a confiderable Number of People came, and Truth favoured us with a pretty open Time.

The 15th we went to *Lyn*, where we had a large Meeting, in which the Power of the Lord God, and the holy Teftimony of Truth went forth eminently againft a dull, carnal Mind, and worldly libertine Inclination, which prevailed too much ; and for the Purity and faving Nature of the Gofpel; and many Hearts were comforted. We went to *Salem* the Day following, and on the 17th, being Firft-day,

we

we had two large Meetings there ; several
soberly-inclined People came in, and thro' the
Goodness and Love of God, Truth's Testimony
and Power was exalted, to the Refreshing of
many Hearts, and the Awakening of others to
more religious Considerations ; so that the
Lord's Cause gained ground over worldly Ease
and Darkness in some good Degree, blessed be
his powerful Name for ever.

The 18th we went to *Newberry*, and on the
19th we had a Meeting near the middle of the
Town, in a Warehouse belonging to Captain
Brown (so called) who offer'd it freely, and was
very loving to us : Many of the Towns-people
came in and about the House, some appearing
afraid to come in ; yet the Word of Life, and
Testimony of Jesus, was evidently manifest
among us in the Love of God, and had a satisfactory Reach and Impression upon many :
We parted with much Chearfulness, and our
Hearts were made truly glad, in that the Word
of Truth prevailed among them.

On the 20th we had a Meeting at *Haveril*
at *Robert Peasley's*, to which a pretty many
People came, and we had a good Season among
them, Truth in part prevailing. The 21st we
were at a Meeting at *Elmsbury*, which was
pretty large, it being Friends Monthly-meeting
for the Affairs of the Church ; and it was a
profitable, awakening and edifying Time ; the
living Power of Truth being manifestly among
Friends to our Comfort.

X

The

The 22d we had a Meeting at *Hampton*, which, tho' much dulnefs and flatnefs of Spirit had prevailed upon divers, yet thro' the bleffed attendance of the Lord's Counfel and Power, we had a profitable Seafon. We went the next Day to *Dover* to Friends Monthly-meeting, and on the 24th, being Firft-day, were at the Meeting again, where fome fober People were gathered with Friends, and the Power and Teftimony of Truth was fweetly manifeft among us thro' divine Favour.

The 25th we travelled thro' a long difmal Wildernefs to a Town called *Wells*, being defirous of having a Meeting there, which was held the 26th; but the People were very fhy of Friends, thro' the crafty and falfe Infinuations of the Prieft, who neverthelefs did not appear while we were there. We lodged at an Inn that Night, in our way to *York*, at which place we alfo inclined to have a Meeting; and the 27th, with pretty much endeavouring, we got liberty, and had a little Meeting : Several People came in and fat quietly, others came about the Houfe, but feem'd afraid to come in; yet it pleafed the Lord to own us, and to open in the Word of Life, fo that divers appeared much fatisfied, and were loving to us. We came that Evening to *J. Morrill*'s at *Kittery*, and the 28th went down by water, near the Mouth of *Pifcataway*, and had a Meeting, at a place called the *Point*, with a confiderable number of People, no Friends living there-away; and the glorious Gofpel,

Gofpel, both in Doctrine and living Power, went over all; many were affected with Truth, and the Name of the Lord was magnified.

The 29th we had a Meeting at the Town called *Portfmouth*, in an Inn, where abundance of People gathered, and were in general very attentive and fober; and the Lord's Glory and heavenly Teftimony arofe and prevailed over the Hearts of moft prefent, many of them freely confeffing, it was the Truth which was declared; and we were truly comforted in the God of Strength. We went that Evening to *Kittery*, and on the 30th came back to *Hampton* to the Quarterly-meeting of Friends which began that Day, and we had a good Seafon in the Love of God, among the Minifters and Elders.

The 1ft of the fifth Month, being Firft-day, we had a very large Meeting both of Friends and many others, and the Lord was pleafed to magnify his own Power and Teftimony in divers refpects, greatly to the Help and Edification of Friends, and Satisfaction to the general; and he had the Praife of his own Work, who is worthy for ever. The 2d I was at the Meeting for Bufinefs, where I ftaid a part of the Meeting, and was opened in divers weighty Exhortations, and to recommend to Friends more particular Care, fome hindering things which were creeping in among them, that they might watch in their refpective Places againft the Corruptions of the World; and took my leave of the Meeting, and rode to the

X 2

Burial

Burial of a Friend's Wife, whither a great number of People came who had never been at a Friends Meeting before ; with whom the Lord gave me a bleſſed Time, to their great Satisfaction, and our Comfort. And then went to the *Grove* about five Miles farther, where many more People came, and there alſo the Word and Way of Life was livingly ſet forth, and they ſtaid with great Attention.

The 3d we got up early, and rode thirty-four Miles to a Meeting beyond *Piſcataway-river*, where we had a bleſſed Seaſon in the Life and Power of God, to preach the Truth ; and ſeveral of the People were deeply affected with it. We went that Night to *Francis Allens*'s in *Kittery*, and the 4th had a Meeting in *Newichawanack*, at a Friend's Houſe ; to which came ſeveral other People, tho' greatly afraid on account of the Prieſts ; yet the Teſtimony of Truth in the Love of God, went freely forth among them, and divers were tenderly affected.

The 5th we were at Friends Meeting at *Dover*, where we had a good Opportunity, the Life of Truth, and divine Part of Religion was earneſtly recommended, and prevailed ; and the ſlothful, idle and remiſs were warn'd and admoniſhed. The 6th we had a Meeting at *Quochecha*, at *Ebenezer Varney*'s, where many of the neighbouring People came in, and ſtaid with great and ſolemn Attention, to hear the everlaſting Goſpel declared, whereunto the Lord

furniſhed

furnished us in his living Power ; and Truth was exalted to general Satisfaction, blessed be the Lord God for ever. The next Day we visited several Friends Families, and on the 8th, being First-day, were at Friends Meeting again, where abundance of the Country-people were gathered from all Parts there-about, and the Lord was pleased to own us with his living Presence, and open'd our Hearts in the Things of Salvation in many respects, which went forth freely to the Meeting in much plainness, and living demonstration, to the Establishment and Information of many Souls ; some were convinced of the Truth, and brought to taste of its Goodness, who I hope will continue to walk in it : It was a Day of good Service for the Lord, thro' his gracious Help, who has the Glory of all. The 9th, being about to depart from this Place, many Friends came to see and take leave of us, with whom we had a heavenly bowing Time, in the Life of Truth, which was plentifully with us, greatly to our Comfort, and uniting our Hearts in the Fellowship of Truth. We parted with many Friends there, and others accompanied us to *Stretham*, where a Meeting was appointed at a Friend's House ; to which divers of the neighbouring People came, who were much Strangers to Truth ; we had some Service among them, and came away with true Satisfaction, in the Peace of the Lord our God.

The

The 10th we had a large Meeting at *Elmſ-bury* again, which greatly tended to our Comfort, to encourage the Living, and to awaken ſome ſluggliſh, unfaithful Profeſſors, and to the winning upon the Hearts of many of the Youth : Some of the neighbouring People ſeem'd much ſatisfied, and it was a Time of good Service for the Truth, in the Lord's Power, and thro' his Help : We lodged that Night at *Henry Dowe's*, where in the Evening the Lord gave us a bleſſed edifying Seaſon, in his humbling Love and Power, to the Help of the Family, and our Comfort

The 11th we had a Meeting at *Newberry*, wherein the Lord greatly owned us in his Love and Counſel, for the ſpreading of Truth, and to the ſolid Comfort of Friends in general. On the 12th we had a Meeting at *Ipſwich*, with a ſober, innocent Woman Friend, her Children, and ſome of the Neighbours, together with ſeveral Friends who accompanied and met us here, and had a ſatisfactory Seaſon among them. The 13th we were at a large Meeting at *Salem*, where the Lord opened many cloſe and weighty Things to Friends, in the Senſe of the Life of Truth, tending to their Growth in Righteouſneſs, and Preſervation in the Life and Subſtance of Religion, and helped me to diſcharge my Spirit faithfully, and to a great degree of inward Liberty and Comfort, bleſſed be his holy Name for ever.

Finding

Finding some Engagement remain, and re-vive upon my Spirit towards *Dover* again, I could not be easy without returning back; therefore leaving my Companion, and having another Friend with me, we rode to *Dover* the Seventh-day, though it was extreme hot Weather, and we had several large Ferries to cross, and got to *John Kenny's* in good time. And on the 15th, being First-day, met with Friends who were abundantly glad of my Return, divers signifying their Expectations of my coming again; and the Lord was pleased to give us a good and confirming Meeting, much to the Help of many, especially of some tender-spirited People, who had been reached by the Love and Power of Truth when we were there before.

The 16th I had a large and prevailing Meeting at *Oyster-river*, in the Power and Goodness of the Lord, wherein many Hearts were affected with Reverence and Worship to the Almighty; but I believe the evil Spirit was disturbed, and stirred up a Woman to make a jangle and clamour against the Truth and Friends, but not being able to shew any thing from the Scripture, either against what was delivered there that Day, or against us in any thing, which I desired her to make appear if she could; the People generally blamed her, and would have had her been quiet, for Truth prevailed that Day in many Minds. The 17th I went to a Meeting I had appointed at *Spruce-creek*,

creek, where divers foberly-inclined People came in, much Strangers to the Truth, and its Doctrine ; and the Lord gave us a good Seafon, in the Ability of his Power : Several of the People were very tender, and I believe fome will be gathered, e're it be long, to the Knowledge of Truth.

The 18th I vifited fome Friends Families, and on the 19th had a Meeting at *Andrew Neal's* in *Newichawanack,* which was made in the Extendings of divine Favour, a good Seafon, to the Help and Comfort of many, both Friends and fome Strangers. The 20th I had a Meeting in *Quochecha,* at *Jofeph Eftis's,* near the Prieft's Houfe ; many of whofe Hearers came in, and feveral were much affected with the Life and Doctrine of the Gofpel, which I had to bear Teftimony of, and the Truth gained Ground to our Comfort, and the Glory of God. We went up to *Thomas Hanfon's* that Night, to be fome Encouragement to the Family to keep their Places, and their Truft in the Arm of the Lord, the fure Defence of his People, it being at that time ftrongly reported, that the *Indians* were on the point of commencing Hoftilities againft the *Englifh,* and the People were generally gathering to Garrifons, this Country being almoft a Frontier that way. We had a good Seafon that Evening in his Houfe ; there were two young Women prefent who had been convinced where I was, fome few Meetings before, and they were very tender and

and humble, with some other young People who came in ; so that it was a profitable edifying Season, in the Sense of strengthning Life from the Lord God. The 21st I was at Friends Monthly-meeting, where many Friends gathered, and it was a good confirming time ; the Love and Goodness of Truth being very near, both to help the truly needy, and the stirring up of the unfaithful and negligent.

The 22d, being First-day, I was at Friends Meeting at *Dover*, where gathered abundance of People of many sorts, and our blessed and never-failing Helper was graciously regardful of his own Work, and owned us with his Power, both to inform the unlearned, to warn the rebellious and negligent, to strengthen the Travellers, the Babes, and the tender ; very much humbling Impression having been made upon many young People there-away : We had some precious sweet Seasons, in the Extendings of the Life of Truth that Evening among Friends in some Families.

The 23d I came to *Hampton*, accompanied with many Friends, and had a good settling and reviving Meeting, in the Sense of divine Love, and parted well, and near one another. The 24th I had a large and blessed Meeting at *Haveril*, at *Robert Peasley*'s, and took leave of Friends there-away, under a weighty and tendring degree of the Love and Life of Christ our Lord. The 25th, after some time of weighty Exhortation, and tender Salutation to

Y   the

the Family and Children, which was a comfortable Seafon, bleffed be the Lord our God for ever, I fet out toward *Salem*, and had fome Service at an Inn by the way, to declare the Truth and the Way of its working; of which the People had never heard fo much before, and feem'd glad of the Opportunity, and I was comforted in the Love of God, which was with us fweetly.

The 26th I was at Friends Meeting at *Salem* again, not finding I could pafs eafy by it, tho' I thought I had been clear before, and the Lord gave us a good Time, to the Refrefhing of many, and his great Name was glorified. The 27th I had a Meeting in *Lyn*, at a Friend's Houfe, at the Requeft of fome of his Neighbours; it was a good open Time, in the Love of Truth, which flow'd towards fome, in clear Doctrine and Sweetnefs, but clofe and humbling Warning to fome deceitful Profeffors; fome good Impreffions were made on feveral that Day.

The 28th I came to *Bofton*, and here met with my Companion again; and on the 29th, being Firft-day, we had two Meetings; likewife another on the Second-day, and again on the Third, in Friends Meeting-houfe there; to all which there came a confiderable number of foberly-behaved People, efpecially to the two latter; and Truth's Teftimony went forth freely, and feem'd to have confiderable Influence upon feveral of the younger People particularly,

ticularly, and on some of the young Priest-hood; tho' there were but a few Friends in the place, and some of those few, not what they ought to be in their Conversations; we laboured to have them together select or distinct from other People, in order to advise them to be more wise, and to have more Regard to the Truth and their own Good; and we hope it may be of some Service to them, and to the Truth, and the Comfort and Strength of such poor Hearts among them who love the Truth, and seek the Honour of God; but abominable Pride, Envy and Hypocrisy prevails still higher in that Place, more and more incurring the Lord's Displeasure, which will certainly come upon them as an armed Man, sooner or later, except they seek a place of Repentance in time.

The 1st of the sixth Month we left the Town, and came to *William Chase's* jun. at *Swanzey*, and had a Meeting there the Day following; which the Lord was pleased to own, and bless with his Presence and Counsel, to our great ease, and Friends comfort, and the Lord's Name was magnified. The 3d we had a Meeting over the River at *Nesannett*, to which several People not of our Profession came, and we had a profitable Season, the People appearing much satisfied. The 4th we had a Meeting at some distance from hence, where the People were much Strangers to Friends and Truth, yet they seem'd satisfied with the Doctrine and

Y 2

the

the Teſtimony of it. The 5th, being Firſt-day, we came to *Portſmouth* on *Rhode-Iſland*, where the Meeting was very large, and thro' the Lord's Goodneſs was made a helpful Seaſon, the Life of Truth prevailing over all. The 6th we came to *Newport*, and ſpent ſome Days among Friends there, and went to the Week-day Meeting at *Portſmouth* again, which proved a time of much eaſe to us, thro' the free opening of Life, and Ability of Truth, which greatly prevailed, and revived many Hearts to the Praiſe of the Lord Almighty. The Fifth-day of the Week we had a great and humbling Meeting at *Newport*, under the merciful Attendance of divine Power, which opened us both in warning the looſe and ſelf-lovers, and extended Relief and Help to the Upright and Tender ; and Information to others not of us, pretty many being preſent that Day on account of a Marriage. The Sixth and Seventh-days were partly ſpent in viſiting Friends, ſome Widows, and ſome Sick, and went to *Cannanicot* in the Evening.

The 12th we went to *Kingſton* in *Narraganſet* to a Yearly-meeting, which continued Firſt and Second-days, where many Friends and abundance of wildiſh, airy, and inſenſible People were gathered from divers Places, tho' many of them have long been willing to hear Truth declared ; and certainly the Lord's Goodneſs and Mercy abounded towards them, and raiſed his own Teſtimony among us into great Dominion,

ininion, for the help and warning, and winning upon many ; and to build up the honeſt
Travellers in the holy Faith ; ſo that the Lord
God of Mercies bleſſed the Opportunity, and
his holy Teſtimony gained ground in the
Judgments, and in the Hearts of the People to
his Glory and Praiſe, who is worthy for ever.
We lodged one Night at *William Robinſon*'s,
and the other at *Thomas Rodman*'s, where we
had a precious Time with ſeveral Friends.

The 14th we returned to *Cannanicot*, and
the 15th had a Meeting, to which many of
the People of the Iſland came, among whom
the Lord opened our Hearts and Mouths in
dread and terror to the looſe, and the rejectors
of the Croſs of Chriſt ; they, many of them,
having been a convinced People ; yet healing
Goodneſs and fatherly Love ran ſweetly towards ſuch as were in want of Help ; and it
was made a graciouſly, edifying Seaſon. That
Evening we came over to *Newport*, and on the
16th were at the Week-day Meeting there ;
for my Heart remained under a deep travail
and ſuffering for the Seeds's-ſake, ſome hurtful
Things having crept in among Friends on this
Iſland reſpecting vain, worldly Liberty, which
was a great Obſtruction to the Current of
divine Love, that gathers into, and maintains
in Unity : In this Meeting the Life and Wiſdom of Truth greatly prevailed, many Hearts
were bettered, and holy Strength, I believe,
was gained by ſeveral, to watch and war more

diligently

diligently againſt that Spirit which leads towards the World, and the death and darkneſs of it.

The 17th we went to a Meeting I wanted to have at *Tiverton* on the main Land, where abundance of Friends and others were gathered; and the Lord bleſſed the time with his Preſence and holy Help; and divers not of our Profeſſion, ſeem'd much ſatisfied with the Doctrines declared; we parted under the bleſſed Senſe of the Good-will of God, and I believe many holy Reſolutions were renewed that Day, thro' divine Goodneſs prevailing.

The 18th we returned to *Newport* again, viſiting ſeveral Friends in our way to Comfort, and on the 19th were at both Forenoon and Afternoon-meetings, which were very large, moſt of the Friends upon the Iſland being there, and many other People; and the Lord God of all Power and Mercy was near and among us, in Wiſdom to divide the Word according to many States, making it a precious and bleſſed Seaſon, to the Help of the Lovers of Truth, and warning of the Unruly and Diſobedient: Our Hearts were ſet at liberty, in his Life, to our great eaſe and diſcharge from this part of the Country; and we had to part with Friends, and the generality of the People, in much nearneſs and true brotherly Reſpect, with humble Hearts before the Lord, who was ſo graciouſly near and good to us many ways, and his glorious Name was magnified, which

is

is worthy for ever. We now being at liberty in Spirit to leave these Parts, we set fotwards the 20th early in the Morning towards *Long-Island*, accompanied by many Friends, and came over the two Ferries to *Narraganset* Country, and came to *Westerly* to *John Richmond*'s, where we had appointed a Meeting some time before; which was made a time of great Comfort and Dominion in the goings forth of the Life and Testimony of Truth.

The 21st we came to *New-London* Ferry, and meeting with a Person who was willing to carry us over the Sound the next Day, we lodged at an Inn, and on the 22d took Boat, and had a fine easy Passage, and got ashore early in the Afternoon, and rode up to *South-wold*. The 23d we came to *John Hollock*'s at *Scatanakit*, and the next Day had a Meeting there with a few Friends and others who came in, amongst whom the Lord's Goodness and Counsel reached forth, to our Comfort, and their Help. We came away that Evening to *Bethphage*, and to *Westbury* the 25th, to Friends Quarterly-meeting which began that Day, and continued the 26th, which was First-day, and the Meeting very large, it being supposed there were present near a thousand People; and the Power and Testimony of the Gospel of Salvation extended freely towards them, and prevail'd over many Hearts to the Glory of God.

The 27th we went to *Sequetaoge*, and had a Meeting with a few Friends and some other People,

People, which was a pretty open Season: We came back to *Bethphage* to *Thomas Powel*'s, and had a Meeting there that Evening; and the 28th we went to a Meeting at *Cow-neck*, which was very large, and the Lord made way for his own Name and Testimony, so that many, both Friends and others, were humblingly affected therewith, and praised the God of all our Mercies. The 29th we were at Friends Monthly-meeting at *Westbury*, and had some good Service among them, in the going forth of the Love and Counsel of Truth. We went to *Flushing* that Night, and the 30th crossed the Ferry to the main Land again, to a Meeting at *Memerry-neck*, and had a profitable Season, in the Extendings of heavenly Love and Counsel towards a poor negligent People among them; hereby I was pretty much eased, and the 31st we went to a Meeting at *Benjamin Heaviland*'s in *Rye* Woods, where pretty many People of several Persuasions were gathered, and the Lord favoured us with his Love, and Help to declare the Truth to the Conditions of many of them; the Meeting was of Service to divers, blessed be the Lord our God for his Presence, and helping us to discharge ourselves faithfully from place to place, to the stirring up and Encouragement of many; so that we now found ourselves clear of those Parts, and of *New-England* in general.

The 1st of the seventh Month we came over to *Long-Island* again, to *Samuel Bowne*'s, visiting

ing several Friends in our way, and on the 2d, being First-day, we were at the Meeting at *Flushing*; and tho' divers things seem to have crept in among Friends there, to their Hurt, and which obstruct the Prosperity of Truth; yet the Lord helped to give due Portions in dividing the Word to the profit of many different States, and we were made truly near to the living. The next Day we visited some Friends Families, I hope to profit, in the good-will of Truth; and on the 4th we had a large and precious Meeting at *Oyster-bay*, in a Barn; there were most of the Chief of the place, and several Justices of the Peace present, and the Lord's powerful Testimony prevailed in the Hearts of many of the People, and I believe the Truth will again be exalted in that Place. We return'd that Night to *William Withers*'s at *Westbury*, and on the 5th had a large and comfortable Meeting there in the establishing blessed Life and Love of Truth, wherein we took leave of Friends there-away, and came that Night to *John Rodman*'s at *Bay-side*.

The 6th we were at the Monthly-meeting at *Flushing*, where many Friends were met, and the Lord our God was pleased to favour us with his Presence and Power to declare many profitable and weighty things among them; tending to stir up and engage Friends in doubling their Diligence and Care to discharge themselves faithfully, in Example and in Zeal for the Glory of the Name of the Lord; and it was a blessed time, to the Help and humbling of many : We parted with Friends in Love and Nearness of the heavenly Relation, and lodged at *Samuel Bowne*'s, where also we had a precious time with many Friends, who came there that Evening. The 7th we came to *New-York*, and had a Meeting the same Evening : There are but few Friends, but a pretty innocent People ; with whom, and some others who came in, we had a good and strengthning Opportunity, in the Love of God.

The 8th we came over a part of *Long-Island*, and *Staten-Island*, to *Woodbridge* in *East-Jersey*, and on the 9th, being First-day, we had one Meeting at Friends Meeting-house, and another at *Row-way-river*, at *John Shadwell*'s ; both which were favourably owned by the Lord of Mercies, and his Power and blessed Testimony extended in a comfortable manner to us, and the Help of many, blessed be his glorious Name for ever.

The 10th we had a Meeting back in the Woods at *John Lane*'s, where a considerable Number of People came in, and we had a good Opportunity to declare the Truth among them to Satisfaction, and came down to *John Kinsey*'s at *Woodbridge*. The 11th we went over the Ferry at *Amboy*, and the 12th had a very large Meeting at *Shrewsbury*, wherein the Lord was pleased to open many Things thro' us, to the People in many States, tending to gather the Strangers, and to build up the Convinced

in

in the Power and Counfel of the holy Truth, much to our eafe, and the Confirmation of fome in the way of Righteoufnefs, and the holy Name was magnified.

The 13th we went to *Mannafquan*, where a few Friends live, and had a Meeting with them, to which feveral other People alfo came; and thro' the merciful Help of the Power of Truth, we had a feafonable open Meeting. The next Day we fet out for *Burlington*, in order to be at the Yearly-meeting there, being accompanied by many Friends, and were the 15th at the Meeting for Minifters and Elders, which was the beginning of the Yearly-meeting for the Province of *Penfylvania* and the *Jerfeys*. The Publick-meeting began on the 16th, and continued by adjournment three Days, and the fourth for the Affairs of Truth among Friends; all which were not only very large and orderly, but were greatly favoured with the weighty and glorious Power, and humbling Prefence of the Lord our God, much to the Comfort of Friends, and a heavenly Vifitation to many others: The Bufinefs of the Meeting was managed in the Peace and Wifdom of our heavenly Head, to Friends great Encouragement, and renewing of true Zeal: We parted under a Senfe of the Love and Favour of our gracious God, whofe glorious Name was praifed and magnified, who is worthy for ever.

Th

The 20th we came to *Philadelphia*, to the Week-day Meeting, which was large, there being a Marriage folemnized that Day; and on the 22d went down to *Chefter*, in our way towards *Maryland*, we being not yet clear of that Province. The 23d, being Firft-day, we were at *Concord*, where Friends from many parts gathered; the Meeting was very large, and the Lord's Power and holy Teftimony, in many weighty refpects, extended freely and largely in a prevailing manner. The next Day we vifited feveral Friends Families, and the 25th had a Meeting at *Kennet*, which was large, and thro' the Lord's Goodnefs was made an edifying Seafon. We had a large Meeting alfo at *John Smith's*, at *Marlbro'* the 26th, where thro' the blefled Favour and Help of divine Power and Wifdom, we had a precious and profitable Meeting.

The 27th we had a Meeting at *New-garden*, which was large, and alfo mercifully favoured with the Prefence and Power of the Lord Almighty, whofe holy Word of Wifdom and Counfel was freely opened among us, to the great Comfort and Help of many Hearts. And here we took our leave of many Friends from feveral Parts, in the living Senfe and true Nearnefs of the Love of Chrift our holy Head, with Praifes to God for his Goodnefs and Mercy.

The 28th we had a Meeting at *Nottingham*, which was likewife large, and was made a blefled, ftrengthning, and edifying Time, and

the

the Teſtimony of Truth prevailed amongſt thoſe who were not of our Society. The Day following we croſſed over *Suſquehannah* into *Maryland*, and the 30th, being Firſt-day, we were at a Meeting at *Buſh-river*, where there are but a few Friends, but many of the neighbouring People came in, and we had ſome good Service amongſt them.

The 1ſt of the eighth Month we came down near *Patapſco*, to *Jonathan Hanſon*'s, and on the 2d had a Meeting with ſome Friends who live there-about, and ſeveral other People; and through the merciful Attendance of the Help of Truth, we had a good Time; tho' we found great want of Zeal and Faithfulneſs to the Truth among the Profeſſors of it there-away; yet ſome are honeſtly concerned, and the Lord is mindful of his own work, and the good of his Heritage.

On the 3d we had a Meeting up the River at *Charles Pierpoint*'s, a pretty tender Man, under ſome Convincement, and his Wife alſo, with ſome friendly People there-away; we had a good Opportunity among them, in the reaching forth of Goſpel-love; and I hope the Lord will prevail in his Viſitation, to gather in and build up a People to bear Teſtimony to the Truth there-away The 4th we came downwards to *Henry Hill*'s, near *South-river*, and on the 5th had a Meeting there, where ſeveral friendly People were gathered, and the Goſpel-ſpring livingly opened towards them, making
Impreſſion

Impreſſion upon ſome; and we were comforted in the Lord our gracious Helper. We got over the River that Night, and came to *Weſt-river*, to *Anne Galloway's*. The 7th, being Firſt-day, we were at Friends Meeting there, where pretty many People gather'd from divers places, and the Lord our God was pleaſed to open our Hearts, in his Power and holy Counſel, to their Help; and we were concerned to ſtir up and warn againſt ſeveral hurtful Practices which were creeping in among them, and in diſcharging ourſelves we were filled with the Peace of God.

The 8th we had a full and pretty open Meeting at *Herring-creek*, to our Satisfaction, and were helped to deal plainly, in the love of Truth, with Friends there, and we parted in a comfortable degree of Nearneſs of Spirit, thro' the merciful Extending of divine regard. The 9th we had a Meeting at the *Cliffs*, where there is a good body of honeſt, religiouſly-minded Friends, with whom we had an open, and a ſolid comfortable time to our Satisfacti-on, and their Encouragement in the way and Service of Truth. The 11th we took Boat, with many Friends in Company, and went over the Bay of *Cheſapeak*, in our way to the ap-proaching Yearly-meeting on the Eaſtern-ſhore, which began at *Tredhaven* the 13th, being Se-venth-day, and held till the fourth of the fol-lowing Week, for publick Worſhip, and the Affairs of Truth among Friends. Great num-

bers

bers of almoſt all ſorts of People came thither, and the Lord God was pleaſed to open the glorious Teſtimony of Truth, and the way of Life, in his mighty Power; and the Word of Wiſdom prevailed in a good meaſure, both upon the Hearts of many of the People, and to the great Encouragement of the tender; and alſo to the alarming and rouzing up the indifferent and negligent. Their Buſineſs was managed in much Peace and Amity: They were alſo ſtirred up to more diligence in Plain-dealing, and Care in divers reſpects, which was gladly received by many, and the Lord's Power and Love crowned our Meeting to our mutual Joy and Comfort, and his glorious Name was humbly praiſed, who is worthy for ever; for it is he who doth whatever is well done. After we had taken our leave of Friends in the Love and Peace of God, we went that Night to the Widow *Pitts's*, and the next Day up the Country to *Cheſter*, where we had a Meeting the 19th, and the 20th came to *Cecil* and had a Meeting, which was a good edifying Seaſon, in the free and gracious Extending of the good Will of God, much to our Eaſe and Satisfaction, many of the People in thoſe parts having long been in a poor, lukewarm and indifferent State.

From hence he wrote the following Letter (which is worthy the Peruſal and Conſideration of thoſe who would indeed be religious) to a Friend
lately

lately convinced in New-England, *and his Wife who was at times under some Concern of mind on account of Religion, though then professing among the* Presbyterians, *viz.*

' NEAR and LOVING FRIEND,

'   AS true Brotherly-love and tender well-
'   wishing, has been often renewed in my
' Heart towards thee, thy Wife and Children,
' since I left you ; so of late I have been mind-
' ful of you so often, that I wanted much to
' write a few Lines to you, and am glad of
' the present Opportunity of sending to let thee
' and thy Wife know, that I retain an affecti-
' onate Remembrance of you, in a measure of
' divine Love, wherein I salute you.   And the
' tender Desire of my Heart and brotherly
' Advice to you, according to the Apostle's
' Exhortation, is, that it may be your Care and
' hearty labour to draw near, and feel after,
' sensible Access to the living God, the Foun-
' tain of living Water, and I may be positive
' he will draw nigh to you, to your inward
' Comfort and relieving Satisfaction ; to the
' Enlargement of your Understandings in
' things appertaining to Life and Peace, and to
' build you up, by degrees, in the Experience
' of his Salvation, and of that Redemption
' which the Father, in and through the Power
' and Spirit of his dear Son Christ Jesus, hath
' offer'd to the Children of Men.

' For

' For as the great Mifchief brought upon
' Mankind, and upon *Chriftians*, fo called, in
' particular, by the Adverfary, has been by
' drawing into a Difregard to the pure God,
' who is a Spirit, and from the feeling fenfe
' of divine Favour, and into a Separation from
' his living Prefence and inward Confolation
' to the Soul; fo the great and bleffed Advan-
' tage which is offer'd to Mankind, and of
' which the Lord Almighty would make them
' Partakers, through his Son, is to draw them
' nigh to God again; that through Faith in his
' invifible Power, they may become Witneffes
' of Help in themfelves to war againft and
' gain victory over the Lufts of the Flefh, and
' the World, and by degrees, over all that unfits
' for inward Accefs and fenfe of Acceptance, in
' meafure, in his Sight, for which many Souls
' are in travail; and that the Way may be
' open'd which leads to the holy Mountain
' and Table of the Lord indeed; which tho'
' it is thro' a Baptifm into death to Corruption,
' and an Exercifing and Refining which is un-
' pleafant to the Creature; yet the End is, to
' prepare the Hearts of People to draw near
' feelingly, and to have to approach him that
' is invifible with Acceptance: And while this
' Accefs and Acceptance in the Father's fight
' is not in a certain meafure attained to, the
' very life and marrow of Religion and Worfhip
' is wanting, both in regard to pleafing God,
' and to our own true Solace and Edification.

A a

' Wherefore

' Wherefore, *my Friends*, my Heart cries
' for you, and begs of you, that your chief
' Concern from time to time, may be to seek
' the Lord God, and draw nigh to him thro'
' the Spirit of his Son, given in measure to all
' to profit with ; and he will certainly be mind-
' ful of you, and draw near to you to your sure
' Help and Comfort, and will by degrees rent
' the Veil, and take away the Covering which
' hath been over every Heart. The departing
' from the divine Appearance or Manifesta-
' tion of God in the Heart, through his Spirit,
' whereunto the Lord Jesus and his Apostles
' directed and gathered the true Believers, in
' order that they might be born again, and pre-
' served to his Praise, who called them ; I say,
' the going from this has been the Cause of
' losing the Sense of his pure Love, and Life,
' and Comfort there-through to the Soul, and
' of departing into Forms and Modes, of splir-
' ting into various Sects, contending and striv-
' ing one with another about Names and Sha-
' dows of things : Mens human Apprehensions
' and Interests having become too much the
' rule and bottom of many People, and a feed-
' ing upon Words and Performances without
' Life, which both occasions great Barrenness
' of Heart, and want of godly Conversation.
    ' And it is a certain Truth, that if ever
' Men return aright to God, they must return
' thro' the Spirit, and to feel after his quick-
' ning Power, to give the Soul Light, and Life,
' and

' and Ability to fight the good Fight of Faith,
' and to war against the Enemies of their own
' Hearts, as well as to perform the Duty of
' Worship and obedient Service, which we owe
' to the great and living God, acceptably.

' And blessed be his Name for ever, he is
' nearer to hear the Bemoanings of our needy
' Souls, and to afford them Relief and Access
' to his holy Life-giving Presence, than many
' are aware of ; who yet are seeking abroad,
' and would gladly have the Privilege of Disci-
' ples of Christ without Self-denial, or coming
' under the Restrictions or Discipline of that
' crucifying Power, and Cross of Christ the
' Lord : This has been the case of many of us,
' who having tasted of the Terrors, and in
' part, of the Mercy of the merciful Father,
' we cannot but wish well for others.

' *My Friends*, I am unexpectedly opened to
' spread these Things before you, for your se-
' rious Consideration, in a measure of the Love
' of Christ, desiring your present and eternal
' Welfare ; and I pray call to mind that en-
' couraging Expression of our Lord, that *those*
' *who deny'd themselves of any thing for his Name*
' *and the Gospel-sake*, should have in this Life,
' *many fold*, and hereafter, *Life everlasting* :
' And of the fulfilling thereof, he has in mea-
' sure made many Witnesses, blessed be his
' Name for ever more. And I hope and be-
' lieve, that he hath also given you some
' Earnest hereof already, and will yet make

A a 2

' you

' you experimental Witnesses more largely,
' as you give up to follow him faithfully, to
' your inward Joy and Comfort; tho' as the
' Followers of the Lamb in the Regeneration,
' you may also have to wade through near and
' pinching Strippings and Tribulations of va-
' rious kinds : Yet again I cannot but invite
' and encourage you to draw near to the Lord,
' and he will assuredly draw nigh to you, and
' become your Shepherd, and you shall not
' lack. The Arm of the Lord of Hosts be
' your Leader and Feeder, your Shield, your
' Buckler, and may he cover your Head in
' the day of Battle : For great is the Wrath of
' the Dragon against the Return of the Church,
' and her coming up out of the Wilderness,
' or bewildered State, that she may again en-
' joy her ancient Beloved, her Redeemer, her
' Head and Husband : Thus under a solid de-
' gree of divine Love, which surely extends
' freely towards you, I tenderly take my leave
' of you, and remain, if I never see you more,
' your truly loving Friend,

Maryland, the 20th of the   ' JOHN FOTHERGILL.'
   Eighth Month 1722.

From *Cecil (continues the Journal)* we went
the 21st to *Duck-creek*, to a Half-year's Meeting, to which many Friends accompanied us
from *Maryland*, and divers came from other
places, with some other People ; so that it was
a large Meeting, and continued two Days.
———The Lord was pleased to own us with

his living Presence, and the Opening of the Treasury of his Wisdom and Counsel, both to other People and to Friends; tending to rouze up the negligent, and to encourage the honest-minded. This Meeting helped much towards our Discharge there-away, and the great Name of the Lord was glorified, who is worthy for ever. That day I was seized with an *Ague*-fit, which continued upon me violently till Night, nevertheless I was enabled to go thro' my Service and Travel.

The 23d we came down toward *Lewistown*, to visit some poor Friends there-away, and the next Day had a Meeting at *Coldspring*, seven Miles from the Town aforesaid, and a satisfactory time with the few Friends in that part; tho' the Return of my *Ague* render'd travelling unpleasant and difficult, being very weak and ill. The 26th we had a Meeting at *Mother-kill*, which we had given notice of as we went down; wherein the Lord of Mercies mightily favoured us with Help to declare the Way of Life, to warn the indifferent, and to encourage the honest-minded : And it was a particular time of Mercy to that People, whereof we were humbly glad, and the Lord, who favoured us with Help thro' all our Exercises, and enabled to go on faithfully in his Service, was praised. We came to *Timothy Hanson's* at *Little-creek* after the Meeting that Night, and the 27th, being First-day, were at Friends Meeting there, and tho' I was much indisposed,

yet

yet divine Goodnefs owned us, and we were helped to bear teftimony to the bleffed Truth, which prevailed amongft us to our Comfort, and the Glory of God.

The 30th we had a Meeting near *George's-creek* at Friends Meeting-houfe, where many Friends met us from feveral places, and divine Goodnefs was pleafed to favour us with a profitable time, to the ftirring up of the Loiterers, and giving Relief to the honeft-hearted Travellers. The 31ft we vifited a fick Friend to mutual Comfort, and went back to *John Maccool's*, at *George's-creek*, at Night.

The 1ft of the ninth Month we rode to *Newcaftle*, and had a Meeting with Friends there, wherein the Lord was pleafed to manifeft his Power and Wifdom, much to our eafe, and the Help and Comfort of many. The 3d we were at the Monthly-meeting at *Center*, wherein Truth opened a door for fome Service in feveral refpects; and the 4th, being Firft-day, we were at *Chichefter* Meeting, which was large, and a good awakening time, to the Honour of the holy Name. The 5th we got to *Philadelphia*, the Quarterly-meeting for the County being then to be held there; wherein we had fome good Service among Friends, to mutual Satisfaction and Help in the Caufe of the Lord Almighty.

Being now pretty clear in our Spirits of that part of the Country, fave fome Weight which remained upon me relating to this Place, we

ftaid

ſtaid about two Weeks here; and thro' hard travelling before, and a deep Exerciſe of Spirit attending me in this place, I was much weaken'd yet the Lord was pleaſed to open in his holy Power and Wiſdom, and to ſupport with Abi-lity of Body; ſo that we had many open and relieving Meetings with Friends in the City, (and others who came from divers Places to take Leave of us) whom I was moved both to warn in the Word of Life againſt many hin-dering things growing among them; and to exhort the Elders to be diligent in Example and true Zeal for the Lord; whoſe merciful Hand likewiſe extended freely towards, and prevailed among the Youth; and the honeſt Travellers for the Proſperity of Truth and Righteouſneſs, were much encouraged and ſtrengthned.

The 19th, having a good and ſeaſoning Op-portunity in the Evening before with many Friends at our Lodging, and a bleſſed open time in Supplication with the Family and ſome others, we took our Leave in the Love of God, and went down by Land to *Cheſter*, accompanied by many Friends; the next Morning we took Leave of them and Friends there, and went on board the Ship called the *Globe*, bound for *South-Carolina*, which Place had been before me moſt of the Journey; we ſailed down the River, and next Morning went aſhore at *Newcaſtle*, and had a precious open Meeting with Friends there in the Love of Truth. The 22d we went on board again, and ſet ſail for *Charles-town*, to

which

which Place we had a safe, tho' somewhat flow Paffage, and got well thither the 16th of the tenth Month, being the feventh of the Week, and were at Meeting on Firft-day, with the few Friends in the Place, fome moderate People coming in, and the Lord mercifully owned us, and gave us a good Time among them ; tho' the main part of the People in that Country feem'd a carelefs, dark People, in matters of Religion. We likewife had feveral Meetings in other parts of the Country, wherein the Lord opened freely in his Power and Wifdom, to declare the Way of Life and Salvation to the People. We had alfo divers Meetings in *Charles-town* ; and tho' there are but a few Friends there-away, yet there were fome with whom we were comforted, and to whom our Vifit was of fervice. Divers of the People, and fome of thefe the chief in the Place, were alfo fomewhat reached by the Truth, and were very loving ; but many feemed much above the true *Chriftian* Simplicity. When we had laboured there about two Weeks, and had many Meetings during that Time, and finding our Spirits clear to leave the Place, we took our Paffage for *Barbadoes*, and taking our Leave of Friends in much nearnefs and tendernefs of Spirit, went on board the 28th, and fet fail for *Barbadoes*, and were favoured greatly with the Lord's Prefence and Peace. We had a good Paffage, and landed well at *Bridge-town* in four Weeks, and were gladly received by Friends there,

there, and lodged at *John Oxley's*. We had many Meetings at *Bridge-town*, and in several parts of the Island, both among Friends, and others not of our Profession, who seemed glad of our Visits: But the Decay among Friends in this place, thro' giving way to the Spirit and Friendship of the World, and going from the Cross of Christ, seem'd to make the Way more narrow for the Testimony of the Gospel of Salvation to go forth with the desired Success among other People; yet the Lord God of Mercies was near to us in his Love and Power for our Comfort and Help; and extended very largely and mercifully towards all People, the Professors of Truth particularly, in order to awaken and repair the Decaying, as also to feed and strengthen the few honestly Religious-minded: So that we often admired the Lord's Goodness, and magnified his holy Name.

When we had laboured upon the Island in the Love of God about two Months, both in Meetings for Worship, and in divers Meetings for the Care and Discipline of the Church, in that Counsel and Ability of Truth where-with the Lord favoured us, and bore up our Spirits under and thro' much Affliction of Soul, for the sake of the Cause of Christ, about which many were grown careless; I say, having thus laboured, and now finding our Spirits easy and clear of that Service, and seeing the way open'd for our Return to *England*, by that holy Hand which drew us from our Habitations, we took

B b

leave

leave of Friends in much Love and holy Comfort, recommending them to the Name of the Lord : And on the 29th of the firſt Month 1723, we ſet ſail for *England*, and the 31ſt of the third Month we came a-breaſt of *Portland*, the firſt Land we made, and on the 1ſt of the fourth Month meeting with a Boat at Sea, we hired her to carry us to the *Iſle of Wight* ; the next Day we got to *Portſmouth*, and took Poſt-horſes for *London*, where we came the 3d in the Morning, being Second-day, and got to the Meeting of Miniſters, the beginning of the Yearly-meeting 1723.

Of this Viſit to America, *he gave the ſaid Yearly-meeting the following Relation, viz.*

‘ WE * firſt acknowledge in humble Re-
‘ verence to the Lord Almighty, that
‘ he mercifully favoured us with his Love and
‘ Countenance, very often upon the Sea, and
‘ guarded us thereon from unreaſonable and
‘ wicked Men, into whoſe hands ſome fell
‘ very near us, and brought us ſafe to *Virginia*
‘ after a moderate Paſſage : We then entered
‘ upon our Service in viſiting Friends, and
‘ went towards *North-Carolina*, having many
‘ large and open Meetings, among Friends
‘ and others alſo.

‘ We

---

† *Himſelf and* Lawrence King *his Companion.*

' We came back again from hence into *Vir-*
' *ginia,* and had Meetings in many parts of it;
' and in several where there are few or no
' Friends : In both these Provinces we found
' great Willingness in many People to hear the
' Truth declared, divers of whom appeared
' very loving and tenderly affected. There
' seem'd likewise to be a comfortable Openness
' among the Youth, the Offspring of Friends
' in several places, and rather a Growth among
' some of the Elder, in a religious Care : Yet
' not so much among either as might have
' been hoped for and expected from the La-
' bour, which in the Love of God hath been
' many ways extended towards them ; yet di-
' vine Mercy still reaches freely to them, and
' in some places there is an Increase in Righte-
' ousness, and Truth is in good Esteem : But
' in others, the Love and Friendship of the
' World occasions a Decay.

' In *Maryland* we found there had been
' great Loss, by the Decease of many of the
' Elders, and of the more zealous and con-
' cerned Friends ; yet there are in several parts,
' some who are hopeful and religiously disposed
' among the Younger, and others who are left,
' tho' too few there are of these : A love of
' hurtful Ease and vain Liberties having pre-
' vailed to the Prejudice of some, and hinder-
' ing the Work and Honour of Truth. There
' appears nevertheless, some Openness among
' several of the neighbouring People, and a

B b 2

' gracious

' gracious Extending of divine Love to them ;
' as well as of an helpful hand in heavenly Wif-
' dom towards Friends in feveral refpects, greatly
' to our mutual Comfort and Satisfaction.
 ' In *Penfilvania* we found an enquiring Open-
' nefs in diverts parts among People of feveral
' Profeffions ; fome were convinced of, and
' we hope received the Truth in the Love of
' it : There is a large body of religioufly-
' minded People among Friends, who are
' growing up in a true Care for the Honour
' of Truth ; tho' thefe are mixed with many
' earthly-minded, and fome loofe, libertine
' People, who occafion much Exercife to the
' Right-minded : Yet the Lord's Goodnefs
' and Care is near and over that Country, and
' his Truth profpers in it.
 ' In the *Jerfeys, Long-Ifland,* and *New-York*
' Governments, there are a confiderable num-
' ber of Friends, and in fome places an hopeful
' Opennefs among other People. We travelled
' diligently through thefe Parts, and tho' vain
' Liberties in fome, and too great Carelefnefs
' and Indulgence in others, have ftained or
' obftructed the Progrefs and Dominion of the
' Work and Beauty of Truth ; yet the Vifita-
' tion of heavenly Good-will and tender Love,
' with Defires to help, is very evidently and
' freely extended, in order to repair and build
' up in Righteoufnefs : There are, however,
' fome honeftly concerned Friends there-away,
' among whom we had a fatisfactory Labour,

' in

' in the fresh Visitation of divine Power and
' Love.

   ' In *Rhode-Island* and the Government be-
' longing to it, and *New-England*, we had
' many Meetings, and close Labour, but in
' the whole much to our Satisfaction : There
' is a considerable body of Friends in several
' parts of that Country, and we believe in
' many places, they are rather increasing in the
' Knowledge of the Power of Truth, and in
' Stability in Righteousness and Faithfulness to
' it ; and altho' some hindering and wounding
' Circumstances have attended in divers places,
' yet there is a tenderly-concerned, valuable
' People there-away, both elder and younger.
' We had many Meetings amongst the neigh-
' bouring professing People ; in some places
' but few were willing, or dared to come in,
' but in others we had very large ones amongst
' them, especially towards the East of *New-*
' *England*, and several, we hope, were effectu-
' ally reached by the Power of Truth, and
' received and joined with it in Humility and
' Gladness : And in some parts a very com-
' fortable, tendring Visitation prevailed upon
' many of the Youth among Friends. We
' laboured very diligently, through the Ability
' received, in most parts of this Country, and
' took Leave of Friends in solid Hope, on ac-
' count of the Lord's Work, and much Love
' and heavenly peace in ourselves, with holy
Thankfulness

' Thankfulnefs to the Lord Almighty, the
' great Helper of his devoted Servants.

' Then returning back towards *Penfilvania*,
' &c. we had fome comfortable Service there-
' away, and Friends were encouraged and
' ftrengthned in the Lord: We failed from
' hence to *South-Carolina*, and laboured there
' fome time in the Service of the Gofpel, hav-
' ing Meetings with the few Friends there,
' and among other People: The Lord our
' God was with us to our Comfort and Help,
' tho' the generality of the People feemed but
' cold and very indifferent about true Religion.
' There are but few Friends in thefe parts,
' and but very few who feem to love Truth in
' Uprightnefs; yet fome there are who thus
' love it, and retain the Simplicity thereof in
' a good degree: Thefe were very glad of our
' Vifit, and we were much comforted together
' in the Lord: The People were alfo, gene-
' rally, very loving and chearful towards us.

' Finding our Spirits eafy and clear of thefe
' parts, we failed to *Barbadoes*, having the fa-
' vour of a fafe and ready Paffage, and thro'
' the nearnefs of merciful Regard and divine
' Life and Goodnefs to our Spirits, a Seafon
' never to be forgot, bleffed be the Lord for
' ever. Friends received us with gladnefs, it
' having been long fince any Friends from
' *England* had vifited them: We had many
' Meetings, both among the Profeffors of Truth
' and others in this Ifland, which were to the

' Comfort

‘ Comfort of the living amongſt them ; many
‘ other People ſeem’d glad of the Viſit, and
‘ behaved ſoberly and reſpectfully : But a looſe,
‘ lofty, and irreligious Spirit or Diſpoſition,
‘ hath too generally prevailed upon the Inhabi-
‘ tants of that Place, and to a ſorrowful de-
‘ gree hath obſtructed the ſpreading of Truth,
‘ and has even brought on a Decay or Dimi-
‘ nution of the number of Friends : Yet there
‘ are a few in ſeveral parts of the Iſland, who
‘ retain their Integrity to God, and love, and
‘ are concern’d for his Honour. The Lord
‘ was pleaſed to own us with his Help and
‘ Wiſdom to divide the Word aright, in warn-
‘ ing and ſtirring up the Unfaithful, and with
‘ Encouragement and Comfort to the Lovers
‘ of Truth ; and indeed alſo to publiſh the
‘ Goſpel-doctrine by way of Information to
‘ all : So that we were ſenſible the Day of love
‘ and mercy from God, was yet freely extend-
‘ ed to many in that unworthy place. And
‘ now growing eaſy and clear in our Spirits, of
‘ our Service in thoſe parts, and our way be-
‘ ing open for *England*, we took our leave of
‘ Friends in the Love and Peace of our hea-
‘ venly Father, and had the renewed favour
‘ of a ſafe and good Paſſage to *England*.

‘ And one thing I think good to add, hav-
‘ ing often remark’d it ; that tho’ it fell in our
‘ way, rather in an uncommon degree, to lay
‘ open and teſtify againſt the corrupt grounds,
‘ ways and Practices of the Hireling and Men-

‘ made,

‘ made, pretended Minifters of Chrift of our
‘ time, in feveral Countries, and Societies ; yet
‘ the People heard with unufual Patience and
‘ Thoughtfulnefs, in general, and we alfo
‘ pafled quietly thro’ all our Journey without
‘ any of them appearing, or offering any Di-
‘ fturbance or Difputation : Which we were
‘ thankful for, believing it to be of the Lord’s
‘ Goodnefs and Wifdom, and his invifible
‘ Dread which prevailed, and will prevail in
‘ the Earth : To him, the Support, Defence
‘ and rich Rewarder of his People and Servants,
‘ in Awfulnefs of Soul be afcribed all Glory
‘ and Pre-eminence, with Fear and Praife,
‘ for ever.

From Barbadoes *he wrote the following
Epiftle to Friends of* Dover *Meeting in* New-
England, *viz.*

‘ DEAR FRIENDS,

‘ SINCE I was with you, my Spirit has
‘ often turned towards you, in the mov-
‘ ings of true and near Love, and in tender,
‘ fervent breathing, for your being inwardly
‘ fuftained, ftrengthned and encouraged in an
‘ humble Dependance upon the pure and in-
‘ vifible Arm of the Lord Almighty, and in a
‘ due Devotednefs of Soul to follow him with
‘ full purpofe of Heart : I have wanted an Op-
‘ portunity to manifeft my Remembrance of
‘ you in a few Lines, which I hope I may have
‘ from

' from hence, and herewith extendeth my
' dear Salutation, in that pure engaging Love
' of our gracious God, whereby he hath been
' pleafed to vifit, and overcome many of our
' Souls, and thro' the Operation of the Spirit
' of Judgment, which he hath gracioufly
' mixed with unfpeakable Mercy, he hath
' prepared many Hearts, in meafure, to draw
' nigh to him, and to be made Partakers of his
' living, foul-engaging Goodnefs, and pure
' Life, giving us an Earneft of eternal Com-
' fort.

' And oh ! my *near Friends*, Elder and
' Younger, who have been thus mercifully
' followed, and waited over in long-fuffering,
' and humbled in degree by the inward touches
' of the Love and Favour of the Lord God of
' Bleffings, my Heart groans within me, that
' it may continually be your, and all our Care,
' to labour with due Watchfulnefs, to walk
' humbly before him, to feel after his living
' Power, and to bear his Yoke refignedly and
' chearfully ; that thereby we may be crucified
' to the World, the Evils and hurtful Friend-
' fhip of it ; and with due patience, caft our
' Care upon him, with Refolution to follow
' him wherever, or thro' whatfoever he may
' be pleafed to lead us ; for he is God, and be-
' fides him there is no Saviour, nor Healer of
' the fick or wounded Soul, nor any that can
' lead to durable and certain Bleffing, either
' here or hereafter : And fure I am, his Eye of

　　　　　' Mercy

' Mercy in tender love is over his Children in
' all States, and in all Places ; and is, and ever
' will be a rich Rewarder, and fure Friend in
' times of Need, to thofe who give up all to
' follow his Reproofs and Requirings, not hav-
' ing, or thinking any thing too near to part
' with for the fake of his Favour : Such will
' often have Caufe to fay, *their Lot is fallen in*
' *a good Land.*
' And oh ! that none who have tafted of pure
' Love and divine Sweetnefs in their own Souls,
' as a Spring in a dry place, may ever give way
' to the difcouraging Enemy again, who is
' bufily waiting to hinder, and turn whom he
' can afide from the narrow way, which alone
' leads to Life and Salvation : And as this is
' Satan's Aim, fo he hath many Methods of
' working, either by infinuating, that an
' eafier Way may do, or begetting Difcontent,
' and fetting the Creature into Uneafinefs, in
' the Time of its inward Travail in Pain, or
' to look abroad, and to watch for Occafion ;
' and then he darkens the Mind, the Heart
' hardens, and the Beauty and Excellency of
' the Law of God is loft, and fo for Eafe to
' the Flefh, and prefent Pleafure, there is a
' drawing back and back ; and in this ftagger-
' ing Condition Satan has prevailed to perfuade,
' that all which the Soul hath feen and felt,
' was but a Miftake, and proceeded from fome
' other Caufe : And thus have fome heavenly
' Vifitations been flighted, to the great and
' miferable

' miferable Lofs of many ; which I fincerely
' pray may never happen to any more in any
' part of the World.

' And my Soul humbly begs of the moft
' gracious God, that if any have been hurt in
' their Minds thro' Unwatchfulnefs, after the
' pure Way of Life hath been caft up plain in
' their View, by giving Room to any weak-
' ning Confultations, that he may be pleafed
' mercifully to renew a Day of winning Love,
' and caufe it to arife upon fuch in the Purity
' of its Brightnefs, in their very Souls ; fo that
' they may clearly difcern the Wiles of the
' Enemy, and fee a Way open to turn to the
' Lord effectually, and become fenfible Wit-
' neffes of his Mercy and Salvation ; *fo be it* ;
' *fo be it : Amen.*

' And, *dear Friends*, you of the elder rank,
' I tenderly intreat you to be diligent, and
' careful in walking and in watching for the
' Renewal of your Strength and Capacity, to
' approve yourfelves in all Things, the Lord's
' faithful Followers and Servants, ordered in
' divine Wifdom : And as you are bent in Care,
' to be prepared to give up your Accounts with
' Joy, the Spring of Life and Wifdom will be
' opened to you from time to time, to help
' you to watch over all the Family under your
' eye, and to walk before them fteadily, and
' to their Help and Encouragement.

' And that the young People may all watch
' againft the many Enticements to Corruption,

C c 2   ' and

' and to Liberties, which unfit for divine Fa-
' vour and Love coming in upon the Soul : A
' Stain or an Hurt is foon received, but a Re-
' covery or Reftoration is not to be obtained,
' but thro' Sorrow and Difficulty in divers re-
' fpects, as, I am perfuaded, there are among
' you young People, who have from certain
' Experience with Sorrow to teftify, upon
' whom a gracious Hand from on high hath
' taken hold, in Mercy and Loving-kindnefs ;
' which I hope will never be forgotten by you :
' And thro' fome of thofe who have been thus
' vifited, and touched in Heart by the Finger
' of God's Love, if they keep near to the
' Lord in true reverent Submiffion, I believe
' he will appear and work, and make them
' Inftruments to fhew forth his Salvation, to
' the Praife of his glorious and powerful
' Name ; and to call to others, in the Name
' of the Lord, to come and tafte how good
' he is.

' *Dear Friends*, my Heart is often, as it
' were, among you, in the one Spirit of Life
' and Righteoufnefs, and is ftrongly engaged
' in Sympathy, and travails for your Growth
' in Faithfulnefs to the Lord of Mercies and
' Salvation ; whom as you duly regard, he will
' furely be a Spring of Bleffing to you, and a
' fure hiding place, whatever comes upon the
' Ungodly and Forgetful, whom he will cer-
' tainly vifit in Difpleafure.

' I am

' I am fweetly open in Spirit towards you at
' this time, in the Extendings of immortal
' Love from the great Fountain, the Relief of
' the truly Needy in all Ages, the Staff and
' Strength of true depending Souls ftill, where
' ever they are, and however exercifed, bleffed
' be his holy Arm for ever.   And tho' I feem
' eafy, without expecting ever to fee you again,
' yet you are near me, and I think I cannot be
' unmindful of you, and fhall long and hope
' to hear well of you ; thus with tender En-
' treaty that you may all make a right ufe of,
' and put a true value upon the day and time
' of the Father's love, I commit you to the
' all-fufficient Word of Life and Truth, and
' remain your near Friend and Brother in the
' Truth,

Barbadoes, the 18th of the   ' JOHN FOTHERGILL.
  twelfth Month, 1723.

And before he set sail for England, *he found
himself engaged to visit those who professed with
us in the other Islands, with the following Epistle,
which he intitled,*

' *A* BROTHERLY SALUTATION, *with
' some* Chriftian *Exhortations, to the Profes-
' sors of* TRUTH *in* Antigua, Anguilla,
' Jamaica, *or there-away.*

' MY FRIENDS,

' IT having fallen to my lot, through the
' moving of the Word of Life, to vifit
                                                 ' many

' many parts of the *American* Countries again,
' in the Service of the Gospel of Christ ; and
' being here on this account, a tender and
' brotherly Care hath sprung in my Heart to-
' wards you also, tho' I do not see a way open
' in the Truth to visit you in person, being
' drawn in Spirit towards *Europe* again : But
' still a living Openness is in my Heart to visit
' you with an Epistle, where-with also reacheth
' my hearty and true brotherly Salutation,
' unto all who know and love the Truth as it
' is in Jesus, and manifested thro' the Spirit
' inwardly ; and with tender Entreaty and
' Advice, that you all carefully feel after, and
' wait upon the Lord, for the renewing of in-
' ward Strength, and the Experience of his
' living Power arising and working in you,
' even the redeeming, sanctifying Power of
' the Father and the Son, to quicken your
' Souls, and enable you to serve and worship
' the living God acceptably ; who is the alone
' sure Fountain of true Comfort, the all-suffi-
' cient Helper of his People, and the com-
' passionate Reliever of the poor and needy
' Souls, in all Countries and Conditions, and
' is worthy to be trusted in, obey'd and mag-
' nify'd for ever.

 ' And I pray you consider, that as it is cer-
' tain, the end and tendency of the Visitation
' of the Lord, thro' his blessed Light and
' Truth, by Jesus Christ appearing inwardly
' to the Children of Men, is to bring *from*
           ' *Man,*

' *Man*, and to turn People *to himself*, to be
' taught of him, and so to be established in
' Righteousness: So, whosoever thus in heart
' truly turns, and takes Counsel of him, wait-
' ing diligently from time to time to hear his
' Instructions, and to feel his Power to help
' to cease from Evil, and whatever he mani-
' fests to be disagreeable to his holy Will; to
' learn to come up in doing well: All such are
' and will be regarded in merciful Compassion
' from on high, and the mighty Arm will be
' stretched forth both to feed and help on,
' thro' all the Disadvantages that may attend
' them.

' And it is also certain, that whatever Pri-
' vileges any may outwardly enjoy, none can
' grow rightly, or be preserved in the way of
' Life and Peace, but as Faith is kept in the
' invisible Power of God, and Diligence in
' waiting for a renewed Sense of Life and
' Light in the eternal Word of Power, to open
' Counsel, and give Ability to do his Will, and
' to confess the Son truly, as our Redeemer,
' before Men; wherefore I again earnestly in-
' treat and exhort, in the bowels of the Fa-
' ther's love, you whose Understandings are
' thus in a good measure open'd, to labour
' carefully to draw near the Lord in spirit oft-
' en, in humility and patient fervency, with
' Hearts resigned to follow him fully; and
' assuredly he will draw nigh to you, and feed
' your Souls with Food from his own never-
' failing Treasury.   ' But

' But oh! my Heart is loaded with a for-
' rowful Concern and Travail on the account
' of fome, who have been long fully perfuaded
' concerning the way of Truth and Righteouf-
' nefs ; and have been often very fenfible of its
' holy Reproofs, in order to reclaim them
' from the Evil of their ways, and from the
' corrupt and vain Practices and Friendfhips of
' the World ; and yet continue to live in, and
' comply therewith ; flighting the Reproofs of
' Truth, rejecting the Inftructions and Offers
' of divine Help thro' the Grace of God ; be-
' caufe of the Narrownefs of the way of Life.

' And others there are, who have at times
' been inwardly affected, by the Life of Truth
' appearing to their illuminated Underftand-
' ings, and to have join'd with the lovers of
' it for a time ; yet have grown weary, and
' afhamed of the Crofs of Chrift, and the Sim-
' plicity of Truth ; and fo have hearkened to
' the Whifpering of the old Enemy, and his
' Enticements into vain Liberty, and carnal
' Eafe, wherein fome have fettled again, build-
' ing up what they had, in part, deftroyed.

' Some alfo, may feek to excufe or juftify
' their Doings, by obferving fome, either real
' or fuppofed Miftakes, or evil Actions in
' others, and fo have grown hard, if not envi-
' ous : I fay, refpecting fome fuch People, my
' Heart travails in pain, that they may feri-
' oufly confider, and come to fee their Condi-
' tion in the Day of mercy ; and to fuch of
' them

' them as may see these Lines, oh ! take warn-
' ing, take warning, while Light and Reproof
' from the God of mercy is yet at times visit-
' ing your Souls, in long-suffering and merci-
' ful regard, waiting to quicken you into more
' Faithfulness, and Devotedness of heart to
' follow him ; and to confess the Truth before
' Men, to bear the Yoke of Christ, and learn
' of him, that you may find Rest and Peace
' to your Souls for ever.

' And know ye, you who slight and turn
' away from the pure Truth, and deny or re-
' ject the Cross of Christ, for the sake of pre-
' sent Ease or Pleasure, and who choose the
' Broad-way, that your very Insides in every
' part are seen, and noted of the Lord ; your
' ways are marked by the righteous Judge, and
' a time of terrible Awakening is before you :
' The Almighty will assuredly turn your carnal
' Ease, vain Rejoicing, and foolish Grandeur,
' into bitter Mourning and Lamentation, if
' you do not turn at the Reproof of Truth, and
' with its Instruction, in a day of the merciful
' striving of the Lord's witness with you in
' your Hearts ; which, as a Servant of Christ,
' and your Souls true Friend, I tenderly in-
' treat, and faithfully warn you to consider,
' and lay duly to heart.

' And you, *my Friends*, who have escaped,
' or have been preserved in a good measure from
' the Evils and Corruptions of the World, thro'
' Obedience to the Truth, be diligent in la-

D d

' bouring

' bouring to improve the divine Gift commit-
' ted to you for that end ; so that none of you
' through neglect thereof, tho' you may have
' the Denomination of *Servants*, be at the
' conclusion cast into everlasting Weeping and
' Sorrow, with the slothful Servant. And also
' remember the *Pleaders of Excuses*, mentioned
' in the Parable of Christ, who having been
' invited to the Marriage, and called to the
' Supper, made their several Allegations for
' not coming ; which tho' they related to things
' lawful, yet drew upon them the woful Deter-
' mination, that not one of them should *taste of*
' *the Supper*. For although the great Lord be
' long-suffering, and bears long with the car-
' nal Reasoning of the Children of Men, in
' several respects ; yet he will be found to be
' a God of Justice and Judgment, as well as
' Mercy, and will recompence those who will
' not be prevailed upon to obey the Truth, but
' continue in Unrighteousness, and the vain
' sensual Lusts of the Flesh, with Tribulation,
' Anxiety and Wrath ; while Glory, Honour
' and Peace will be the Portion and Enjoy-
' ment in eternal Life, of all the sincere Fol-
' lowers of the Lamb of God, tho' through
' many Sorrows and humbling Fears.

' Wherefore lift up your Hearts, you *honest-*
' *minded*, in reverent Hope for the renewed
' Appearance of divine Life to your travelling
' Souls, for it is truly reviving, and is the one
' Fountain of true Joy, Encouragement and

' Strength

‘ Strength to all the Children of God, in every
‘ Part of the Earth. And walk circumfpectly;
‘ be diligent and careful in meeting together,
‘ fuch as conveniently may, or fit down toge-
‘ ther in the Name of the Lord, to wait upon
‘ him, if but two or three in a place ; it being
‘ the Promife of Chrift himfelf, and will for
‘ ever be fulfilled, that *fuch he will favour with
‘ his Prefence*, in all places, whether in greater or
‘ in lefs Congregations ; and this is the Life and
‘ fubftantial Edification of living Souls, which
‘ truly qualifies to worfhip acceptably : And
‘ wherever Coolnefs or Neglect herein is given
‘ way to, or continued in by any who are con-
‘ vinced of the Truth, and the Way of wor-
‘ fhipping the Father in Spirit, by inwardly
‘ waiting for divine and fpiritual Food and
‘ Relief ; where this Indifferency and Neglect
‘ prevails, there Weaknefs in religious Con-
‘ cerns, and Dulnefs refpecting Duty towards
‘ God, always follow ; and the Way and Pre-
‘ cepts of Truth become wearifom, and the
‘ Enemy of Souls furnifhes with one Excufe
‘ or another for fuch Indifferency and Declen-
‘ fion from neceffary Care ; and fo Darknefs
‘ gradually creeps into the Heart, and a Dan-
‘ ger of ftumbling, fome on one thing, fome
‘ on another, increafes from lefs to more, till
‘ great and lamentable falls fometimes hap-
‘ pen, which may prove utterly deftructive
‘ in their confequences : Yet the Deftruction
‘ of fuch, is altogether of themfelves, for the

D d 2

‘ Lord

' Lord Almighty hath offered sufficient Help
' for all states and circumstances, however dif-
' advantageous, through his Grace and Truth ;
' yet will he be enquired for, and waited
' upon by all, that they may be made Expe-
' riencers of his Salvation. Oh ! good is the
' Lord, worthy to be feared, waited upon, and
' obeyed faithfully for ever, saith my Soul this
' time, in the immediate sense and view of
' the free reachings forth of his powerful Arm
' of Salvation, healing and nursing Goodness ;
' especially towards humbly concerned Hearts,
' that are sincerely desirous to be helped to
' grow up obedient Children to the everlasting
' Father, which I humbly beg may become,
' and continue all your and the whole Family's
' Care, in true Sincerity to the end.

   ' And here I would have concluded these
' lines, having already exceeded my expecta-
' tion when I began them in the Love of
' Truth, and that Plainness and Sincerity
' wherein is the truest Friendship ; but one
' thing yet bears weight with me to propose to
' your serious Confideration, *viz. What is the*
' *chief cause or end of your settling, and continu-*
' *ance, where I am very senfible many Difadvan-*
' *tages attend you in respect to Religion ?* If it
' be under an Apprehension of some inward
' Restrictions to bear testimony to, and for the
' Truth amongst that People ; then I pray
' confider, and be careful to live so near the
' Truth, and a truly religious Zeal, in faith-
                           ' fully

' fully following the heavenly Light and In-
' ſtructions thereof, that you may be Lights
' indeed ; and keep in due Moderation and
' Juſtice in managing your Affairs, and be
' careful to order yourſelves, and your Youth,
' who have any, ſo as to walk according to
' the ſimplicity and plainneſs of Truth ; thus
' will you keep out of, and bear teſtimony
' againſt the vain Ways, Words, Faſhions,
' and corrupting Friendſhips of this World :
' How elſe are you like to be really of Service,
' or Examples to others in the way of Truth,
' or capable of ſhewing forth that Redemp-
' tion, which there-thro' is offered from God
' to the degenerate World ; or juſtly hope for
' his Countenance inwardly, or his Bleſſing to
' attend your Affairs.   Yet if this be your In-
' ducement, and is from time to time accom-
' panied with this godly Care, whatever be the
' effect or event reſpecting others, the Lord's
' Care will be over you, his gracious Ear will
' be open to the cry of your needy Souls, and
' he will ſhew himſelf to be your Shepherd,
' and you will not lack.

' But if the chief Motive be a Regard to
, preſent or temporal Intereſt, it is not reaſon-
' able to hope for, or expect the Privilege of
' his holy Countenance upon your Souls, or
' ſucceſs other ways ; and it happens too often,
' that thoſe who are chiefly under the Influence
' of preſent Views, become indifferent with
' reſpect to a true Concern of Heart, and ſo
' give

' give way to a halting and mixing with
' worldly Liberties in Converſation, and be-
' come rather a Reproach and Cauſe of ſtum-
' bling to others, who may be awakened to
' ſome religious Thoughtfulneſs, and look to-
' wards thoſe for Encouragement ; but I hope
' better concerning ſome of you in particular,
' tho' I thus write.   Nevertheleſs there is great
' danger of coming to loſs in the beſt Reſpect,
' and more eſpecially concerning your Off-
' ſpring, who have their Education and Con-
' verſe with and among thoſe who too gene-
' rally are not only Strangers to the Truth and
' its Simplicity, but many of them wholly
' over-run with vain, wicked, and corrupting
' Converſation ; ſo that what you gain for
' yourſelves, and for them, may be an occaſion
' of ſtrong Temptations to thoſe who follow
' the ſight of their own eyes, into wicked and
' ſinful Practices, which lead (no condition of
' Mankind who give up to them excepted) to
' a woful and miſerable end at laſt ; and
' whether Parents be clear of their Blood,
' may be queſtioned.

  ' Theſe things have ſtood much in my way,
' in my deepeſt Thoughts reſpecting Friends,
' particularly on theſe Iſlands : and I am in-
' clined to recommend them thus to your
' Conſideration, tho' far from deſigning to put
' an unneceſſary Conſternation upon any ho-
' neſtly concerned travailing Soul, that is wait-
' ing in fear and care to know the Lord's
' Counſel

' Counsel and Ordering in such weighty things.
' But I would have all stirred up to such a ne-
' cessary Concern of Spirit, that you may be
' helped to live, and to do whatever you do,
' to the Glory of God; and so may have the
' Comfort and Blessing of his divine Favour,
' and that he may be your Ruler and King;
' and in becoming so, he will assuredly save,
' preserve, and gather his humble Subjects to
' his heavenly Kingdom in eternal Life, where
' all Sorrow is at an End, and the wicked cease
' from troubling any more; which my Spirit
' is renewedly engaged to travail for on your
' Behalf, and the whole Heritage of God, as
' for my own Soul; that his great and glorious
' Name may be renowned thro' the Earth, as
' he is worthy, worthy, for ever.
' Thus having discharged my Spirit of the
' Exercise which hath grown upon me towards
' you, and according to my Understanding, in
' the Way which Truth hath opened, in true
' Sincerity; I take my leave in the Extendings
' of the Love of Christ, wherein I remain your
' true and real Friend,

Barbadoes, the 23d of the   ' JOHN FOTHERGILL.'
  first Month, 1722-3.

The

The Year after his Return from America, *he visited Friends in* Ireland ; *of which Journey he left the following Account.*

HAVING been under a weighty Concern for some time to visit Friends in *Ireland*, and perceiving my way to be open'd for that Service, about the 27th of the fifth Month 1724, I set forward and went by *Sedbergh*, and was at Friends Monthly-meeting there, and the next day at *Preston* near *Kendal*, at the Burial of an ancient Friend ; from thence pretty straight to *Whitehaven*, staying one Night with *James Dickenson :* On the First-day we had a Meeting within the Walls of the new Meeting-house which was building there ; and the Lord's Power and Testimony prevailed among a very large Assembly, greatly to our Satisfaction and Encouragement.

I got well over to *Dublin* the Seventh-day following, being the 8th of the sixth Month, towards which place I found my Mind rather pressed with some weight of Concern, so that I could not hasten from it : I staid two First-days, and had several other Meetings with Friends, wherein the hidden Virtue and Power of Truth enabled to bear a plain and faithful Testimony for God, to the Help of the Upright and my Ease ; especially the latter First-day, in both Meetings, my Heart was opened in the Power and Doctrine of the Gospel towards Friends and others, and the Name of the Lord God was glorified.

My

My Spirit was then eafy, and I fet out for the North parts firft, and went to *Drogheda*, feveral Friends accompanying me ; we had a Meeting with a few Friends there in the Evening, and rode the next day to *Rathfryland*, near which place we had a Meeting the 19th, where feveral of the neighbouring People came in, and the Lord gave us a good time, the Love and clear Teftimony of the Gofpel reaching forth to our Comfort.

The 20th I had a large Meeting at *Lurgan*, wherein a clofe fearching Labour became my lot among Friends, which ended indifferently well to my Satisfaction.

The 22d I had a Meeting at *Monallen*, and went to *Lurgan* again that Night. The 23d at *Ballinderry* Meeting, which was very large both of Friends, and many others of different Profeffions ; and the Lord's Power and Gofpel-teftimony livingly and freely reached forth among them, in much Plainnefs and Authority, much to my Satisfaction and Eafe of Spirit ; and the great Lord and Helper of his Servants, had the Glory and Praife of all. After this I vifited two ancient Friends, *Thomas* and *Tobias Courtney*, with whom I was comforted in the Love of Chrift.

The 24th I had a Meeting at *Lifburn* ; the Power of Truth owned us to Friends, and my Comfort and Help.

The 25th and 26th I had Meetings at *Antrim* and the *Grange*, and the 28th at *Colerain*,

E e

where

where, befides Friends, pretty many People of other Profeffions came into the Meeting; the Power of Truth open'd my Heart and Mouth amongft them in much Plain-dealing and Honefty; both for the clear Information of the People, and Warning to fome loofe ones, as well as Comfort of the few upright-hearted. After Meeting we walked about a Mile to vifit a poor ancient Friend, to fome Profit in the Love of God. The next day I came back to *Ballynalee*, to a Mens Six-weeks Meeting, for the Care of the Affairs of the Church in that part, and the 30th was at a publick Meeting for the Worfhip of God, where feveral other fober People came in: We had a good time in the Love and powerful Extending of the Arm of Truth; the Upright in Heart were ftrengthned and encouraged in the Lord.

The 31ft I had a good, feafonable and edifying time with Friends at *Dunclaudy*, where alfo were feveral other fober People, towards whom the Gofpel reached freely, and had fome Impreffion.

The 1ft of the feventh Month I had a Meeting at *Ballynaroan*, and a prevailing fweet Seafon among fome tender People; and another the Day following at *Redford* near *Charlemount*, to a good degree of Satisfaction.

The 3d I rode to *Ballyhagan*, and had a Meeting there, where the Lord's power was plentifully with us, and the Gofpel-teftimony fpread in a prevailing manner, in warning and

awakening

awakening the Indifferent; in Confolation and holy Encouragement to the Well-minded, and the glorious Name was magnified.

On the 6th I was at two very large Meetings at *Lurgan*; and thro' the Goodnefs and Help of the Lord's power it was made a profitable Seafon to many: My Spirit was truly eafed thro' faithful dealing with the forgetful and lukewarm; and in a free extending of a planting and relieving Miniftry, which the Lord gave me that Day: Thro' which labour I was much eafed, my Duty being difcharged in that part of the Nation.

The 8th I had a little Meeting with fome few Friends, and feveral other People, at *Caftle-fin*, and went to *Coothill* that Evening, and lodged with *Terrence Cayle*, who with his Wife are of the native *Irifh*, yet had received the Knowledge of the Truth in the Love of it, and I hope will continue to grow therein. The next Day I had a pretty good open Meeting with Friends and divers others; who were very fober and attentive, and feemed very glad of the Opportunity.

The 11th I went to *Oldcaftle*, to a Meeting there, where we had a good and profitable Seafon, in the prevailing of divine Love, to the Help of the People; and on the 13th I was at Friends Meeting at the *Moat*; a large and good Meeting it was, in the living Authority of Truth, to the Comfort and Help of many; and the Lord God of Goodnefs and Mercy was glorified.

E e 2

The

The next day I went with several Friends to *Bally-murry* in *Connaught*, where a Meeting had been settled some time; and on the 15th had a pretty open helpful Meeting there, in the reaching of the Love of Christ, yet in much plain dealing and faithful warning to keep to Truth, that so they might be blessed.

The 16th I had a Meeting with Friends and some other sober People at *Walterstown*, and the Lord's Power and Testimony prevailed comfortably, and his Name was glorified.

The 17th I went to the *Moat* again, where we had a large and blessed helpful Meeting, in the extending of divine Love and Wisdom; and another the day following, with Friends and several civil People who came in, at *Lismoiney*.

The 19th I rode to *Birr*, and had a Meeting there, and went that Night to *John Ashton*'s, where we had a Meeting the next Day, and many of the neighbouring People came in; and the Lord was pleased to own us with his living and powerful Presence, freely opening the Word of Life; and we had a precious, pure, helping, seasoning Time with several Friends, who came in again that Evening; ever blessed be the heavenly Arm, which is the alone true Helper. The 21st I rode to *Woodhouse*, not far from *Cashell*; we had a little, but blessed Meeting at *John Bowles*'s the 22d, and the Day following another at *Joshua Fennel*'s, at *Kilcommon*. The 24th I had a pretty large and

good

[213]

good Meeting at *Clonmell*, with Friends and some sober People ; and another the 25th at *Youghall*, where the Mayor of the Town, and many others besides Friends came in ; and the Power and Testimony of Truth, through the Lord's Goodness prevailed, and it was made a good Season to many.

The 27th, being First-day, I was at two large and powerfully helpful Meetings at *Cork*, in the free Extendings of the Wisdom and Life of Truth, very much to my Ease and Comfort, and of many others ; and the 28th I was at their Mens Meeting, where I had some Service for Truth in several respects, to the Help of Friends in the Affairs of the Church.

The 29th I went to *Sheperreen*, and had a powerful, precious Meeting, in the free Reachings of the Gospel-life and Doctrine towards the few Friends there, and many neighbouring People who came in. The 30th I came back to *Castle-Salem*, and had a merciful Season in *William Morrice*'s House, in the free goings forth of a Visitation of divine Love towards him and his Family, and came again to a Meeting appointed at *Bendon*.

The 1st of the eighth Month I had a large Meeting at *Kinsale*, of many sorts of People, wherein the living humbling Power and Gospel-doctrine mercifully prevailed over many Hearts, to mine and Friends true Gladness ; and the glorious Name was magnified. The 2d I went to *Cork* again, where we had a precious,

edifying

edifying and satisfactory Meeting, to our true Comfort; in the sense whereof we took leave of one another, and with several Friends I came to *Mallo*, and the 3d to *Limerick*; where on the 4th, we had two large and precious Meetings, in the free Extendings of divine Love amongst us, to the Help of many; and on the 5th we were favoured with a strengthning, helping Opportunity before the Meeting for Business began, it being the Province-meeting, and was carried on peaceably, with proper Concern, and Friends parted comfortably. On the 6th I was at Friends Week-day Meeting for the Town, for which many Friends staid; and divine Power, and heavenly Virtue and Counsel sprang up and spread amongst us, to our Encouragement, reverently to trust in, and follow the Lord God of Mercy and Salvation, whose glorious Name had the Honour, worthy, worthy, for ever.

The 7th I had a Meeting with a few Friends at *Tipperary*, and some other People who gathered with them; but it seemed a cold place as to Religion. I went from thence to *Cashell*, where on the 8th I was at a Marriage of a couple of Friends, and the Lord was pleased to open his Gospel-doctrine, and lift up his own Power in an eminent manner, to our great Gladness and Satisfaction.

The 10th I had a Meeting at *Knockbally-magher*, pretty much to our Comfort; and the next Day was at two Meetings at *Mountrath*, wherein

wherein several weighty things were opened and declared, in the Life and Power of Truth, to the Help and Establishing of Friends in the Way and Practice of Righteousness.

The 12th I went to *Ballynakill*, and had a serviceable Meeting there that Evening. The 13th returned to *Mountrath*, to the Burial of a Friend, where I had an open, solid time in declaring the Truth amongst a large number of People, who were in general attentive and sober. The 14th I had a large and good relieving Meeting, thro' the Lord's Goodness plentifully extending to the Comfort of the Honest, and close Warning in divine Counsel to some earthly, wrong-spirited Persons there; and that Evening had another Meeting with some Friends at *Ballycorrell*; the 15th another at *Athy*; another the 16th at *Ballytore*; and went the 17th to *Catherlough*, where the Province Meeting began that Day; and the Lord our God, the sure Helper of his People, favoured us with his holy Presence, in a weighty, strengthning manner, to our great Comfort: The Affairs of Truth were managed in Diligence, and the peaceable Spirit of the Gospel. I lodged that Night at *Gregory Russel's*, where we had a precious time in the Evening. The 18th, being First-day, I had a large, weighty, and heavenly Meeting, and Friends parted in much Comfort and Warmness in the Truth, thro' divine Favour. I went that Night to *Samuel Watson's*, at *Killconner*, where on the

20th

20th I had a pretty open Meeting with Friends, in the Love of Chrift.

The 22d I had a large and edifying Meeting at *Waterford*; and the 23d I went to *Rofs*, where I had a Meeting with a few Friends, and fome other People who came in, though but a poor hard place. The 25th I was at a Monthly-meeting at *Lamb's-town*, pretty large and folidly profitable, though with fome heavy and clofe Labour amongft Friends, becaufe of divers things being out of good Order; yet the Love and Power of God mercifully reached forth amongft us, and his Name was glorified, to whom all is due.

The 26th I had a Meeting at *Wexford*; and the 27th another at *Ballyna-carrick*, which was a very clofe, fearching, warning time; yet healing to the Upright, and it was made a good Seafon. The 28th I had a Meeting at *Cavladine*, which was a pretty helpful time, to our Comfort, but with fome clofe Warning to fome ftiff-necked People; the 29th another at *Ballyna-clare*; and the 30th another at *Afkin-thynny*, where the Lord gave us a precious, comfortable Seafon, in the free goings forth of his awakening Power and Love, which much healed my deep travailing Soul, and his pure Name was glorified.

The 1ft of the ninth Month I had a large Meeting at *Ballycane*; and the 3d another at *Wicklow*. The 4th I came to *Dublin*, and was at a bleffed Meeting with Friends there the 6th.

On

On the 7th the Half-year's meeting began,
which continued four Days, and the Lord our
God graciously favoured us therein, by owning
and helping with his powerful Presence and
Wisdom, greatly to our Comfort ; and Friends
parted in Peace and heavenly Nearness, with
living Praises to the Almighty.

Whilst he staid at Dublin, *he wrote the
following Lines to Friends of* Wensleydale
Meeting, viz.

'MY *near* and *dear Friends*, who love
' Truth itself, and want to be what
' Heaven would have you, I beg of you all re-
' member, *It is I*, faith the Lord of old, *that
' will build and plant*; it is he, it is he, and no
' Hand else, that can do for Souls, what right
' Minds want. And he sees every where, both
' those who live upon something else, without
' the sensible Enjoyment of him, (who dwell
' often, nay much in dry Lands) and the truly
' hungry pained Souls, whom nothing else but
' the renewedly working, and secretly feeding,
' strengthning Power, and Hand from Hea-
' ven, can satisfy. Oh! these Criers and Fol-
' lowers on in humble Steadiness for heavenly
' Help, heavenly Bread and Water from the
' Hand of the all-mighty, all-seeing, and graci-
' ously tender Father ; these, these indeed, will
' be helped, and will grow in certain feeling,
' and redeeming Knowledge : And thus must
F f   ' every

‘ every degree of the Lord's Family, old and
‘ young, wife and lefs knowing, be led, and
‘ nurfed, and taught, and fed, and grow in the
‘ one Root, the one Life, and in the one Sub-
‘ jection, where Peace, Harmony, Onenefs of
‘ Heart, and the helpful running of the one
‘ healing Virtue is indeed witneffed. Oh !
‘ Elder and Younger, feel after it, ftoop till it
‘ runs thro' you, and then you will worfhip
‘ the Fountain, and grow in Care ; firft, and
‘ above all, over your own Spirits, and then
‘ in true Care in the Lamb's Spirit, over and
‘ towards the Houfhold : And yet the Sword
‘ and Hand of the Lamb of God, and Saviour
‘ of Souls, muft be known, both inwardly,
‘ and lifted up, by the Servants of Chrift, in
‘ Wifdom and Zeal againft Unrighteoufnefs,
‘ and the many Products of *Efau*'s Mountain ;
‘ the unbridled, flefhly Will and Affections of
‘ Man, which too many amongft the Lord's
‘ People would gladly have mixed amongft the
‘ Plants of Righteoufnefs, and would have vain
‘ Liberty, and darkening Carnality faved alive ;
‘ which is the Caufe of Death reigning over
‘ fome, inftead of Life : And the rebellious,
‘ felf-faving, unfaithful, turbulent Houfe of
‘ old *Saul*, rather grows ftronger in fome than
‘ the Houfe of *David* ; the confiding and
‘ humbly devoted Man. Well, *my dear* and
‘ *truly beloved Friends*, a pure, bright Open-
‘ nefs is over me, towards you at this time,
‘ beyond my expectation ; and leads me thus,

‘ in

‘ in the Love of him who appeared in the
‘ *Burning-bush*, (yet even that was in order to
‘ open a way for Deliverance and Help to
‘ *Israel*;) and whose loving, helping Hand hath
‘ been and is extended towards you, for the
‘ building of you up in Righteousnefs, and in
‘ the pure feeling Senfe of his faving Health.
‘ Oh! he is merciful and long-suffering, watch-
‘ ful over the needs of all the living, and in
‘ particular is mindful of the poor and low, yet
‘ fervently concerned Hearts ; even to the very
‘ leaft and weakeft, the moft humbled in true
‘ fear, amongft the whole Houfhold. Oh !
‘ haften, haften to draw near him, and feek
‘ his Face, that you may be prepared for him
‘ to fhine upon you ; for in his Prefence there
‘ is Life and fure Help, and true Welfare ; and
‘ that you may thus fare well indeed, is the
‘ Defire of your true Friend,

‘ JOHN FOTHERGILL.’

On the 12th of the ninth Month *(continues
the Journal)* I had a Meeting with Friends and
feveral other People at *Ballyhays*, to pretty good
Satisfaction.   The 13th at *Timahow*, and went
the 14th to our dear Friend *Thomas Wilfon*'s at
Thornwell. The 15th I was at a large and folidly edifying Meeting at *Edenderry*. The 17th
at *Kill*, and the 18th again at *Edenderry*. The
20th at the *Moat*, and the 22d had a Meeting
at *Jacob Fuller*'s to good Satisfaction.

F f 2

The

The 25th I was at Friends Monthly-meeting at the *Moat*, much to our Comfort and Strength in the Lord; and had a Meeting that Evening at *Lifmoiney*.

The 27th the Province-meeting began at *Edenderry*, and continued for the Affairs of Truth and publick Worſhip three Days, which the Lord was pleaſed to make a glorious heavenly and ſtrengthning Seaſon to Friends, and reaching to many others, and the moſt holy Name was glorified. That Evening and the next Morning I was at *Thomas Wilfon's*, where heavenly Life and Goodneſs very humblingly and ſweetly overſpread my Soul with many Friends, uniting us in a near manner at our parting from one another.

The 30th I went to *Dublin*, not knowing then but that I might go readily for *England*; but ſome heavy Exerciſe grew over my Spirit for ſeveral Days, and my way was blocked up at preſent for *England* (tho' I had ſome good Opportunities with Friends at *Dublin*) and under this mournful Exerciſe my Heart opened towards ſome Places in the North again, and alſo towards *Newport*, &c. in *Connaught*, which I had ſeen little of before; and in giving up in my heart to go, my Mind was ſet at liberty in living Sweetneſs again; and our Friend *Benjamin Holme* being there, and inclined to go that way, we went the 7th of the tenth Month to *Drogheda*, and had a Meeting there that Evening, ſeveral Friends being with us.

The

The 9th we had a large and pretty open Meeting at *Rathfryland*, in the Inn where we lodged ; and the 11th we went to *Lurgan*, where the Province-meeting began that Day, and continued two more : Several Services fell in the way here amongst Friends and the neighbouring People, towards whom the Lord was pleased to open my Mouth in his Power, fully to my Satisfaction and Comfort in coming thither at this time.

The 13th in the Evening we had a very large and powerful good time among the soberly-inclined People at *Warrenstown*, in *J. Greer*'s House, where we lodged ; and the 14th we went to *Lisburn*, and had a precious open Meeting that Evening with Friends and many of the Towns-people.

The 15th we went to *Newtown*, a place where not any of our Friends lived, and had a large Meeting in the Sessions-house ; the People generally were very civil.

The 16th we had a very large Meeting in the Court-house at *Belfast*, to our great Satisfaction, the People being unexpectedly loving ; there were no Friends in the place.

The 17th we came back, and had a Meeting at our ancient Friend *Tobias Courtney*'s ; and another large precious Meeting at *Lurgan* that Evening, much to my Ease and Comfort.

The 18th we went to *Ballyhagan*, and had a good little Meeting there that Evening with some few Friends, at *Thomas Greer*'s near *Charlymount*.   The

The 19th I set forward with *Benjamin Holme*, and some other Friends towards *Connaught*, and the 20th being First-day, we rode to *Inniskillin*, and that Afternoon got the Liberty of the Court-house, and had a large, good Meeting with the People of the Town, no Friends living near the place. The 21st we rode to *Ballyshannon*, and got a little Meeting of the Towns-people in our Inn that Night, and the next Day got to *Sligo*, and had a Meeting there the 23d in the Sessions-house, the Sheriff and several more of the People being very loving.

The 24th we rode to *Ballina*, but had much Trouble on the Way from the Waters; it being a very rainy Season, and we Strangers to the Road: But very providentially for us some Men came into our way, just before we came to a Bay on the Seaside, so that we had them to guide us over the Sands, we riding to our Horses Bellies, and often deeper, above a Mile, which we could not safely have done without their Assistance. We found no Friends here, nor many *English*. The 25th we went to *Castle-bar*, and got the 26th to *Newport*, where there are a few Friends; we staid here several Days, and had three large Meetings in the Court-house to our Satisfaction, through our Father's divine Help, many sober People coming in: And we had some good Service most of one whole Day among the few Friends there, whom we left in a good degree of
nearness

nearnefs in the Love and Covenant of God, to whofe heavenly Teaching and Help they were recommended. The 30th we came to *Gerſhon Boate*'s at *Dunmoor*, and had a good prevailing Seaſon that Evening, in the free Extendings of the Goſpel towards ſome civil People who came to our Meeting

The 1ſt of the eleventh Month we came to *Mary's-town* to *Gerſhon Boate*'s jun. and had a good and large Meeting of Friends and others the next Day, and ſome good Service with the Families in the Evening.

The 4th we had a peaceable and bleſſed Meeting in *Athlone*, many of the People, and the chief of the Town came in, and were very tender ; for the Power and Love of God was plentifully ſhed abroad among us to our Comfort. The 5th we had a Meeting at *Jacob Fuller*'s, a powerful and bleſſed time in the free reaching of divine Love to Friends and many others ; and a ſeaſonable good Meeting at the *Moat* the next day, and the day following a large and heavenly Meeting at *Richard Holme*'s, among many other People, to general Satisfaction ; and another that Night, to Comfort and good Service in the Love of Truth, at *Liſmoiney*.

The 9th we went to *Henry Fuller*'s at *Bally-tore*, and had a large and comfortable time in the Father's love with ſome Friends there that Night. The 10th we went to the Province-meeting at *Caſtledermot*, which held two Days, and

and Friends were helped in the Lord's Service together, and parted in Comfort. We came back to *Ballytore*, where we had a large Meeting in the Evening.————

If a Journal of the remaining part of this Visit was by him kept, it is either mislaid or lost: but the following Extract of a Letter wrote from this Place, to a Relation in Yorkshire, *dated where the Journal breaks off, will in part supply the Deficiency; to which is added an affectionate Memorial of his fervent Regard to the Friends of his own particular Meeting, from the same Place.*

' Dear Cousin G. M.

' IN fresh and near Love my dear Salutation
' often and now reacheth to thee and Mo-
' ther, with all my near and dear Friends
' about you, tho' under pain of Heart that I
' am unexpectedly so long detained from you;
' but for the free Assurance renewedly, that
' the heavenly Hand and holy living Power
' engageth me here for the good of Souls, and
' helping to build up the House for the Praise
' of the King of Righteousness.
' When I wrote to thee in the ninth Month,
' I thought I should have been with you in the
' tenth; and came to *Dublin*, not knowing
' but I might leave this Nation; but in the
' way a load of Sorrow and Weight grew
' upon me, and for most part of two Days I
' was

‘ was exceedingly diſtreſſed, till Life ſprang,
‘ and ſet ſeveral Parts of the Nation before me,
‘ both amongſt Friends and others ; and I was
‘ freely given up to turn back again, yea, to
‘ go wherever Truth required. Many Friends
‘ had ſaid, they could not but admire, if I
‘ went then away, and rejoiced at my being
‘ thus turned about. I had wrote again to thee
‘ at that time, but that I had ſent ſome Ac-
‘ count to Friends at the Quarterly-meeting at
‘ *York* of my Stay, from whence I conclude
‘ you heard where I was. I have travelled
‘ very cloſe during a Month, with great toil ;
‘ but ſatisfied as much as I could wiſh, that I
‘ was in the Lord’s Counſel and Work. I
‘ and three other Friends were ſeven Days and
‘ Nights, and had Meetings among other Peo-
‘ ple, without coming to any Friend’s houſe,
‘ and travelled hard, having in that time rode
‘ near 300 Miles in almoſt conſtant Rain, which
‘ hurt my Health ; however the glorious Name
‘ of the Lord was with us, and was magnified.

‘ When I had near gone thro’ this Service,
‘ inſtead of being able to look towards home
‘ with Chearfulneſs, there ſeemed like Dark-
‘ neſs to ſtand betwixt me and *England*, and
‘ my Heart is ſtill drawn another way, and to
‘ go thro’ the other Part of the Nation again ;
‘ which I dare not omit, or turn my back
‘ from, come what may : For Truth ſtill
‘ ſeems to open a Door for my Labour, wider
‘ and wider, both within, and to thoſe with-

G g

‘ out ;

' out ; fo that I have now no Expectation of
' feeing you before the middle of the firſt
' Month.————I hope to let thee hear farther
' from me when I get ſomewhat more diſ-
' charged, and am able to look homewards, or
' otherwiſe. I reſt this Day, which is more
' than I have done for many Weeks, yet am
' now pretty well in Health, only ſomewhat
' low at times, when I think of home, and my
' unexpected long Stay from you and my poor
' dear Children, for whom my bowels yearn
' in Love and tender Care, that they may be
' ſober, and ſeek to fear and love the Lord,
' and in ſo doing fare well ; and thus may you
' all fare well, fare well. I am thy loving
' Friend and Couſin,

' ·JOHN FOTHERGILL.

' *P. S.* Mayſt let Friends ſee the few Lines
' incloſed, *viz.*

' *To Friends of* Wenfleydale *Monthly-meeting*
' *in* Yorkſhire·

' DEAR FRIENDS,

' ALTHO' it is ordered that I am very un-
' expectedly detained from you thus long,
' yet holy Goodneſs hath been and is pleaſed
' to favour with renewed Confirmation to my
' full Satisfaction, in the daily attending my
' low and deep travailing Soul, with living
' Light

' Light and Help in his pure Prefence, both
' for daily Food and Qualification for the
' Lord's Service, wherein you are often truly
' frefh in my near Remembrance; both many
' particulars who are, I hope, waiting inwardly
' in Heart for pure heavenly Miniftration; and
' alfo in a general way : And deeply is my Soul
' often engaged in Prayer, that heavenly Help
' may frequently fpring in your Souls, and en-
' courage you fecretly, and engage your Hearts
' for the Caufe of the Lord in every refpect.
' And that you may, both Elder and Younger,
' Male and Female, be Encouragers and
' Helpers one of another in the Ways of
' Righteoufnefs, and to true Bleffednefs. And
' oh! *my near Friends*, that you may all thus
' labour in Heart and Soul, and feel after the
' loofening, fpringing of immortal Life ; to
' look to, and follow the Drawings of the pure
' Love of the Lord God, the Redeemer, the
' Succourer, the Strengthner of all the true
' and honourable Servants, young and old, in
' all Ages. So will Hearts be difintangled from
' the hurtful, weakning Affections towards
' Vifibles of all kinds, and will be gradually
' brought into more Dominion in feveral re-
' fpects, and fo will you grow both in the
' Knowledge of heavenly Favour, and in quiet
' Truft in that invifible, living Power, which
' is the fure Comfort of the Righteous, in
' and through their unpleafant, heavy Places,
' and which leads to fure Bleffing every way.

G g 2

' And

‘ And I pray mind the Work and Bufinefs of
‘ the Lord’s Houfe and Family, in the Lord’s
‘ Time, with due Diligence and Faithfulnefs,
‘ in your feveral places: So may, and I believe
‘ will, both Ability and Peace, and holy en-
‘ gaging Comfort from the living Rock of all
‘ the righteous Generations, be often with
‘ you ; and you will often fare well, and be
‘ nearer and favourily helpful one to another.
‘ And thus with thefe few poor Lines, freely
‘ and very nearly reacheth my dear Salutation
‘ to all the Living amongft you, I remain your
‘ *near Friend* and *engaged Brother* for the help
‘ and building up of all the Lord’s Children
‘ and People, to the Glory and Praife of the
‘ Lord God of Mercy and Salvation, worthy to
‘ be trufted in and followed fully for ever.

‘ JOHN FOTHERGILL.’

Towards the end of the Year 1725 *(as a
fhort Journal informs us)* he vifited fome of the
South parts of *England*, travelling with great
diligence through *Lancafhire, Chefhire, Staf-
fordfhire,* to *Birmingham,* having Meetings in
his way, as alfo at this Place, to his folid Satisfaction. From hence he went thro’ *Worcefter,*
into *Glocefterfhire,* and to *Briftol,* where he
was at feveral Meetings, and of the two laft,
being Firft-day, he notes that ‘ they were large,
‘ and the Seafons weighty, in the Attendance
‘ of the Gofpel-power ; the holy Teftimony
‘ whereof

' whereof was exalted, and prevailed over Cor-
' ruption and Vanity, to the Comfort of the
' Upright, and the Difcharge of his Spirit in a
' great degree, and the Name of the Lord God
' was humbly praifed and worfhiped.'

He went from hence thro' *Bath* into *Wilt-
fhire*, having Meetings in his way ; and at *La-
vington* an Evening-meeting, to which came
many fober People of the Town, among whom
the Lord opened his Heart and Mouth, in the
Gofpel-teftimony, which went forth freely towards them, and the Encouragement of the few
Friends in that Place. At *Broomham* Meeting,
where he was on a Firft-day, many of the
neighbouring People came in, as well as many
Friends, and the Lord favoured the Time with
his Power and holy Prefence, and exalted his
righteous Teftimony over all. From hence he
went to the *Devizes*, where he had a large
Meeting that Night, to which feveral of the
more confiderable People of the Town came,
and behaved foberly ; and the Doctrine of the
Gofpel fpread over all with weight, to general
Satisfaction, and the Glory of God, who alone
is worthy, and whofe Power, he adds, ' fuf-
' tained my bodily Ability, thro' much ex-
' tremely fpending Labour there-away, in a
' wonderful manner.'

After this he had a Meeting at *Melkfham*,
which he mentions as ' a clofe or plain-dealing
' Seafon ;' alfo at *Calne, Charlcot, Chippenham,*
and *Corfham*; which laft, he obferves, ' was
' very

‘ very large, Friends from many other Meet-
‘ ings being there ; and I was opened, *says he*,
‘ and helped to preach the Gospel in its own
‘ Power and Counsel, which through divine
‘ Goodness prevailed, to the Help and reviving
‘ of many, and to my great Ease of Spirit in
‘ that part of the Country, having been much
‘ exercised under a weighty Sense of a luke-
‘ warm, earthly Spirit among many Professors
‘ of Truth there-away ; yet the Lord rose
‘ against it, to the Awakening of several to
‘ more religious Fervency.’

He went from hence to *Marshfield, Dead-martin, Hullington* and *Tedbury*, at which Places he had Meetings which were pretty profitable and satisfactory. At *Nailsworth* he was at two Meetings, which were large, consisting both of Friends and other People of different Professions, and the Power and Testimony of the Gospel arose amongst them, to a good degree of Satisfaction. From this Place he went to, and had Meetings at *Penswick*, where he had a blessed strengthning Time, thro’ heavenly Goodness and Mercy ; and so to *Cirencester, Slow, Cambden, Bridgenorth,* and *Shrewsbury.* At *Namptwich* in *Cheshire* he had a Meeting at an Inn, which was an open time, in the free spreading of the Gospel, among many sober People, in the Love of God. After this he had Meetings at *Newton* and *Franley* in the same County ; from thence to *Wooldale* and *Hightown*, at both which Places he had satisfactory

factory Meetings, and got to *York* the 24th of the firſt Month, ' where, *ſays he*, Friends were ' truly comforted together, in the Power and ' Love of God, which attended the Meeting ' for our Help in his Service. From hence, *he* ' *adds*, I returned home, with Peace and true ' Satisfaction thro' the Lord's Favour, whoſe ' holy and great Name had, and hath the ' Praiſe, who is worthy to be feared, ſerved ' and magnified for ever.'

Whilſt he was upon his late Viſit in *Ireland*, he received an Account of the dangerous Indiſpoſition of one of his * Sons, in whom, tho' he was not then twelve Years of Age, ſuch Indications of ſolid Piety and Prudence above his Years, had appeared, as to render his Life very deſirable, and this Account the more afflicting to his Father ; who nevertheleſs was enabled to reply by Letter, that ' tho' he had all the ' Tenderneſs and Affection of a Parent for his ' Child, yet being ſatisfied he was from him

' in

---

* William Fothergill, *He died not long after of a tedious and painful Illneſs, which a peculiar Evenneſs of Temper, often tender'd and encouraged by a Senſe of divine Regard and heavenly Support, enabled him to bear with exemplary Patience and Reſignation. Many of his affecting Expreſſions are ſtill remember'd by thoſe who were then with him ; as well as many Inſtances of his Care and Fear, during the Time of his Health, not to offend the Almighty ; the ſweet Influence of whoſe awful Preſence, ſeem'd often to be upon him.*

' in the Counfel and Service of the Lord, he
' muft fubmit all to divine Difpofal.'

In the Year 1726, having performed the
feveral Services then before him, and finding
himfelf at liberty to engage in his temporal
Concerns, he began Houfe-keeping again, and
apply'd himfelf with diligence and alacrity in
the care of his Family and Bufinefs : Yet not
fo as to neglect a due Attendance of Meetings,
both for Worfhip and Difcipline, being feldom
abfent, whilft difengag'd from other publick
Service, from the Monthly and Quarterly-
meetings for his own County ; often attending
thofe of the neighbouring Counties likewife, as
well as the Yearly-meetings in *London*.

In the Year 1727 he married *Elizabeth Buck*
of *Netherdale*, a Perfon of a grave, becoming
Deportment, and fuitable Age ; with her he
lived in great Affection and Tendernefs the remaining part of his Life, fhe furviving him
not much more than a Year.

The next Account that we have of any publick Service, was a Vifit to Friends in *Wales*
and the South of *England*, of which we have
the following Relation.

BEING drawn in Spirit to vifit *Wales*, and
fome other parts Southwards ; in the fore
part of the fecond Month 1732 I began my
Journey for that end, and went by *Manchefter*
and *Chefter*, and fo to *Bala* in *Wales*, where
the Yearly-meeting for that Dominion was
held

held this Year ; and great was the Concourse of People, who in general behaved civilly, and were very attentive to the Testimony of Truth, which was livingly declared by many Friends, in the free movings of the Power of Truth that mercifully attended and assisted Friends in the several Services of that Meeting.

From thence I went with *John Goodwin* to his House at *Eskergaugha*, and was at the Meeting there the Day following, being First-day, wherein Truth prevailed to Friends Comfort, and the Help of some ; divers of the neighbouring People, then present, being under some Convincement at that Time.

From this place we travelled thro' a mountainous Country and difficult Roads to *Llandewy* in *Cardiganshire*, to *Thomas Evan's*, and had a little Meeting with a few Friends thereabouts the next Day, and went after Meeting to *John Reese's* in *Caermarthenshire*; but a Fair happening to be near the place, we could not have the Meeting before the Day following, when we had a good little Meeting with Friends there-away in the Morning, and then rode pretty fast to *John Bowen's*, to a Meeting which had been appointed there before. The Day following I travelled into *Pembrokeshire*, and came to *James Lewis's* House, not far from *Redstone*, from whence we went the next Day to *Haverfordwest* : Here I staid till the Fifth-day following, and had several Meetings with Friends, wherein, through the Help of Truth,

H· h

Friends

Friends feem'd fomewhat rouzed up in the way of their Duty, to their profit. From thence I came to *Jamfton*, and had a pretty good Meeting there, and took my leave of Friends of that County.

On the Sixth-day I came to *Laghorn*, where there are but few Friends, yet had a good Opportunity amongft them, and feveral others who came in and heard the Teftimony of Truth with appearance of Gladnefs.

The next Day I came to *Paul Bevan*'s at *Swanzey*, and the Day following, being Firft-day, was at two Meetings there, wherein the Power of Truth prevailed and gained Dominion, to the Help of many, and the Almighty was glorified.

From thence I came to *Trivereeg* to *John Bevan*'s, and next Morning had a little Meeting there, and went that Night to *Elifha Biddle*'s at *Pontipool*, where I had feveral Meetings to our Help, thro' the Lord's owning of us, bleffed be his Name.

The next Firft-day I was at *She-newton*, where there was a pretty large Meeting, which, through the Help of Truth, feemed to be of fervice. The Day following we croffed the *Severn* and got to *Briftol*, where their Yearly-meeting was begun; and it pleafed the Lord of all our Mercies eminently to own and help his People, greatly to our Comfort, and the Exaltation of his own Teftimony, which feem'd to make Impreffion on many Hearts, and the

glorious

glorious Name of the Lord our God was magnified.

I staid several Meetings after this in the City, much to my satisfaction, and from thence went to the Quarterly-meeting for *Glocestershire* held at *Thornbury*, which was large, and the Power and Goodness of the Lord was graciously extended among Friends, to the Comfort of the honest-hearted, and for the stirring up of the negligent amongst them ; for divine Counsel and Virtue was strongly with us, in the Love of God.

I went that Night to *Sudbury*, and next Day to a Meeting at *Melksham* in *Wiltshire*, where the blessed Truth, and its own Testimony, arose and prevailed to our Encouragement.

The next Day I had a large Meeting at *Charlcott*, and another that Evening at *Caln*, which the Lord manifestly owned, and made truly helpful to the Upright in heart, as well as awakening to the dull and earthly-minded.

The next Day I had a Meeting at the *Devizes*, where the Presence and Help of the Lord was truly comfortable, and confirming in a dependance upon him, to the Praise of his own Name. That Evening I rode to *Marlborough* to a Meeting appointed there. The number of Friends there is but small, and are weakly in Religion ; yet Help reached towards them in the Love of God.

From hence I went to *Newbury*, and the Day following, being First-day, had two

 Meetings

Meetings pretty much to satisfaction, and there seemed reason to hope, that Friends there, who had formerly been hurt, may yet recover in a religious Mind, and become a good Meeting.——

The Account of this Journey breaking off here, and no other mention of it occurring in any of the Papers he has left, makes it probable, that he went from hence to the Yearly-meeting at London *pretty directly, and was prevented by other Occurrences there from continuing it to his Return home.*

He attended the Quarterly-meeting at York, *as was usual with him, when disengaged from other Services, and went from thence to* Scarborough, *where he staid some time, it being the* Spaw-season, *and many People of Note then frequenting it.*

The Year following he was engaged to visit some of the Southern parts of England *again, and has left the following Account of it, viz.*

IN the Year 1733, a fresh Concern came upon me to visit some of the South and West parts of *England*, and the Time to set forward seem'd to be in the latter part of the ninth Month: I accordingly left my Family the 20th, and was at *Leeds*, *Wakefield* and *Hightown*, and to *Bradford*, where my Friend *Benjamin Bartlet*, being under a Concern to go with me, was making ready for the Journey, and on the

30th

30th we set out for *Sheffield*, where we staid First-day, and then went pretty directly into *Warwickshire*, where we had Meetings at *Badgley* and *Wigginsal*, and on the Seventh-day got to *Birmingham* ; where on the Day following we had two large Meetings, which were preciously attended by heavenly Power, much to the Comfort of the living, and tending to rouze up the negligent, to our great Gladness in the Lord.

The 2d of the tenth Month we went to *Wolverhampton*, and that Evening had a Meeting with the few Friends in that Place, to which came many soberly-behaved People, towards whom the Love of God extended, much to our Comfort.

The 3d we had a Meeting at *Dudley*, wherein Truth owned us, to the Help of Friends ; and the 4th we went back to *Birmingham*, to a Burial, which was attended by a large number of People ; and thro' divine Favour, it was made a time of profit to many.

The 5th we went to *Sturbridge*, and the 6th to *Broomsgrove* ; at both which places we had Meetings ; and on the 7th to *Worcester*, where on First-day we were at two Meetings, to pretty good satisfaction ; as also a comfortable Season in the Evening, with a pretty many Friends who came to see us, at *John Corbyn*'s.

On Second-day we went to *Evesham*, where on the Day following we had a Meeting with Friends, and rode that Night to *Tewksbury*, and

had

had a Meeting with Friends there that Evening, which the Lord was pleafed to attend with
his Power, to our great Encouragement.

On Fourth-day we went to *Glocefter*, and had
a comfortable little Meeting with the few Friends
there that Evening ; and another at *Nailfworth*
on Fifth-day. The next Day we had a Meeting at *Slattenford*, where Friends from divers
other Places met us, and the Lord was pleafed
to comfort and encourage our Hearts together,
in the bleffed fenfe of his living Power.

On Seventh-day we came to *Bath*, and had
two Meetings there next Day, and rode to *Briftol* the Third-day Morning, to the Meeting held
there that Day, wherein we were favoured
with the fenfe of ancient and divine Help to
our Comfort. We ftaid at *Briftol* a Week,
and had feveral Meetings there, one of which
was very large on account of a Burial ; thro'
all which Opportunities the ancient Power and
Prefence of the Lord owned and ftrengthned
us, and the Lord God was magnified.

The 2d of the eleventh Month we went to
Portfhed, and had a pretty large and profitable
Meeting. On Fifth and Sixth-day we had
Meetings at *Sittcot* and *Bridgwater* ; and from
hence to *Taunton*, *Minehead*, *Milverton*, *Wel-
lington*, *Spiceland*, and *Columpton* ; in all which
places we had Meetings, and fome profitable
Seafons in them.

On Firft-day we were at a pretty large
Meeting at *Exeter*, and the next Day had a
good

good time, and some good Service with Friends there in their Monthly-meeting for the Affairs of the Church. On Third-day we had a Meeting with Friends, and some Neighbours that came in at *Abbot-Caswel*, and another next Day in the Evening at *Totness*. On Fifth-day we went to *Kingsbridge*, and had a comfortable Meeting with Friends there ; and another on Sixth-day in the Evening at *Hulyton*, to which came several sober People, with whom we had a good Opportunity. On Seventh-day we went to *Plymouth*, and on First-day had two remarkable Meetings there, thro' the powerful working of Truth. On Second-day we went to *German*'s in *Cornwal*, and had a blessed Meeting with Friends there that Evening. On Third-day we went to a Meeting at *Liskard*, to which many Friends came from distant places, and the Lord helped us graciously to our Comfort. On Fourth-day we had a Meeting at *Loo*, where the Lord's Power and Wisdom plentifully owned and relieved our Souls, and much encouraged Friends.

On Fifth-day we went to *Austil*, and had a large and helpful Meeting there, through the Arisings of divine Power, tending to establish in the Faith, and in the Practice of the Gospel. We lodged that Night at *Samuel Hopwood*'s, who went with us on Sixth-day towards the *Land's-end* ; near which Place, at *Sennan*, we had a large and open Meeting on the First-day following, and then came back to *Penzance* to

a Meeting

a Meeting that Evening, to which came many of the Towns-people. On Second-day we had a Meeting with Friends there-abouts, at *Market-Jew*, and came that Night to *Fal-mouth*, where on Third-day we had a Meeting with Friends, which the Lord our God greatly favoured in the powerful Extendings of his Gospel-life and Wisdom for Friends Help, in a saving manner. On Fourth-day we had a Meeting at *Key*, where some other People came in, and Truth was pleased to own us, and open us towards them, for their true Information, and the Comfort of Friends.

On Fifth-day we went a-cross the Country to *Warebridge*, on Sixth-day to *Port-Isaac*, and had a good Meeting with Friends, and a pretty many soberly-behaved People, thro' the free Extendings of the Virtue of the Gospel. We lodged at *John Scantlebury*'s, who went with us on First-day Morning to a place called *Dennis*, where we had a glorious and precious Meeting in a Field, with many hundreds of People who were met there, and behaved with remarkable Sobriety. We afterwards rode to *Austil* to *Samuel Hopwood*'s, where we had a good Opportunity with several Friends who came to see us that Evening.

On Second-day we came to *Milton*, and had a good little Meeting with Friends who live there-about ; another on Third-day at *Colling-ton*, and went on Fourth-day to *Oak-hampton*, where on Fifth-day we had a Meeting, in which

which the Lord favoured us with his living Prefence, and enabled us to publifh the Teftimony of the Gofpel among fome fober People of the Town, who came in; and for the Help of Friends, who had been exercifed by a wrong and dividing Spirit, which had enfnared fome of them, and particularly a Man and his Wife, with whom, and fome others, we had much labour after Meeting.

On Sixth-day we came to *Exeter*, and on Firft-day we had a large and helpful Meeting, in the Love of Truth, to the humbling and true Benefit of many. On Second-day we were at their Monthly-meeting for the Affairs of the Church, where we had fome Service, in the continued merciful Helpings of Truth. On Fourth-day we had a Meeting at *Chard*, of which previous Notice having been given, feveral Friends met us there from divers Places; and that Night we had a large and weighty Meeting at *Ilminfter*. On Fifth-day we had a large and baptizing Meeting at *Long-Sutton*, thro' the merciful prevailing of the Gofpelpower; and another in the Evening with Friends at *Somerton*. On Sixth-day we went to a Meeting at *Glaftenbury*, which was pretty large, and an edifying Seafon, in the prevailing of the Power of Truth, and the almighty Helper had the Glory.

On Firft-day we were at a General-meeting at *Puddimore*, to which fome fober People came, as well as pretty many Friends, and

Truth

Truth extended comfortably towards them. On Second-day we had a pretty large Meeting at *Shipton-mallet*, of divers sober People besides Friends, and the Love and Power of the Lord our God were amongst us.

On Third-day we came to *Froome*, and had a Meeting there in the Evening, which was very large, and of various Professions, many of whom attended to the Testimony of Truth, which ran freely forth amongst them; and we were much eased in that Meeting, and comforted in the Lord.

On Fourth-day we came to *Bradford* in *Wiltshire*, and had a Meeting with Friends there, and lodged at *Joseph Hull*'s, where several Friends came to see us, and the Lord gave us a good Season together that Evening.

On Fifth-day we came to *Tedbury*, and had a Meeting there with Friends, and some others who came in, to our Comfort, in the sense of divine Mercy and Regard extended to us.

On Sixth-day we had a Meeting at *Cirencester* in the Evening, which was to our Satisfaction; as were likewise two Meetings which we were at on the First-day following at *Shipton*.

On Second-day we went to *Benjamin Kidd*'s at *Banbury*, and the next Day to a Meeting at *South-newton*, where Friends from several other Meetings came, and the Lord our God mercifully favoured us, and gave us a blessed Opportunity together.

On

On Fourth-day we went to *Warwick*, where we had a Meeting among Friends, truly to our Comfort, in the prevailing of the Lord's Power: We came to *William Gulson*'s at *Coventry* that Night, and the next Day had a large Meeting there, wherein the Love and Power of Christ gloriously prevailed, and the Lord our blessed Helper had the Honour, who is worthy for ever. On Sixth-day we had a Meeting at *Nuneaton*, where many sober People came, and the Gospel of Salvation extended freely towards the Meeting, and had a comfortable Impression on many Hearts; we came back to *Nathaniel Newton*'s at *Hartshill* to a Meeting on the First-day, where many People from distant parts were gathered, both Friends and others, and the Lord opened the Testimony of the Gospel of Salvation, through Faith in his Name, in a precious manner; and we parted with Friends in a near sense of the Love and Power of God, and to his Praise.

On Second-day we set out for the North, visiting several Friends by the way, and came that Night to *Derby*.

On Third-day we visited some who were lately convinced in that hard Town, with whom we were comforted, and left them in hope. We came that Night to *Breech*, expecting to have had a Meeting there that Evening, but the intended Notice had failed; so came to *Chesterfield*, where we had a Meeting on Fourth-day, wherein the Arm of the Lord our God

I i 2

reached

reached mercifully for the help and building up in the moſt precious Faith, to our Gladneſs and Comfort ; tho' we were very ſenſible of a loſs to the Meeting, by reaſon of ſeveral Friends being abſent.

On Fifth-day, being the 6th of the firſt Month, we came to *Bradford*, being both well, and in true Love and Nearneſs one to another. ———

Among the Papers containing an Account of this Viſit, was the following Epiſtle to a Quar-terly-meeting which they were prevented from attending in Perſon, viz.

' DEAR FRIENDS,

' ALTHO' we had once a Deſire and hope
' to be with you at this Meeting, yet
' now it is otherwiſe order'd ; nevertheleſs
' ſome Concern reſts with us to ſend you a few
' Lines, in a near and encouraging Salutation,
' in a ſure Senſe of our Father's Love to you
' all, who have been born of incorruptible
' Seed, by the humbling Workings of the
' Power of the Word of God, which liveth
' and abideth for ever ; and who have a careful
' Concern at heart to be nouriſhed and quick-
' ened by its freſh Springs of Life, which is
' the Light of Men, in a religious ſenſe, thro'
' all Ages : We having to hope and believe,
' there are ſuch among you, who of neceſſity
' muſt often be under deep Affliction of Spirit,
' both

' both for the fake of our profeffed Brethren,
' and efpecially for the Honour of Truth, and
' the Peace and Welfare of the Church.

' And deep longing is in our Souls, and we
' accordingly with Earneftnefs advife, that you
' all may feek rightly for the powerful Influ-
' ences of this bleffed and incorruptible Seed
' in yourfelves, fo that you may be born of it,
' into the heavenly Relation and Union, by
' that divine Word which ever lives ; and fo
' will you become fpiritually-minded, and Par-
' takers together of that one Life, which hath
' made the Lord's People one in Heart : And
' by, and in the Light of this divine Life,
' the Faithful have received a true Underftand-
' ing and found Judgment, and are likewife
' preferved in Onenefs, both of Judgment and
' Practice, in confeffing Chrift before Men ; for
' God is one, and his Way is one for ever.

' But, on the other hand, many amongft
' us, fuffering the Earth, and the Flefh with
' its by-ends, to cover or load the divine Seed,
' or its Appearance in their Hearts, know not
' what it is to be born of it, and fo come not
' into the heavenly Relation and Brotherhood,
' nor to be Witneffes of the one Life arifing
' in, and leavening their Hearts and Spirits into
' true Godlinefs ; nor what it is to become
' Walkers in the Light, in the one Way, and
' one Practice, to the Glory and Honour of
' the one Faith, and Order of the Houfe

' and

‘ and Family of the one Truth, and un-
‘ changeable God.

‘ Oh *Friends!* that you may be prevailed
‘ with to apply yourselves to confider thefe
‘ Obfervations duly in yourfelves ; and be
‘ helped to feek the Power and Life of the
‘ Word, and to wait for and walk in the one
‘ heavenly Light, fo as that you may know it
‘ more and more, and be baptized into the
‘ true Onenefs, and may follow the one ever-
‘ lafting High-prieft abundantly more, and to
‘ your own unfpeakable Comfort.

‘ But you may remember, fome of the
‘ ancient profeffed Believers were fo negligent
‘ and unhappy, as to continue in the carnal
‘ Mind ; and fo Divifions were amongft them,
‘ and various, felfifh, and pernicious Practices ;
‘ fome efteeming Perfons more than Chrift the
‘ Truth, which, tho’ they were fuch as were,
‘ or had been rightly prepared, and fent in
‘ his Name for their Gathering, was highly
‘ offenfive to God :   And as the fame Caufe
‘ will produce the fame hurtful Effects, we in-
‘ treat you, our *Friends,* even thro’ the County,
‘ both Elder and Younger, in order to avoid
‘ and to be helped out of thefe Inconvenien-
‘ cies and Danger of greater Hurt, feek after,
‘ and wait with due Diligence to feel the
‘ Power of the Word of Life to fill your
‘ Hearts, and alfo for frefh Arifings of the
‘ pure humbling Life and Light thereof ; fo
‘ will you become a more living People, and
‘ much

‘ much more truly religious and zealous for
‘ the Lord, yet in that Wisdom which comes
‘ from the Lord Jesus Christ, the one Head
‘ of the true Church ; and your Eyes will be
‘ opened and kept open, and your Ears too,
‘ to see and distinguish the true Shepherd
‘ and his Voice, from the alluring, enticing,
‘ seducing Stranger’s, both respecting the Gain,
‘ and the Liberties of the Spirit of the World ;
‘ and concerning that crafty, self-seeking, con-
‘ tentious Spirit, which hath captivated some
‘ in divers places, to their Hurt and Shame
‘ already, as well as in a sorrowful degree in
‘ some other parts, to the scandal of Religion :
‘ And of which Spirit, and deceiving Endea-
‘ vours to sow Discord, and scatter into by-
‘ ways for its own Honour and Advantage,
‘ without any true Regard to the Honour of
‘ God, *be you all warned and stand clear*, left
‘ any should become Instruments thereby of
‘ more Hurt and Confusion, than yet hath
‘ been amongst you.

‘ Thus have we endeavoured to discharge
‘ ourselves towards you, in the certain Sense of
‘ the Love and Good-will of God, which hath
‘ not only opened our Understandings and
‘ Hearts on your Account in divers respects,
‘ but seemed to point out this Way to discharge
‘ ourselves towards Friends of your County,
‘ that it may be more generally seen, if you
‘ be willing to send Copies hereof to them,
‘ which we desire ; and remain your truly
‘ loving

‘ loving Friends in the Sincerity of the Gof-
‘ pel of Chrift, our Lord and Saviour, and
‘ Law-giver.

The 9th of the twelfth   ‘ JOHN FOTHERGILL,
  Month, 1733-4.
                          ‘ BENJAMIN BARTLET.’

In a Letter to a Friend, dated from Port-
Ifaac, *upon this Journey, he gives the following
Account.*

———— ‘ My Health is fuftained mercifully,
‘ and holy Help afforded to live, and labour
‘ in the Service for which I am drawn here-
‘ away; in a manner which occafions reve-
‘ rent bowing of Soul before the Lord, and
‘ revives my Faith in his Name, who hath, as
‘ it is his due, the Praife of all: And tho’ it is
‘ a Time of great Lownefs here-away, refpect-
‘ ing that Dominion, which Chrift fhould have
‘ in the Hearts of his People; yet the Father’s
‘ Love in Mercy often ftrongly runs, and in
‘ part prevails, to the Comfort and Joy of the
‘ truly inward: And the fearching, piercing
‘ Labour, at times, makes fome Impreffion,
‘ giving to hope, that it will not be quite in
‘ vain. However, the Arm of the Lord is
‘ working, and helps the truly Honeft, where-
‘ of we have a fhare of Rejoicing in him, and
‘ holy Thankfulnefs for his humbling Help
‘ from day to day; and my Heart is deeply
‘ reverent at this Time in mentioning divine
                                        ‘ Mercy

‘ Mercy herein.   We have been through one
‘ Side of *Somerfetfhire*, moft of *Devon*, and at
‘ the *Land's-end* in this County : We expect
‘ it will be near three Weeks before we get
‘ thro' *Somerfetfhire*, from whence we propofe
‘ to go homewards pretty readily.

‘ J. F.’

About the Year 1733 his fecond Son, *Thomas
Fothergill*, died in the twenty-fecond Year of
his Age ; of whom, our Father has been often
heard to fay, that *he never once difpleafed him* ;
And as he had *feared* God, and *honoured his
Parents* from his youth upwards, fo he felt his
Diffolution approaching without Terror, and
departed in Innocency and Peace. And fo
manifeft was the religious Awe that was upon
him, both in Meetings, and in his general
Converfation, as often to imprefs the Beholders
with a fenfe thereof, and to excite fome that
were lefs regardful of their Duty in this refpect,
to more diligence.

After he return'd from this laft Vifit, he was
not any long time together abfent from home :
He vifited neverthelefs many of the neighbouring Meetings, and was often concerned, by
Letters to advife, both fuch of his Children
as were not under his immediate Tuition,
alfo many particular Perfons, as well as fome
Monthly and Quarterly-meetings, to mind the
Day of their Vifitation, and humbly, feri-

K k

to seek the Lord and his Truth ; and so was he
often the instrumental means of Assistance and
Encouragement to many in their religious Duties. As some such Letters have been preserved,
that were wrote about this time, we thought
it not improper to insert some Extracts from
them in this place, *viz.*

' DEAR SON,

' IT is not unpleasant to have necessary Occa-
' sions of writing to thee given me, because
' I doubt not but to hear from me is very ac-
' ceptable : And as a degree of divine Love, I
' believe, tinctures my Spirit, both in remem-
' bring and in writing to thee ; I hope there
' may some helping Encouragement attend it,
' and profitably affect thee in the best Sense ;
' which, as a Longing or Desire hath been
' begot, and some Tastes afforded thee in the
' Father's Good-will, he will not neglect, tho'
' he suffers a plunging into Sorrow, and Doubt
' of getting rightly along, to attend ; in order
' to keep best Care and Pursuit necessarily vi-
' gorous, and secondary things in their places ;
' which is the Safety, Beauty and true Riches
' of Men. For heavenly Care leads to a quiet
' and ballanced sort of living and walking
' here on Earth ; a Favour and Privilege of
' unspeakable Advantage, and which Multi-
' tudes deprive themselves of, by bending their
' chief, and many almost their whole Appli-
' cation to seek Terrestrials ; and so want the
' Stay

' Stay of all Stays in needful times. Thus
' near Love and Care in my Heart, ceaseth not
' to prompt me to desire and long for thy
' right Improvement, which I am still given
' renewedly to hope will be granted.'——

—— ' My true Salutation attends thee, under
' a continued Desire that thou mayst often re-
' verently and duly keep in mind, from whom
' all lasting Good comes, and whose Addition
' to our Endeavours, gives the valuable Im-
' provement, and that labouring to walk and
' act in steady Regard to, and Hope in God,
' will bring the most holy Quiet, and Serenity
' of Mind at home, and gain the most truly
' honourable Regard abroad; and at the same
' time help to walk safely on this Sea of Glass,
' to which this World may be well compared;
' wherefore look carefully to Truth, and the
' Beauty of its Simplicity, and thou will have to
' behold the reeling, chaffy Spirit, and Ways of
' this World, rather with an eye of scorn than
' love, and be thankful that thou art in mea-
' sure already gather'd and set above it. And
' it will be good to consider also, that though
' Diligence is a great and necessary thing, and
' in seeking divine Favour the most profitable,
' because therein is all Treasure, both for Time
' and Eternity, and there is certainly a Blessing
' from God on the truly diligent; yet it may
' likewise be necessary to remember, that the
' *Race is not always to the Swift*, but Patience,

K k 2

' with

‘ with the Exercife of Faith in the hidden
‘ Arm of Power, brings to fee great things
‘ many ways : And thus, *dear Child*, may the
‘ Hand of the God of the Living be with thee,
‘ and guide thee in his Counfel, and to his
‘ Praife ; and this is my earneft Longing for
‘ thee.’————

———— ‘ Thy lownefs and doubtful ftyle, on
‘ the greateft Account, affected me nearly, yet
‘ hath not been very painful to me, becaufe
‘ every Birth (of divine Appointment) is at-
‘ tended with prefent Uneafinefs, and in a
‘ certain, and fometimes very heavy manner ;
‘ and the Senfe of the Danger and Difficulty,
‘ tho’ fometimes it fwells to a difcouraging de-
‘ gree, yet hath this Effect with the Honeft ;
‘ it improves Fear and Care with earneft and
‘ humble Diligence, in walking mindfully,
‘ and breathing the more hungrily after the
‘ Succour and Stay of the invifible Hand,
‘ which delights in doing his Children good,
‘ and feeding yet with feeming Shortnefs of
‘ meafure, and without that Difpatch of the
‘ Work which the Creature would have ; fo
‘ that it requires Time to learn neceffary Pa-
‘ tience, and what it is to live by Faith ;
‘ wherefore, *dear Son*, as a wife Man hath
‘ exhorted, *with all thy getting get Under-*
‘ *ftanding* ; I accordingly intreat thee, to feek
‘ principally after Improvement in Acquaint-
‘ ance with the fanctifying Hand, and to
‘ learn

' learn the Way and the End of its turning;
' and also that Stilness is required, when we
' see that no Hand but the Lord's can open the
' Way, and bring the long'd-for Help; and
' yet that Help and Salvation is to be looked
' for reverently and hopingly; and in so ap-
' plying on our part, the Lord our gracious
' God doth, and will delight to regard, and
' work so, that his Arising may fill the Soul,
' and engage it in present Gladness, and
' strengthned Faith in his Arm, and renewed
' Trust yet to travel on: And thus his gracious
' Workings bring forth Praise and holy Ad-
' miration, to his great and mighty Name,
' wherein alone is that Salvation, and those
' Riches, that are good for all.
' May the feeling Knowledge hereof, and
' an humble Hope and Trust to be guided and
' ballanced by the invisible holy One, guard
' and stay thee, thro' the unsettling Struggles
' that may attend thee: For betwixt the Con-
' verse and Pursuits of the unmortified World,
' however polish'd by human Endeavours, and
' the earthly Nature in ourselves, with the gild-
' ed Appearance of Penetration, Comprehen-
' siveness of Reasoning and Finesse, of many
' among the more learned part of Mankind,
' and the little, low, yet pure and powerful
' Seed, which at times makes itself known
' indisputably, yet hides itself again: Creatures
' are liable to dangerous Tossings; and good
' Beginnings, Ideas, and Desires of God's own

' begetting

' begetting, have unhappily miscarried, and
' instead of coming nearer the Experience of
' Salvation being as Walls and Bulwarks about
' them, in a quiet Habitation ; too many (for
' want of carefully looking towards the true
' Port) have been gradually, by one Wave after
' another, carried off to Sea again, and ship-
' wreck'd in the loose, unbottomed Concep-
' tions and Interests of this World. Wherefore
' cleave close, I pray thee, to the immoveable
' Rock, the spiritual Appearance of the Father
' and the Son, in whom is all Might, and all
' Sufficiency ; and I fully believe he will be
' thy God, thy Saviour, thy Shepherd, to lead
' and feed thee, thy Shield and exceeding great
' Reward. *Amen.* The best Love is fresh up-
' on me towards thee to my Comfort ; and
' hath drawn me thus to make these Observa-
' tions for thy Caution and Encouragement in
' the best Pursuits.'————

———— ' As my Mind hath been concerned
' in much affectionate Care on thy Account,
' and sometimes a lively Hope hath affected
' my Soul with Comfort, that thou might
' become a Man for God, and so to walk in
' his Fear, that he might be pleased to ma-
' nifest his gracious Care over thee ; so I am
' under both humble and anxious Desires, that
' thou may watch against the Pollution of the
' lying Vanities of this corrupting Age, and
' the Spirit of the World ; being well and
' thoroughly assured the divine Being requires it

' at

‘ at our Hands, and is only well pleaſed with
‘ thoſe who walk uprightly before him, and
‘ are truly afraid of, and therefore ſteadily
‘ ſtrive againſt, leaning to any Thoughts or
‘ Practices which are contrary to the divine
‘ Mind, either in greater or in leſſer matters;
‘ and they have the eaſieſt Work of it, who
‘ are the moſt duly reſolute in early time, and
‘ firmly ſtand and walk according to Under-
‘ ſtanding; whereas bending a little here, and
‘ a little there, (for which Excuſes will be
‘ ready at hand, but of the evil one’s preparing)
‘ and yielding and leaning aſide, always weak-
‘ ens and enſlaves, and renders that dwarfiſh,
‘ which the Lord of all Power would make
‘ ſtrong, healthy and ſound, and able to walk
‘ in his way with Alacrity.’————

In the Year 1736 *he made the neceſſary Pre-*
parations for his third and laſt Viſit to America,
which had been before him a conſiderable Time:
From the ſhort Minutes he kept of it, we have
tranſcribed the following Narrative, and inter-
ſperſed ſuch Epiſtles as have come to our Hands,
that were wrote in this Journey.

SOME Exerciſe having been upon me ſome
Years to viſit the Churches in *America*
once more, it now became weighty and clear
before me, that the proper Time was come for
the Performance of that Service; I therefore
prepared myſelf for the Journey, having the
Concurrence and near Unity of my Friends,
and

and left my dear Wife and Family the 17th of the second Month 1736, and went to *Leeds*, and had several Meetings amongst Friends, as I found it with me, in my way by *Manchester*, *Warrington*, thro' a part of *Cheshire*, *Staffordshire*, and by *Coventry*, *Alesbury*, *Jordans*, and so to *London*. Having many good Meetings, in the sense of the Love and Power of Truth amongst Friends, in many places.

After some Weeks stay with Friends at *London*, in the Labour of the Gospel, under the merciful Assistance of the Power and Love of God, my Spirit being clear and at Liberty, and a Ship being ready, I went on board at *Gravesend*, in the Ship called the *Jane*, bound for *Philadelphia*, the 9th of the fourth Month: We set sail the next Day, and arrived safe and well at *Philadelphia* the 6th of the sixth Month, having an easy, good Passage, and more especially so, because of the Favour of the lively sense of the divine Presence being often renewed, under which my Soul humbly worshiped God, who is worthy for ever.

I lodged at *Israel Pemberton*'s, but staid not long there-away, finding my Mind most drawn to hasten towards *Maryland* and *Virginia*, and set forward the 14th of the sixth Month, several Friends accompanying me to *John Richardson*'s, near *Christen-creek*; and from hence to *Newcastle*, *Cecil*, and so over *Chester* and *Choptank* Rivers, having several profitable Meetings in the way. And not far from the Banks of this last River, we had a Meeting in a
Forest,

Foreſt, at one *Jeremiah Jadwin's,* amongſt a People little acquainted with the Doctrines of Truth; yet pretty many gathered there, behaving with Sobriety and Attention, and the Power of Truth came into dominion amongſt us, much to our Satisfaction: After Meeting we lodged with one *Richard Cooper,* a loving, generous old Man, and a Perſon of Note in that part of the Country.

The 1ſt of the ſeventh Month I had a Meeting at *Little-creek,* from whence many Friends accompanied me to a Meeting at *Mother-kill,* which the Loving-kindneſs of God very mercifully regarded, and gave Friends comfort in his Preſence, amongſt a poor unfaithful People.

On the 4th we had a Meeting at *Lewiſtown* in the Court-houſe, which was a pretty open, profitable Seaſon. Alſo on the 5th at *Coldſpring,* and another in the Evening at *Charles Dingy's,* both to good Satisfaction. From hence I ſet out for *Virginia,* and Notice having been given in the Country, we had a pretty large Meeting on the 9th near *Swanſgut,* a little within the Confines of *Virginia,* which was to good Satisfaction in the Aſſiſtance of Truth, though I had the *Ague* then upon me.

On the 10th, as ſoon as I could bear to ride, *Edward Mifflin* and I ſet forward, and came that Night to *Paul Crippin's,* a Friend near *Muddy-creek,* where formerly a Meeting had been ſettled; but by gradually mixing with the Spirit of the World, and ſo into Marriages

L l   with

with others out of the way of Truth, the Elders being dead, the Youth turn'd their backs of Truth, and the Meeting was quite drop'd : I had no freedom to appoint a Meeting there, and so set out the next Day towards *Neswaddacks*, where Notice had been given of our Intention to have a Meeting there the next Day, which was the first of the Week. The Meeting was held in the Meeting-house where formerly there had been a pretty number of Friends, but now they are near gone, through the Love of the World, with its Enjoyments and Liberties; so that a Meeting is hardly kept there; but pretty many of the Neighbours gathered, and **we** had a Meeting, which was comfortable to me, in my Faithfulness to the Lord; tho' they seem'd to have but little Sense of God, or the Operation of Truth; for indeed a Cloud of carnal Indifferency appeared to me, to have overspread almost all that part of the Country in an uncommon manner.

From hence we set out for the Yearly-meeting on the *Western-shore*, but by the Difficulties we met with in crossing the Bay, one Day of it was over before we arrived : We had however two Days Meetings with a solid religious body of Friends there, and a pretty many others, whose Behaviour was sober and commendable; and the Lord our God was pleased to bless the Opportunity with his Presence and Wisdom, to the Satisfaction of many, and his holy Name was glorified. We visited several Friends

Friends here-away, and then went towards *Carolina*, having Meetings in divers places, one especially near *Perquimons-head*, which was large and satisfactory ; and another at a new Meeting-house near *Perquimons-river*.

On the 25th I went from hence towards *Paspitank-River*, and was at a Meeting of Friends there the 26th, which was made in good measure comfortable, to God's honour, to whom it is due : And tho' I was exceeding weak, by reason of a very sharp Return of the *Ague*, which came upon me the Day before, yet on Third-day following we had a Meeting up the River at *Amos Trueblood's*, chiefly consisting of other People, which, in the Lord's Help, was much to our Satisfaction. I had likewise a Meeting at *Little-river*, and another up the same River, tho' very weak in body.

The 1st of the eighth Month I got to *Perquimons*, where the Yearly-meeting was held for *North-Carolina*, and began that Day ; it was pretty large, but I was scarcely able to sit the Meeting, thro' the Violence of my Disorder. On the 2d the Meeting was still larger, and I was enabled to declare the Truth, in its own Ability and Wisdom, to the Help and Comfort of the Upright : And the Power and Love of Truth tended much to season and fit Friends to transact the Affairs of the Church, which were that Day brought before them. The Meeting ended the next Day, but I was too much indisposed to attend it.

On

On the 4th I set out for *Virginia*, full of Peace, tho' very weak, and the next Day had a comfortable Meeting at *Thomas Newby's*, with some Friends and other neighbouring People. Also the Day following another at *L. Buffkin's*, which was pretty large and comfortable. Thro' the Lord's Goodness my Indisposition now began to wear off, and I was enabled to travel with more ease. On the 7th I had a Meeting near *Joseph Pleasant's*, where through divine Mercy, which was graciously amongst us, we had a good Season. I staid here visiting Friends in their Families in the Neighbourhood two Days, and on the 10th, which was First-day, was at a Meeting not far off ; and had a merciful and livingly edifying time that Evening, with several Friends who came to see me, with *Joseph Pleasant's* Family.

The 12th I went over *Nancemond-river* to *Western-branch*, where I expected to have had a Meeting that Day, but the Notice had fail'd ; so I staid at *Abraham Rixe's* till Fifth-day, and went to the Monthly-meeting for the Church-affairs, which was large and peaceable. From hence I went to a Meeting at *Rascoe-neck*, and came up near *Western-branch* to a Burial. The 17th I was at a General-meeting at *Western-branch*, which was very large, and thro' divine Favour a good time, my Spirit being very much at Liberty ; and I was clear'd of that Part of the Country. I then turned up the Province to have some Meetings with a few

Friends

Friends that were gone to settle there, and had one the next Day at *Robert Rixe's*, another the Day following at *John Denson's*, and another the 21st at one *John Thorp's*, where we had a blessed Time, thro' divine Help, amongst a People who were nearly, if not altogether Strangers to Friends and the Doctrine of Truth, who nevertheless behaved with Sobriety and Attention.

From hence I travelled forward, and had Meetings near *James's-river, Appamattack-river*, and other places: And the 1st of the ninth Monh had a Meeting at *Wyke Hunni-cutt's*, amongst his Neighbours and some Friends, to good Satisfaction. And the next Day had a precious establishing time toward Friends, thro' the Lord's Mercy, and to his Glory, at a Meeting at *William Lead's*, near *Wynoke*. Also at *Curles, Black-creek*, and *Swamp*, and turn'd back the 6th to see Friends at a Monthly-meeting, where I took leave of many Friends of that Part of the Country in much Love and comfortable Nearness. Next Day I went to *Cedar-creek* Meeting, where the Truth much comforted me, and opened blessedly relieving and establishing Doctrine to the People; and we had some good Service among pretty many Friends whom we went to visit. The Day following we had a Meeting at *John Cheadler's*, to which a pretty many People gathered from a considerable distance, and we had a good Meeting; as also another good

open

open Meeting, where none that I heard of had been before, at one *Thomas Warren's*, who was under fome Search after Truth, and a fober Man.

On the 11th I fet forward thro' the Wildernefs, in order to vifit a new fettled Country, far up in the Mountains, and that Night got Lodgings at a friendly Man's Houfe in the Fork of *Rappahannock-river*, and rode the next Day over fome high and ftony Moutains, a Man being with me as a Guide, who was a Stranger to the Way as much as myfelf, yet thro' the good Care of our God we got over *Shanadore-river* to one *Chefter's*, who was very courteous to us, his poor Circumftances confidered, which was alfo the more acceptable, as I expected nothing but to lodge in the open Woods that Night.

The 13th we went to *Abraham Hollingworth's*, a Friend, near *Opeck*, and the next Day, being Firft-day, I was at a Meeting with fome Friends and divers others, at the Meeting-houfe near *Alexander Roffe's*. The 15th I came back to *Abraham Hollingworth's*, in order to be at Meeting the Day following near *Shanadore-river*, which was held at *Robert Mackay's* the younger, and was pretty open and comfortable. On the 17th we had a Meeting at *Ifaac Perkin's*, to which came the greateft part of Friends of that new fettled Country, wherein the Love and Wifdom of Truth appeared much to my Eafe, and their Eftablifh-
ment

ment in Religion. The next Day I had a good open little Meeting at *Richard Beeson*'s; and on the following, another with some Friends and divers others at *John Smith*'s. On the 20th we cross'd *Potomack-river*, and travelled over that high Ridge called the *Blue-mountains*, and having miss'd our Way, with great difficulty we got to *John Baile*'s at *Mannockacy*, and was at the Meeting there the 21st, and took leave of Friends there-away. From hence we set out towards the Head of *Patuxen-river* in *Maryland*, and in two Days hard riding we came to *Samuel Plummer*'s, and travelled down towards *Patuxen-mouth*, and had a Meeting with a few Friends there on the 26th, to our Comfort. This is the lowest Meeting in the Province.

The 1st of the tenth Month we had a Meeting at *Herring-creek*, and another the next Day at *West-river*, where Truth opened me in a very close-dealing and warning manner to some loose People, as well as truly comfortable to the Upright in Heart. On the 3d we had a Meeting near the upper part of *Patuxen*, and went that Night to *Gerrard Hopkins*'s the younger, where I had some Service for Truth; in shewing how the Youth were in divers respects departed from it into the Spirit and Ways of the World, and the unhappy Consequences thereof in divers Instances. We had a Meeting next Day at *Elkridge*, which was of good Service, and another the Day following at a Friend's

Friend's Houfe at *Patapfcoe*. From hence I went to *Bufh-river*, and had a Meeting with Friends there-away, and another at *Deer-creek*, to fome good Satisfaction.

We got over *Sufquehannah-river* on the 11th, tho' with fome Difficulty, by reafon of the Ice driving down upon us, and went that Night to *Henry Reynold*'s in *Weft-Nottingham*, and on the 12th was at Friends Meeting there, which was large and folid, and had a precious Opportunity amongft them. After this I went forward towards *Philadelphia*, having Meetings at feveral places, as at *Eaft-Nottingham*, *London-Grove*, *New-Garden*, *Kennet*, *Newark*, and *Chichefter*, which laft was pretty large, many Friends being there from divers places; from whence I went home with *John Salkeld*, and on the 22d got to *Philadelphia*, and the Day following was at Friends Week-day Meeting, where we were gracioufly favoured with heavenly Help, much to our Comfort. I ftaid there-about till the Firft-day following, when the Lord was pleafed to blefs us by his Power and Love, much to our Humiliation in his Prefence, in three publick Meetings.

The 27th I fet out again into the Country, and had a Meeting that Day at *Plymouth*, and a large one the Day following at *North-Wales*, (it being their Monthly-meeting for Bufinefs) wherein we were comforted together; and alfo the next Day at *Perquiomin*, which thro' heavenly Help was a truly good Seafon. The

31ft

3 1ſt I had a comfortable Meeting at *Maiden-creek*, and the 2d of the eleventh Month ano-ther at *Oley* with Friends there-away, which was much to my Eaſe, and the Comfort of the Upright-hearted. I had Meetings likewiſe at the *Furnace* near *Manatania*, and at the *Great-Swamp*, which Truth made a truly good time to many ; alſo at a place called *Plumſted*, and a large one at Friends Meeting-houſe near *Buck-ingham* ; and from thence I went to *Wright's-town* and *Falls*, at which Place I had a large and truly edifying Meeting. I had likewiſe Meetings at *Trent-town*, *Burlington* and *Briſtol*, to which Friends came from ſeveral diſtant places.

The 16th I was at *Niſhaminy* Meeting, which the Lord of Mercy and all Power glor\iouſly owned to the Comfort and Help of many ; and his mighty Name was worſhiped. We had another Meeting that Evening at *Adam Har-ker's*, where I lodged, much to the Edification of the living. The 18th I had a Meeting at *Rye-bury*, and the Day following another large and profitable Meeting at *Abington* ; from whence I went to another at *Horſham*, and croſſing the *Sculkill* into *Cheſter* County, was at *Calne* Meeting on the 23d, being Firſt-day, and ſo to *Uchland* and *Goſhen*, where, thro' the Lord's Goodneſs, we had a large and precious Meeting ; and another the Day following in the Valley ; alſo at *Radnor* and *Newtown* : And from hence to a Meeting of Miniſters and Elders at *Hart-*
M m

ford,

ford, where on the 1st of the twelfth Month a General-meeting was held. The next Day, through the Help of Truth, we had a precious Opportunity at *Springfield*, the Day after at *Derby*, and the next at *Merion*, which was large and edifying. From hence I went with some Friends who came to meet me, to *Israel Pemberton*'s at *Philadelphia*. On the 5th was a Quarterly-meeting of Ministers and Elders, and the next, being First-day, I was at three Meetings, wherein divine Regard very comfortably owned and helped us. The 7th I was at the Quarterly-meeting of Business for the County, which was large and peaceable; and on the next Day at the Youth's-meeting there, which, through the gracious Goodness of the Lord, was made a blessed time to many.

I left the City on the 9th, and had Meetings at *Chester* and *Middletown*, and was at the Quarterly-meeting of Ministers and Elders at *Concord*, where I staid over the First-day, and also the Meeting of Business for the County the Day following, which thro' divine Goodness were large and edifying.

The 15th I was at the General-meeting at *Providence*, which was large, and a heavenly time. The 16th I had a Meeting at *Birmingham*, which was large and solidly profitable: Another the next Day at *Bradford*, and the Day after at *London-grove*, where many Friends from other Meetings met me, and the Lord our God was pleased eminently to own and

bless

bleſs our Meeting to our true Comfort and Joy in his holy Preſence. From hence I went to *Sudbury* and *Laycock*, where I had Meetings, and another on the 23d, in my way to *Calne*, at a Friend's Houſe, which was made through divine Goodneſs, a very edifying time to Friends, and many of the Neighbours who came in: No Meeting of Friends had been held there before. I returned from hence to *Philadelphia*, where I ſtaid near a Week, and had ſome ſatisfactory Service in divers caſes.

On the 1ſt of the firſt Month, being Third-day, I had a Meeting at *German-town*, from whence I went over the River into *Jerſey*, and had Meetings at *Woodberry-creek*, *Pileſgrove*, and *Salem*, which laſt was large and edifying, thro' the Love and Wiſdom of Truth. The next Day I had a precious Meeting at *Alloway-creek*, and the Day following another at *Greenwich*, wherein heavenly Help in divine Favour was bleſſedly with us, and the Name of our God was magnified.

The 9th I rode to *Cape-May*, and the next Day had a comfortable Meeting with ſome Friends at *Richard Townſend*'s; as alſo the Day following a pretty large and edifying Meeting with Friends near *Jacob Garriſon*'s. The 12th we croſſed the River, and the Day following had a large Meeting, and an open, precious Time, in the Love and Power of the Goſpel, at *Great Egg-harbour*; as alſo another pretty large Meeting higher up on the Shore, at *Robert*

M m 2

Smith's

Smith's the Day following. That Night we paſſed over a dangerous Marſh and River to *Little Egg-harbour*, where on the 15th we had a Meeting with Friends there-away, to our true Comfort. From hence we paſſed thro' the Wilderneſs to *John Eſtaugh*'s near *Haddonfield*, and on the 18th was at a Quarterly-meeting there, wherein the helping Hand of the Lord was with us to his Praiſe.

The 19th I went to *Philadelphia*, and was at a Meeting of Miniſters and Elders, in the Beginning of their Half-year's-meeting for the two Provinces, which continued two Days, and was eminently owned with the helping Power and Preſence of the Lord. The Half-year's-meeting being over, I ſtaid till the Monthly-meeting for the City, where I had ſome Service for Truth, and comfortable Satisfaction. I then went into *Jerſey*, and was at a large Meeting on the 27th, being Firſt-day, at *Haddonfield*; another at *Cheſter* on the Day following; and a large and weighty Meeting near the Widow *Evan*'s that Evening.

The 30th I went to a Meeting at the *Falls*, in the County of *Bucks*, where a Marriage was that Day ſolemnized; and divine Power and Goodneſs owned us greatly, to our Comfort. I came back the next Day, and was at the Meeting at *Burlington*, which the Lord was pleaſed to bleſs with his Love and powerful Appearance; and his holy Name was humbly worſhiped and glorified.

The

The 1st of the second Month I had a Meeting at *Cuchocas*, worthy of awful Remembrance; and the 3d a great Meeting near *Mount-holly*, wherein Truth opened and prevailed in a ftrengthning manner. The next Day I was at *Burlington* Monthly-meeting, which was much to our Help in the Lord, and our great Encouragement in his Service. The next Day I had a Meeting at *Old-Springfield*, and on the Day following near *Upper-Springfield*, which was large and a profitable Seafon.

The 7th I was at a large Monthly-meeting at *Chefterfield*, wherein the Power and Love of God eminently appeared amongft us. The next Day we had a Meeting at *Mansfield*, and a bleffed open Meeting the Day following at *Burden's-town*, among a foberly-behaved People. The 10th, being Firft-day, I went to *Stonybrook* Meeting, and on the 12th had a large Meeting, and a precious open Seafon, amongft a mix'd People at *Allenflown*; and another the Day following at one *Mofes Robins*'s, where a confiderable number of People of other Societies gathered, and we had a good time with them. The 14th I went to a place near the Sea-fhore, called *Good-luck*, where the Day following I got a Meeting among the People there-about, and went to a place called *Squan*, where Notice being fpread among the Neighbourhood of a Meeting to be held the next Day, we had on the 17th a large and

helping

helping Meeting, thro' the gracious Assistance of the Lord our God. After Meeting I went near *Shrewsbury*, and the 20th had a Meeting at *Middletown*, in a *Baptist* Meeting-house, among some soberly-inclined People of several Professions, which was to good Satisfaction. That Night I went to *Shrewsbury*, and had a Meeting there the next Day, and another not far off the next, which the Lord our God owned to his own Praise. I staid amongst Friends here-away till First-day Morning, and had a very large Meeting at *Shrewsbury* again, and went that Night to *William Hartshorn*'s, and had some Service in the Family that Night, in the Love of Truth, to good Satisfaction. The 25th I was at Friends Quarterly-meeting, which was large, and a precious Season ; next Day had another great Meeting, chiefly among the Youth, and set out that Evening on my way to *Woodbridge*, where I had a Meeting the 28th, and another at *John Shadwell*'s the next Day, where a considerable number of People gathered, among whom I had a good Opportunity.

The 1st of the third Month I had a Meeting at *Plainfield*, and went from thence to *Long-Island* and *New-York*, where I had also a Meeting, and another on the 4th at *Newtown* in *Long-Island*, to which came several well-disposed People, and the Lord made it a precious time. The next Day I was at the Monthly-meeting for Business at *Flushing*, wherein Truth was graciously with us, to our Comfort.

Comfort. On the 6th I went over the Sound to *Weſt-cheſter*, intending to have had a Meeting there that Day, but the Notice had failed; I viſited ſeveral Families of Friends, and having appointed a Meeting there that Day-week, went to *Ryewoods*, near which Place we had a large Meeting the 8th, being Firſt-day; another the Day following at *North-caſtle*, and the next Day another at *Horſneck* in *Connecticut* Government. The 11th I had a Meeting at *Whiteplanes*, where there are but few Friends, but many of the neighbouring People gathered with us, and the Love and Power of Truth was very comfortably amongſt us. The next Day I was at Friends Monthly-meeting near that Place, where moſt of the Friends there-away gathered, and many other People likewiſe; and in the heavenly Opening and Aſſiſtance of Truth we had a bleſſed Seaſon together.

The 13th we had a Meeting at *Weſt-cheſter*, according to Appointment, and went afterwards to *Samuel Bowne*'s on *Long-Iſland*, who had accompanied me this Week. On the 15th, being Firſt-day, I was at the Meeting at *Fluſhing*, which was large; from hence I went towards *Cow-neck*, and had a Meeting there; and a large one the Day after at *Matinicock*, which was made to many a ſolidly, helping, and eſtabliſhing Time. I had Meetings likewiſe at *Oyſter-bay*, *Weſtbury*, and a precious Opportunity in the enlarging of the Life of Truth at *Bethphage*. The

The 24th I went to a Meeting at *Seckitauga,* where the good Arm of the Lord was eminently with us to our true Comfort, and the Help of divers. The next Day I was at Friends Monthly ‐ meeting at *Weſtbury,* which was large, and Affairs well conducted : And the Day following went to a place called *Rockway,* where we had a Meeting in a Barn, and the Lord of all our Mercies was gracioufly mindful of us : We went after Meeting to viſit a Woman Friend, in a weak, low Condition, with whom we were comforted in the fenfe of the Prefence of Truth.

The 27th we went to *Fluſhing,* *John Bowne* being with me, where the Yearly-meeting for thefe Parts began, and continued four Days, part for Worſhip, the reſt for the Affairs of the Church ; the publick Meetings were very large, and the Goodneſs and Mercy of the Lord God owned them, and enabled us in his Service, to the Help of many, and exalted his own everlaſting Gofpel-teſtimony, and his glorious Name was worſhiped and magnified.

The 31ſt feveral Friends fet out with me towards *Rhode-Iſland,* tho' I was now in a poor, weak, fpent Condition, as to bodily Ability, afid capable of travelling but flowly, the Weather being exceeding hot, yet I was meafurably fupported with inward Help and Hope in the Arm of the Lord's All-fufficiency. We paffed thro' *Connecticut* Government, and came to *James Perry*'s, in the *Narraganfet* Country, and the 5th
of

of the fourth Month, being First-day, were at *Kingston* Meeting, and the Day following at a Monthly-meeting there. On the 7th I had a Meeting on *Connanicot-Island*, where some Friends met us from *Newport*, and we were favoured with a comfortable Time, in the Prevalency of divine Goodness, and got that Evening to my Brother-in-Law *John Proud's*, in *Newport*.

On the 9th the Yearly-meeting began at *Portsmouth*, and a large, precious Meeting it was; I returned to *Newport*, where the Yearly-meeting continued, and held four Days, the Affembly being large and peaceable, and at times comfortable in the Arisings of the mighty Power and Love of God, who had the Glory and Praise. The 15th I had a large and edifying Meeting at *Tiverton*, and lodged at *Joseph Wanton's*, where we had a good little Meeting that Evening. The next Day I had a Meeting at *Seconnet*, and a large one the Day after at *Coaxet*. The 19th, being First-day, I was at *Cushanet*, where we had a large and good Meeting, in the Lord's merciful Help; as also at *Peniganset*, *Rochester*, and *Succoneset*. From whence we went down to the Water-side, and went aboard a Sloop with many other Friends, and got well over to *Nantucket* the 23d, and on the 24th the Yearly-meeting began there, which was large, and continued four Days, to true Satisfaction, and the Name of the Lord was glorified.

N n

The

The 28th I went over the *Sound* again, but paſſed the Night in an open Boat, and got into *Baſs-river* near *Yarmouth* the next Day, and had a Meeting in *Plymouth* the Day following, where no Friends live, nor had there been a Meeting there near thirty Years; many of the People came to it, and almighty Goodneſs mercifully owned us, and enabled to preach his everlaſting Goſpel, much to the Peoples Satisfaction, who behaved very civilly.

The 1ſt of the fifth Month I had a Meeting at *Pembroke*, and rode that Evening to *Boſton*, and the 3d, being Firſt-day, went to the Quarterly-meeting at *Hampton*, where many Friends and others gathered; the next Morning Friends tranſacted the Affairs of the Church, and had a publick Meeting afterwards: The Lord our God was gracioufly pleaſed to own our Aſſemblies in his Power and Wiſdom, to his own Glory, and much to the Edification and Comfort of many Souls. On the 5th I had a Meeting at *Stretham*, which was an open, bleſſed time; and another large one the Day following at *Quochecha*, to good Satisfaction.

On the 7th I had a Meeting at *Dover*, to which Friends in that part of the Country generally came, and alſo many of the *Preſbyterian* People, who heard of my being come to thoſe parts again, (having in a former Viſit to this place, had good Service for the Lord in theſe parts) and we had a glorious, powerful Meeting in the Name and Love of God, which

was

was great among us that Day. I lodged at *John Kenny*'s, where we had a precious Opportunity with many Friends that Evening. The next Day we had a Meeting at *Portfmouth*, in the Court-houfe, to which the People flocked in great numbers, and behaved foberly; and the Power and Doctrine of Truth had Impreffion on many Hearts. On the 9th I had a Meeting at *Hampton*, and another the Day following at *Almfbury*, which was large, and thro' divine Help, a glorious and ftrengthning Time to the honeft-minded, profitable to many I hope, and not to be forgot.

I had a Meeting the 11th at *Haveril*; and the next Day a large and folidly profitable Meeting at *Newbury*, many of the People coming in, and confeffed to the Truth. The 14th I had a large Meeting with Friends at *Salem*, and another at *Marblehead* in the Townhoufe next Day; wherein the Lord's Power, and the Doctrine of the Gofpel, prevailed among the People to their Help. I went to *Lyn* that Night, and had a large and good eftablifhing Meeting there next Day.

The 17th I came to *Bofton*, and had two large and comfortable Meetings there; many People came in, and behaved foberly: Alfo another the Day following, to good Satisfaction, and in the Evening moft of the Friends there, gathered to a Friend's Houfe, and we had a Meeting, which I believe was profitable; and here I took my leave of Friends in thefe parts.

N n 2 The

The 20th I was at the Week-day Meeting at *Mendham*, and went from thence to *Uxbridge*, were we had a Meeting, and another the Day following with a few well-inclined People at *Ralph Earle*'s. From hence I went to *Shrewsbury*, and had a little Meeting the next Day at *Lancaster*, with some who professed to be Friends; and from thence I returned to *Mendham*, where I was at a pretty large Meeting the 24th, and had some good Service with a few Friends in the Evening. On the 26th I had a large Meeting at *Wansokit* in *Providence* Woods, but found many of the People very little acquainted with the Power and Baptism of Truth, yet the Lord God of Mercies open'd my Heart, and enabled me to labour, I believe, to some of their Advantage, as well as to my own Discharge in the Lord's Service. The next Day I had a pretty open, serviceable Meeting at *Shanticote*, tho' Carnality was prevalent among them; and on the Day following another at *Greenwich*, indifferently satisfactory, thro' divine Help, amongst a barren People: I staid at *Thomas Fry*'s, a generous, friendly Man, tho' not of our Community, who had also some good Children. The next Day I was at *Warwick* Meeting, and the following at a Yearly-meeting at *Providence-town*, which was large, and to some Satisfaction.

The 1st of the sixth Month I had a large and pretty good Meeting at *Smithfield* Meeting-house, through heavy and faithful Labour, in
divine

divine Help: Another the Day following at *Ebenezer Woodward*'s in *Taunton*, and the next Day at *Swansey*, which was large on account of a Burial, and satisfactory in a good degree, tho' the pure Life of Truth seems to be low there-away. From hence I went to *Free-town* and had a Meeting there, and also at *Sandwich*, which was pretty large; and on the 9th I had a Meeting at *Mannimay*, among some friendly People, which was much to our Satisfaction; and another at *Bass-pond* the next Day, and one the Day following at *Rochester*.

The 12th I had a large Meeting at *Penigan-set*, and the 14th, being First-day, was at a Yearly-meeting for Worship at *South-Kingston*, which held two Days, the Meetings being large; and the Name of the Lord was gloriously high, and humbly magnified on our parts. The 16th I had a Meeting at *John Richmond*'s in *Westerly*, a great and blessed time in the Love of God; and another the next Day at *John Mumford*'s; after which we came down to the Ferry at *Connanicot*, but could not get over till the Day following, and went to the Meeting at *Newport*, where on the 21st, being First-day, we had two very large Meetings, to which many Friends came from distant places to take leave of me, and the Lord of all our Mercies was pleased to open my Heart and Mouth largely amongst them in his Power and Counsel; and we parted with Comfort in his Love. In the Evening I had a

blessed

bleſſed time with ſome Friends of the Town, in the melting love and ſenſe of the pure Preſence of our heavenly Father, who had and hath the Praiſe and Glory for all his Mercies and gracious Help. Next Morning we took a near and affectionate leave of one another, and I ſet out for *Long-Iſland*, and landed next Day at *Oyſter-pond-point*, and came to the upper part of *Southwold* that Night, and lodged at an Inn, where many of the Neighbourhood flocked in, and we had a ſerviceable Meeting with them.

The 24th I came to a Friend's named *John Hallack* at *Seatakit*, where we had a Meeting next Day, and came that Evening to *Bethphage*, from whence we went to the Quarterly-meeting at *Weſtbury*, which began there the 26th, the Meeting for Miniſters and Elders being held that Day, and a large publick Meeting, and another for Buſineſs the Day following. The 28th, being Firſt-day, there was a mighty Concourſe of People, and the Lord our God made it a precious time, in the help of his Wiſdom and glorious Power. The next Day we went to *Thomas Pearal*'s, where divers Friends coming to viſit us, we had a Meeting that Evening; another at *Cowneck* the Day following, and got to the Monthly-meeting at *Weſtbury* on the 31ſt.

On the 1ſt of the ſeventh Month I had a large and good Meeting, thro' merciful and heavenly Help, at *Fluſhing*, it being alſo their
Monthly

Monthly-meeting; and the next Day another at *Newtown*; and one in the Evening at *Richard Hallet*'s, at whofe Houfe I lodged; and there took leave of many Friends of that Ifland, in the Love and Power of the Lord our God. I came to *Woodbridge* in *Eaft-Jerfey* the next Day, and on the following was at the Meeting there; and on the 5th at a bleffed open Meeting at *Elizabeth-town,* where no Friends live, and that Night came back to *John Shadwell*'s: The next Day we went up the Country to a place called *Whippaning,* where a few friendly People live, with whom I had a precious and comfortable little Meeting, and the next Day another with a few Friends at *Libanon*; and fo to *Bethlehem, Wrightftown* in *Penfilvania,* and *Middletown*; at which laft places I had large and folidly profitable Meetings, and took leave of Friends there, under the fenfe of the Power of Truth. From hence I went to *Frankfort* and had a Meeting there, and came to *Philadelphia* that Night. After ftaying the Week-day Meeting next Day, I went over the River *Delaware,* in order to be at the Quarterly-meeting for *Glocefter* and *Salem,* which were held the 16th; and on the 17th I returned to *Philadelphia* to the Yearly-meeting there, which continued feveral Days, and thro' the merciful Attendance, and bleffed Help of divine Goodnefs, it was made a glorious, comfortabie, ftrengthning time, and Peace and Unity appeared eminently amongft Friends.

(Of

(Of which he gives some farther Account in a Letter to one of his Sons, viz.)

————— ' As to myself, I am, I think, some-
' what miraculously supported as a Creature,
' and am in good Health pretty generally, and
' expect I may be so discharged, respecting the
' Continent, as to be free to go towards *Bar-*
' *badoes* in about two Months. The Yearly-
' meeting at this place ended last Night ; it
' was exceedingly large, and, upon the whole,
' generally acknowledged to have been very
' edifying, strongly good and helpful divers
' ways, and very much to my Ease and hum-
' bling Gladness in the Lord our God, and
' never-failing Helper.   And Friends in gene-
' ral are in a good degree of Harmony.—————
' My Heart is nearly affected with the best of
' Love towards thee and for thee, that nothing
' short of Rain from the divine Presence may
' satisfy thee, for this is what only prepares the
' most acceptable Sacrifice, *a broken and con-*
' *trite Spirit*, wherein is true Light and dura-
' ble Joy : Thus farewel, farewel, saith thy
' nearly affectionate Father, to the best of my
' Capacity in every respect, which I hope thou
' art, and often will be, profitably sensible
' of.

' J. F.'

On the 22d of the seventh Month (*continues
the Journal)* after the Yearly - meeting was
over,

over, having some Concern remaining with me towards *Maryland*, I set out for the *Western-shore*, and went that Night to *Chester*, and had Meetings at *Bush-river*, near *Patapscoe*, and at *West-river*; where I staid at *Joseph Gallo-way*'s about two Days, visiting several Friends Families there-away, and was at the Meeting again on First-day, which was pretty large.

The 4th of the eighth Month I had a pretty large Meeting at the *Cliffs*, wherein Truth blessedly owned us, and enabled me to labour much to my Discharge of that part of the Country. Next Day I had a Meeting at *Her-ring-creek*, and took leave of Friends there, returning again to *Joseph Galloway*'s.

On the 6th I set out with some Friends for the *Bay*, in order to be at the Yearly-meeting near *Choptank-river*, and got well over: On the 8th, being First-day, the Yearly-meeting began, and continued five Days, some of the Meetings being very large; and the Power and Testimony of Truth comfortably prevailed among the People, to the true Satisfaction of Friends, and the almighty Name was magnified. After the Yearly-meeting was over, I had a Meeting at *Tuckahow*, and a pretty large open Meeting near *Choptank-head*, among some People who made little profession of Truth, yet the Love of God extended freely towards them, wherein we rejoiced.

On the 16th I was at a large Meeting near *Little-creek* on *Delaware-river*, it being their

O o

Yearly-

Yearly-meeting, and continued two Days, many Friends and others were prefent, and the bleffed Truth owned us, mercifully prevailing to many of our Comfort, and the Lord our God had the Glory. After this I had Meetings at *Duck-creek*, *George's-creek*, *Newcaftle*, and a pretty large one at *William Shipley*'s at *Williamftown*, alfo at *George Kiffen*'s, *Kennet*, and *New-garden*; at *Concord*, *Providence*, and a large heavenly Meeting at *Gofhen*. I went from hence to *North-Wales*, and was at two Meetings there, wherein divine Goodnefs was manifefted to our Comfort, and the holy Name was honoured.

The 31ft I was at a Monthly-meeting at *Abington*, which was large, and on the 1ft of the ninth Month had a Meeting at *Horfham*, which was greatly to my difcharge, and the Comfort of many. The next Day I had a Meeting to true and great Satisfaction at *Trent-town*, and another the Day following at *Burlington*, in order to be fully clear, with Satisfaction, of that Place, After this I had a Meeting with Friends at *Briftol*, and the next Day was at three large Meetings at *Philadelphia*, being Firft-day. The next was their Quarterly-meeting, and the following a General-meeting, moftly of Youth, which was made, thro' the Goodnefs and Help of Truth, a precious, eftablifhing Opportunity. I ftaid that Week in the City, and was at the Meetings as they fell in courfe, and the Firft-day

following

following was made truly satisfactory and comfortable.

On the 14th I had a Meeting at *Fairhill*, wherein divine Wisdom and Power very eminently dignified the Opportunity to our Joy in the Lord. The next Day I went to a General-meeting at *Chester*, which was very large and satisfactory; and we parted in true Love and Nearness in the Love of Christ our Lord. On the 20th I had a large Meeting at *Salem*, and was at the Quarterly-meeting there the Day following, with good Satisfaction; as also the next Day at the Youth's-meeting, which was large, and made thoroughly satisfactory in discharging me of those Parts.

The 23d I had a blessed Meeting with Friends at *Pilesgrove*, and the next Day was at a General-meeting at *Haddonfield*, wherein the Lord our God graciously owned us, and blessed our Meeting, giving us to part one from another in a living Sense of his Love and Power; and his glorious Name was worshiped and praised. I came that Night again to *Jos. Cooper*'s, and the Day following to *Philadelphia*, where I staid till the 8th of the tenth Month, and had divers great and heavenly Meetings; and after a very open and solidly edifying Meeting, I took leave of Friends there in much true Love and Nearness in Spirit, and heavenly Unity in the Lord.

I then took passage for *Barbadoes*, in company with a Native of *Berytus* in *Syria*, (about

 sixty

ſixty Miles north of *Jeruſalem)* who being oppreſſed by the *Turks*, and ſtripped of his Poſ-
ſeſſions, had been obliged to ſeveral *European*
Princes for indulging him to aſk the Benevo-
lence of their Subjects. I had ſome ſatisfactory
Converſation with him, which induced him to
be very affectionately courteous to me, and was
I believe of ſome ſervice to him in a religious
Senſe, tho' we could converſe very little but by
an Interpreter. We had a ſafe Paſſage, thro'
ſome very ſtormy Weather, and landed in *Barbadoes* the 9th of the eleventh Month 1737.

From Barbadoes *he wrote the following Epiſtle
to Friends on the Eaſtern-ſhore in* Maryland.

' DEAR FRIENDS,

' IN the Extendings of the Love of Chriſt,
' the great and bleſſed Shepherd of the
' Lord's Flock every where, am I concerned
' to remember you, and ſtirred up to write
' a little to you, as a tender and brotherly
' Salutation ; and I earneſtly intreat you all,
' carefully and weightily to conſider, that the
' moſt neceſſary Concern and Work of our Day
' here, certainly is to ſeek for experimental
' Knowledge of Reconciliation to God the
' Father, thro' the Obedience of living Faith
' in the Name of Chriſt, and the renewing of
' the holy Spirit ; and ſo to live, walk, and
' labour in and with our heavenly Talent or
' Gift, that we ſhew forth and promote the
' Righteouſneſs

' Righteousness and Purity of the blessed Gos-
' pel-day, as Lights to the World, but most
' immediately and directy so, to those of the
' same Profession with us.

' And I am fully satisfied, that the gracious
' Regard of almighty Goodness is a fresh ex-
' tending towards you, in order to help you,
' both to wait and to live more comfortably in
' the Dominion of Truth in yourselves ; and
' to enable you, in the Life and Wisdom of
' Truth, to be more serviceable in your Fami-
' lies, in the Society professing to be of you,
' (so lamentably decaying in your parts) and
' also to the Nighbourhood : For if the
' redeeming Power, and sanctifying Life of
' Christ, the one true and blessed Head and
' Shepherd, did but shew itself and its hea-
' venly Effects suitably, thro' the more know-
' ing and more active, or chief part of the
' Society, it is indisputable with me, that the
' Lord's Work of gathering many to be living
' Stones, and building People up a spiritual
' House, in Order and godlike Beauty, would
' prosper, and recover Strength and Lustre
' among you : For you would be helped to
' speak in one Life, one Zeal, and one Lan-
' guage of Wisdom, to the Joy and Comfort
' of the honestly-minded, who some of them,
' tho' they may be at a distance in divers re-
' spects, yet are at times looking for *Zion*,
' but cannot see such Beauty amongst her pro-
' fessed

' feſſed Chiefs, where they have expected it to
' appear, as to convince them, *this is ſhe.*
  ' And ſome others who are lamed in part,
' and depraved in ſenſe, yet are not quite dead,
' but are now and then awakened to ſee and
' feel ſomething of their own dark and be-
' wildred Condition ; who if they had proper
' light ſhewn them, and were ſtirred up to
' look wherein they have turned aſide, (which
' is but your and all our Intereſt and Duty to
' be devotedly concerned for) ſome ſuch I be-
' lieve would yet be gathered nearer, would be
' reſtored in themſelves, and would add Help
' and Beauty to the Lord's Family : And the
' Mouths of thoſe who mock and contemn
' the Repairers, would, in the Lord's Counſel,
' be ſtopped, or turn to their own Shame and
' Sorrow ; and the ſeeming Strength of the
' Arm of ſuch uncircumciſed, would appear
' to be mere Weakneſs, and like Briars and
' Thorns in the Way of the Lord of Hoſts.
  ' So, *dear Friends, Brethren* and *Siſters,* be
' rouzed up into upright Inwardneſs of Appli-
' cation in Soul, to have your own Hearts
' ſearched by the Finger or Power of God ;
' and that its Love and Virtue may help and
' lead you in faithfulneſs to labour in the Work
' of the Lord, that you may be fully clear of the
' Blood of all : And I fully believe the bleſſed
' Maſter-builder and great Huſbandman, will
' yet add a Bleſſing to your ſincere Application,
' both inwardly for your own Help, and to
                            ' others ;

' others ; for his Eye is towards you for good,
' and towards the Work he hath begun in
' your parts.

' And I beg it may ever be remembred,
' particularly by the more active for Religion,
' either as Minifters, or other Helps in the
' Government of the Church, that Exhorta-
' tion, Advice, or propofing the beft of Rules
' for neceffary Practice, are not like to produce
' much good Effects, if the Tincture and Sa-
' vour of the Spirit of Religion and Gofpel-
' power do not accompany fuch Labour, and
' fhew itfelf in the Life of fuch Perfons ; for
' that leads into, and gives Dominion over our
' own Spirits and Tempers, and wafheth from
' the defiling Love and Spirit of this World,
' with its corrupting Friendfhips and felfifh
' Views, which have hurt many inwardly, if
' not flain and laid wafte Multitudes.

' But oh ! to humble, clean and enlivened
' Hearts, the frefh feeling of the Life of Truth
' revives Faith under Difficulties and Difcou-
' ragements, and gives both Beauty, Authority
' and Room, and never fails to render People
' really ufeful, and Helpers to repair and
' build up, according to the feveral Talents
' received : Nor can any thing below this
' heavenly Life being felt and yielded unto,
' make any effectually ufeful ; but Weaknefs
' and Decay in Practice will ftill follow and
' fpread : For the carnal Mind, and flefhly
' Wifdom, tho' there fhould appear fome out-
' ward

' ward Strictness, will often find Excuses for
' not doing one thing, and for doing another,
' as best suits present Advantage or Pleasure to
' the Creature ; and hence have come those
' numerous Divisions, Enmities, Contentions,
' and variety of Practices, Parties, and evil
' Liberties into the professed *Christian* Church-
' es, and in part amongst us as a People, under
' which, you and the Cause of Christ in your
' Province suffer.

' However, I am persuaded the Lord of
' Heaven and Earth is graciously mindful of
' you, of his Cause, and of many poor, in-
' wardly distempered, and lamed (by their evil
' lusts) amongst you, in order to extend Help,
' and to make you Helpers one to another,
' thro' Holiness of Life, and wise and living
' Zeal ; and therefore, *dear Friends*, be en-
' couraged in labouring to live, to exhort, re-
' prove, invite and provoke to love as occasion
' may offer, with *Christian* diligence, and with-
' out Partiality : So will Light yet break out
' from Darkness, and the darkning, reasoning
' Spirit of this World, will gradually be si-
' lenced, and the Testimony of Truth, in its
' several ancient and holy Branches, be again
' seen clearly, as they are the Fruits of the
' Life and Light of the everlasting Gospel ;
' and will be borne openly and faithfully for
' Christ's sake : And thus you, as his Children,
' will be abundantly more honoured and
' owned with his living, glorious, healing

' and

' and ſtrengthning Preſence : And ſo inward
' Salvation, outward Fruitfulneſs in Righteouſ-
' neſs, with freſh Anointing, and raiſing up
' of helpful Inſtruments for various Services
' in the Church, and the good of Mankind,
' will yet again grow among you, to your Joy
' and Honour, and to the Glory and Praiſe of
' the unchangeable, holy Lord God Almighty,
' ever worthy to be loved, feared, obediently
' truſted in, and magnified for ever. Thus,
' *dear Friends*, my Soul longs for you, and
' the Father's Honour, and in his Name ſa-
' lutes the Living. I am your true Friend, and
' an earneſt Seeker of your preſent and eternal
' good.

' JOHN FOTHERGILL.'

' If I have been very preſſing and earneſt
' with you, and not without danger of of-
' fending ſome, yet know ye, it is from a clear
' View that the Lord of Heaven and Earth,
' who ſees all things and Perſons as they are
' in reality, is both willing and deſirous to help
' and quicken you, and to repair his Work
' and Plantation among you in this Province ;
' and to water and dreſs it, that it may be-
' come both more comfortable in itſelf, and
' more beautiful ; he therefore uſeth various
' means to induce and encourage you to ſeek
' the Lord in good earneſt, to know him to
' work in, for and with you, for that great
' end, to prevent greater Deſolation, and For-

P p

' ſaking,

' faking, which is like to overtake you, thro'
' the Rebellious and Negligent, to more fcan-
' dal and forrow of heart.

   ' I am now clear, and I befeech that you
' may make proper Ufe of this and all other
' Favours, both in thinking of it carefully,
' and fpreading it as may be judged neceffary ;
' and I feem rather moved with defire that this,
' or a Copy of it, may go to Friends over the
' *Bay :* Tho' at prefent my Hope feems weak
' of fome, of their regarding any thing that
' may be for their effectual Help. But the un-
' changeable God, his holy Truth, and faithful
' Labourers in his love and fear, will be clear,
' and have Comfort in themfelves from him
' whofe Ear grows not heavy, that it cannot
' hear in any Land or Age ; Glory and
' Thankfgiving be to his Name for ever and
' ever.'

           Barbadoes, the 23d of the
           twelfth Month 1737.

*All the Account that remains of his Vifit to
this Ifland, and of his Return, we believe is
contain'd in the following Letters to one of his
Sons in* England, *viz.*

Barbadoes, *27th of the eleventh Month* 1737,

—— ' I was brought hither well about fixteen
' Days ago, in 32 Days from *Philadelphia*, yet
' do not find myfelf free to leave the place fo
' foon ; and therefore as a Veffel is juft going
                                 ' hence

‘ hence for *London*, I cannot well omit writing
‘ a little to inform thee, that I am thus far on
‘ my way, and eafy in the hope and fenfe
‘ of the Father's favour.——If this Ship had
‘ ftaid two or three Weeks longer, I fhould
‘ have been in hopes, I might have left the
‘ Ifland with Eafe; but I dare not, as it is:
‘ And yet it is queftionable, whether another
‘ will fail for *England* in lefs than two Months,
‘ which is fomewhat hard for me to think of,
‘ both in refpect to the Unpleafantnefs of the
‘ place, from the extreme Heats, the fmall
‘ number of Friends, and the general Remote-
‘ nefs of the Inhabitants from Religion.——
‘ Tho’ I am eafy in Refignation to all-wife
‘ Difpofal, and full of Thankfulnefs, under
‘ the bending Senfe of gracious and ftrong Ex-
‘ tendings of divine Good-will to many of the
‘ remote; and of fatherly, fuccouring Encou-
‘ ragement to the few fpiritually-minded here.
‘——May Rain from Heaven bedew thy Soul
‘ and Underftanding; and cherifh and revive
‘ the Lord's Heritage every where.——

‘ J. F.’

Barbadoes, 12*th of the fecond Month* 1738.

——‘ Nearly affectionate and careful Re-
‘ membrance of thee, induceth me to endea-
‘ vour to let thee hear from me as often as I
‘ well can in this long Abfence, which Wif-

P p 2

‘ dom

' dom hath seen good to order; under which,
' for that reason, I am humbly chearful in re-
' verent hope; and for the present we must
' submit to be yet longer separated than I ex-
' pected, when I last wrote. No Vessel hath
' fail'd hence to any part of *England*, that I
' know of, nor is likely to do soon for *London*,
' so that I conclude to take Passage in one
' bound for *Lancaster*, and which intends to set
' sail in two or three Days; being now very
' desirous to be gone hence: Tho' I hope never
' to forget the merciful Nearness and Goodness
' of Truth to me here; both in affording the
' renewed sense of heavenly Life, and in pre-
' serving my Health. —— I cannot well add
' much, nor is much more in my Thoughts
' at present; but may say, that tho' this is a
' poor irreligious place, yet both many of the
' People, and the few Friends here, are very
' loving and respectful; and I hope I shall
' leave the place with inward Ease to myself,
' and Reputation to Truth. From thy truly
' loving Father,

' J. F.'

Lancaster, 2d *of the fourth Month* 1738,

' DEAR SON,

' HEREBY thou wilt understand, I am
' brought safe to my native Land again,
' in which I very humbly acknowledge mer-
' ciful Goodness and Preservation, still en-

' gaging

' gaging and engaging in Love, Fear and re-
' verent Truſt towards the moſt gracious,
' almighty Lord God, of whoſe Goodneſs,
' Power and Mercy, there is no End. I
' ſtrongly intended to have come by way of
' *London*, had any Paſſage offer'd with a pro-
' bability of my reaching the Yearly-meeting;
' but when this ſeemed unlikely to happen, I
' rather choſe to come to this place, where
' I arrived laſt Night, after a Paſſage of ſix
' Weeks betwixt Land and Land, but thro'
' very rough hard Weather, for the Seaſon of
' the Year: But I was always preſerved quiet,
' inwardly eaſy, and ſteady in hope. I am
' pretty well in Health, as well as eaſy and
' ſweet in Spirit: Worſhip and Praiſe be to the
' holy Author of all good.—So with dear Salu-
' tation in holy living Love to my near Friends,
' (and there are many ſuch) and to thyſelf, I
' remain thy ardently well-wiſhing Father,

' J. F.'

From Lancaſter *he went directly to his Habitation, which was then in* Netherdale, Yorkſhire,
*where he was joyfully received by his Family and
Friends, with humble Gratitude and Reverence
to that holy Power which had through all preſerved him to their Comfort. He ſet out ſoon
after for the Quarterly-meeting at* York, *which
was large, and attended by divers Friends from
ſeveral parts of the Nation, who were truly*
glad

*glad of his Presence among them on that Occasion,
which indeed was solemn and edifying in many
respects, in a very eminent manner.*

Whilst he was on this Visit in America, *he
wrote the following Epistle to Friends of the
Quarterly-meeting at* York.

' DEAR FRIENDS,

'IN the solid sense of the uniting, heart-
' warming, strengthning, supplying Love
' and Life, in and thro' CHRIST our Head,
' Lord, and Captain of all our Salvation, doth
' my Spirit and Heart very nearly salute you ;
' and you may be assured, tho' I am drawn, by
' the Father of the living Family, outwardly
' from you, who are the most near part of it
' to me, yet am I very often with you, in the
' Union of the one heavenly Power and En-
' gager of Hearts for the health and well-being
' of *Zion,* and for her growth in that Sound-
' ness and Beauty, with which God would
' bless his People and Family ; and for the
' Prosperity of which great and good Work,
' our gracious God hath gathered and baptized
' many Spirits among you, into a deep and
' daily Concern ; and who also suffer and
' mourn in Soul before the Lord, when Things
' and Practices happen, and are fallen into,
' which weaken and stain, and wound parti-
' culars, and dishonour the Cause and Name
' of the Lord our God.

' And

' And in this Care and Exercise am I still
' with you, who thus travel for the Health
' and Comfort of the Flock of God, and for
' the Help of the Weak and Unwise, that the
' Name of the Lord may be magnified in the
' Earth; and in this have we cause to hope
' and be encouraged, that divine Help, in the
' sense of our Father's Love and Presence, con-
' tinues graciously to visit with renewed Help,
' both to live and labour; and he with whom
' all fulness dwells, doth not forsake.

' Wherefore, *dear Friends*, I tenderly intreat
' all who love the Lord Jesus Christ in since-
' rity, to hope in the divine Power and Life
' which ever lives, and fervently to wait for
' the daily fresh Anointing of it, from whence
' alone you, and all have, and ever must have,
' Enlargement of Life in yourselves, whereby
' to live; and of Light, Wisdom and Strength,
' to act any way to good purpose in God's
' House.

' And I fully believe the Spirit of the Lord
' will lift up a Standard against the Enemy,
' who is at work under various Disguises, as-
' saulting the Work of the Gospel, and will
' help the Lord's People to be more and more
' bright in Life, and successful in Labour;
' but besure be honest and true in your Lots
' and Posts, both when you are collected to
' act in a body, Males apart, and Females
' apart, for the Propagation of Peace and
' Purity, and the Beauty of Truth, and to dis-

' courage

' courage the Appearance and Operation of the
' defiling and enticing Spirit of Unrighteouf-
' nefs; in which Work, both Male and Fe-
' male fhould be juft and faithful to God, as
' well privately in Families, as more publickly
' in the Churches. And as you are thus faith-
' ful, you will be true Friends to the younger
' and weaker, and one to another; but you
' cannot be fo, if Self and Flefh, with its li-
' bertine ways, be fheltered, and fought to be
' faved, rather than that the holy equal Line,
' and Judgment of Truth fhould be extended,
' and have its ftraight way.
  ' And I particularly befeech you, *my beloved*
' *Sifters*, to be encouraged and ftirred up,
' humbly and with Hope, to feek the Lord,
' who will be Wifdom and Strength; (for all
' have Need of both) and if you in Faith and
' Meeknefs feek the Lord for his Help, you
' will be enabled to act more ftrongly, wifely
' and fuccefsfully in fulfilling your Part of
' building and beautifying the Houfe of God,
' to your own Comfort and Joy, in feeing the
' Father put his own Image and Life of Righ-
' teoufnefs more and more upon your Sex,
' and the Youth among them. And I am fure,
' if the Brethren live in, and to the Life of
' Religion, they will both be Examples to you
' of Diligence, in Life, in attending Meetings,
' and in zealous Watchfulnefs, to encourage
' the good, and to admonifh the loofe and
' diforderly; and will alfo put you forward,

' and.

' and ſtrengthen you in doing your parts
' faithfully.

' Thus, *my dear Friends*, do you ſeek divine
' Help together, and alſo in your particular
' Reſidences and Seivices; and I am fully per-
' ſuaded, the everlaſting Father of all Comfort,
' and of divine Light and Ability, will add
' a Bleſſing to the Cries and Labour of his
' People, and make many inſtrumental to re-
' pair and recover decaying and lean places.
' But how is it very likely that the lower, or
' more feeble outwardly, ſhould do much to-
' wards ſo great a Work in many reſpects, if
' the more knowing and ſtrong, as Creatures,
' ſhould mind themſelves, and their temporal
' Affairs, more than the Life of Religion, and
' the Concerns of Truth and Righteouſneſs.

' And you younger People of that Meeting
' and County, towards whom my Bowels have
' often moved within me in the Love of God,
' ſeek to have room made in your Hearts for
' Chriſt, that he may reign in you, and be
' your Saviour and Shepherd; and he will yet
' more baptize you into Death to Vanity, and
' a Senſe of Salvation, and make you a Gene-
' ration to his own Praiſe; that from age to
' age, the Name of the mighty God may be
' great and renowned in the Earth, and in that
' beloved County.

' Thus, *my near Friends*, my brotherly
' Greeting in the Goodwill of God the Father,
' runs to you in a manner which I hope many

Q q

' of

' of you can feel; and be comforted and en-
' couraged in the Lord and in his Service, for
' he is good unto his People: And you may
' know that the good Arm of Truth, which
' drew me over the Sea once more, hath
' mercifully helped and affifted to travel and
' labour with Diligence, and often to humbling
' Comfort. I have now been at the moft
' Northern part of *New-England* where any
' Friends live, and hope to be at *Bofton* in
' about a Week, where Friends are fomewhat
' increafed, and the People civil and courteous,
' as they now are in many, if not moft other
' places.'

This Epiftle was dated at Hampton *in the
Eaft of* New-England, *the* 5th *of the fifth
Month* 1737, *and accompanied the following one
to Friends of* Wenfleydale *Meeting.*

' *My near and truly beloved Friends,*

' ALTHO' it hath pleafed the everlafting
' Father and bleffed Comforter of his
' People, to feparate me outwardly, far from
' you, by the Engagings of his Love towards
' the Inhabitants of thefe Countries, yet his
' uniting Love and pure Goodnefs hath, and
' doth often lead my Spirit nearly to remem-
' ber, and hiddenly to vifit you, and run as it
' were among you, from one to another, in a
' particular manner, and often to breathe for
' your Edification in your Meetings; and

' in

‘ in such tender and divinely enlivened Desires
‘ for your best Help and Feeding, that I could
‘ gladly have wrote something of a brotherly
‘ Salutation e’re now, if I could have sent it
‘ to you when my Heart was so opened. But
‘ I have been some Weeks, and am under a
‘ fresh nearness, and living, careful, well-wish-
‘ ing for you, and your prospering in the Sal-
‘ vation of God, so that I just steal a little time
‘ to write, hoping to meet with an Opportu-
‘ nity to send it e’re long : And herewith freely
‘ reacheth a degree of the Love of God, thro’
‘ my Heart unto you, which Love hath often
‘ affected many of us with earnest longing for
‘ the Help and Favour of its glorious Author
‘ and Spring : And through Faith in him that
‘ is invisible, and honest care to be subject to
‘ the Operation of his humbling Hand, we
‘ have been gathered into a near and heavenly
‘ Relation, some nearer, and others at more
‘ distance or behind, according as the divine
‘ Influence of the Love and Power of God in
‘ Christ hath been joined with, waited for,
‘ and cherished, in order that we might be
‘ thoroughly baptized and purged : And as this
‘ heavenly Hand and Fan of God hath been
‘ kept under and longed for in Fear, lest any
‘ thing in us should escape or get up again,
‘ that is offensive to that pure, all-seeing Being,
‘ the Lord’s People’s true Nearness and Oneness
‘ is increased.

                    ‘ *My*

' *My dear Friends*, both elder and younger,
' who can run and read this Language with
' humble Hearts before the Lord our ever-
' living Rock and Fountain of all good, be
' you encouraged humbly to hope in, and pa-
' tiently, yet diligently to wait for more and
' more of this pure and winnowing Salvation,
' and you will feel almighty Goodnefs and
' Power to carry on the great Work he hath
' begun in you, for he is well able: But where
' heavenly Goodnefs is with-held from the Soul,
' and where little or no pure Accefs in holy
' Stilnefs is experienced, there hath been want
' of true and honeft fubmiffion to the Influence
' and fifting Operations of the Love and Power
' of God, the one everlafting Father of the
' living; or an hiding of fome Idols, or falling
' in Love with fomething which unfitteth for
' drinking of the heavenly Wine; and thence
' comes Coldnefs towards the Purity of Reli-
' gion, and Barrennefs touching the inward
' Knowledge of God and his Salvation, unfea-
' foned Hearts, and unfavoury Language and
' Converfation at times, more and more ftupi-
' fying themfelves, and fometimes darkening
' and dangerous Imaginations are followed,
' which fcatter into By-ways, through Infinua-
' tions of the wicked Subtilty.

' Wherefore, oh *my beloved Friends!* I befeech
' you carefully and fteadily mind, and dili-
' gently wait for, and truft in the invifible and
' incorruptible Seed and Power, which ever lives,

' is

' is ever pure, and ever sufficient to carry on and
' perfect his great and glorious Work of Re-
' demption ; and is also well able to assist and
' furnish with Wisdom and suitable degrees of
' Ability, for every Engagement and Service
' which he leadeth unto ; tho' we be poor, and
' often nothing but poverty and emptiness, as
' indeed we should be, till divine Life and
' Goodness spring in again, for which, quiet
' and awful Attendance is our Duty. And
' thus the holy almighty Workman will be
' with, and operate in his own Family ; and
' as we lean towards him trustingly, in pure
' desire to be helped to follow him uprightly,
' we shall not lack, nor ever be confounded.

' *Dear Friends*, my Life in Christ, the one
' living Head all the World over, is often with
' many of you in a rejoicing manner, and in
' strong Desires that you may all feel it more
' and more to wash and fill you, and so give
' you to drink into the one Spirit of Truth
' and heavenly Unity.

' And that the Elder among you, while
' a little of Day remains, may heartily seek
' to be redeemed ; a great, but absolutely
' necessary Work, for Time is but short to
' many : And let the Younger carefully seek
' that true Godliness, which the Touches and
' Winnings of divine Love would incline and
' lead all to : For this is the only infallible
' way to Blessedness here, and for ever ; as
' also to be fitted for Service every way, as
' well

‘ well as to Honour and true Efteem among
‘ Men.   Thus may the Love of God, and the
‘ Power of his Chrift, prevail with, and fill
‘ you more and more. *Amen.* And may know
‘ I am not difcouraged from hoping I may be
‘ favoured to fee you, and my native Country
‘ again ; divine Love led me from you for the
‘ Lord's Caufe-fake, and hath been near to di-
‘ rect and fupply with Affiftance, as much to
‘ my humble Admiration and bowing my Soul
‘ in Thankfulnefs, as in any part of my Life,
‘ and I believe to fome Service to others ; the
‘ great Being of all Power hath the Glory, for
‘ he alone is worthy : And tho’ I have been
‘ helped to travel very diligently, and to a
‘ good degree of difcharge, yet fo much is yet
‘ before me, that I expect not to fee *England*
‘ in lefs than ten Months, if my Life be pro-
‘ longed ; but I am given up freely in Defire
‘ to the Father's Will, if he will but plainly
‘ lead and help.   Now, in ever-living and pure
‘ Love, and ftrong Defires for all your Salva-
‘ tion and beft of Comfort, in and thro’ free
‘ Accefs to the Father of Might and Mercy,
‘ thro’ Jefus Chrift our Lord, where we have
‘ alfo to worfhip livingly ; I once more falute
‘ you, and remain your truly loving Friend
‘ and Brother to the living in *Ifrael*,

‘ JOHN FOTHERGILL.’

*To thefe Epiftles it may not be improper to
fubjoin the following Teftimonial of his Labours
and Travels in the Miniftry in thefe parts of
America, in a Certificate from Friends there to
the Monthly-meeting of* Richmond, *of which he
was then a Member. It is felected from many
others which he brought from divers places, as it
feems to be the moft comprehenfive of the peculiar
Nature of his Labours and Services, viz.*

' To our Friends *and* Brethren *of the Monthly-*
   ' *meeting of* Richmond *in* Yorkfhire, *or,*
   ' *where elfe this may come.*

' WE falute you in the Love and Fellow-
   '   fhip of the Gofpel : And whereas our
' worthy Friend and Elder *John Fothergill,*
' hath been concerned now in his advanced
' Years, to undertake a third Vifit to thefe
' Parts of *America,* in the Service of the Gof-
' pel ; and with great Diligence, fincere and
' hard Labour, for the Honour of God, the
' Good of Souls, and the Difcharge of Duty,
' hath travelled thro' near, if not all the Meet-
' ings of Friends in *New-England* ; in which
' Service the Lord hath been pleafed to own
' and enable him, in an eminent manner, not
' only to point out, and fhew to the Children
' of Men, their fpiritual Maladies ; but alfo
' moft clearly to direct, and movingly to in-
' vite, unto Chrift the *Phyfician of value,* for
' a fure and certain Cure, greatly to the Re-
                       ' lief

' lief of the oppreſſed, and Rejoicing of thoſe
' who are concerned for *Sion*'s Proſperity.
' His Deportment and Converſation being alſo
' weighty and edifying, adorning the Service
' and Station whereunto the Lord hath ap-
' pointed him; wherefore the Faithful have
' dear Unity with him, and ſincerely deſire his
' future Preſervation every way, that in the
' Lord's time he may be conducted home to
' you and his Family in Safety, with Sheaves
' of Peace in his Boſom.

' *Signed at and in Behalf of our Quarterly-*
' *meeting held on* Rhode-Iſland, *the* 13*th of the*
' *eighth Month* 1737, by forty-ſix Friends.'

In the Year 1739, *when the Winter Quarterly-
meeting at* York, *which he attended, was over,
he ſet out for* Norfolk; *which County, part of*
Suffolk, *and* London, *had been before him ſome
time, yet not ſo diſtinct and clear as he moſt loved;
of which he gave the following inſtructive Account in a Letter to one of his Sons, dated from*
Sutton *in* Lincolnſhire, *the* 3*d of the eleventh
Month, viz.*

———— ' Tho' I have been unuſually long
' without writing to thee, both on account of
' having little material to adviſe of, and being
' under ſome uneaſy Uncertainty about my
' real Duty reſpecting this little Journey, which
' hath cauſed me more Exerciſe by Night and
' by

'by Day, than many greater: Not through
'my own Unwillingness to go any where, if
'I may but be thoroughly satisfied of the Fa-
'ther's Mind; but from a Fear, whether
'Truth itself required, and drew to it, tho' it
'hath stood almost constantly before me much
'of the time since I saw thee: But I longed
'for more clear, living Engagement; that
'even after the Time which seem'd to be
'pointed out was come, I got not to a full
'Conclusion till about three Weeks before I
'came away. In this Unsettledness I was
'backward in writing, and when I came to a
'Conclusion, my time was much employ'd in
'leaving matters suitably: And thus I have
'been tossing in much fear and littleness, yet
'under, I think, an honest Devotedness; and
'so have been thus long, in a sort, hid from
'thee: Tho' I found not much Necessity of
'writing, except to manifest my truly tender
'and earnest longing of Soul for thee, and for
'thy Help in the way of Blessing, which, be
'assured, is continued as honestly as I am ca-
'pable of. I may farther inform thee, that I
'hope to reach *Warwick* next First-day but
'one, that County, and the upper or western
'part of *Suffolk* and *Essex*, having most place
'with me.——Meeting-time being come, I
'must bid *Farewel,* and am thy loving Father,

' J. F.'

R r

After

After having vifited the Counties above-mention'd, he came up to *London* the beginning of the Month following, and ftaid therein vifiting the Meetings of Friends in and about the City, during feveral Weeks, to the Help and Encouragement of many, and the faithful Difcharge of his Duty. He return'd by *Uxbridge*, *Jordans* and *Wiccomb*; at which places he had pretty large Meetings, and to fome Advantage, tho' attended with deep labour, yet with humbly gladdening Help: From thefe parts he went directly home, where he arrived in Health and Peace.

He attended the Quarterly-meeting at *York* in the firft Month following, where his Company was, as ufual, acceptable; as his Example was helpful and edifying, both in Meetings and out of them.

Tho' under very great Weaknefs as to Health, he came up to the Yearly-meeting in *London* in the Year 1740, and it being the firft after his Return from *America*, according to the general practice of Friends, and at the Defire of his Brethren, he gave a concife and inftructive Account of his late Vifit to thofe parts, the State of Friends, the Increafe of the Society in fome places, and its declining State in others, with the Caufes which had moft obvioufly contributed thereto. He obferved, that as the Elders of the People were preferved in Frefhnefs and Zeal, under a diligent Care for the Growth of fpiritual Religion, Truth increafed,

good

good Order was preferved, the Difcipline kept up, and the Youth in many places tender and hopeful. On the contrary, where thofe who were of the firft Rank, both in refpect to Age and Situation of Life, declined in their religious Care; where the Spirit of this World fuppreffed the tender Defires after Riches of a durable nature; there Weaknefs, Diforder and Unfaithfulnefs, was too obvious, and a daily Decay of real Piety, as well as of Numbers, prevailed, to the Grief of the honeft-hearted, and the Lofs of thofe who unhappily fuffer'd this corrupting Spirit to take place. He pointed out, in a clear manner, the different parts where thefe Effects appeared, with that deeply affecting Sorrow which pierced him, when amongft thofe whofe Conduct occafion'd it.

This Summer, being engaged in fome little domeftick Affairs, he was not much abroad long together, tho' he attended feveral diftant and large Meetings in his own County; often remembring his abfent Friends and Children with true Affection, and manifefting his Care for their trueft Intereft; one of whom he writes to in the following manner: — 'But above all, 'my longing is for thy fpiritual Accefs, and 'Enlargement in the heavenly Paftures, under 'the leading and putting forth of the one 'heavenly Shepherd, which I ftill hope, as 'well as often humbly breathe for on thy ac- 'count, being well fatisfied of thy fincere 'Defires; which if properly retain'd, and

R r 2   carefully

' carefully cherifh'd on thy part, I cannot but
' comfortably hope, heavenly Help will mer-
' cifully regard ; fo be it, *Amen.*'

And in another Letter to the fame, dated
the 27th of the tenth Month 1740, he has
the following memorable Expreffions.

' I have been, and am, thro' merciful Fa-
' vour preferved in ufual Health, and attended
' with beft Peace and Comfort in our heavenly
' Father's Goodnefs ; tho' in the manifeft Ap-
' pearance (as I have often looked at it many
' Months) of a *fevere threatning time of Dif-*
' *trefs, in divers cafes, to this Nation* ; and
' if we be not quickened and excited hereby
' to Diligence, in feeking to lay hold of eternal
' Treafure, the Love and Favour of the bleffed
' infinite Rock and Fountain of all good, we
' fhall be more inexcufable than others of
' Mankind who know not fo well, and clearly,
' where and how to feek Happinefs and Re-
' fuge indeed ; which I often inwardly long
' and breathe in Spirit we may lay fuitably to
' heart. But after this little hint of what is
' much with me, I fhall take notice of fome
' of thy Remarks on thy late Journey, (into
' *Holland* and *Germany)* and firft tell thee, thy
' Account of thofe People called *Menonifts,* and
' *Moravians* (as I fuppofe they call themfelves)
' exactly agrees with my fecret and fettled Idea
' of them both ; for I believe both, and the
' latter efpecially, have had, in fome meafure,
' their Eyes opened ; but they fet Man to
' work

' work to form, and imitate Religion, and
' to build, without digging properly to find
' the Rock: Yet many from their pious In-
' tentions make a Shew for a time, and some
' Good may turn out of it: But it is a matter
' to be lamented (as I have very often thought)
' that there should be, as it were, an universal
' and continued Propensity prevailing, amongst
' the *Germans* especially, to run away with
' Speculation; and thereby so many valuable
' Springings, and Glimpses of the heavenly
' Day, should have yet brought forth or pro-
' duced no more durable Fruits, in experi-
' encing Salvation in reality. But it ever will
' be true, *no following Christ acceptably with-*
' *out submitting to the Cross*; which hath al-
' ways seem'd to me to be the place, at which
' that Country people in particular, as almost
' all Nations in general, have miscarried.—
' May the Plough of God take more effectual
' hold amongst them, is my heart's Desire:
' And may this Consideration strengthen thee
' in fearing, and even loathing a sort of living
' and delighting in, or being at ease in
' barren Speculation, even of best Things or
' Principles; but be still more and more ani-
' mated to seek daily Bread from the ever-
' lasting Father's own hand, who will hear
' and answer in due time the sincere and pa-
' tient, tho' hidden Criers for it; and thereby
' such will grow in the living Root, and bear
' Fruit in due season, to the Father's Praise

and

' and Honour.   I falute thee with this Breath-
' ing frefh upon my Soul for thee, which hath
' been often with me, when by my long Silence
' I have feem'd almoft to have forgot thee.'——

In the latter part of the Year 1741, he vifited Friends in fome of the northern Counties,
travelling through the Bifhoprick of *Durham*,
fome parts of *Northumberland*, from thence
into *Cumberland* and *Weftmoreland* ; of which
Journey, all the Account that remains, is contained in the following Letter to a Relation,
wrote foon after his Return, dated the 6th of
the ninth Month 1741, *viz.*

——— ' I cannot lofe Hope, nor almoft full
' Expectation, but that the divine Power,
' which can do all Things, will one time or
' other mercifully help thee, if thou labour in
' Watchfulnefs and Patience, to look to him
' for Salvation in true Diligence, fincere Re-
' fignation, and holy humble Truft ; and that
' he will refine thro' various manners of deal-
' ing, and diftreffing Difpenfations, his beloved
' Sons, whom he would make chofen Veffels
' in his Houfe : And with fuch an Eye, I be-
' lieve he hath looked upon thee, fomewhat
' like as upon *Jacob*, when a Stone was his
' Pillow ; yet the Lord of all Power and
' Majefty was in that Place, tho' *Jacob* knew
' it not.   And fo have fome others been made
' Witneffes, that he in Mercy and gracious
' Goodnefs,

' Goodnefs, was even working in and near us,
' when fometimes the Heavens feem'd like
' Brafs, and the Earth like Iron, and Fear and
' Sorrow furrounded: Thus he hath, and will
' winnow and refine, and will fhew that none
' elfe can fave ; and yet that he forfakes not
' thofe who would have no other God but
' him, the ever-living and all-powerful One,
' everlaftingly worthy to have all our Hearts,
' and to be trufted in, waited for, and praifed
' for ever. A Meafure of his glorious Love
' and Mercy covers my Heart at this Time,
' and bows my Spirit in humble Worfhip to
' his moft worthy Name : But I cannot ex-
' prefs like many others, according to my
' Views, and muft therefore leave what I have
' hinted for thee to gather the Subftance, as
' thou art capable. I am as well in Health,
' thro' merciful Support, as I have been many
' Years, and was favoured with Help from the
' beft Hand, in the little Journey through the
' northern Counties, to as much humbling
' Gladnefs in the Lord, as I have almoft ever
' known ; tho' we met with feveral afflicting
' Cafes, befides the common Heavinefs, or
' want of proper Hunger, which is more or
' lefs almoft a general Hurt. ———— I faid *we*,
' above, for I had the Opportunity of the good
' Company of *Michael Lightfoot* moft of the
' Time.'————

He

He continued at Home during the Winter, except attending the Quarterly - meeting at *York*, which when able, and not engaged in other Services, he seldom missed ; but Travelling began now to be very difficult and painful to him, from a constant and sharp *Strangury*, the too frequent Companion of advancing Years, and the Effect of unwearied Diligence in Travelling.

In the Spring of 1742 he found himself engaged to pay a Visit to Friends in *Oxfordshire*, and after he had discharged this Service, he came up once more to the Yearly-meeting in *London*, wherein, upon divers Occasions, he manifested the same living, holy Zeal, under the Conduct of heavenly Wisdom, for the Prosperity of Truth and Righteousness, which had often been conspicuous in him on these solemn Occasions. In the same Year he visited Friends in *Ireland* once more : This Concern had long remained upon him, as he expresses it in a Letter, *as a Debt to that Nation :* He left no farther Account of this Journey, than of the Places where, and the Times when he had Meetings ; it may however be remarked, that even at this Time of Life, and under great bodily Infirmity, his Care was as great as ever, that his Ministry might be as little burdensome to Friends as possible ; for it appears from the Account he kept, that he was at upwards of sixty Meetings in about eleven Weeks, and travelled in the same Space of Time above 670 Miles :

Miles: He intended to have communicated to a Friend a more particular Account of this Visit, and of the State of Friends in that Kingdom, but was prevented by Indifposition, and other intervening Services. The following Paf-fages from fome Letters wrote in this Journey, will not perhaps be altogether unacceptable.

———— 'My Hands and Thoughts, *(fays he,*
' *in a Letter to a Friend foon after he fet out)*
' have been bufy in haftening to difcharge
' myfelf of this Debt to *Ireland*, and I now
' hope for a Paffage thither, the firft fuitable
' Wind.——I am but in a low and heavy
' State of Mind, and fhould be very doubtful
' of being helped to live and act properly, but
' that a Grain of Faith is preferved; which
' hath heretofore often ftaid my Mind in pa-
' tient waiting, till merciful Supply of Food,
' and Ability to labour again, hath been ex-
' perienced from the all-fufficient and only
' rightly relieving Hand; and here is my cen-
' ter in reverent Truft, where, as we endea-
' vour fteadily to keep, duly attending for
' frefh Help that we may be what we are,
' thro' the Grace from on high, I believe we
' fhall not be neglected or forgotten of the all-
' knowing Fountain of every good Thing.'——

And in another Letter from *Dublin*, to one of his Sons:

S f   ' Thro'

———— ' Thro' merciful Support, I am as
' well, I think, as when we parted, tho' as I
' ride in pain, more or lefs, it occafions fome
' Fear, but doth not much dejeſt me, becaufe
' hitherto I have been helped along thro' Dif-
' ficulties, in the Father's Drawings, above
' reafonable Expeſtation ; and I am comfort-
' ably encouraged to hope in that fupplying
' Hand in every refpeſt.————May alfo know,
' that as the Time I had thought of came near,
' I became fo loaded, that every domeſtick
' Concern was almoſt uneafy to me : I came
' by *Warrington* and *Sutton*, but was forced to
' ftay three Days at *Chefter* for Wind ; I had
' a good and eafy Paffage, and came hither
' on Third-day Morning, to part of Friends
' Meeting, to my own and fome others
' Comfort.'————

He ftaid here till after Firft-day, and then
went towards the Southern parts, and to *Cork*
in about three Weeks ; and fo to *Mountrath*,
from whence he wrote the following Account.

———— ' I have kept clofely ftirring along,
' and much employ'd to anfwer the End of
' my coming, as diligently and honeftly as I
' know how ; which thro' continued merciful
' Help and renewed Supply, hath been hitherto
' as well, or rather better borne as to the Body,
' as well as in the chief Refpeſt, than I dared
' to hope for : And I am thus far thankfully

' eafy

' eafy on my own part, tho' thro' deep Labour,
' and at times much Sorrow ; yet I am glad I
' am here, becaufe of the bleffed favour of
' Help to pay this Vifit; and alfo in that I am
' fenfible of the ftrong Extendings of gracious
' Regard to this Nation, and even thàt the
' Dead may hear, and be made to live.

' I have been round the Southern parts, and
' am now near the middle, going Northward;
' and hope to be at *Dublin* at the Half-year's-
' meeting, and have fome Expectation that I
' may be clear by that time to return.'————

And foon after he got home, he wrote to
the fame Perfon, that ' he was thankfully eafy
' for gracious Help, thro' his late Journey, on
' divers Accounts.' And often faid, ' It was
' like removing a Weight from his Shoulders.'
After his Return, he continued much about
home, vifiting the neighbouring General-
meetings, and attending the Quarterly-meeting, as his Health, which daily grew more
precarious, permitted. The Winter proving
very inclement, it injured his Health ftill
more, and prevented him during great part of
the Spring from going abroad : His Care neverthelefs for the Profperity of Truth, was as
frefh as ever, his own inward Strength being
gracioufly renewed, as he often expreffed with
reverent Thankfulnefs to thofe about him, as
well as occafionally to his abfent Family ; for
whofe Prefervation and Increafe in divine Ex-

                    perience,

perience, and steady patient Progress in the Paths of Humility and Dependance, his Soul was often most deeply engaged.

In the sixth Month of this Year he attended the General-meeting at *Pickering* in the County of *York*, to which he got with some difficulty; but, as he mentioned in a Letter wrote in his Return home, he was soon satisfied in the Meeting in himself for the Journey. These Meetings which are held once a Year, are commonly very large, and held in an open place, to which some thousands of the neighbouring People resort, and at this time many of them behaved attentively, tho' it is not always, that so much can be said in their Behalf.

He continued very weak during the Winter of 1743, going but little abroad, and scarce being able to converse much with Friends, who came to see him at home, without feeling great Weakness afterwards, but his Fervour of Mind towards the best Things decayed not, nor diminished in the least. About this Time writing to a Friend, he says, ' that tho' he ' was more than a little afflicted in Body, yet ' he was not forsaken of the everlasting Helper.' And soon after to the same, in the following lively and affecting manner, *viz.*

' The *Christian* Affection accompanying ' thine, affords me more comfortable Satisfac- ' tion than I can describe, or thou can well ' conceive ; but it is to be considered as the ' merciful Operation of the all-knowing, all- ' good

‘ good and blessed Power, bringing into a
‘ Capacity of more helpful Oneness and Sym-
‘ pathy than bare Nature can do, and hum-
‘ blingly strengthens both Fear and Hope in
‘ his Arm for Help and Preservation in his
‘ way, thro’ what is yet before us here : In a
‘ renewed Consideration, and a degree of the
‘ sense of his manifold Mercies, and Fatherly
‘ Regard and Succour hitherto, my Heart
‘ worshipeth his Name, and greets thee in
‘ Love and living well-wishing.’——

During this Confinement at home, pursuant
to a secret Inclination of his own, strengthen’d
by the Request of his Children and divers
Friends, when Health and Opportunity permitted, he wrote that part of the Journal which
the Reader has been acquainted was finish’d by
himself, and continued adding to it by little
and little, till within a few Weeks before his
death. He got with some Difficulty to the
Quarterly-meeting at *York*, and was enabled to
bear the fatigue, and long sitting in the Meetings for Business, beyond his Expectation, as
he intimated to one of his Sons, in a Letter
wrote soon after ; part of which it may not be
improper here to insert, as it is another Indica-
tion of his deep Gratitude to Heaven, and the
holy Awe, which accompanied him in all
‘ things.—‘ Thine, *says he*, was very acceptable,
‘ being accompanied with a relish of religious,
‘ as well as natural Love and Nearness, which
‘ both comforts at present, and encreaseth

‘ reverent

' reverent Truſt in, and Regard to the al-
'. mighty Source of all our Good and true
' Help ; who hath hiddenly, yet mercifully
' cared for us many ways, and requires our
' Conſideration as ſuch, in order to encourage
' and inſtruct, in humble Confidence, yet with
' Watchfulneſs towards him, that he may be
' our Shepherd, thro' time, and his glorious
' Name may be renowned here and for ever.
' Bear with me, *dear Son*, in thus reaching
' towards thee in the living ſenſe of Mercy ;
' the ſtaying Comfort whereof is highly wor-
' thy of our ſecret Notice, and ſometimes our
' ſolid Commemoration.'————

In the Spring, 1744, he found himſelf engaged, tho' very weak in body, to ſee Friends
once more at their Yearly-meeting in *London*,
being accompanied by our ancient Friend
Boſwell Middleton, for whom he had a ſingu-
lar Eſteem : He came by *Sheffield*, *Mansfield*,
Nottingham, *Leiceſter*, and *Northampton* ; at
which Places he had Meetings with Friends to
Edification. His Weakneſs render'd it difficult
for him to bear the large Meetings for Buſineſs,
nevertheleſs he attended them, and under that
exemplary, reverent, watchful Frame of Mind,
which render'd his Company truly acceptable
and ſerviceable.

He return'd by *Nottingham*, where he had a
Meeting on Firſt-day with Friends, to his Satisfaction, expreſſing in a Letter, that ' ancient
' holy Help made the Viſit truly eaſing to
' him.'

' him.' From hence he went to his Monthly-meeting, where Friends were glad to see him; and home to his Family at *Knaresborough*, to which Place he removed this Summer.

Having rested a little at home, he attended the Midsummer Quarterly-meeting at *York*, which in a Letter wrote to a Friend soon after, he observes, ' was large of Friends, as well as ' many others not so called; and more satis-' factory and edifying, than sometimes at this ' Season, the Business being also transacted in ' a very amicable Manner ; *and concludes,* ' Tho' my Stomach will take but little Food, ' nor always keep that little, which weakens ' the Body much ; yet I think, my better Part ' is almost uncommonly supply'd in divers re-' spects, much to my Comfort, and reviving of ' my Faith in the heavenly Influence, which ' is Strength in Weakness, and will be, where ' his only worthy Name hath the Praise.'

About this time it came before him to visit Friends towards *Bristol*; and the circular Yearly Meeting at *Worcester* was particularly in his view, towards which places he set out in the sixth Month by the way of *Marsden-height*, and from thence into *Cheshire*, where he visited several Meetings, wherein, as he writes to a Friend, *Truth helped and strengthned him to pay some Debt, to his comfortable Ease :* From hence he came to *Shrewsbury*, where he had two Meetings, and then passed into *Herefordshire*, where he visited Friends pretty generally ; and

concludes

concludes with obferving, that ' tho' in this
' Journey his natural State was but feeble, and
' attended with divers Difficulties, yet he was
' not doubtful but he fhould be affifted, in
' Mercy and Favour, to difcharge himfelf of
' the Debt which had feem'd to grow and re-
' main upon him, the way he was going, to
' fuch a degree, as to return in holy Quiet:
' And, *fays he*, I afk no Queftions farther, but
' to be helped to live to the ever-living Being,
' the little time he may fuffer me to continue
' on this fide the Grave.' He was enabled to
reach *Worcefter* Yearly-meeting, and therein
to bear a noble *Chriftian* Teftimony to the All-
fufficiency of that Power which had preferved,
fupported, and guided him in the way that was
right and well-pleafing, in degree, and is likewife able to do the fame for all the Children
of Men. From hence he went to *Briftol* and
Bath, vifiting the Meetings of Friends in and
near thefe places, and was helped to labour
faithfully, and in much Plainnefs among them,
to his own great Relief and humbling Comfort, as he often expreffed in his Letters on
this Journey.

He left *Bath* the beginning of the eighth
Month, and travelled homewards by eafy Jour-
neys, having Meetings with Friends as Opportunity offer'd. He got home by the End of
the Month, but in great Weaknefs, the Weather having proved unufually wet and cold,
had greatly affected him; fo that after his Return

turn he feldom got abroad, but continued vifibly declining (and not unperceived to himfelf) during feveral Weeks, fometimes with fhort Intervals of Eafe ; in one of which he wrote, ' that he thought himfelf fomewhat better, ' and that he might put on fome time longer, ' and with lefs Mifery than he had endured ' the laft two Years ; yet, *fays he*, I may be ' miftaken, as my Recovery is fo flow, that ' in a Week it is fcarcely advanced perceptibly.' And then concludes, ' As I have no Depend- ' ance on human Affiftance but from thee, ' nor any Correfpondence which affords me ' like Comfort and Satisfaction, I muft beg ' thy frequent Remembrance, and to hear ' from thee as often and freely as Leifure will ' permit ; and be affured, my hearty careful ' Defires for thee, in every true good, not only ' is enliven'd by the ftrong Ties of Nature and ' Affection, but are more riveted and ftrength- ' ned, by many a gracious Spring of living ' Goodnefs, from the almighty Helper of his ' People, who have trufted in him and feared ' him. Thus, *dear Son*, farewel, farewel, ' faith thy affectionate Father,

' J. F.'

With thefe affecting Expreffions ended a Correfpondence, which afforded the ftrongeft Satisfaction that any thing in this life could yield : The Letter was dated the 15th of the tenth Month, from which time he gradually

T t

declined

declined till the 13th of the eleventh Month following, when he peaceably expired; leaving to his Family and Friends the comfortable Aſſurance of his being gone before, to enjoy that unmixed Happineſs which is the Portion of thoſe who prefer a conſcientious Diſcharge of Duty to God, their Families and the World, though attended with Labour, anxious Care and Solicitude, to all the falſe, tho' gilded Purſuits, which the Spirit of Deception throws in the way of Mortals.

What happen'd in this Interval was communicated in a Letter, ſoon after his Deceaſe, by a Perſon who attended him Night and Day, with the Diligence that filial Duty, and a juſt ſenſe of his Worth required, *viz.*

———— ' From the time he left *Bath* he
' felt himſelf gradually declining, and was very
' much indiſpoſed when he got home; this he
' attributed to the Coldneſs of the Weather,
' and expected, a little Reſt and Warmth
' might tend to his Recovery; but he ſenſibly
' declin'd ever after he got home, and more
' than he ſeem'd to be aware of.————

' He got to Meetings during ſome Weeks
' after his Return, and his Teſtimony was
' as lively and powerful as ever : He was
' confin'd within doors about ſix or ſeven
' Weeks, and while he could bear to ſit ſo
' long, the Week-day Meetings were kept in
' his Houſe.————In the laſt four or five Weeks
' his old Complaint, which had at times af-
' flicted

‘ flicted him extremely, abated very much, and
‘ he could sit or lie four or five Hours without
‘ making water, and this without much pain.
‘ —— He several times expressed his Satisfac-
‘ tion and inward Peace, in having performed
‘ his last Journey, saying, *his Shoulders were*
‘ *a good deal lightened by it; and was reconciled*
‘ *to his Grave, if he was now to be taken away;*
‘ *but should incline to write something more (by*
‘ *way of Journal) if the Lord saw meet to raise*
‘ *him once more.* I was very attentive to his
‘ Conversation, being never from him, but
‘ when I could not avoid it: When almost all
‘ other Expression failed, he was observed to
‘ repeat the following, in a very fervent and
‘ emphatick manner, viz. *Heavenly Goodness*
‘ *is near, heavenly Goodness is near*; thus ac-
‘ knowledging to the last a sense of the Lord's
‘ Presence. The two last Weeks he slept al-
‘ most continually, Day and Night, his Me-
‘ mory and Capacity being very much impaired:
‘ He was quite in a State of Mildness, and the
‘ Innocency of a Child; and tho’ it was satis-
‘ factory to see so much Sweetness about him,
‘ yet it was at the same time afflicting to observe
‘ his Strength and Faculties exhausted: ’Twas
‘ the only Satisfaction I could then enjoy, to
‘ do every thing in my Power to one of the best
‘ of Parents, and the worthiest of Men, tho’
‘ sometimes the most cutting Affliction I ever
‘ felt, to see him languishing, and at the
‘ same time not able to express his Wants:
‘ The Day preceding his Decease he was

T t 2

‘ restless

' reftlefs and uneafy, but at laft expired very
' quietly, without Sigh or Groan, about Ten
' in the Forenoon on the Firft-day, and was
' buried on the Third-day following : We
' were favoured with the Company of feveral
' worthy Friends from divers parts on this Oc-
' cafion, and indeed the Time was folemn, and
' by fome never to be forgot ; feveral lively
' Teftimonies being delivered, both on Truth's
' Account, and to the Memory of fo worthy a
' Man, who is gone from a Series of Pain and
' Exercifes, to receive the Reward of his faith-
' ful Labours.———

' A. F.'

Tho' the following Letters are without Date
or Superfcription, yet as they may poffibly fall
into Hands to whom they may be of ufe, it
was thought proper to infert them : In giving
Admonitions of this kind, he was always efpecially careful, not to divulge to any the Errors
or Faults he laboured to amend.

The firft feems to be wrote to the Friends of
a particular County, but as no Addrefs remains,
it is left to thofe who are concern'd to profit by
it : It feems by the Hand not to have been
written long before his Deceafe.

' DEAR FRIENDS,
' BEING often brought under fome nearly
' affecting Confiderations, refpecting the
' ftate of the Church in your County, it hath
' appeared

' appeared to me, there are *three Things* which
' are particular Hindrances to the Prosperity of
' Friends in the Life and Substance of true
' Religion; which I am stirred up to put you
' in mind of with tender and brotherly Cau-
' tion: The first is an *inordinate Pursuit of the*
' *Riches and Enjoyments of this World*; another,
' the *want of honest Care and Zeal to keep clear*
' *of, and stand up against that vile Practice of*
' *clandestine Trading*, which is indeed but one
' Effect of the Cause already mentioned; ano-
' ther Thing is, *want of due Care in all those*
' *who are active and concerned in managing the*
' *Affairs of the Church, to be such as truly fear*
' *God, and hate Covetousness; and such as feel*
' *reverently after heavenly Help to act and judge*
' *for the Lord, and not for Man.* Wherefore,
' as I look upon a due and right Concern upon
' Friends in this respect, to be greatly condu-
' cive to the Churches Good, its Peace and
' building up in the holy Faith; it is fresh and
' tenderly in my Mind to intreat you all,
' carefully to consider, that *the Wise Man's Eye*
' *is in his Head:* And it is an everlasting Cer-
' tainty, that the right Wisdom that enables
' any to act for the true Good of the Church
' of Christ, must be *received from Christ the*
' *Truth, and the Head of the Church:* And
' whoever seeks to be ordered, and to act in it,
' will always seek God's Glory, and the Sup-
' pression of every thing that is contrary to it,
' and without respect of Persons; and also to

' walk

‘ walk as Enfamples to the Flock in the Prac-
‘ tice of Godlinefs and *Chriftian* Self-denial.
‘ And to be thus helped, the Renewing of the
‘ Holy Ghoft, the only true Helper, is abfo-
‘ lutely neceffary to be carefully waited for ;
‘ and thus would Mens Hearts and Minds be
‘ loofened from the captivating Fetters and
‘ Bias of the Earth, and fo be render'd bright
‘ Examples to one another, fhewing forth the
‘ Effects of true Fear towards God, in fhun-
‘ ning every evil Way : And fo would that
‘ bafe Part of Robbery be avoided with juft
‘ Care, and teftified againft to the Honour of
‘ the righteous Principle of Truth, and the true
‘ Peace and Tranquility of Soul, to fuch as
‘ obferve it, be eftablifhed. Thus would Friends
‘ in that County profper in the faving Know-
‘ ledge of Chrift abundantly more, and become
‘ more fruitful in Righteoufnefs, and more true
‘ Way-marks to the many Enquirers for the
‘ Way of Salvation amongft you ; the Love and
‘ Peace of God would more plentiful abound in
‘ you fecretly, and unite you as profeffed Chil-
‘ dren of one Father, which my Soul reve-
‘ rently and fervently begs before the Lord our
‘ God, may become your joyful Experience
‘ in an abundant manner ; fo will you fare
‘ well indeed, to the Glory and Honour of
‘ the divine Name, which is worthy, worthy,
‘ for evermore.

‘ J. F.’

A Copy

A Copy of a Letter to a Friend in the Miniſtry.

' MY FRIEND,

' SOME Days ago, as I was riding alone,
' thou was ſuddenly brought to my Re-
' membrance, and divers Conſiderations re-
' ſpecting thee enſued, in true Care for thee,
' for thy Safety and Comfort, and for the
' Good of the Cauſe of Truth ; which Con-
' ſiderations have made ſuch Impreſſion on
' my Mind, as to prevail upon me to commit
' them to writing. I queſtion not but the Love
' and Power of Truth hath had a good degree
' of Prevalence in thy Mind for Regeneration,
' and hath begotten Love to the Lord's Work
' in the Earth, and ſome Engagement at times
' to be active therein. Now, a ſure way to
' grow right, is to have a true and watchful
' Care, to feel and know certainly the firſt
' Work, *Regeneration*, to be duly carried on,
' to be *crucified with Chriſt* ; and ſo pure Love
' to Truth itſelf will grow predominant, and
' other Loves be buried. Then a thorough
' Care to attend with Patience for certain; and
' intelligible Requirings, and heavenly Help,
' upon every Occaſion of acting for Truth ;
' thro' which humble Care, the divine Hand
' filleth Veſſels more and more with Food,
' with Light and Aſſiſtance to act according to
' his Pleaſure, to his Honour, and the Edifica-
' tion

' tion of the People in their several Stations,
' amongst whom we converse or labour.

' The farther Counsel which arose, and is
' with me (not from any Uneasiness on any
' particular Account, but for thy right Help)
' is, *labour innocently to be and to do what*
' *Grace would make thee, and lead thee into* ;
' and be content with its Wages ; for it gives
' or makes way for, as much Regard and
' Freedom from Men, as is meet for us. Have
' a care of *too much Talking and Conversation* ;
' so we may better remember, that no Incon-
' sistency be observed in it, and there may be
' less occasion or room for sinking into un-
' profitable Drooping or Reservedness. I know
' it is also rather profitable, to be moderately
' concerned about some temporal Affairs, with
' inward Fear, till we become assured of a
' distinct Requiring to leave it.

' J. F.'

We shall conclude this Account of the Labours and Services of our dear and honoured
FATHER, with some Testimonies concerning
him: The first is taken from the Account
given to the Quarterly-meeting of *York*, by the
Monthly-meetings of *Richmond* and *Knaresborough*, to which he successively belonged ;
the Purport whereof is as follows :

THAT

THAT though he was born of religious Parents, and religiously educated, yet he was made sensible in his early Years, that neither Tradition, outward Regularity, nor any thing short of real inward Purification of Soul and Spirit, would render him acceptable in the Sight of the Lord; he therefore gave up his Heart to him, who thro' the effectual Operation of his divine Grace, baptized and gradually purified his Spirit, and prepared and fitted him to be an useful Instrument in God's Hand, and an able Minister of the Gospel of Peace and Salvation; to which Service he was called, when but young, and readily gave up, not suffering the Things of this World to take up his Mind and Time, but laboured diligently and faithfully therein from his young Years, to the Conclusion of his Days.

And as by the blessed Teachings of the holy Spirit, he grew in Experience, both in the Mysteries of the heavenly Kingdom, as also of the Workings of Satan in Opposition thereto; so he was qualified, and often had to detect his Snares, and to point out the Way that leads safely to eternal Rest; which he did with an holy Zeal and Fervour, becoming one who had a deep Sense of the great Value of Souls, and the Dangers they are environ'd with in this State of Probation, and of the awful Majesty of the divine Being.

He travelled much in this Nation in the Service of the Gospel, in *Scotland* likewise, and

Wales

Wales : He visited *Ireland* several times, and thrice he crofs'd the Seas to *America,* in the same Service, to the Comfort and Edification of the Church, leaving Seals of his Miniftry in many places. — He had always a Regard to the well-approved Practice of duly acquainting his Friends, and having their Unity and Approbation ; and was careful to perform the Service required, with as much Expedition as poffible, choofing rather to fuffer Hardfhips, than to lofe Time, or be burthenfome to Friends, *even in the latter Part of his Life, when he was attended with great bodily Afflictions.*

His Teftimony was awakening, found and edifying, deliver'd in the Demonftration of divine Authority ; for he handled not the Word deceitfully, nor endeavoured to pleafe itching Ears ; but as he waited to be endued with Wifdom and Power from on high, fo he was enabled to fpeak home to the Conditions of the People ; For *he who cut* Rhahab, *and wounded the* Dragon, *put a fharp Sword into his Hand againft Hypocrify and Wickednefs, and againft fuch as held the Truth in Unrighteoufnefs* ; yet to the Afflicted, and thofe who were travelling toward *Zion,* he had often to adminifter both fuitable Advice and Confolation.

He was zealoufly concerned for good Order and the Difcipline of the Church, and was remarkably qualified for the Management of its Affairs, being of quick Apprehenfion, an extenfive Capacity and deep Judgment ; and

could

could exprefs himfelf aptly, copioufly and ftrongly ; and as he diligently attended both Monthly, Quarterly, Yearly, and General-meetings, fo he was of very peculiar Service in them, approving himfelf a wife and able Counfellor, faithful and juft to God and Man.——

His Converfation was exemplary ; being humble, fteady and fincere, doing the Work of an Evangelift, and making full proof of his Miniftry, in *Patience*, *Temperance*, *Vigilance* and *Fortitude*, enduring Afflictions, and ufing even the Neceffaries of Life with Moderation. He was kind and affifting to his Friends, pleafant and helpful to his Neighbours, fkilful and induftrious in managing his temporal Affairs for the Benefit of his Family, over whom he had a true paternal Care : Being a loving Hufband, an affectionate Father, as well as a faithful Friend, and a living Minifter, and acceptable to all forts of People.

He departed this Life at *Knarefborough* in *Yorkfhire*, the 13th of the eleventh Month 1744, and was honourably buried in Friends Burying-ground in *Scotten* near the faid Town, the 15th of the fame Month, aged 69 Years, having been a Minifter near 50 Years.

The clofe and affectionate Friendfhip that had fubfifted between him and our worthy Friend *John Hayward*, during great part of their Lives, has engaged the latter to give the following Teftimony to his Memory.

A

A TESTIMONY concerning our dear Friend JOHN FOTHERGILL.

AS the Memory of good Men should live, we find ourselves sometimes engaged to hand down to Posterity our Knowledge of them. And I have to say concerning our deceased Friend, that in his publick Ministry he was a *Strength and Comfort to my Soul* in my early Days, as well as at many times since; and I doubt not but that many others have the same Testimony in themselves to give concerning him. And my Judgment is, that he was a living Minister, a Man shunning Applause, and always endeavouring to keep down Self in all its Appearances; an inward Seeker after divine Manifestation, a constant Reprover of forward Spirits, but a true Helper of the Faithful and Sincere, however weak or fearful. A Man of a strong and clear Judgment, both in spiritual and temporal Affairs, steady in his own Conduct, as well as in the Discipline of the Church; zealous in maintaining the *Christian* Testimonies profest by us, and industrious in his outward Affairs, when not engaged in the Service of the Gospel: And I doubt not in the least, but that *he is gone to everlasting Rest.*

JOHN HAYWARD.

The

The Perufal of the preceding Sheets will doubtlefs inform the intelligent Reader, what manner of Perfon he was, whofe *Memoirs* they contain, and render any additional Teftimony the lefs needful. His Children neverthelefs find themfelves engaged, in Juftice to the Memory of fo worthy a Parent, to mention,

THAT it is well remembred by feveral of them, with what Earneftnefs he endeavoured, in the yearning of Compaffion, to imprefs upon their tender Minds, a Regard to the divine Witnefs in their own Breafts, often gathering them about him, placing fome upon his Knees, the reft ftanding before him, whilft he minifter'd Counfel to them, according to their Capacities, the Tears defcending from his Eyes : Which Seafons have often been revived in fome of their Remembrance, on various Occafions to their Profit.

And as he had no greater Joy than that his *Children fhould walk in the Truth*, fo it was his Care to be exemplary to them therein, in all *Plainnefs*, *Temperance*, and *Godlinefs*, encouraging every Appearance of good, difcouraging the contrary, and admonifhing and reftraining, as occafion required; watching over their tender Years with true paternal Care and Solicitude for their prefent Welfare and future Happinefs, to the utmoft of his Power.

As he thus difcharged his Duty towards them, fteadily and faithfully, fo his Conduct reached

reached the Witnefs in their Minds, and convinced them early, that nothing could fo effectually endear them to him, nor entitle them to his peculiar Regard, as a ftrict Conformity to his Precepts and Example, not only in refpect to Plainnefs and Sobriety, but alfo in coming up in a truly religious Life and Converfation : And that his impartial Regard to Truth in the inward Parts, would lead him to treat thofe who fuffered themfelves to be mifled by the Deceivablenefs of Unrighteoufnefs, with Difregard and juft Reproof : So that they have had at times to acknowledge with Gratitude to the Moft High, the Happinefs of their Lot, inafmuch as a diligent Application of Heart to feek and fear the Lord, whom he ferved continually, was the fure Way to a beloved Father's Affection.

And tho' his principal Endeavours were, that his Offspring might be made Partakers of that Bleffing which makes truly rich, the Poffeffion of Truth in themfelves, as the moft excellent Inheritance ; yet he was not unmindful of their temporal Good, but provided for them liberally, according to his Circumftances, placing them in fuch Stations in Life, wherein, by Induftry and Care, they might be render'd eafy to themfelves, and ufeful to others.

And tho' for a Time he had not the Satisfaction to fee the Travail of his Soul for all his Children fully anfwer'd, and no fmall Affliction attended him on that Account, yet he faithfully

laboured

laboured in bowels of Compaſſion, and paternal Tenderneſs, for the Help and Recovery
of ſuch of his Family, from whoſe Conduct
his Anxiety aroſe ; endeavouring by the moſt
pathetick Application to awake to a Change.
and Reformation of Heart ; ſeeking by In-
treaties, by Reproof, by Tears, and every
Method a Heart repleniſh'd with divine and
fatherly Affection could ſuggeſt, the Recovery
of ſuch as had ſtray'd from the Father's Fold.
After a Series of painful Labour, ineffectually
beſtow'd, he was enabled to caſt his Care
upon the Lord, who releas'd his burthen'd Soul
from the Weight he had long borne ; and we
doubt not heard and beheld his ſtrong Cries,
his Tears, and humble Interceſſions, and anſwer'd beyond his Expectation, renewing his
Viſitation to them afreſh, and by his mighty
Hand brought into a State of Acceptance.

This, they think it their Duty to acknowledge, in order to ſtir up other Parents to the
like Care ſo to live, as to anſwer the Witneſs
of God in their Children, and having their
own Minds ſeaſon'd with the Savour of the
Goſpel, they may ſay in Word and Deed,
follow me as I follow Chriſt : And ſhould their
Offspring turn aſide from the way of Purity,
theſe Parents will be helped to labour for the
Recovery of their Children ; and if not ſuc-
ceſsfully, yet it will be to their own Eaſe, in a
holy Conſciouſneſs of Diſcharge of Duty.

In

In all the Stations of Life his Teſtimony was confirmed and embelliſhed by a Conduct becoming a Miniſter of Chriſt, whom he ſerved faithfully, and with great diligence, and by a daily inward dwelling with the Spring of Wiſdom and Light, his Mind was often open'd, and his Spirit ſuſtained, to ſecret Worſhip. When his Hand was upon his Labour, his Delight was in the Law of his God, to meditate therein Day and Night, and to talk of his Statutes, in his Houſe to his Family, and thoſe with whom he convers'd ; and many times, by a Tranſition from earthly to heavenly things, inſtructed and edify'd the Minds of thoſe preſent.

In his publick Teſtimony awful and weighty, being endued with true Wiſdom, ſtrong and immoveably bent againſt all Unrighteouſneſs, quick in diſcerning, and powerful in detecting the Myſteries of Antichriſt, who has ſought to ſtupify the People with the golden Cup, and thereby to ſpread the Power, and enlarge the Borders of the Kingdom of Death. As a Flame of Fire was he to the Rebellious and Stubborn ; but refreſhing as the Dew on *Hermon* to the honeſt Traveller, miniſtring Counſel and Comfort to the drooping Soul, being not only an Inſtructor, but a Father to many : zealous and wiſe, in the Support of the Diſcipline eſtabliſhed amongſt us, impartially and honeſtly executing Judgment and Juſtice ; no Family Connections (not even his own) could bias

him

him from laying the Line upon Offenders, and from a steady Endeavour to keep clean the Camp of God; in which Labour he was often successful, being made a *Terror to evil Doers*, and a *Praise to them that did well.*

Thus conducted, in every Station of Life, he became honourable amongst Men, and greatly esteemed by those of superior Rank who knew him; being adorned with that Dignity which Truth confers on its faithful Followers: One of his Acquaintance, a worthy Magistrate, in a Letter to one of his Sons, soon after his Decease thus speaks of him. — 'I 'must own my Weakness; I could not refrain 'paying some Tears to the Memory of my 'departed Friend: At first I thought it a 'mournful, but after a short Recollection, a 'pleasing Tribute; for though Death be the 'Wages of Sin, yet it opens to the Reward of 'a well spent Life; I therefore ought not to 'mourn, but to rejoice at his receiving his '*Reward,* that *inexpressible, happy,* and *eternal* '*Reward* prepared for him.'

To conclude. The mighty God, who visited him in his Youth with the Discovery of his saving Power, who thereby cleansed him from Unrighteousness, and sanctified him to himself a chosen Vessel, supported him in all his faithful Labours by Sea and Land, covered his Head in all Conflicts, and by whom his Bow abode in Strength, became his Evening-song and Stay in the Decline of

Life;

Life; that heavenly Goodness he had ever prized as his chiefest Joy, remained as a Seal upon his Spirit, that *he had pleased God, and was accepted of him.* In this, after having served God in his Generation, he fell asleep, and was, we doubt not, gathered to the Assembly of the Just, to continue that glorious Employ, which was his principal Delight on Earth, to *worship, adore and magnify the Lord God and the Lamb for ever.*

It does not appear at what time the following Paper was wrote; nor whether it was ever copied and given abroad for general Service: It appears by the Hand to have been done pretty early in his Life, and most probably the first he wrote; yet as it contains divers weighty Advices, it may still have its Service, and is therefore added to the rest, *viz.*

A

A
Faithful Warning,

SOUNDED

In the BORDERS of the CAMP of ISRAEL.

READER,

THE *Cause of my setting Pen to Paper at this Time, is a Desire to discharge my Duty to God, and to clear my Conscience towards my Brethren in the Creation, in order to stir them up to Circumspection in what relates to their Duty to their Creator, in answering the tender Motions of his holy Spirit given unto all Men, whereby they may come to be acquainted with God, and with his Son Jesus Christ, whom to know is* Life eternal : *And that thus they may come to witness the Lord to be on their side, in the Day that is approaching ; which to those who do not know their Peace to be made with God, will be a terrible one : Fear will take hold within, and Troubles without ; and Distress on every hand. Therefore, sober Reader, that thou may take the Wise-man's Counsel, which is to*

X x 2

acquaint

acquaint thyself with God, and be at Peace, *is my hearty and earnest Desire, who am a Lover of thy Soul, and a Friend (according to my Power) to all Mankind.*

J. F.

DEAR *Friends and Brethren in the holy Seed,* in which our Relation stands, where-ever scattered throughout the whole World: Unto you doth the Salutation of endeared Love reach, and flows from the divine Fountain thro' my Heart at this time; earnestly desiring all your Preservation, in the continual Remembrance of the Goodness of God to your immortal Souls; who once were seeking from Mountain to Hill, and from one Profession to another, as many thousands, as good as we were, are doing at this Day, and who are seeking the living among the dead, where he is not to be found.

And oh! methinks I see how glad many were in that Day, that the Lord thought them worthy to come to the Knowledge of the great Mystery, hid from Ages and Generations, and now revealed, even *Christ in us, the Hope of Glory :* And how willing were many in that Day, to deny themselves, and to take up his Cross to their own Wills and Desires, so that they might obtain Favour with him, who had given his Son a Ransom for them, altho' it was through the Loss of all ; And thus many came to witness with the holy Apostle, in

measure,

measure, a being *crucified to the World*, and the *World to them*, by the *Cross of Christ*, under which it was their Delight to dwell. Thus the Favour of God was obtained by many, which was more to their Souls than the Increase of earthly Riches; and the Lord was well pleased with them, and delighted to honour them with his glorious Presence, which, blessed be his most worthy Name, many Souls have good cause to say, he has not with-held from those whose Care and chief Concern it has been to live to his Honour, desiring nothing more in this World, than that God's Will may be done by them; considering, that the End for which he has been pleased to afford them Time, Strength and Understanding in this Life, was that they might spend them to his Praise, and the Honour of his Name, and to walk so before him, as that he may delight to bless them, in providing all things necessary for them. And thus, *dear Friends*, we come to receive the Benefits, and to reap the true Advantage of the Death and Sufferings of Christ, who died for all, according to the holy Apostle's Testimony recited above, that *henceforth we should live no longer to ourselves, but unto him who died for us, and rose again:* For tho' he died for all, yet here was, and still is the Danger of forfeiting, or depriving ourselves of Justification by him; by *living to Self*, and not to him, in Obedience unto Righteousness: Which my Soul earnestly desires may never be the State of any, whom

God

God in his infinite Love hath given to believe in the Light of his dear Son, the Rock and Refuge of all the Righteous for ever.

And, *dear Friends and Elder Brethren*, unto whom my Heart is now opened, and deeply affected with the free Extendings of God's ancient Love, whereby the Lord hath brought us to be acquainted with himself, and one with another ; in which Love I am concerned to defire you every one to confider, how wonderfully the Lord has ftood by you, and helped you thro' many Straits, and hath been Mouth and Wifdom, Tongue and Utterance, and hath never failed in the needful Time, as you have leaned upon him, and ftood in the Senfe of your own Nothingnefs without him : And let us ftill remember, that without the Help and Affiftance of God's invifible Power, we are this Day as weak, and as unfit as ever, to act or perform any thing that will either tend to the Honour of God, or the Propagation of his pure Truth, and confequently to the Comfort of our own Souls, or edifying the Church. Wherefore, in the Confideration of thefe Things, I cannot be eafy, but in Reverence to God, with a venerable Efteem for the faithful Elders, in good Will to the Church of God, and in order to clear myfelf of that Neceffity which remains upon my Spirit, I am willing to give forth this Caution, believing I have many Witneffes, who will be ready to fet their Seals to the Truth of it. Therefore, *dear Brethren*, keep near to the
Lord,

Lord, with whom is everlasting Strength, and he will fill you with heavenly Wisdom, which is first *pure*, then *peaceable, gentle*, and *easy to be intreated* to that which is good ; and will make your Labours and Exercises effectual to his Honour, the Peoples Comfort, and the Good of his Church, which he is bringing up out of the Wilderness, and has many to add to her, who are yet unwilling to come in ; and for whose Sake the Lord has long spared this Nation, and hovered over it with an Eye of good.

And now to you who make Profession of this pure holy Principle of Truth, which God in his great Love hath revealed in you, and convinced you of, so that you have professed to believe, that as it is obeyed and followed, it will lead to God, and yet do not shew your Faith by your Works, nor bring forth Fruits of Righteousness, which are always the Fruits of true Faith ; I am earnest with you to con-sider weightily, wherein true Religion con-sists : Is it in a *bare Profession of the Truth* ; *a giving up the Name to God?* Or is it in *well-doing* ; in *obeying* this pure Principle of Truth we profess, so as to come to be saved by it, and redeemed out of the crooked Ways and bye Paths of this sinful World ? Remember *Cain* of old ; he offered an Offering, as well as *Abel* ; but *Abel*'s Offering was accepted ; *Cain*'s re-jected : And what was the Reason ? The Lord himself declares it, in speaking to *Cain* : *If*

thou

*thou doſt well, ſhalt thou not be accepted ? And
if thou doſt not well, Sin lies at thy Door.*
Thus we may ſee plainly, that true Religion
doth conſiſt in *well-doing* ; falſe, in *evil-doing :*
No matter what the Profeſſion hath been, or
is ; for it is not the *Hearer* of the Law, but
the *Doer of it*, who is juſtified before God.
And tho' many may be ready to ſay, *they have
but little Knowledge, and can but do a little* ;
and *others, that they are concerned in the World,
and cannot well avoid it* ; *or be ſo circumſpect
as they would be, or as they ſee they ſhould be* ;
and ſo loſe their Buſineſs, and bring Shame
upon themſelves, their Families, and the Society. And here the Enemy works all manner
of ways to keep his Hold in the Heart of
Man, the Place where God ſhould predomi-
nate. But unto ſuch as may reaſon on this
wiſe, I would ſay in the Words of our bleſſed
Lord ; *to him that hath but little*, if he be
faithful, *more will be added* ; but he who is not
faithful in a little, is not like to be faithful in
much ; and therefore is unfit to have it. And
if the Lord in his Mercy hath brought any
to the Knowledge of Good and Evil, and
by the Light of his holy Spirit hath taught
them what is Righteouſneſs, and what is Unrighteouſneſs, as bleſſed be his honourable
Name for ever, he has done to many, they will
be inexcuſable : And he hath promiſed unto
thoſe who ſeek the Kingdom of Heaven, and
his Righteouſneſs, that *all other Things ſhall be
added,*

added, as he fees meet : Now thofe who know what is Righteoufnefs, and do not purfue it, how can they expect the additional Bleffing in this World ? Or what juft Foundation of Hope have they to enjoy that glorious Habitation which God the Lord has prepared for the Righteous only, when this World to them is at an End ? Which if they are deprived of, the Lofs is difmal indeed, and which all the Riches a Man can poffibly acquire, can never make up. To all therefore, who are in any meafure fenfible of the Requiring of God, through the Spirit of his Son, by whom he fpeaks to his People, according to the Author of the *Hebrews* ; methinks a Warning, in the pure Love of God, founds aloud through my Heart to come away and meet the Lord, who hath long hovered over you ; and be rouzed up to Zeal and Circumfpection, while time is offer'd unto you ; and it runs through my Soul in great Dread and Fear towards God, and Love to the whole Univerfe, to fay on this wife, *that as fure as ever Chrift wept over* Jerufalem *in ancient Days, becaufe he would have gathered them together, as a Hen gathereth her Chickens under her Wings, but they would not ; fo furely he mourns over the Inhabitants of this Nation, at this Day* ; whom, in his tender Love, he hath brought in fome degree to be acquainted with the Spirit of his Son, even the Spirit of Truth, which, as it is followed, leads into all Truth, and out of all Error and Untruth. Thus

Y y

gathering

gathering Peoples Minds into Covenant with their Maker, and into one Spirit, whereby they become Sheep of one Pasture, Children of one Father, and often are fed as at one Table ; which the good Shepherd is daily spreading for those who follow him with all their Hearts, as well as in Profession : A Sense of his Goodness to his faithful Followers, at this Time affects my Heart in so strong a manner, as that Praises spring in my Soul to him, the divine and inexhaustible Ocean.

But still, *my Friends*, methinks I would expostulate a little with you farther on this Subject ; I mean concerning *Jerusalem*, whose Inhabitants our Saviour so often would have gathered ; it does not appear, but that as they were a People of one City, so they were of one Profession, and yet wanted to be gathered ; let us seriously consider what was the Reason of it : Their Minds, their Affections, wanted to be gathered into Covenant with God, and into Obedience to his holy Spirit, whereby they might have been led thro' the outward Ceremonies, into that which was within the Veil ; and for want of a Willingness to be thus gathered, they came to a miserable Disappointment ; *the Things that belonged to their Peace, were hid from their Eyes.* Now, in the Fear of God, I desire all you who are making Profession of the precious Truth, seriously to consider, how far your Minds are gathered by it, and whether your Wills are subjected thereby

unto

unto the Will of God, and brought into Covenant with him ; or you are gathered in Name only, and your Minds are at liberty to wander in the World, and after the Things thereof, in an inordinate manner ; which the Lord takes Notice of, and beholds with a dreadful Countenance ; the Senfe whereof doth make many poor exercifed Souls to lay themfelves as in the Duft, before the Lord, on the Behalf of fuch, being fatisfied that the Day of God is haftening on apace, wherein all Coverings will be found too narrow, that are not of the Spirit of Truth. Haften therefore to come under its Government, all you who are making Profeffion of it ; that fo in this fhattering Day which is approaching, you may be of thofe who have a Right to fly to the Name of the Lord, which was, and is, and ever will be, a Place of Refuge to the Righteous. For methinks I hear, as it were, the Noife of a Day near at hand, wherein it will be faid to the Righteous, *be righteous ftill* ; and to the Filthy, *be filthy ftill.* Let all therefore be rouzed up to the Work of Sanctification, thro' the Operation of the Power of Truth, while it is called *To-day* ; this my Soul and Spirit doth deeply travail for, my Heart being filled with true Love and good Will unto all Men, defiring nothing in this my prefent Exercife, but that God's Will may be done by me ; and that his Love may be embraced by all, in laying Things rightly to Heart, and turning from the Spirit of this

Y y 2

intangling

intangling World, which is in danger to hinder you, if tampered with, from coming up in that Zeal, and Courage, and Boldness, that God would furnish you with, as you give up freely to his Work. And indeed, *Friends*, here is great need of Faithfulness, and Zeal in Practice, and close Discipline, in maintaining and managing the holy and good Order, which God in his great Wisdom hath instrumentally established amongst us; and that in the Authority and Wisdom, which the Lord is endowing his waiting People with, whose secret Labour it is, *that* Zion *may become the Glory of Nations,* Jerusalem *the Praise of the whole Earth.*

And *dear Brethren and faithful Sisters,* whose Exercise none know but the Lord alone, tho' you can in measure sympathize one with another, and you mourn sometimes because the Work is heavy, and but few who are willing faithfully to join, and put their Shoulders to it, yet be not dismayed nor discouraged; the Lord is able, and also willing, in his own Time, to send forth more Labourers into his Harvest, and he will bless your Exercises to you, and grant you to see the Fruits of your Labours, to your unspeakable Joy; this is my Faith, and herein is my Soul often borne up above close Exercises, believing the great and powerful God is desirous, that *his Camp should be cleansed:* For it seems to me, that there are abundance of People who are not of our Society, who will confess to the Truth in Words, and have

their

their Eyes very ſtrictly upon us, to ſee if our
Actions agree with our Principles, and our
Conduct anſwers the Profeſſion we make.
Therefore, *dear Friends*, join Hand in Hand,
and ſet Shoulder to Shoulder, and go on in the
Name and Fear of the living God; his Power
will be with you, and his Angel will be your
holy Companion: And as you thus keep in
the gentle and meek Wiſdom of God, that
which would ſeem to obſtruct and withſtand
the Work of Truth, will be made to fly before
you: *So will the Mountain of the Lord be eſta-*
bliſhed above all other Mountains, and his Hill
be exalted above every Hill; many ſhall flock
unto it; and the Name of the Lord ſhall become
more and more famous in the Earth; which
that it may be, the Souls of a little Remnant
deſire more earneſtly than to ſee the Increaſe
of any viſible Thing.

A

Tender Visitation

OF

ENDEARED LOVE,

FLOWING

From the divine Fountain, towards the whole Flock and Family of God, wherever scattered.

From one who is a Lover of Souls, and a Traveller for the Welfare of ZION.

JOHN FOTHERGILL.

My Bowels, my Bowels; I am pained at my very Heart; my Heart maketh a Noise within me; I cannot hold my peace, because thou hast heard, oh my Soul! the Sound of the Trumpet, the Alarm of War. Jer. iv. 19.

UPON the 24th Day of the eleventh Month 1699, as I was walking solitarily to our Week-day Meeting, and pondering in my Spirit, as at many other times, upon the things that belong to the Welfare of the Church of God, there fell a weighty Concern upon me

to

to vifit Friends with this following Epiſtle; and finding a Neceſſity to remain upon me, in the conſtraining Love of our heavenly Father, I do hereby ſalute you all, who in any meaſure are come to taſte of the good Word of Life, (which is even ſo near as in the Mouth and in the Heart) and of the Powers of the World to come.

Dear Friends and Brethren,

DWELL, I beſeech you, in a ſenſe of the great need you daily have of renewing of this Taſte, and in the Remembrance of God's inexpreſſible Love to your Souls, in diſcovering unto you the way of Life; even unto you who ſate in Darkneſs, and under the Region and Shadow of Death, now is Light ſprung up, according to Scripture-teſtimony; and as you have walked in this Light, the Light of the glorious Son of God, which has ſhined as from on high into your Souls, you have come to behold the Baits and Snares of your Souls Enemy, ſo that many have been made to pour forth their Souls to God, in a Senſe of the need they were in of a Saviour, and of his having heard them in an acceptable time, granting them Ability to eſcape the Evils they had been overcome with, and giving them Victory over that which had been Maſter over them; and thus many have been made Conquerors, and more than Conquerors, thro' him who hath loved them; thro' whom, not only inward, but

even

even outward Enemies, have been in a great degree fubdued, and made willing to be at peace with 'them. This hath been the Lord's doing, and indeed it is marvellous in the Eyes of many to this Day ; and I have Faith to believe it will never be forgotten by them : But it is their chiefeft Concern how to demean themfelves fo, as that they may anfwer the great Love of God to their Souls, not in the leaft doubting, but as they thus live, all things in this Life will be added, as the Lord fees convenient.

My Heart is filled with the Aboundings of God's Love towards you, *my dear Friends,* who are thus concerned, and herein - I can dearly falute you, with the Knee of my Mind bowed to the Lord Jehovah, in whom is Safety, that he may preferve you ever mindful of him, and low before him, waiting, as at his Footftool, to hear the gracious Words that proceed from him ; confidering, that of yourfelves, and without him, you can do nothing that will further the great Work which he hath called you to be engaged in.

And thus as we all keep in Self-denial, and under the daily Crofs, the Crofs of Chrift, which the Apoftle faid, *was to them that were faved, the Power of God,* 1 Cor. i. 18. we fhall dwell under his Power, and the Operation of the Spirit of Truth in ourfelves, and be made inftrumental in the Hand of the Lord, in our refpective Places and Offices in the Church,
every

every one confidering, what his Duty and Station in the Body is: For if we are Members of the Church, we have each one fome Service in it, either greater or lefs; and that all who profefs themfelves to be of her, may be ftirred up to confider what this is, and to be diligently engaged in performing it, to work while it is called To-day, before the Night comes, wherein none can labour, am I at this time concerned; that fo the End, for which the Lord reached unto us, and vifited our Souls, may be anfwered by all to his Honour and our Comfort: And I cannot but earneftly defire, that all may be rouzed up faithfully to purfue after this point, in this time of Peace and outward Quiet, (if it pleafe the Lord to lengthen it out to us yet a little longer) that when we are called to account, we may fo have numbered the Favours and Mercies of God to us, as to be able to give up our Accounts with Chearfulnefs.

And oh! what fhall I fay or write that may prevail upon you, whom God hath been pleafed to call by his Grace, and to reveal his faving Truth in you; how fhall I prevail upon you, to fhake yourfelves from the Duft of the Earth, and come away in Faithfulnefs and Obedience to your Call, in Zeal and Boldnefs for your heavenly Captain; and no longer to confer with Flefh and Blood, nor reafon with the Spirit of the World, which hinders your Growth, and makes you dwarfifh, fo that there is but very little Fruit on fome of you,

Z z   upon

upon whom the Lord hath beſtowed much Labour. And altho' ſome of you, as to Age, might have been Teachers of others, yet have you need that others ſhould teach you, tho' you may not be very willing to hear of it, but be ready to ſay, in order to excuſe or cover yourſelves, that *you have known the Truth many Years*, and *have openly profeſſed it* : But let me tell you, in the Fear and Dread of the powerful God, That a Knowledge of the Truth, or a Profeſſion thereof, is not ſufficient; nay, altho' it has been ſo obey'd, as that you have come out of the open Profaneneſs of the World, which may well be called the open Streets of *Babylon* ; yet if you do not obey its Requirings, ſo as to bring forth Fruits meet for him who hath given you ſo many refreſhing Showers of his pure Love, and come out of the ſecret Chambers of *Babylon* alſo, you will be in danger of ſuffering great Loſs, more ways than one : For God is determined to lay her waſte, to make her a Heap of Ruins ; and Woe will be to all thoſe who have been delighting to drink in the Cup of her Fornications, whatever their Profeſſion or Appearance have been ; and the Day of her Sorrow is haſtening with Speed.

Therefore, *my Brethren and Siſters* in Profeſſion, my Heart being full of Goodwill, I am led, in the conſtraining Love of God, to warn you all to beware of the Merchandizes of *Babylon*, eſpecially the Pleaſures of this

fading

fading World, and to have a care that they do not prevail upon the Minds of any, so as to get between you and the Lord, or separate you from the Love of God, manifested unto you thro' his dear Son, and the Light of his holy Spirit; but that all who have come to believe in the Light of Christ, may so live, as that they may shew their Faith by Obedience unto Righteousness, which is always the Fruit of true Faith: *For as the Body is dead without the Spirit, so is Faith without Works dead also.* James ii. 26.

And as you come up in Obedience to him in whom you profess to believe, he will lead and guide you into all Truth, in the way of Holiness, which is the only way to Rest and Peace: Thus you will be *Israelites* of God in Heart as well as in Profession, and your Ease will be to dwell alone ; no more to be numbered among the Nations, neither in their Worship, which is in the Alienation from God ; nor in the polluted Ways and Customs of the World, which is what my Soul desires, and is the End of my present Exercise ; and that it may never happen to any whom God has visited in this Day, as it did to some of the *Israelites* formerly, who lived to see a Time, wherein they were ready to lament that *the Summer was over, the Harvest ended, and they ungathered:* Which State, my Soul earnestly breathes to God may never happen to be any of ours, to whom he has graciously given a Summer-season unto; but

Z z 2

that

that we may embrace his tender Love, which is extended towards us; for which, and his numberlefs Tokens of Mercy and Favour vouchfafed to us ever fince we were a People, my Soul in Reverence (with many more) doth bow unto the living Fountain; and feeling his pure Love to fill my Soul at this time, I am made to fing Praifes to God who dwells on high, and is alone worthy, worthy, World without end.

And as you, *my elder Brethren*, who have known the Truth many Years, I cannot but fay (in Humility of Soul before the Lord, and with a true Efteem for *faithful Elders*, as the Words ran thro' my Heart when this Exercife came upon me) lift up your Eyes and fee how white the Fields are unto Harveft; do not you fee how many there be who do not yet profefs with us, but are fo far convinced as to confefs, that it is the Truth which is held forth amongft us: And now their Eyes are attentively upon us, to fee how we come up in the practical Part of our Religion, in Care, in Zeal and Circumfpection in all our Undertakings: So that I have fometimes faid, That in many Places verbal Teftimonies are not fo much wanting, as a Care in anfwering our Teftimony and Principles, in all our Behaviour and Deportment amongft the Sons of Men: The want whereof doth often hinder Truth from prevailing, and ftands in the way of thofe who are not yet of this Fold, yet whom the Lord waits

to

to gather into it : For the sake of such he hath staid his Hand, which hath long been stretched out over this poor Nation : Wherefore let all be stirred up to see, if nothing lies at any of your Doors, or remains undone on your parts; but that you come up in a holy Zeal and Boldness for God and his Cause upon Earth, that so the Beauty and Glory of the everlasting Truth may shine forth to the World thro' you all. *Let your Lights so shine in the World*, that they who see your good Works, and holy Care, *may glorify your heavenly Father :* This doth my Soul earnestly intreat for you all.

For it would be a dismal thing indeed, if any whom God has set to be as Way-marks to others to walk by, to be as the Salt of the Earth, as the primitive *Christians* were, and the true *Christians* are, should thro' Negligence or Indifference rather, be hinderers of others, until the time of Gathering be over : Would not such be in danger of being guilty of the Blood of others? In the Fear and Love of God therefore, let all lay these things to heart, turn to the Light of Christ in your own Bosoms, and consider of your ways, and see by it, how the matter stands between God and your Souls; whether you have not resisted, as *Jerusalem* did, until they were left in Darkness, and could not discern the things that belonged to their Peace? Whether you have answer'd the Call of the Lord in Obedience unto Righteousness, and thereby brought Honour to God?
Or

Or have otherwife by Negligence, or Liberty taken to fulfil the Lufts of the Flefh, caufed the way of Truth to be evil-fpoken of? If it hath thus been with any who profefs the bleffed Truth, methinks the Trumpet of the Lord founds very loud to fuch; and with yearning Bowels of true Goodwill, I cannot but warn fuch, to feek the Lord with your whole hearts, if happily he may yet be found of you: And altho' it be in the way of his righteous Judgments, (which is the alone way to Redemption, and is for the prefent not joyous but grievous) yet embrace it, and be willing to bear his Chaftifements, while he condefcends to mix them with Mercy: For this I muft fay, that thofe who will not bow under the Judgments which God Almighty is offering in love, they muft bear his Indignation, when the door of Mercy is fhut upon them in the Day that is approaching, when the Sinners, altho' in *Zion*, fhall be afraid, and Fear will furprize the Hypocrite, even all fuch who profefs themfelves to be what they are not in reality. Oh! how fhall I write, or what fhall I fay, to clear myfelf, and eafe my Spirit of that Weight of Exercife which refts upon me in true Love to all? Let me fay unto all, who make mention of the Name of the Lord, *depart ye from Iniquity*; and in the Words of our bleffed Lord, fpeaking to the *Jews* that had believed on him, *If ye abide in my Word, then are ye my Difciples indeed; and ye fhall know the Truth, and the Truth*

fhall

shall set you free. They then alledged, *they were* Abraham's *Children,* and consequently *free :* But our Saviour replied, that *if they were* Abraham's *Children, they would do the Works of* Abraham ; but he tells them plainly, *they were of their Father the Devil, and his Lusts would they do.* You therefore who are the Children of believing Parents, have a care I intreat you, of trusting to this Plea of the *Jews ;* it is a Covering that will prove too narrow ; an Excuse that will do your Souls no good ; and if you are not following your Father's Steps in the Way of Regeneration, and working the Works of Righteousness, you will stand condemned as the *Jews* were, and your Profession will be of no avail.

Therefore, as you believe in the Light, see that you walk in it, while it shines upon you, that so you may become the Children of the Light and of the Day, Children of God, Heirs and Coheirs with Christ in the Kingdom of his Father's Glory, which will be of more Value in a dying Hour, than all the Pleasures of the World, were it possible for a Man to obtain them. Let me therefore recommend you to the *ingrafted Word, which,* as it is obeyed and followed, *is able to save the Soul :* It is not far from any, but nigh at hand, even *in the Mouth and in the Heart,* that it may be both heard and done. Thus as all come up in Obedience unto the Word of Truth, you will draw down the Favour of God upon you, and

the

the Lord will be as a King to defend you, a Rock of Refuge in the fhattering Day that is near at hand, when the Lord will hide his faithful Children as in the hollow of his Hand.

Remember, *dear Friends*, how the Lord's Love was manifefted over thofe exercifed Ones, who were in pain for the Welfare of *Jerufa-lem*; on thefe he fet his Mark for their Safety, whilft thofe who beheld the Abominations with Eafe and Unconcernednefs, perifhed with thofe who worked them, tho' they might not be found with them in open Profanenefs; but they had all one fare. Thefe Things have been left for our Inftruction, and my Soul defires that we may thoroughly confider them; then I believe a Concern would be begot in many Hearts who are now at Eafe, that we might grow rich towards God, and bring forth Fruits to his Honour; and not to feek ourfelves, or the Favour or Friendfhip of the World. For thofe who do fo, and are more concerned herein, than in confidering how they may be-have, fo as to be worthy Receivers of the many Bleffings, both fpiritual and temporal, which he hath favoured us with, may be af-fured, that the all-feeing Eye of God is over them, and he fees them with Difpleafure, tho' they may think themfelves fafe and rich, and may create to themfelves Peace, and deck themfelves with God's Jewels, yet their Peace may be broken when they have the greateft Need of true Peace, and their Riches become

come Poverty and Want; which I heartily desire may never be the State of any whom God hath visited with his glorious Truth.

And this Word lives in my Heart to you all, whether old or young, rich or poor, whom the Lord hath concerned to labour for the Good of his Church, whether in a publick Testimony, or in a more private manner; oh! see that you come up in your proper Office, in the Dominion and Authority of the pure Truth, and keep close under the Government of your heavenly Captain, who hath engaged you in his Warfare against the Enemy of Souls; and beware of consulting with Flesh and Blood, or giving way to the reasoning part; for this weakens your Hands as it gets room, and is the Work of the Enemy, who seeing himself dethron'd in you, and the Lord concerning you to help to overturn his power in others; I know great are his Endeavours to hinder such in their Progress, and many are the Snares he is making use of: Therefore, *dear Friends*, keep true to your Leader, whether it be little or more that the Lord requireth of you; let your Eye be singly to him, your Faith fixed in his Power, and the Enemy with all his Agents will be put to flight: And as you abide in the Word of his Patience, you shall grow strong in the Lord, and in the Power of his Might. And notwithstanding some may be ready to think, that tho' they get one step forward one Day, yet they lose it another; and so are ready

to faint in their Minds, and let in Difcouragements; let me caution you, *my tender Friends,*
againft admitting thefe Things to have too
much place in your Thoughts; for God, who
hath begun the Work, if you abide in his
Counfel, will carry it on, and perfect it in his
own time, to his Praife and your Comfort. Be
faithful therefore in your feveral Conditions,
and think not God's time long, but wait for
it: Remember *David,* and how long it was
e'er he came to rule in *Ifrael,* after he was
anointed King by the Prophet, and how many
Trials and deep Exercifes he underwent, info-
much that he feared he fhould one Day fall
by the Hand of thofe who fought his Life:
And certain it is, that many whom the Lord
has Service for, he is pleafed to try with various
Exercifes, in order that they may be experimental Witneffes for him, of his great Power.

Neither let any defpife the *Day of fmall
things,* but be faithful in the *little;* if the Lord
fee meet he can *add more:* But thofe who are
not faithful in *little,* how are they like to be
faithful in *much?* and therefore are unfit to
have it. See therefore, *my Friends,* that you
quit yourfelves like Men and Women for God,
in your feveral Services, whether in publick
Teftimony, or in Affairs relating to Difcipline
and the good Order of the Church; that fo
nothing may be wanting on your parts; that
how foon foever the Lord may come to take a
View of his Vineyard, in order to clear it of
the

the fruitlefs Branches, which he hath long
beheld with a fparing Eye, and plentifully
watered them with the Showers of his Love,
you may be clear of the Blood of fuch, having
difcharged your Duty every way towards them ;
and methinks, *Friends*, I find it to reft upon
me to fay, *this Day draws on apace* ; a Day
wherein he will make it plain, who are on his
Side, and are following him faithfully ; and
who they are, who profefs to follow him, and
yet live to themfelves, and in the Liberty of
their own carnal Hearts : My Soul is in deep
Heavinefs many times for fuch, tho' they are
often the moft unwilling to confider Things
aright ; and fometimes the moft forward to
judge hardly of the Servants of the Lord, who
are made willing to fpend and be fpent for the
Glory of God, and the Good of his People ;
and of whofe Labour and Travel, both in
Body and Spirit, the Lord takes notice, and
they fhall not go unrewarded, as they continue
faithful unto God ; unto whom they look in
all they take in hand, and dare not fpare, neither for Favour, Affection, nor any Thing that
is here below, when the Lord opens their Un-
derftandings ; and thefe *fhall reft from their
Labour*, in endlefs Happinefs, and *their Works
fhall follow them*.

And unto you who have kept your Integrity,
and are as Fathers and Mothers in *Ifrael*, for
whom I have a reverent Efteem in the Lord ;
unto you a Word dwells upon my Spirit, in the

A a a 2

pure

pure Love of God : *May you ever remember the Days of your Youth, and how tenderly the Lord dealt with you ; how he led you even on step by step, and often passed by the Infirmities and Weaknesses that attended you :* And when you were in danger of missing your Way, you, whose Desires were good, did not he condescend to *inform your Understandings, lead you as by the Hand, and help you into the Way again?* Thus did your heavenly Father deal with you, in his tender Love and Mercy : And as you keep these Things in Remembrance, they will engage your Minds to be watchful over, and very tender towards those who are but as Children, (as you once were) in whom the Lord is at work, and forming them for his Service, to promote the Good of *Zion,* and the Welfare of *Jerusalem* ; for which many of you have faithfully laboured in your Day. And now the Lord is stirring up many, whom he will make valiant for him, and his Truth upon Earth, as they stand faithful unto him, when many of you are gone to your Rest. And therefore, *dear Friends,* receive the Word of Exhortation ; and wherever you see any tender breathing Babe, that hath its Father's Stamp upon it, altho' it appear weak, and in a stammering manner, if you can discern that its Longing and Desire is for the Prosperity of Truth, and of the glorious Work of God, how can you but be glad thereof ? And if it happens that such an one should at any time miss its way, either on the right hand or on the left, how

ready

ready should the wife in Heart be to inform, and extend a Hand of Help in the same Love wherein God dealt with you in your Childhood: And as you are thus preserved in the pure meek Spirit of Jesus, your heavenly Head, it will abundantly add to your Authority, and beget the more Care in those you are thus concerned for, to answer your Advice, and to keep close to the Requirings of God; and it will also give you the greater Weight with such as are justly blameable. Thus will the Government of Christ, the Power and Authority of the Gospel, more and more prevail over that which is of the Flesh and fleshly Will, thro' your keeping in the Dominion and Dignity of Truth: And thus will the Church of God be adorned with her own Robe, with the holy Spirit of the living Lord; and her Members will love and cherish one another, every one acting in its own Place and Station, be it never so small or low; the Circulation of heavenly Life will then be witnessed, and all will go on to the Glory and Honour of the great God, who is worthy for ever.

And be sure, *my Brethren*, as much as in you lies, keep in the meek, gentle, condescending Spirit of Love one towards another; so that nothing may ever get place amongst you, that may grow to Hardness, or cause Grudgings to arise in any of your Minds one towards another, for this will insensibly eat as a Canker, to the weakening of your Strength and

and Authority unawares ; but fo give way to one another, in the Liberty of Truth, that you may grow up in the bleſſed Fellowſhip of the glorious Goſpel, as that all who behold your *Chriſtian* Behaviour one towards another, may have Cauſe to ſay, *you are the People of God, and taught by his holy Spirit :* And thus you will be a good Example to the very hindermoſt of thoſe amongſt whom you are concern'd, which will be a Means to faſten and ſet home your ſeveral Services upon all you are engaged with : You will alſo be kept near and dear one unto another, in the *Unity of the one Spirit, the Bond of laſting Peace ;* which, as you abide in, the Enemy, with all his twiſtings and twinings, will never be able to break, nor deprive you of. Therefore, *my Brethren,* join Hand in Hand, and ſet Shoulder to Shoulder in this weighty Work, the Promotion of God's bleſſed Truth, and go on in the Name and Fear of the Lord, in Self-denial, (which reaches a great way, if truly conſidered) and under a Senſe of the daily Need you have of his Aſſiſtance : This doth my Soul earneſtly intreat of you all, being filled with a Senſe of the Goodneſs of God, at this very Moment, and drawn forth therein much more than I did expect. But having now eaſed my bowed Spirit of that which has remained as an Exerciſe upon me, I ſhall now conclude, earneſtly wiſhing the Welfare of you all ; and the Lord, ſaith my Soul, multiply his

Mercies

Mercies and the Visitations of his pure Love, with the Peace of his holy Spirit, upon his whole Flock and Family. To God the Father, through Jesus Christ, be everlasting Glory, Honour and Praise, who is worthy, worthy, now and for ever.

JOHN FOTHERGILL.

Wensleydale in Yorkshire, the 21st
  of the twelfth Month 1699.

F I N I S.

www.ingramcontent.com/pod-product-compliance
Lightning Source LLC
Chambersburg PA
CBHW021713110726
47902CB00005B/1174